Contents

***

To the people who try, try again,
even when it's really fucking hard.
—
Luckily, you can do hard things.
Like, *really hard* things. *wink wink*

Chapter 1

Finley

"You know, watching you out there during practice, it was like you were just another coach," Patrick remarks, surprise lacing his tone. Like, somehow the fact I'm a woman would change my ability to be the head coach for a professional men's hockey team.

Fortunately, Paddy here is not the first man to make a statement like that while somehow thinking it's a compliment. Though I do wonder for the third time in as many minutes how *this* is the man they picked to interview me for a sixty-minute segment on the leading sports network.

Instead of making a smart-ass remark before systematically walking him through exactly why it's comments like his that make women in sports feel singled out, I do what Sabrina, the head of the Denver Yeti's PR department, has drilled me to do for the last nine months since I became the first female head coach in professional hockey history: I fucking smile.

And I swear I see Sabrina relax from the corner of my eye. It makes me want to stick my tongue out at her, but I manage to keep it together. See? I'm super damn professional.

I continue, answering Patrick's statement as if it were a question, "The mechanics of hockey are the same no matter what level you're playing at, or if you're coaching a men's or women's league. Sure, there are a few differences, but that's true as you move from high school to college to the farm league to the pros, too. As far as experience goes, I *am* just another coach out there."

Patrick nods. "And the men all seem to respect you."

Truly, where did they find this guy?

"I've found respect is earned, and when you're working with professional athletes, you earn their respect by making them better. I've been with most of these guys for two to three years now. We worked together during my time as an assistant coach, and we saw success at the end of last season when I was interim head coach. These men have been working with coaches for years, and when you're able to help them get just a little bit better—to increase their speed or their stats by a percent or more—well, they don't care if you're a man or a woman."

The truth is, the team has been great. From the summer interns to the owner, the Denver Yeti have been nothing but professionals. There were a couple of comments from guys on the team when I first joined as an assistant coach a few years back, but every coach learns to expect that. Whether you're a man or a woman, the players test you to make sure you're worth their time.

Fortunately, I'm damn good at my job, and the players recognize that.

When Burt, the previous head coach, had a heart attack on the bench last season, I stepped into the interim head coach position, and there was no pushback, no testing. The players were nothing but supportive. But I'd already proven my worth.

Though I'm enough of a realist to know that respect based on performance is conditional. One mistake, and it can all crumble. Which is why I don't plan on making any mistakes.

"And is that a lesson you learned from your father, Hall of Fame coach Hal Blake?" Patrick asks, his face alighting like a little boy on Christmas morning—the same face almost any hockey fan gets when talking about my dad.

"It is," I reply. "My dad is known for his ability to make players better, and I was fortunate enough to be the one person in his life he got to coach from the time they were in diapers."

Patrick laughs. "I'm sure it's helpful having your dad's support and experience to call on whenever you need it."

Ah, so *now* we're going with the nepotism angle. Love it, Paddy. Love it.

Probably not the place to mention that my dad actually called up the Yeti's GM, Greg White, to suggest I wasn't ready for the head coach position when the interim job unexpectedly opened up. Hell, he all but said it again today during our weekly call. But I've proven to him that I'm worth his support before, and I'll prove it this season, too. Turns out, I enjoy proving men wrong.

"I'm fortunate to have worked with a number of excellent coaches throughout my career, including my dad, as well as other men's and women's coaches at various levels. No one makes it to this stage without a roster of mentors they've learned from." Another planned answer delivered with the winning smile Sabrina loves so much. I should win some sort of award for the performance I'm putting on right now.

The interview with Patrick continues, the focus moving from the fact I'm a woman with a famous coach for a father to the current challenges with the Denver Yeti roster. My answers are clean, precise, and fully Team Yeti.

Patrick turns to face me fully, his smile suggesting he's about to spring a hard question on me. "So, let's talk about the defense. A lot of analysts have been surprised by how many points the Yeti have let the other teams score this season."

"Our defense isn't performing as well as we'd like," I tell the truth, even though Sabrina would argue it'd be a better move to try to spin it. But building a culture of accountability has been my push since I took over as head coach. And I think it's working. The players joke about it sometimes, but I truly believe in doing what you say you'll do and owning it when you don't. Despite our defensive struggles, we don't have any internal drama. The players know what is expected of them, and we own our outcomes, naming mistakes, addressing them quickly, and learning from them to move forward. And I can't preach accountability if I'm not willing to live it myself, even when it makes me look less than ideal. Like now.

"Our defense is young," I continue. "This is a building year for us, and you're seeing some of that right now. But I have full confidence that we're going to be where we need to be to make it deep into the playoffs this year. Pike has really started to come into his own, and with his leadership, the team is going to rally."

The unspoken truth is Pike *has* to come into his own. We're three months into the season, and if he doesn't, I'm not sure the team will get where they need to be by April. We spent our entire coaches' meeting this morning discussing this very thing. Then my defensive coach, Rob McCall, and I had a long conversation with Pike about how we expect him to be more vocal on *and* off the ice.

Another fifteen minutes pass by before Patrick finally states, "One final question, Finley."

As much as it crushes my soul, I reply, "Of course," rather than asking him if he calls all coaches by their first names or if it's just the ones with vaginas. I love watching men squirm when I use the V word.

"Where do you see the Yeti at the end of this season?" he asks.

I smile, a real one this time, and I don't miss the way it makes Patrick shrink back just slightly.

"Holding the Cup above our heads, of course."

There is no other option.

I shake his hand, thanking him for his time, before making my way over to Sabrina. "What's next?"

"They want footage of you with the coaching staff. You with a clipboard, watching film, in a meeting room," she reads from the tablet in her hand.

"Real or staged?" I ask, imagining the cameras zooming in on my video coach, Dr. Sutton Pearce, as she navigates through her ridiculously named computer files. "Defenderella" was the one she opened this morning before dropping a truth bomb on Rob and me about the state of our defense.

"Staged, Finley, always staged. We can't have the general public calling you the 'Ice Queen' like the guys do."

"I *am* the queen of this ice, Sabrina." I honestly love the nickname, not that I would ever let the players know. Who wouldn't want to be given a royal title that screams badass?

She sighs. "You know that managing your image is a key portion of my role, right? As the head coach, you're the face of the team."

I wink at her. "Then you're welcome for giving you such great material to work with."

Sabrina looks slightly shocked, and I realize she rarely sees the sass I keep so carefully hidden. "You know, the fact that you look like you could be a model does not, in fact, help us. It's hard to make hockey fans take you seriously when you're on repeat in their spank bank."

I shake my head. "I played on the boys' hockey team for four years in high school. I may have had my own changing space, but that certainly didn't stop me from hearing *exactly* what they thought. Boys are gross, and that rarely changes as they age. I learned quickly that results are the only way to earn their respect. So the men of Colorado can jerk off all they want to an image of me lifting the Cup, but I'll still be the best damn coach in the league."

"You should've said that during your interview!" Charlotte Langford's voice echoes from behind us as we walk down the long hallway that leads to the coaches' offices. "And, turns out, I should've been more prepared to change out the interviewer."

I pause to let her catch up with us, blinking at her bright outfit. The hot-pink blazer she has on matches her heels perfectly, and the bright blue shirt and matching pants underneath should look ridiculous, but somehow, she pulls it off. The only reason I manage to match is because, besides my black power suits for game day, I spend one hundred percent of my time in team-issued sweatsuits.

"How did we get lucky enough to have Patrick?" I ask.

Charlotte laughs, picking up on the sarcasm in my tone when most people wouldn't. She lived in the apartment across the hall from me for a little over a month a year ago, and due solely to her outgoing personality, we became friends. Despite our work schedules dominating the majority of our spare time, she's still the one person I can fully be myself with.

"God, he was the worst, wasn't he?" Charlotte asks. "I swear, we did our due diligence. You've seen him. He did that interview with that one quarterback who finally decided to retire. You know, what's-his-face? Tim?"

I shake my head at her, hiding my amusement behind a face of ice. "Your dad is the owner of the Colorado Stallions, Charlotte. How can you possibly not know the name of arguably the most famous quarterback of all time?"

She circles her pointer finger in front of my face, her hot-pink nails flashing. "Don't give me that look. You know I've never cared about the football side of Dad's business. Why would I want to watch a bunch of grown men running around, throwing balls at each other, when I could be helping build a global entertainment business? I, personally, booked Jaxon Steele for five nights at the stadium. Singing like that while running across a stage? Now *that's* impressive."

"He sure is pretty," Sabrina agrees.

Um, hell yes, he is. Unfortunately, that buzzing on my wrist informs me I have yet another coaches' meeting before the game tonight. "Well, I've got to get to my meeting so I can have a fake one before my real one. Is there anything else you need from me, Charlotte?"

"Besides your forgiveness for somehow being associated with a company that hired Patrick?" Her smile says she knows I'll forgive her. "No. Just please don't let it ruin our friendship. I like Taco Tuesday, even if you're gone like every Tuesday."

"I have—"

"To work," she cuts me off. "I know. And travel all the time. And your games start so late. Luckily for you, my schedule is equally as crazy, so I don't judge you for it. But you'd better plan on being my plus-one to the Jaxon Steele concert. Don't forget *I* saw you dancing with a hairbrush to 'If You Love a Girl.'"

"No way," a deep voice chirps. "Ice Queen does not sing into a hairbrush." Lefevre slings an arm around Charlotte's thin shoulders.

I blink at him. Twice. One of the best parts of being known as Ice Queen is I can make these huge-ass men do almost anything just by glaring at them. It's a real power trip.

"I mean." He coughs, his boyish face dropping. "That is clearly untrue. Coach Blake would never engage in such ridiculous, fun behavior."

I shake my head. Twenty-five-year-olds are so easily manipulated. "Precisely, Lefevre. Now, don't you have some cardio to do?"

"Nah, I finished—I mean," he says, backing away when he realizes it wasn't a question but a command. "Yes. Yes, I do."

And just as quickly as he came, he's gone again.

My watch vibrates again, notifying me that I'm truly about to be late.

"I've got to go," I announce. "Can you have your assistant work with Paige to figure out which day will work for me to join you at the concert?" I ask Charlotte.

She shakes her hips. "I knew it. You're secretly a Steelie."

I wink. "It's not a secret. I'm basically his number one fan. Ask my hairbrush."

Chapter 2
Finley

"Coach Blake," Rob says as he knocks on my open office door. I'm working through my overflowing inbox before heading to the arena for our game, and happy for the distraction.

"What's up?" I smile at my assistant coach.

"I've got that list of veteran defensemen you asked for. Want to walk down together and review it as we go?"

I close out of my email, flagging two interview requests to come back to after the game.

"Yes. Thank you for turning it around so quickly. After the conversation with Dr. Pearce this morning, I don't want to waste any time convincing White we need a veteran defenseman." The GM argued against trading for one this summer, but even he has to admit that our team needs the support only an experienced defenseman out on the ice can provide.

After slipping into my black suit jacket, I do one final check in the mirror. No flyaways have escaped my ponytail, no lipstick on my teeth, and—oops, an upside-down Yeti. I twist the lapel pin on my jacket before tightening the back so it can't flip again. Real drunk mascot energy when it does that.

Game day ready, I follow Rob past my assistant, Paige, and into the hall.

As we walk, he hands me a list with six names on it, and I scan through them quickly, all players I'm familiar with. My eyes snag briefly on the final one, and I force my body not to react to my high school crush who almost certainly forgot I existed after we spent a mere fifteen minutes together when I was sixteen. Instead, I make myself peruse the list again, thinking through each of them, trying to be unbiased.

"Thanks, Rob. Let's cut Erikson and Kane before it goes to the front office, but otherwise, I think any of the other four could be what we need to help build some confidence and experience on the ice."

"Great." He crosses out both names, and some of the tension in my chest loosens. "I'll drop this by White's office. He knows to expect it?"

"I briefed him earlier after our conversation with Pike."

Pre-game flies by in a blur of flashing lights, loud music, and ice-blue-and-black jerseys. The guys know Chicago is projected to make it deep into the playoffs this year, and despite it still being fairly early in the season, the energy in the locker room is reaching a level just this side of too much. I knock twice, giving the men a chance to cover their dicks before I enter. It's really more for me than them, but I think we can all agree it's better not to have flaccid penises out and about.

I give my pre-game speech, keeping it short and sweet like always. It's J.D. Dalton's job as captain to get them pumped up. My job is to remind them this is just another day at the office.

The first period is a bloodbath. Our defensemen let the energy of the place feed them as they push harder and faster than they normally would—than they likely *should*. I scan the ice, cataloging the movement of the players on both teams, noting when our lines start to get gassed.

"Well, you've got to give it to Pike," Rob says as we huddle in my office between periods. "He's stepping up."

I nod in agreement. Leadership doesn't come naturally to him, but he's trying. He's done everything we asked of him during our meeting. "He's not going to have a voice tomorrow if he keeps it up, though," I observe.

After a very quick debrief, we head to the locker room. I quickly talk through adjustments with the team, focusing primarily on our defensemen, but our forwards haven't been perfect, either.

The second period starts better. Our breakouts are cleaner, the defense tighter, and Pike is doing exactly what we asked. He's loud, more assertive, and the rest of the team is feeding off his energy.

Li hits their winger at the red line, and for a moment, it feels like the momentum is finally turning. The next line keeps up the pace, and I can feel the season turning in front of my eyes.

Li and Pike are back out on the ice for their second shift when the Guardians' top line comes flying down the ice on an odd-man rush, the crowd rising. Li hesitates, for no more than half a second, but Pike crosses hard into the lane to cover.

He gets there, ready to blow up the play entirely.

Shit. "PIKE! BLINDSIDE!" I yell, but it's too late. My heart flies into my throat, knowing what's about to happen.

Their forward slams into Pike at full speed, causing his body to fly backward as his legs crumple beneath him.

Pike goes down hard, his gloved hands going instantly to his knee. Not screaming, not moving. Just that tight, breathless pain every hockey player recognizes.

"Fuck," Rob mutters from beside me, and I couldn't agree more.

Li reaches Pike as the referee blows the whistle. I watch, doing my best to keep my expression neutral. Using Li as leverage, Pike tries to stand but goes right back down. The trainers leap over the boards, and Pike is helped off the ice slowly, one bulky arm around each of the two trainers, barely touching his right skate to the ground.

The crowd claps, worried murmurs rippling through the arena.

"Go with him, Dr. Lowell," I tell the team doctor as they shuffle past me. I've seen the way Pike's knee buckled before, and I know what it means: Pike's out, likely for the season.

I force myself to exhale. He'll be lucky if it's not the end of his career. A career that, just today, I asked him to do more with. To give more.

And he fucking gave it *all*.

I'm laser-focused for the rest of the game, being more vocal than I normally would be as the team struggles to find its rhythm. I know I'm distracting them as much as I'm helping, but the guilt of pushing Pike to overextend himself overrides my logic, causing me to overstep my role as head coach.

We lose 2–3, Volkov playing an extraordinary game to keep us that close when the shots on goal were 49–20.

"Update," I demand when I meet Dr. Lowell, waiting for me in the hallway after the game.

"Torn ACL. He's out for the season."

Despite the guilt eating at my chest, I force myself into my Ice Queen role. I go through the motions of reassuring the team, show nothing but calm confidence as I talk to my team, and then answer the press' questions.

Now is not the time for emotions. Now is the time for White to get me a goddamn defenseman.

***

"I think Gus Reed is our best bet," I announce, walking into the GM's office at eight the next morning.

I've been in the gym for the last two hours, hoping to find a place of clarity as my feet pound miles into the treadmill. When that didn't work, I tried pushing my body to its limit with a heavy-lifting circuit, but still… nothing. White arrives punctually at eight each morning after dropping off his twins at daycare. So, I've been stewing in my own office, waiting for him to arrive.

Pike was our sole hope to get our defensive lines together. Now, well, now I need White to make a trade.

There are four names on the list we gave White yesterday, and I need him to pick one. Hell, I needed him to have picked one six months ago when I said we needed more experience on the team, but he said it was a building year. That may be all well and good for him, but I'm the first female head coach in the history of professional hockey. My first season can't be a building season—it looks terrible for those of us breaking glass ceilings in all industries. And, even if you put my need to represent *all* of womankind aside, the average tenure of a head coach is a little over two years. The average for a GM is almost double that. It's a lot easier for him to argue in favor of a building year when he's far more likely to survive it.

"Coach Blake," White starts, but I cut him off. I need to make my case before he turns me down.

"I know Jenson is better statistically, but I spent hours last night watching film. He doesn't have the same off-ice presence as Reed. Reed is the guy we need to get all the lines in order."

White narrows his eyes at me. "How much sleep did you get last night, Finley?"

"Enough." I fight the urge to take a long pull from the half-empty coffee cup in my hand.

"I know you well enough to know you watched our game film at least once. Plus, you're telling me you watched film of *at least* two other players, though I'd have to guess you watched the film of all four of the names you had Rob leave on my desk. That's what? At least four hours of film after last night's game, when you didn't get home until... let's call it midnight just for easy numbers?"

"Dr. Pearce had compiled a film for each of the four men. I wasn't watching full games."

The smile White offers me makes me slightly jealous of his daughters. He must be a great dad.

"You have to take care of yourself, Finley."

"I am. No first-year fifteen for me," I reply, patting my stomach and trying to lighten the mood. I can sleep when I'm certain I'm going to get a next season with the Yeti. Plus, it's not like I could've relaxed enough last night to get any quality rest, anyway.

White shakes his head, not commenting on my weight either way. See? Great girl dad. "I'm not your mom, so I'll let you worry about your health, but as GM, I am going to remind you that it's my job to handle scouting and building the roster. Your job is to take the players I give you and make them a better team. Which means, no spending hours watching films of players to make the decision about who to recruit for me. I have an entire team we pay to do that, Coach. You *coach*."

"I'm part of the team, too," I say. "I want to make sure I'm giving you the information *you* need to get me the players *I* need."

"And I will. I know you're thinking about the conversation we had last spring about bringing on a veteran."

He's right. I am thinking about that conversation. And about how he didn't choose to listen to me.

People always seem to think that the hardest part of being the first female head coach is the trolls on social media, but the truth is, it's questioning the motives of the people I respect. Of the ones I work with every day and have a professional relationship with. It's not knowing whether White would've told a male coach in his first season that he needed to focus on his health, or if he would've told him to double down and praised him for his extra work.

Greg White seems like a good guy, but at the end of the day, it doesn't matter. The only way I can ensure I'm treated the way I want to be is to be the best—and I can't do that without damn good defensemen.

"But," he continues, "I still believe that if Pike hadn't gone out last night, he would've gotten there. And then we would've been solid for the next two or three seasons. Veterans aren't the play for the future—not that it matters now."

"I agree, but we need someone for *now*."

Greg taps his desk once. "Well, luckily for you. I, too, did some work last night. And some this morning, also. As of ten minutes ago, we traded our second-round draft pick and one of our defensive prospects from the Kodiaks to the Florida Cyclones."

My heart skips a beat as I realize what that means milliseconds before he says it. Only one defenseman would possibly be coming to us from Florida. The one I didn't want because of that pesky little crush.

"Beckett Kane is officially a Denver Yeti. He lands tonight."

Chapter 3

Beckett

"Did you make it okay?" my agent asks over my headphones as I weave through the Denver airport.

"Yup," I grunt. It's... fine. I'm lucky the Yeti had a team apartment vacant that I could move into literally the same day. Supposedly, it's furnished and fully ready to go. Which is why I only had to bring two bags with me. One with my gear, and one that's essentially just underwear and a suit to wear for the game on Saturday, in case the rest of my things from my old place don't make it in time. Not that I left much in my Florida condo. I've never understood players who have loads of crap in their homes when we spend so much time on the road.

"There is supposed to be someone waiting for you at Door 506 in a black pickup. And the woman I talked to assured me they'd have everything ready for you, including a full closet of Yeti sweats and T-shirts to get you through until the moving company gets there."

"Great," I reply, certain it'll be done. Logistics coordinators for hockey teams are like fucking magicians. I have no idea how they do it, but everything I need is just *poof* there.

"It *will* be great." Vic is trying to remain positive despite knowing I'm pissed.

"Well," I deadpan, "people have always told me I look good in ice blue."

I can practically hear my agent roll his eyes through the phone. "I'm aware you're not happy about the trade, Beck—"

"Name one client of yours who has *ever* been happy about a mid-season trade, Vic," I demand.

"Mikey—he hated the left winger on the Tempest and wanted the fuck out. Look, you knew it could happen. The Cyclones wouldn't agree to including an NMC in your contract. We discussed it. Almost no players get full no-move clauses after thirty, even if they're a franchise guy or a star goalie. You assured me it didn't matter what jersey you were wearing so long as you got to keep playing."

"Yeah, well, I didn't think I was going to be joining a new team mid-season."

"Didn't know you were so passionate about the Cyclones," Vic says in my ear as I make my way to the correct floor for my ride.

"Just don't want to have to go through all the new-player bullshit again."

I don't want to risk getting put on the IR if an overzealous doctor gets a little too anxious about my hip is what I *really* mean. But that's not information my agent—or anyone else for that matter—needs to know.

"Beck, they got you on a plane *hours* after the contract was signed. There's no way they're planning to do anything other than throw your old ass out on the ice. They needed you like, yesterday."

"I'm not fucking old, Vic."

"In the world of mere mortals, true. When it comes to professional sports, you're definitely flirting with it."

The extra time I have to put in to keep up with my teammates seems to support that claim. And it's not just extra time on the ice. My strength-and-conditioning regimen is a perfectly structured plan, delivering maximum benefit with the least harm to my body. My recovery days are honed. My stretching routine would make a professional yoga instructor look like an amateur. I eat only what I'm told, never allowing myself the cheat days I did in the past. But it will all be worth it if it keeps me on the ice.

I walk through Door 506 and spot a black pickup idling a few paces away.

"Thanks for that, Vic. I've got to go. They're here. Really excited to make small talk with whatever intern they sent to pick me up."

"Hey," Vic says, and I slow down. "This is your chance, Kane. I know how badly you want that C on your chest like your dad had. The Cyclones weren't going to give it to you, even if Guthry had retired before you. Remember that when you show up to practice tomorrow. They literally traded for you because they needed the leadership. Be the fucking leader."

"You're right," I mumble. After hanging up with Vic, I notice for the first time that the man sitting in the front seat of the pickup staring at his phone isn't some scrawny intern. No, if things go the way I want them to, it's my new linemate, Evan Li.

"Li." I tap on the window. He lifts his head, a smile forming as he rolls the window down. "Hey, Kane! Just a second. Larsen will help you with your bags."

A big guy hops out of the backseat and sticks his hand out. "Matt Larsen."

"You're the rookie?" Grasping his hand, I try to remember the roster information I studied on the plane.

"Sure am. Let me throw your bags in the back for you."

I shake my head, moving to the bed and heaving my gear bag over the side. "I've got it."

Once we're back in the car and on the move, I ask, "How did you two get chauffeur duty?"

"Coach asked whether anyone wanted to or if she should send the intern. Larsen volunteered, and I figured I'd drive since we need you to be alive to be of any use to the team," Li jokes.

"That's so unfair. I'm a fucking fantastic driver," Larsen says from the back.

"Sure. As long as you believe speed limits are more suggestions and the point of driving is to see how many times you can cross the lines in the middle of the road."

The rookie grins, his head leaning into the spot between the front two seats. "Is that not how you win the game?"

I chuckle as Li whacks his friend's head.

"Plus," Li adds, "we live in the team apartment building, too, so it was easy for us to be the ones to pick you up."

We spend the rest of the drive chatting. It's something I'd normally be annoyed by, but Vic's parting words are still circling in my mind, reminding me that this could be my one chance to prove I deserve to be a team captain.

Li pulls his black pickup into an underground parking garage, handing me a packet with my key and apartment information. We drag my bags out of the truck bed, and Li silently grabs one before heading toward the elevator.

"My guy! Do you know who else lives on this floor?" Larsen asks as we step out of the elevator, still happily following as Li and I carry my bags down the wide hallway.

I shrug. "Literally just moving in, Rookie, how the fuck would I know?"

He chuckles. "Too true. And to be fair, I've lived here since the start of the season, and I only found out when I rode the elevator with her after the game the other night."

"Oh, shit," Li says, and I glance at him. "Really? I know she lives in the building, but I've never seen her here."

"Children," I interrupt as we reach the door with my number on it. "Who are we talking about?"

"The Ice Queen," Larsen practically shouts at the exact same time Li replies, "Coach Blake."

As if summoned, the door behind me opens. All three of us turn to stare as a tall woman walks out in black joggers and a Yeti mascot T-shirt. Her dark hair is pulled back into a sleek ponytail, and her eyes—they're almost the exact same shade as the blue in the club's logo.

Fuck, she's gorgeous.

I mean, pretty. No. Good-looking. Fuck. What am I allowed to say about my head coach's appearance? That she's attractive?

Nothing. Almost assuredly, saying nothing is the right answer.

Her appearance is surprisingly something the internet articles failed to accurately capture when I was reading up on the plane about my new coach. I'd heard the news about the first female head coach when she was brought on last year, but our teams haven't met this season, so I hadn't had a reason to care. Since I learned I was coming to her team, I read a number of articles about her and her coaching style, but I clearly should've paid more attention to the pictures. Or at least read a vanity piece or two about her. There's something vaguely familiar about her that I can't seem to place.

"Shit." Larsen steps slightly behind me, almost as if he's trying to hide his bulking frame.

"Ah, Rookie," she chides, and the smallest twitch of her lip makes me think she's enjoying messing with the kid. "You think I haven't heard you dumbasses call me Ice Queen before? Why do you think I make you do sprints so often?"

"Sadistic was my guess," he mumbles, though when she chuckles, he gives her a small smile.

"Maybe a little." The gleam in her eye tells me she thinks the assessment is amusing. My college team had a female assistant coach, and she was the toughest person in the room at any given moment. When I heard I was getting traded to the Yeti, some of the guys tried to offer condolences about being traded to her team. However, after working with Coach Green in college, I have no doubt Coach Blake will be just as good as any other coach on the ice. Hell, as sad as it is, she likely has to be better than her male counterparts for her to have made it this far.

"Anyway." Coach Blake's eyes finally meeting mine. "I didn't realize they were moving you into this unit. I guess we're neighbors now."

"Yeah." I hold out my hand. "Beckett Kane. Nice to meet you."

She stares at my hand for a moment, and just as I'm about to awkwardly pull it away, she reaches out and shakes it, her grip surprisingly strong. Or, maybe not surprisingly, considering she's a hockey coach.

"Coach Blake." She looks at Larsen. "Not Elsie, never fucking Elsie."

"Wait, I thought your first name was Finley?"

The rookie and Li are both laughing as Larsen explains, "No, Elsie, like Elsa, like—"

"Fucking rookies," Coach Blake mutters, moving back into her apartment. "See you at practice, Kane," she shouts as she shuts the door behind her.

"I cannot believe you're living across the hall from Coach."

The two men help me carry my belongings into the apartment, Larsen unreasonably excited to learn I have the exact same layout he does. He then proceeds to ask me a million questions about whether I have a wife or girlfriend who will be moving in with me. If my family is going to be coming out for my first game as a Yeti.

As I continue to tell him no, even when he almost pityingly asks if I have a goldfish or something, I realize how isolated I've let myself become.

And when they finally leave, taking their chaos with them, I've never felt more alone.

Chapter 4
Finley

"I am excited to be in Denver and to join the Yeti. So far, I've seen nothing but the highest level of play and professionalism from every level of the organization: from the coordinators who helped me get everything here on short notice to the players to the coaching staff," Beckett Kane says from his seat in the media room.

Beckett *fucking* Kane.

And damn it, if he isn't just as handsome, just as composed, as he was when he helped me with my slap shot when I was sixteen.

Not that I'm paying attention to that. Or the fact he doesn't remember me. Even if it was a long time ago—and literally lasted for less than twenty minutes.

Okay, even I can admit that the nineteen-year-old version of him pales in comparison to the chiseled *man* in front of me.

I'm trying not to take it as an insult that White traded for one of the players I'd specifically crossed off my list, but it's not as easy as I'd like it to be. I had my reasons for not wanting Kane on my bench. Like the fact he clearly didn't read the PR prep package he was given before this interview, or he would know that we only mention the coaching staff on this team when absolutely necessary.

"And how *do* you feel about playing under the first female head coach?"

And *this* would be why. Just what we didn't want to happen. To somehow turn this interview into yet another chance for the press to try to twist some player's comment to make it seem like I'm anything other than your average head coach.

Kane glances up, his dark brown eyes meeting mine from where I stand in the very back of the room. I lift my coffee cup to my lips, covering my mouth and wishing I had a dry-erase board to hide behind instead.

Give them nothing.

"She's not the first woman coach I've worked with. I respect those who've managed to break into the field. Plus, when you get to be as old as I am," Kane says, earning him a chuckle from the reporters, "you've been through a number of first practices with a new team. And I can honestly tell you the practice today under Coach Blake was no different. She knows her stuff, and I'm excited to be a part of an organization willing to do things a little differently in order to make sure they're giving their fans the best possible team to cheer for."

"Not too shabby," Charlotte remarks next to me, and I jump.

"When did you get here?" I ask quietly, again using my coffee cup for cover.

She shrugs. "I was promised a hot new veteran. Didn't want to miss the show. And I'm glad I didn't. Damn, Mr. Kane is a hottie. And apparently not an idiot—or did your PR team tell him to say that?"

I shake my head. "We, in fact, told him to stay away from the coaching staff in general unless he's specifically mentioning Rob."

"So, he's going to get the wrath of Finley when he gets down from there?" Charlotte nods toward the podium where Kane is still answering questions.

"As good as the answer was, I need to know my team can follow directions."

We stand in silence, listening to Kane's response to a question about leaving the Cyclones, until Charlotte turns to me and whispers, "As someone who climbed the corporate ladder on the media side of the industry, I want to tell that man to smile more when he's up there, but unfortunately, he just looks damn good with that slight glare. Like, okay, Daddy."

Daddy energy, for sure.

I suck in a deep breath, intentionally focusing on the bald head of Billy Carlson, my least favorite reporter, to keep myself from following Charlotte's train of thought.

Beckett Kane is my player.

"Charlotte, let's maybe not risk my entire career by saying that in a room full of reporters?"

"Ah, come on, Finley. They know he's hot. Look at the way Carlson is salivating over there."

I lift my cup again before whispering, "He's likely already plotting how to spin some story about how women can't coach men. You know, he said—"

"That you would be gone in less than a year? Yes. You've mentioned it. I've already renewed my membership in the Carlson-Hater's Club."

"It's a lifetime membership," I remind her, earning me a large eye roll.

"You're getting good with the coffee cup." Charlotte tracks my hand. "Though, now everyone's going to think you're tired."

"Every adult on this planet is tired. I think it's okay."

"Maybe we can get a coffee company to sponsor you. Then, no one can say anything about you walking around with a cup all the time. You're not tired, you're a damn good brand ambassador."

I let out a chuckle that I quickly stifle. "Shit, Charlotte. That's the kind of creative thinking we need around here. Are you sure you don't want to be an assistant coach?"

Charlotte raises an eyebrow at me, the look of distaste on her face almost comical. "Don't take this the wrong way, but I'd literally rather die."

"How could I *possibly* take that the wrong way?" I joke.

"But you should meet my friend Sage," Charlotte continues. "Or maybe you already know her?"

I shake my head.

"Sage Sinclair? She's the GM for the Denver Miners."

"Oh, sure." We've been introduced at a few parties, though I had no idea she was friends with Charlotte. I suppose it would make sense that they, as heiresses to athletic empires in Colorado, would be friends.

"Ugh, of course you're both too busy watching boys play with balls to actually be friends with the cool women in the room," Charlotte pouts.

"No balls in hockey," I tease.

She nods thoughtfully. "I've noticed that the few times I mistakenly went home with a puck pusher."

"You know, it feels like more than once might not be a mistake."

"Well, there was one time with—"

I shake my head. "Nope. Don't tell me. I made the team doctor and the team captain give the safe-sex, don't-be-an-idiot talk before the season started. Other than that, I want to know less than nothing about what the players do outside this building."

"Oh, boo. That's so boring."

"I cannot know about their sex lives and still pretend to take them seriously. They are twentysomething-year-old men with unlimited options for bad decisions. Honestly, getting nauseous just thinking about it."

"So boring," Charlotte says.

When the reporters' questions move from interesting to redundant, Sabrina calmly steps behind Kane, thanking everyone for coming and effectively shutting down the interview.

I say goodbye to Charlotte, who slips out a side door, headed to put out some fire about the rider for the musician who is performing in the arena tonight. Then, I make my way down to the practice ice.

The team built a new practice facility that connects to the main arena itself three years ago, and it's now one of the nicest facilities in the league. I have to admit, it's an improvement from having the practice facility over twenty minutes away in some strip-mall-looking complex. A few of the players who've been in Denver for a long time and have families here have houses down by the old practice arena, but the majority of the guys made the same decision I did and live in an apartment or condo downtown, since everything is here.

"Kane," I call, catching up with him in the hallway. He's in a black jacket with the number four in Yeti blue on the left sleeve.

"Coach," he replies, stopping in the middle of the hallway to wait for me.

"You did well at practice today."

"I'm excited to be part of the program."

I raise an eyebrow, daring him to keep lying to me. "Is that so?"

"The Yeti have a lot of potential."

"You were traded from the number-four-ranked team to one that is having trouble finding its footing after the season has already started," I say, crossing my arms over my chest. "I might not have played professional hockey, but I've been around long enough to know that, unless you hated your old situation for some reason—in which case there would've been feelers out there that we would've run into when we started looking for a veteran defenseman—you are *not* pleased about a mid-season trade. Don't bullshit me, Kane, we have a culture of accountability here."

"Fine," he replies, crossing his arms and widening his legs, a mirror of my stance. "Even though I knew it was possible to be traded mid-season, I never thought it would happen to me. I, like every other professional athlete, have enough of an ego to think I was far too critical to the Cyclones to be so easily removed. It's not the best feeling knowing that I was wrong—that I wasn't needed. But I'm here now, so I'm planning to make the best of the opportunity."

He holds my gaze, something most of the younger players avoid. I've been told the icy blue of my eyes—the one that is so close in color to Yeti blue—can be intense. Though I'm pretty sure it's because the guys don't know how to turn off their inherent need to flirt with anything that isn't an asexual blob, so they make the wise decision not to look at me.

"Good." I tap his chest once before quickly pulling away. Fuck. "Because you *are* needed here."

He nods once, his hand moving to rub the spot where I poked him.

"Now, go read your damn PR brief, like you were supposed to before you met with those reporters. I want you in my office at three to talk about your role on this team and what, exactly, it is that I need from you."

"You've got it, Coach," he answers, still standing there as I turn to walk away. "But for the record, I read every single thing they gave me. I just don't agree with the strategy. I'm playing for you. I'd mention the coaching staff in that answer on *any* other team. I'm not going to change that because you're a woman."

My heart skips a beat at the sincerity behind his words. I truly believe Beckett Kane doesn't see this as anything other than him playing for a new coach. Unfortunately for him, he's wrong. The club has paid a lot of money for a marketing team—one that specializes in the psychology of change—to figure out the best way to pull professional hockey into a new era.

And that way is to control the narrative. Control the optics. Control everything.

It works out well since I'm *very* good at control.

"I'm not asking you to change it because I'm a woman, Kane. I'm telling you to change it because I'm your fucking coach. Now, don't you have a meeting with the team doc to get to?"

I sigh. Why must the men in my life make everything harder?

Chapter 5

Beckett

"I'm not exactly worried about that hip flexor," the doctor says, clicking on the tablet as he scans through the files the Cyclones sent over. "But it does seem like your range of motion isn't what it should be."

"I get by just fine," I reply, not lying, but not telling the whole truth, either. Over-the-counter pain pills may be my best friend, but I'm a thirty-four-year-old hockey player. It's a price I'd gladly pay for the ability to keep playing the game.

Doctor Lowell gives me an appraising stare, one I meet with a slight glower of my own. "I've been working with professional athletes for almost as long as you've been alive, Kane. You can bluster and bullshit me all you want, but I've learned you lot are the least reliable patients in the world—and I have to tell you, basically everyone lies to their doctors."

I nod toward the screens on the walls, the ones showing my data from all the sensors and monitors I've been hooked up to since I got here. "A lot harder to lie when you know how many breaths I took in the last twenty-four hours because my stats are lighting up your walls like a stalker's wet dream."

Doc lets out a chuckle. "The team does love data. I'm not sure what Dr. Pearce does with it all, but she comes up with some pretty amazing results from her models. I know you're new around here, but you'll see soon. We've got young players, and not everything can be solved through data analytics, but the Yeti are on the cutting edge, and it's going to start paying off here in a year or two."

Now *that* I can get behind. I don't know that I feel one way or the other about all the monitoring—Li made a pretty sound argument for it this morning when he noticed I had biometric monitors taped to various parts of my body—but I'll take whatever help I can get to make sure I can still play the next couple of years.

When I was out on the ice with my new team, I saw the potential the doc is talking about. With the way they're *almost* where they need to be to be great. And I'm going to be there with them. Holding the Cup over my head while wearing that C patch on my jersey.

Doc looks through my records one more time before turning his stare back to me. "You sure you don't have any pain you want to tell me about?"

"I'm sure."

"Because you don't have any, or because you don't want to tell me about it?" he asks, sitting on the stool next to the bench I'm on.

I decide to be at least a little bit honest with him. "I'm thirty-four and a professional hockey player, Doc. Thirty-four-year-olds have pain. But you saw my routine. I'm prepared to manage it, and it's not going to slow me down on the ice."

I walk out of Doc's office a few minutes later, moving past the PT tables and into the weight room, where the rest of the defensemen and a few of the forwards are getting their workouts in for the day.

"Kane!" Larsen yells, abandoning his position as Li's spotter as he rushes over to me. Fortunately, there's someone from the trainer team to step in as Li completes his bench presses.

"Rookie," I say, glancing back to where he just stood with Li.

He follows my gaze. "Oh, he's fine. I was bored after I finished my workout, so I told him I'd spot him. But Jeff was mad at me for taking over his job anyway."

"Not mad, Larsen," the trainer replies. "Annoyed."

"Anyway, a few of us are planning to go out tonight. Dinner, drinks. That kind of thing. Want to come along?"

I shake my head. "Nah. Not tonight. I'm busy."

"Come on. What could you possibly be busy with?"

I mentally run through everything I still need to do today, including interviews with three private chefs recommended to me by the team and other professional athletes in the area who work with Vic. Now is the time to buckle down, to focus on making sure my body is ready for peak performance. Not going out for dinner and—God forbid—drinks.

"I—" I halt, Vic's words coming unbidden to my mind. The ones reminding me that *this* is my chance. And maybe there's something to being friends with the guys if I'm going to lead them. Guthry always invited the rest of the Cyclones over to his place for dinner or game nights.

"I'm not big on going out," I admit. "But I do have a few interviews with private chefs lined up. I'm sure I could convince them to make extra food if a few of you want to come over to my place for dinner before you go out."

Larsen nods enthusiastically. "Yes. Yep. I'm in. I'm definitely in." He whirls to look at Li. "Evan! Chef tryouts at Kane's tonight. You in?"

Li grunts out a "yep" in the middle of his set, as Larsen takes in the rest of the room. "Probably don't want too many. Your table only seats four, anyway. Oh, I know. Hammer lives in our building, too. I'll invite him. Plus, he and I have been talking about sharing a chef. And it's always good to have the enforcer on your side." He winks.

I let his excitement bounce off me, regretting ever making the offer. How do I attract the golden retrievers on every team?

"Rookie. Calm down," I tease. "You're going to eat like five variations of mostly plain meat and vegetables. Maybe a sample-sized breakfast smoothie if you're lucky."

His eyes widen. "I fucking love banana smoothies. Do you think they'll use that salted chocolate protein powder in it? I hope so."

I shake my head. "I don't know. But I've got a meeting with Coach to get to. Be at my place at five, okay?"

"Done. I'll be there. *We'll* be there," he says as he heads back toward Li, a noticeable pep in his step. "I'm so pumped."

***

"Go on in," Coach's executive assistant directs when I approach her desk, not even bothering to look up at me. "She's been expecting you, Beckett."

It's weird hearing my first name in the barn. Almost everyone in the professional sports world calls each other by their last names, whether they're players or not.

"Thanks," I reply, moving past her and into the office. Coach Blake sits behind a large wooden desk, wearing a black Yeti jacket, her dark hair pulled back. It's the exact same thing she's worn every time I've seen her, and I immediately feel guilty for noticing it.

I don't think I ever thought about what Coach Mack was wearing.

"Coach," I say as I step in front of her desk.

Her piercing blue eyes flick from her computer screen up to meet my gaze, and I feel the hair on my arms rise.

I guess I'm more anxious about this meeting than I realized.

"Kane. Please, take a seat," she replies, gesturing to the chair closest to me.

She locks her screen and turns her chair to face me, giving me her full attention.

"Doc just sent me all your intake documents. You're officially cleared to play. Welcome to the Yeti."

A wave of relief rolls through me; muscles I didn't even realize were tense relaxing.

"Thanks, Coach."

She nods. "Now, I know you're a solid player in your own right, but as you might've guessed, that's not the only reason you're here."

"You need a leader for your team."

"I need a player who's *going* to be a leader," she corrects. "And, apparently, you're the guy for the job."

I tilt my head slightly. That's an interesting way of putting it.

"Apparently?" I ask.

Coach Blake tilts her head as well. "You're a solid defenseman. Your turnover rate is practically nonexistent, your gap control is excellent, and your read on developing plays is one of the best I've seen. That said, I need someone to step up on and off the ice to help the team gel. Our coaching staff is highly competent, and, technically, our players are some of the best out there—even if they're a bit young. But they aren't clicking. Aren't coming together as a team when they're on the ice. Because—much to my annoyance—there is only so much a coaching staff can do to create those connections. That has to come from a player."

She thinks about it before flicking her gaze back up to meet mine.

"It has to come from *you*, Kane."

I nod. "I can do that."

"I know you can." Her eyes search mine, and I swear a flicker of disappointment moves across her features before she moves on. "But I also haven't seen a lot of evidence of that in the film I've watched recently."

I clench my fist against my thigh, forcing myself not to react, her words like a brand against my ego. What is this deficiency in me that coaches seem to spot but I remain blissfully unaware of? "Okay. Can you be more specific?" I ask, something building in my chest, causing the air between us to feel more alive.

"Of course. You're smart, and you play well. You're consistent. But I need more than that. As I'm sure you likely guessed, my plan is to put you on the first line with Li. Evan is solid, even though he doesn't trust his instincts as much as he should. But the second line needs just as much of a veteran presence as the first does. They all do."

"Okay," I say, not hiding the skepticism from my voice. I'm not the fucking coach. How does she expect me to impact the lines I'm not even on? After years of putting my head down, focusing on what *I* can control, this feels wrong. Like wearing a skate that's too big or playing with someone else's stick.

Coach Blake gives me a small smile, as if she can read my discomfort, and something tells me it's not something that she shares often. Then she starts walking me through it. The defensemen on the team. The support they need.

"You're going to be paired with Li. He has good instincts, but he questions them. Overanalyzes everything. He does best when he knows what to expect, but, as we both know, that's not hockey."

"I can't make him trust himself," I grumble.

Coach Blake's dark eyebrows dip toward each other. "And yet that's exactly what I need you to do. But you can't do it through drills or talking to him about it. He grasps it in theory. You need to show him that *you* trust his instincts. If he respects you, which I have no doubt he will, that will have more impact on his trust in himself than anything else."

With each word, I not only get a clearer sense of what she needs from me—and what likely caused me to be looked over for captain by the Cyclones—but also how Finley Blake was the woman who managed to break this particular glass ceiling. She's fucking smart, not only when it comes to the game but the players. And despite the frigid exterior I saw at practice yesterday, I'm starting to realize it might be an act. She seems to truly care about the men who play for her. At one point, she even pulls up video clips of Larsen on her computer and walks me through what they've been working on.

"He's young, but he's damn strong. See how explosive he is? He doesn't need you to tell him what to do; he's had coaches his whole life. He needs to know that when he does something stupid, you've got his back. Because he *is* going to do something stupid. And he'll do it so hard and fast that it creates waves of chaos on the ice."

By the time my meeting with her is done, I have an entirely different perspective of what it means to be a leader on a team.

And I can practically see that C on my black-and-blue Yeti jersey.

Chapter 6

Finley

I drop my grocery bags and my black backpack to the ground outside my door, digging into the pocket with the Yeti mascot on it to find the key to my door.

"Hey, Coach," a low voice says behind me. I quickly pop up, key in hand, to see Kane moving down the hallway, followed by a petite blonde woman. His six-foot-three frame looks giant in comparison.

My stomach tightens, just slightly, as I glance between the two of them. I'm... annoyed. I just had a major conversation with Kane about how we need a leader on this team, and what? He immediately went to the bar next door to the arena and picked someone up?

Of course he did. He's Beckett Kane.

Just because he isn't one of those players constantly making the news thanks to his evening activities doesn't mean he isn't like that. It just means he's smart enough to be discreet. Which doesn't surprise me. After spending over an hour in my office with him today, it's clear he is intelligent—and not only about hockey. Honestly, it felt more like a strategy session with one of my coaches than it did talking with a player... which I will not be digging into any further at this time.

"Evening, Kane." I meet his eyes. Something hot and irritated crackles up my spine. I move my gaze to the woman—beautiful, bright smile, two inches shorter than me, despite the heels she's wearing. "Well, I'll leave you two to—"

The elevator dings, and the doors slide open, revealing Larsen and Li, looking like the human version of puppies as they tumble out, wearing matching Yeti joggers and T-shirts.

"No way! You invited Coach?"

I look between the three of them, suddenly very sure I *do not* want to know what's about to happen in that room.

Not my business. Not my business. Not my—

"What are you boys up to tonight?" I ask, deciding it *is* my business. Because a good coach cares. Not because I'll wonder about this forever if I don't find out.

Kane slowly lifts one eyebrow as if to say, "Boys?" Luckily, Larsen is here, and he's always ready to talk.

"Dinner. Kane is trying out private chefs, and he invited us along."

I blink once, digesting what I heard. Is this Kane's usual MO, or is he taking my request to become a leader on and off the ice seriously?

"Did he not invite you?" Larsen continues. "I'm sure there's enough room." He looks at Kane. "Right?"

Kane pauses a beat too long, so Larsen changes his focus to the woman I'm now realizing must be the chef. "Right?"

There's slight panic in her eyes, and I can only assume she's trying to mentally calculate how she's going to add another plate of food from the cooler bag slung over her arm, which probably should've been a sign earlier that this wasn't a date.

"Unfortunately, I have plans tonight, but thanks for the offer… Larsen." I add the last part with a slight smirk toward Kane.

My players certainly don't need to know those plans consist of a steak salad for dinner, prepared by yours truly from a salad-in-a-bag kit and my leftover filet from last night's dinner, and three to five hours of watching film.

"Oo, big date, Coach?" Larsen asks, and the way Kane's shoulders bunch makes me want to laugh. Clearly regretting inviting the rookie over for dinner. As psychotic as he makes me, I secretly love the chaos energy Larsen brings.

"Dude." Li punches his friend in the arm.

I bite the inside of my cheek to keep from smiling. "Larsen, what makes you think that's an appropriate question?"

"Thought it was worth a try," the large man says. "I got Grumpy McGrumperson over here"—he points at a scowling Kane with his thumb—"to invite me to his place for dinner, so I thought maybe it was my lucky day or something. And I'm a nosy fucker who happens to know nothing about you."

"It's going to stay that way, too," I reply before unlocking my door. "Good luck, Chef."

I shut the door to the sound of another player exiting the elevator and joining the fray. I really should've considered the fact that I live across the hall before telling Kane to step up his leadership game. A clear miscalculation on my part. I just hope he doesn't start parading women around every night.

I rest my forehead against the closed door, annoyed that I care. Annoyed that it even crossed my mind. And slightly annoyed that Kane doesn't remember the fifteen minutes he spent helping me with my slap shot. It has lived rent-free in my head since I was sixteen, but apparently holds less than zero mental space for him.

Which is fair. And not at all something I should be annoyed by. Which I recognize.

Shoving the irritation down, I move through my evening routine, the occasional sounds from across the hall reminding me of how isolated I've become.

It grates. Especially when I hear the high-pitched laugh of a woman. The chef.

Because she can laugh and flirt with random men. She didn't have to sacrifice everything to achieve her dreams. *She* doesn't have the world waiting for her to make one mistake and take it all away.

After a quick dinner in front of my laptop, I change into the shorts and T-shirt I prefer to sleep in and pull the Falcons' film up on my TV. With my notes folder open on my screen, I get to work, preparing for our next game.

I'm through the first period, almost no notes written, when I pause and rewind the play, forcing myself to focus as their forward scores the first goal of the game. He's fast, but not unstoppable.

Voices drift through the door, and I tiptoe to the peephole, not at all proud of myself for my curiosity. The chef is saying goodbye, and Kane steps out into the hall with her.

I watch, like a complete stalker, as he shakes her hand, thanking her for her time. His hand looks large compared to hers, and I imagine what it must feel like to have its strong warmth wrapped around—oh, for crying out loud. I clearly have let my personal life go stagnant for too long if I'm suddenly envisioning Beckett Kane's hand wrapped around mine in a way that is certainly not suitable for a player and their coach.

"All right, boys, fifteen minutes until option two is here," Kane announces as he walks into his apartment.

Oh, hell. Of course they're trying out multiple chefs. Why can't they just go home so I can get back to my usual routine?

I debate emailing Paige to see if she can get Kane assigned to another unit, but decide against it. These are still early days. Asking for a player to be moved, or even for me to move out of the building, would cause a level of gossip that I neither need nor want in the middle of the season. A season that's already decided to be a huge fucking pain in my ass.

Instead, I silently move back to the couch, grabbing my headphones from my backpack as I pass. Deciding I need a distraction, I make a call to the only person likely to answer at this time.

"Hey, Dad," I say once the video connects.

"Finley, is everything okay? Shouldn't you be watching film?" he asks, clearly confused about why I'm calling him now, rather than waiting for our usual check-in.

"I'm making my way through the Falcons' last game as we speak," I reply.

"That Lancaster is fast. Shows off too much with his stick-work, though."

"Indeed."

We sit in silence for a beat, and I question why calling my dad felt like a good option. He has always been there for me, but we don't do feelings. We don't do easy conversations or banter. We don't do—well, anything that isn't hockey.

He finally offers, "And you got Beckett Kane."

"I did."

"He'll be a strong addition for your team. White clearly knows what he's about over there."

"He does," I agree. Even I can see that I might've been a bit dramatic in cutting Kane from my original list.

"Plus, they can probably do some fluff piece about two kids from a few miles away ending up on the same team—one as the coach, one as the star player." Dad laughs. "Did you know he's from Superior?"

"Read it in the packet the team put together," I answer, with no intention of mentioning to my dad that I met Kane once before. Or that he hasn't left my mind since he showed up outside my front door, disrupting the modicum of equilibrium I've tried so hard to achieve.

I mean, just look at tonight. It should've been one of the most productive evenings of my week. Home early from the arena, a good dinner, and a few hours' worth of film watched with actionable notes to discuss with the coaches tomorrow. Instead, I've been distracted by the party across the hall.

And whose fault is it? The same man I clearly *didn't* choose to be on my ice, and yet, somehow, is. Beckett *fucking* Kane.

That's who.

"... why it's so important that you let Rob handle him. He's older than you, Finley. He's not going to take a woman telling him what to do well," my dad says, still talking about Kane, though, apparently, now he's moved on from fun biographical facts to reasons why I'm not fit to coach him.

All my players are younger than me, but besides Sutton, none of my assistant coaches are, so I've moved on from the fact that I'm in charge of men many years my senior. It never crossed my mind that I should worry about Kane being three years older than me.

"I understand, Dad."

Rob is the defensive coach, so he will work most directly with Kane, but at the same time, my dad's worry doesn't reflect my experience today.

"I do think he respects me, though," I continue. "We had a long conversation about what I expect from him, moving forward, and he seemed receptive."

"Of course he did. Kane's a smart man. He didn't make it this long by making an enemy of the coach on day one. Trust me when I say, he's not happy to be on your team."

Some people might think it's harsh coming from the man who had me in skates before I could walk, but not me. Sure, my dad may have always been my harshest critic, but it's only because he holds me to the highest levels of perfection. And if anyone is interested in arguing that it's an "unhealthy parenting dynamic," like my one and only long-term boyfriend, Travis, did, well, the results speak for themselves. Literally no other fathers ever will be able to say their daughter was the first female head coach in professional hockey. And just wait until I'm holding the championship trophy over my head—then he really will be proud of me.

"I'll talk to Rob," I concede, though my stomach turns at the thought. I'm the head coach. I shouldn't need to ask Rob to handle a player for me. A player who, so far, seems to have no issues with me. And even if he does, well, he can do what veteran players do: retire.

But my dad knows this sport better than anyone else. Even if he's not been coaching for over a decade now, he's still one of the most respected minds in hockey. So, if he thinks I need to be worried about whether Kane respects me or not, I will.

Chapter 7
Beckett

Working with PR teams is something I've always hated. I understand fans love to know what I eat for breakfast on game day, or who has the strongest grip, but the truth is, it goes against everything in my nature. I don't want the world to know my business. Which is why I'm annoyed to be currently sitting in the conference room with an assortment of players and staff in a meeting called by Sabrina, the head of the PR team.

I'm only three weeks into my time with the Yeti, and I need to be focused on hockey. Especially after we dropped a game to the Cyclones last night. After winning the last two at home, I *wanted* the victory over my old team last night. Shit. I *needed* that victory to show everyone it was a mistake to trade me mid-season—even though I'm starting to find my groove with the players here in Denver.

Unfortunately, that wasn't in the cards. Pretty hard to win if you can't score. The 0–1 loss hit hard, and all I want to do is be out on the ice right now, working to get better, not sitting in a damn conference room.

"Thank you all for taking the time to come in today," Sabrina starts. "We're just waiting for two more before we begin."

I stare at the time on my phone's lock screen, wondering how long this will take. I have at least another two hours left of training and recovery before I can head back to my apartment. As the numbers change to ten o'clock, Coach Blake walks through the door. There's something about her hair that's slightly different today, making her face look softer. It's...

"Thanks for waiting," a man says, and I realize I failed to notice that Coach Blake was followed in by none other than Ken Peterson, the owner of the Denver Yeti. *Fuck.* Now is not the time for distractions. This must be serious if the owner is getting involved.

Mr. Peterson offers, sitting down, "Sabrina, this was your brainchild. Why don't you take it away?"

"Thanks, Ken." Sabrina smiles widely as she clicks a button. At the end of the room, an image appears on the TV. "I'm excited to announce that you all will be participating in a very exciting new PR campaign: 'The Great Yeti Challenge.'"

She looks around the room as if expecting applause, but when she gets none, she smooths out her ice-blue blazer and forges ahead. "In pre-established pairs, you all spend the next two months participating in a series of five challenges, all of which will be recorded and broadcast on social media. A winner will be picked each week."

No. Nope. Not happening. I *will not* be competing in challenges.

"This is just what the team needs to really get the fan base behind us," Mr. Peterson praises from his seat next to Sabrina. "The Mountaineers did something similar last year, and the basketball games' attendance increased by almost fifteen percent within the first month." He smiles at us, like that should be enough of a reason to do some ridiculous challenge.

I look around the room to see how the rest of the group is responding. Dr. Pearce is in full student mode, her e-pencil poised on the top of her device, ready to take notes. Li is watching her like he's trying to decide whether he needs to take out his notebook, too. Larsen is—*Oh, Jesus, Murphy, they're going to pair me with Larsen.*

I enjoyed having the guys over to my place a few weeks ago, but Larsen is a golden retriever who someone fed a bowl of sugar and then set loose a basket of squirrels. He stops by my place regularly now that he knows where I live, and frequently invites me to come over for dinner or to come play video games with him and Li. It's... Okay, it's actually pretty fun, but it's also a lot. When I was in Florida, I spent time with people socially once every couple of months at most. I'm okay with some Larsen in my life, but I know if we get paired together, it will be too much. I'll bark at him, and like the puppy he is, he'll be devastated. And then I'll have to live with that on my conscience.

Sabrina walks us through a series of five challenges, including a bake-off, a talent show, an obstacle course with other Colorado pro athletes, a trivia contest, where we answer questions about our partner, and a surprise final event that she won't give us any more information on. She didn't even break when Larsen stuck out his bottom lip and begged.

"And finally," she says, "the moment you've all been waiting for—the teams."

I catch the quick glance Li gives Dr. Pearce, and a tug pulls on the side of my lips. Does Li have a thing for Pearce? I guess in my new role as team leader—despite the lack of C on my jersey—I should talk to him about why falling for a coach would be a good way to ruin his career.

"J.D., you're pairing with Rob," Sabrina informs them, nodding toward the two men as J.D. pats Rob on the shoulder.

"Team Dad!" Larsen jokes, earning him an eye roll from both men. Though I hate to admit it, J.D. isn't half bad as a captain.

He has the guys' respect, even if he wasn't able to get the defense straightened out.

Sabrina ignores him and continues with her list, "Lefevre and Dr. Pearce."

Li's shoulders slump ever so slightly as Lefevre lets out a whoop.

"Björk, you're with Volkov." The two high-five, and I laugh as Larsen starts poking Li in the arm.

"Please tell me I'm with anyone except the rookie," Li pleads.

Sabrina laughs. "Li and Larsen. How could I break up the bromance?!"

Li drops his head into his hands. "Please don't call it that."

"Dude!" Larsen exclaims, dropping a heavy arm over Li's shoulder. "We're going to kick ass!"

"Everly, you're with John," Sabrina tells the two youngest people in the room by far, both here for college internships.

"Team Intern!" Larsen laughs. "You two are going to get crushed."

I look around the room, realizing I'm the only player left. And the only other people in the room are the owner, my coach, and the head of PR. Who the fuck—

"And that leaves Beckett and Coach Blake."

Coach's head jerks up from her phone. "No." She looks back down as if that's the end of the conversation. I mean, I don't want to partner with her, either, but that's pretty fucking rude.

Sabrina sighs, looking to the owner for support.

"You're an important part of this team, Coach Blake." Mr. Peterson focuses his attention on Coach. "We need you out there."

"Ah, she's just scared that Li and I are going to kick her and Kane's ass," Larsen teases, shooting me a wink.

A wink.

The kid has a death wish.

I swear Coach's brain is working overtime to try to figure a way out of this—not that it seems likely with the *owner* telling her she has to. Finally, she nods once, and says, "Fine, but what do I get when I make Larsen cry because I've beaten him so badly?" The smile that threatens to spill from her lips makes my heart do some unexpected calisthenics.

Sabrina laughs. "That's the spirit. And a great question." She clicks to the next slide. "The winning team gets to pick our partner charity for next year. In addition to a visit by the team, the organization will also receive a million dollars from the Yeti Foundation, an amount we anticipate the fans will double over the course of the season. And, obviously, bragging rights. We've been working on a little something the champions will be able to display in their lockers, too."

"Or on their desks," Coach Blake cuts in with a pointed look at Larsen.

"Or on their desks," Sabrina agrees before she answers the last few questions from the group. She ends the meeting with a reminder that the first event will take place in two weeks at the culinary school across town.

I take a deep breath. It's fine. PR is a distraction from the game, but at least this will be on off days. Hopefully that means the social media team will leave me alone before the games since they'll already have a lot of footage. I wonder if that was the PR team's plan all along. I know the competition concluding before we move into our final playoffs push had to be strategic.

Larsen starts chirping about their team taking home the W as soon as we walk into the hall. I shove him into the wall, chuckling when he mutters a curse. Unable to be kept down, he immediately bounces back and starts talking to Li about getting their new chef to train them for the cooking challenge.

"Kane," Coach Finley calls from behind me. "Do you have a minute?"

"Sure," I reply, turning to face her fully. "Want to meet in your office?"

She waves the idea off. "I just wanted to let you know I'm not going to be the best teammate in this competition. I mean, I'll try while we're there, but I'm either all-in or all-out when it comes to competitions. My focus needs to be on getting this team into the playoffs. I don't have hours each week to spend training with a chef to win a silly cook-off."

"Understood," I say. "I'm not looking to do much more than the minimum that's required, either. I've got a team to lead—I mean a team to be the leader of," I joke, reminding her of the way she told me she leads the team.

The right corner of her mouth lifts slightly. "Indeed. And *I've* got a team to lead."

Chapter 8

Finley

"Oh, hell, no." I shake my head. "Certainly not."

"I didn't pick them." Kane slips the apron over his head and ties the strings around his waist.

"Where's Sabrina?" I ask, looking around the large room set up for the cooking competition.

I'm not sure how the last two weeks passed so quickly, but somehow, the practices and games flew by when all I wanted was for time to stand still, so I never had to do this ridiculous challenge.

On the plus side, our defense is *finally* getting it together. We've won eight of our last twelve games, including one against the Chicago team who took Pike out of commission.

Kane shrugs his large shoulders. "Avoiding you, if I had to guess. I don't think it was an accident that she had someone from her team give me our aprons."

Fucking Sabrina.

"For the love. I cannot wear this," I groan taking in the monstrosity they expect me to be filmed in. The apron is designed to look like a yeti body with your head replacing the mascot's. It's ridiculous. And worse, *it's an apron.*

"We're all wearing them." Beckett looks down at his chest, now completely covered by the yeti apron. "It's not a big deal."

That is so much easier for him to say. No one is going to see him in that and all of a sudden think his place is in the kitchen. In fact, with his black T-shirt that is tight in just the right places, he looks like a DILF about to go grill some hamburgers at the family picnic.

"I guess these are going to be a fundraising item," Beckett comments. "Honestly, I think Sabrina and her team are onto something. People are going to love this."

He looks at my face and holds up his hands. "Woah. No need to blame me. I'm just doing what I'm told."

"I'm not blaming you," I say. Unless he means that as a member of the male population, then, I'm *totally* blaming him and, in all fairness, the female half of the population, too. "I'd just prefer not to wear fucking aprons."

"Coach, are you annoyed about this as well?" Larsen asks, barging into our conversation.

"Obviously, Larsen."

"Right?! I told Li the yeti body is dumb."

I nod. I'm not sure how Larsen became my ally in the crusade to ditch the aprons, but I will take what I can get.

"They clearly should've done our bodies wearing, like, Yeti-branded boxers," Larsen continues. "Like the bikini ones, but for guys. Or yours could've been a bikini one. Oh, man, yours would've been awesome. Can you imagine a little black bikini—"

Larsen is cut off as Li, with a look of absolute horror on his face, pulls him away from me and the ungodly number of sprints he was about to be told to go skate.

I swallow the laugh that's about to escape me at Larsen's ridiculousness when I realize Kane is staring at my stomach, his gaze vacant.

"Um, Earth to Kane?"

He shakes his head, dragging his focus back to my eyes.

I hold out the apron. "I've made an executive decision: I'm not wearing this."

"Then don't. I'm, personally, not willing to appear anything but an active participant for something the owner seemed overly invested in, but that's just me."

I glare at him, then, begrudgingly, put the apron on, pulling the strings tight behind me. As someone who *desperately* needs the owner in her corner, the man has a good point.

"You look," Kane starts, running a hand through his dark hair, "ready. You look ready."

"Well, looks can be deceiving, because I am, in fact, a terrible cook." I purse my lips, realizing that's not quite correct. "Unless it's a big piece of protein and a salad coming straight from a plastic bag."

He smiles, and it disarms me slightly. This might be the first real smile I've seen on him. Kane has been stepping up at practice lately, and while I occasionally catch him joking around with the other guys—usually exchanging good-natured insults with the other defensemen—he's not a guy who smiles frequently.

"This might be rough," he warns, and I nod.

"Hopefully, Sabrina is one of the judges—it'll serve her right for making us do this."

Kane chuckles, and I realize I've said more than I usually would've. Exposed a glimmer of my nonprofessional side.

***

"Do you know anything about making cupcakes?" I ask, forcing myself not to grind my teeth as Larsen and Li sprint toward the supply shelf behind us. I *hate* losing.

We're in a teaching kitchen, with cameras trained on us from every angle. If it's not the social team in our faces, recording on their cell phones, it's the professional cameras of our PR team set up to capture each of us.

"I'm pretty sure I haven't eaten a cupcake in the last decade," Beckett mutters, massaging a point on the back of his neck as he scans a vanilla cupcake recipe in front of him. "Jesus Christ, how do those two dumbasses already have their ingredients?"

I follow his gaze to where Li and Larsen are back at their station, setting out bags and tubs of God-knows-what.

"Okay, it's supposed to be Yeti themed," I say, trying to work through this. "So, we could do ice rinks, skates, or jerseys?"

"Do you have a secret cupcake talent you've been keeping from the world?"

"No." I shake my head. "But for the record, if I did, I would *certainly* keep it from the world. Plus, how hard can it be?"

"I mean, hard?" he asks. "Isn't that the point? To make us look like idiots?"

Knowing that running out of time is a real issue in the cooking shows this event is based on, I force myself to focus, looking through the recipes the PR team set out for us to choose from. "Too bad for them, I'm pretty good at not looking like an idiot, even when I have no idea what I'm doing. Okay." I tap the vanilla recipe in front of him. "I think we go vanilla on vanilla. If it turns out neither of us is good at decorating, we can at least call them snow mountains or something."

"Smart," Kane says. "Or we can draw lines and turn them into rinks. Though vanilla on vanilla is the worst flavor combination, and taste is half of the score."

"I like vanilla with vanilla. It's what I had every birthday growing up."

Kane's look of disgust makes me want to give him a good uppercut to the solar plexus, but instead of resorting to violence, I put down the recipe cards.

"I'm open to your suggestions."

"You call the plays, Queenie."

Queenie?

"I *will not* be going by Queenie," I declare. Ice Queen is fine. It evokes small amounts of fear. Queenie feels like I'm on a throne doing story time with the kingdom's four-year-olds.

Though if the smirk pulling across Kane's face has anything to say about it, he seems to think otherwise.

I'm forced back to this ridiculous competition when the interns run by giggling.

Splitting up the work is our best bet, so I announce, "Okay, I'll get the cupcake ingredients, you get the frosting."

We make our way toward the shelves in the back, both spending more time searching for one ingredient than Li and Larsen spent getting all of theirs.

"Not that one," I hiss as Beckett grabs the bag of sugar. "Yours calls for powdered sugar."

Beckett raises one eyebrow, looking down at his armload of ingredients. "Yeah, which is why I have it right here." He lifts his right elbow, where there is a plastic bag full of white powder tucked. "This sugar is for you."

I look down at my arms and then again at the recipe. Fuck. How did I miss that?

"I figured we'd make healthy cupcakes," I say.

Beckett walks away, headed back to our station. "No one wants that, Coach," he calls over his shoulder. "No one."

We get to work on the cupcakes, measuring ingredients and dumping them in.

"It says to slowly pour in the dry ingredients. How slow do you think is slow?" Kane asks.

I eye the mixer in front of us. This thing is intimidating. My mom passed away when I was three, and it has been Dad and me ever since, which means I've used a mixer exactly zero times in my life.

I pinch the bridge of my nose. "I have no idea."

"Okay, well, I definitely have some vague memories of going too fast with my mom and ending up with flour all over the kitchen. So, I think we need to go pretty slow. Though I'm worried we aren't going to have enough time."

"They only have to cook for twenty-four minutes." I read the instructions for what feels like the millionth time.

"Yeah, but then they have to cool before we can decorate them."

I look at where his finger is tapping, ignoring the way the muscles in his hand flex. "Can't we just stick them in the freezer, or something, to get them to cool?" I ask.

"I mean, maybe?" he replies, working the silver machine with much more confidence than I feel.

Silently, we scoop the cupcakes into their liners, and Beckett shoves them into the oven as I set the Yeti-branded egg timer on the counter.

"Frosting?" I ask.

"Frosting," Kane agrees, a look of resignation on his face.

As Kane combines our ingredients, I scope out the competition. Sutton is meticulously adding their powdered sugar to the mixer. She angles her wrist again and again, pouring slightly more of the white powder into the bowl each time until, clearly fed up, Lefevre grabs the silver cup from her hand and unceremoniously dumps the whole thing into the silver bowl at once.

Her entire demeanor screams outrage until a puff of white dust shoots up and covers Lefevre's face.

I laugh loudly and gently bump my arm against Kane's to make sure he doesn't miss out on the hilarity. The hairs on my arms tingle as a static shock passes between us at the contact.

Kane pulls his arm away abruptly as Sutton shouts, "Culture of accountability, Lefevre!"

Following the noise, he chuckles. "At least we've got them beat."

"I don't know," I say. "Sutton seems like the type of person who might secretly be crafty and will crush the decorating portion of the competition."

Kane leans closer to me, his warm breath dancing along my ear when he murmurs, "What does someone who's secretly crafty look like?"

I examine Sutton closer. "She just has that vibe that she knows what Mod Podge is."

"What the fuck is Mod Podge?"

"Glue?" I shrug. "I don't know. Do *I* look like someone who crafts?"

I turn to face him, my gaze trailing over his jaw before finally landing on his dark, coffee-brown eyes.

"Does Lefevre cook for himself?" Kane asks, jolting me out of the staring contest I seem to have been the only contestant in.

I shrug. "I'm not sure. I let the nutritionist handle that."

"And here I thought you were the type of coach who didn't know how to delegate." His eyes widen as he turns to look at me fully, his hands going up in a defensive gesture. "I didn't mean that."

The timer rings, and I decide to ignore his comment. Because what does that even mean? He's been here for over a month, and I've never once asked him about his nutrition. Honestly, I couldn't give a shit as long as he performs, which he has been. As much as it pains me to admit.

"Saved by the bell." I drop down in front of the oven, peering in at the little mounds of white inside. Neither of us has any idea how to tell whether a cupcake is cooked the appropriate amount or not, and since we're running short on time, we decide to pull them out.

"I think we need to do that," Kane says, subtly nodding toward Li, who is fanning his cupcakes with a baking sheet.

"You don't think sticking them in the fridge is the way to go?" I ask.

Kane considers it, glancing back at the large, walk-in fridge off to the side of the room. "No one has gone in there since we've gotten eggs."

"I see your point," I agree. "I'll fan; you work the mixer to see if you can make a few more colors. Probably black and Yeti blue?"

"I'm on it," Kane replies with a nod. "It'll match your eyes."

I gape at him. That was, yup. Super normal and not at all making my body turn weird temperatures.

He clears his throat before quickly grabbing the little box of food coloring. He stares at the instructions on the back like it's his first hockey contract, and he can't believe it's really real. His cheeks turn red, clearly embarrassed to have admitted that he—what?—noticed I had eyes.

Finally, I turn back to our cupcakes, tentatively picking each one out of the tray and setting them on the little wire thing Li has his on before fanning them. We work in silence for the rest of the allotted time, our arms occasionally bumping as we both work side by side. It's distracting in a way that makes me glad I have my own office. I hate sharing space with others.

"Holy buckets!" I exclaim, looking over at the cupcake Kane is working on. "You *are* a crafter."

It's a masterpiece. He's only done one in the time it's taken me to make three of the cupcakes into little ice rinks, but shit. His yeti looks like the one on the timer in front of him.

No wonder the social media team has all been over here, phones focused on him. I assumed it was because he's by far the most attractive player here, but no—he's actually fucking good at decorating cupcakes.

Kane looks up, his cheeks turning slightly pink. "Yeah, no, yeah. I don't think I've ever actually frosted a cupcake before."

"I call bullshit," I say, then, remembering my role, I wink at the camera now trained on me. "Don't let the secret out of the bag too soon, Kane."

Directly behind me, Sabrina laughs, and I almost jump. Jesus. When did she get there?

Kane keeps his eyes trained on his cupcake, slowly using a dark purple we're calling black to create the wide-open mouth of the yeti.

"You totally know what Mod Podge is," I whisper.

"Mod what?" His lips lift into a small grin.

Even though I know I shouldn't, I laugh, and it's well worth it when a proud smile creeps across his face.

Then, we fall into an easy silence as we both work, trying to get these cupcakes frosted before time runs out.

"Faster, Kane," I hiss, watching the time tick down on the large clock in front of us. I've frosted a total of nine cupcakes, six that could *possibly* pass as rinks and three that are just large, black circles I'm calling pucks.

"I'm hurrying," he replies, his tongue sticking out between his teeth as he concentrates on the hockey stick the yeti is holding.

"Time!" Sabrina yells as Kane puts the finishing touches on it.

He looks up, smiling, before his eyes drift to the cupcakes I decorated. "What the fuck is that?" he whispers, a snort-like sound accompanying the question, as Sabrina does some sort of recap up front.

"Rink." I point at the white ones. They look fine. Better than I anticipated. "And those are the black pits of my soul."

Kane snorts again.

"Or we could call them pucks if you think the judges would be opposed to soul cupcakes."

"Pucks, right. You'd think that would've been... easier."

I breathe in, reminding myself that I can never, under *any* circumstances, be caught rolling my eyes on camera. Even if it's almost painful keeping myself from doing it.

"Hey, thanks. And, if you didn't notice, they're decorated. All nine of them."

Sabrina claps her hands, drawing everyone's attention. She then proceeds to walk around the room, making each group show off their cupcakes before the three judges take a bite.

We all know the interns are going to lose—the smell of their burning cake batter wafted through the place as soon as they opened their oven—but the rest is a mystery to me.

The judges let out gasps of delight when Larsen uncovers their cupcakes, showing off excellent replicas of the team jerseys, each with a different name and number. After the judges try theirs, Larsen picks one up and, with a dramatic flair, flashes Kane his name and number before taking a giant bite out of it. *Fucking Rookie.*

Finally, it's our turn.

"Wow!" the woman on the left exclaims. "These look just like the mascot!"

Kane dips his chin while the other two judges look at the pucks. One has his eyebrows drawn down so far; the only explanation is that he's taking a break from judging cupcakes to solve world hunger.

"Coach really carried the team with the pucks and the rinks, though." Kane offers me a slight smile. One that definitely doesn't make my insides swirl.

"The lines are impressive. Very straight," the enthusiastic woman gushes.

The three judges take bites of the cupcakes, letting us know they're pretty good before moving on.

What feels like an hour later, Sabrina finally announces the judges' scores. Li and Larsen, unsurprisingly, won with their jerseys and apparently "very tasty" chocolate cupcakes.

"And, in an unexpected twist," Sabrina says, "Coach Blake and Kane came in second. What a team, those two!"

A warmth spreads through my chest at her comment that I immediately shut down. *Oh, fuck.*

I'm barely paying attention as she moves on to announce J.D. and Rob squeaked out a third-place spot over Björk and Volkov; my brain is still stuck on her declaration about us being a good team.

I force myself out of my head long enough to laugh with everyone else when the team captain and Rob chest-bump in their yeti aprons before quickly packing up the extra cupcakes to leave in the front-office breakroom.

"Here." Kane takes a few out of my box and putting them in a different one. "We'll give these to the poor interns who burned theirs."

I nod, not sure what to do with my hands. Or my face. Or my voice.

Kane glances at me. "Not a bad showing for two people who don't know what Mod Podge is." He emphasizes the word *two*.

I shoot him a sarcastic smile. That man totally knows what it is.

"We *do* make a pretty good team, Coach."

I open my mouth to brush him off. To make some snarky comment about not needing anyone on my team, but that's not true. I did need him today. And he's right. We *do* make a good team.

Which is exactly the problem.

"Well, as long as you keep pulling out hidden talents, I think we'll be okay." I grab the box of cupcakes and make a beeline toward the door—not even taking the time to pull off the stupid yeti apron. I have to get out of this room and away from whatever it's doing to my heart rate.

Chapter 9
Finley

"Congratulations on a great game tonight, Coach." Ken Peterson steps in my path as I make my way from the media room to my office after a 2–1 victory over Las Vegas. His wife is next to him, looking ready to go to high tea at the Brown Palace in her suit jacket and pearls.

"Thank you, sir," I respond, shaking his outstretched hand. "The Phantoms are a tough team. It was a good win."

"It was an impressive show the men put on out there. Our defensive line, especially, is looking good."

Too good, in fact. I find myself tuning out everything other than Kane's almost supernatural ability to know where the other players are going to be, rather than focusing on the bigger picture.

"Yes, sir," I reply, waiting for him to continue with his recommendations for next game.

"Well," he says, gesturing to his wife that he's ready to leave, "keep up the good work."

Wait. Does he not have any suggestions for what we should be working on? What we need to be doing next? He's fully ingrained himself in the ridiculous PR competition, but *that's* all he has to say to me when the team is in the middle of a major rebuilding year and barely on the cusp of making it to the playoffs?

"Always," I reply when I realize all he wanted to do was tell me, good game. As he and his wife walk away, hand in hand, I feel flat. Almost hollow. Definitely not the swell of pride I expected to feel from my boss telling me I'm doing a good job as the head coach, when I've worked my whole life to get here.

"Why does your face look like that, Coach?" Larsen asks as he, too, exits the media room. After scoring one of our goals tonight, he deserved to be in there. And the media love him.

"What does my face look like?" I ask, tipping my head to one side, attempting to bait the rookie into saying something dumb. It's becoming my favorite pastime.

Larsen's gaze flitters between my eyes and my mouth, clearly trying to figure out a way to describe what he sees there. "You know, like you took a drink of an old protein smoothie only to realize everything has separated and there's a thick film of something gross on the top."

"That's—" I start, but Larsen cuts me off, "Oh! Did you hear about the name the public has given you and Kane's team?"

"What do you mean?" I ask.

"Like, they're calling us L-squared. Yours isn't as cool, but that's not your fault. You two don't have the same chemistry we do."

"Fuck." Li pauses mid-step as he walks by with the third-pair guys. "Are you talking about the stupid trending team names again?"

"Woah," Larsen exclaims, looking slightly offended. "I wouldn't go so far as to call theirs trending. And L-squared isn't stupid."

Li sighs. "If I hadn't been with you the entire time after the bake-off competition ended, I would've sworn you started it yourself."

"I consider that to be one of the greatest compliments you've ever given me, honey," Larsen replies, fluttering his eyelashes and pretending to kiss Li.

Li shoves him, and the two start tussling there in the hallway.

"Oh, hey, Dr. Pearce," I call, catching sight of Sutton's dark brown hair from down the hall.

"Fuck," Li groans as I speed away, desperate for any reason to escape that conversation.

"Coach," Sutton replies, her eyes never leaving the tablet in her hands. "I don't have my analysis yet."

"Not a problem," I say, falling into step next to her. "I just needed to escape those two."

Sutton's eyes momentarily flash to the two grown men still play-fighting as she shrugs. "Do you know the amount of adrenaline currently pumping through their bodies?"

"Do... you?" I ask, not sure whether she's quizzing me or genuinely interested.

"The best guess I have based on sports physiology is it's approximately twice—maybe even three times—what it should be at rest, even this long after a game. During peak-play stress, such as a fight or last-second goal attempt, it would likely reach six to ten times their normal amounts," Sutton answers as if she's lecturing a class. "If you would let me take blood samples pre- and post-game, I could get you a more precise answer."

"Not necessary, Dr. Pearce."

She sneaks one more glance over her shoulder before we turn the corner and leave the men. "The conclusion is they still have significantly elevated levels of adrenaline, which is known to cause disruptions to their emotional regulation."

"Finley!" a chipper voice yells from down the hall.

I force a smile, mostly because I know it annoys Sabrina to no end when I do it. "Yes, Sabrina?" I ask.

"We need you to come to the post-game family area to meet a special guest."

I try to avoid the family area whenever possible, but this is fine. This is what head coaches do. They shake hands and kiss future nepo babies.

At least I have something in common with the babies.

"Good game out there tonight, Queenie," Kane says as we pass by him, a heaping plate of salmon and rice in front of him as he cools down on the stationary bike. "Your call to switch the pairs there at the end was just what we needed, even if Li and I would never admit to being tired that early."

Damn it. Why is that swell of pride I couldn't find earlier suddenly making an appearance now? Maybe it's delayed pride? Obviously, I don't care what Kane thinks, so it can't be that.

I mentally shake it off. Not the point. "I don't care how well you played tonight, Kane. I will make you do sprints if you continue to call me that."

He smiles, and damn it, it makes me want to smile back, even though I know it means he's going to keep calling me Queenie. I'm not sure how Kane always seems to pick up on my teasing when no one else does, but it's somewhat endearing. And also irritating. Where's the joy if I can't make the players scared of me?

"Beckett," Sabrina interrupts. "I could use you, too, actually. Just for a minute."

Kane swings his leg over the bike, placing his weight on his right side a fraction too carefully. It's a subtle hitch, but I catch it, nonetheless.

"I'm coming." He falls into step beside me, plate of food still in hand.

"Are you okay?" I ask.

"Of course," Kane replies, his eyes on his food.

"While I've got you two," Sabrina interrupts, glancing over her shoulder at us as she continues down the hallway, never slowing her stride. "You are the only team that hasn't submitted the nonprofit you'd like to work with if you win the competition. Do you know who you'd like to compete for?"

"I thought they weren't due to you until end of day tomorrow," I respond, worry beginning to gnaw at my stomach that I missed a deadline.

"They aren't. I figured I'd ask since I have you both."

I meet Kane's gaze, and he offers a slight shrug. Guess it's up to me, then.

"Who have the other teams picked?" I ask, pretending I don't want to duplicate answers rather than needing inspiration.

"Rob and J.D. picked a nonprofit that supports veterans as they transition out of the military. Li and Larsen chose one that has something to do with sea lions—"

"Sea lions?" Kane interrupts. "But we're nowhere near the ocean."

I nod in agreement. What a weird choice for the two of them to make. Rob's choice doesn't surprise me at all—he has a lot of family who have seen active combat—but sea lions in Colorado?

"That doesn't change the fact that they need help, Kane. They are an important species for ocean health and are essential to marine ecosystems," Sabrina says, and I can practically hear Li telling her the exact same thing.

"We can do better than that," Kane whispers. "Not that I'm against sea lions or anything. It's just..."

"We don't live anywhere near the sea?" I ask, conspiratorially. "That."

We follow Sabrina into the family area, and I put on my best meet-someone-important smile.

"Ah, it's the fake smile," Kane remarks, his tone almost sad.

I whip my head toward him. This is the smile Sabrina made me practice. It does not look fake. "This *is* my smile, Kane."

"Okay," he says, as if it doesn't matter to him either way.

"I hear someone wanted to meet the first-ever female head coach," Sabrina singsongs.

"Go get 'em, Queenie," Kane jokes, stepping back as I step forward and run directly into... a girl wearing a soft beanie, mask, and a Kane jersey. After switching her stuffed yeti to her left hand, the girl sticks out her fist for a bump.

"Hi, Coach Blake. I'm Lilly."

I tap my fist to hers before dropping into a squat in front of the young girl, surprised by the instinct to meet Lilly at her level. I glance at the two women standing on either side of her, trying to understand what this is.

Damn it, Sabrina. A heads-up would've been nice.

"Hi, Lilly. Did you get to see the game?" I ask.

Lilly nods, looking at the woman in a puffy jacket with the words Wishes and Wings embroidered on the left breast. "It was my Wings Wish."

"That's so cool." I can feel everyone's attention in the room focused on me. "Are you a hockey fan?"

"Yeah. I'd started learning to play when I was diagnosed. Now I'm in the hospital a lot, so I can't go to the practices, but I still love it."

"I'm sorry to hear that," I reply, glancing at the woman I assume is her mother, hoping for some kind of guidance here.

"But," Lilly says, a smile on her face, "I watch almost every Yeti game with my dad."

"Oh, really?"

"Yeah, but he works nights, so we usually record them and watch together the next day. When I turned seven a few months ago, my parents put a TV in my room, so I could watch some of the games before I go to bed."

I nod, searching the room for her dad. There doesn't seem to be a man nearby, so I decide not to question it. "That's a smart way to do it. What was your favorite part of the game tonight?"

Lilly bites her lip and looks at her mom, who shrugs. "She asked you."

"When you yelled at the boys, and then they started playing better. Usually, Kane is the one doing the yelling, but tonight it was you. He's my favorite player, but you're my favorite coach in the whole world."

"Well, gosh," Kane mutters from behind me, as I bite the inside of my cheek to keep my emotions under control.

"How did you become a fan of Kane's so quickly?" I ask the girl. "He's barely been here long enough for the store to get his jersey in stock."

"They had it in by his second game!" Lilly explains. "I always hated playing the Cyclones because Kane would make us lose. They were idiots for getting rid of him."

"Lilly!" her mom scolds.

"What? Dad agrees with me."

"Would you like Kane to sign your jersey?" I ask, clearing out of the way.

She nods, and Kane takes my spot, having Lilly turn around so he can sign her back. He jokes with her as he does it, and I can't take my eyes off the pair of them. He's gentle and kind. Not that I could imagine anyone being anything less to Lilly.

Lilly's mom steps up next to me. "I really appreciate you both taking the time to do this. Lilly's had"—her voice breaks with emotion—"a really rough year. You don't know how much it means to her to get to meet you both like this. She's been using my phone to watch the videos from your cooking competition. Even asked me to bake vanilla cupcakes with vanilla frosting last night."

"I'm so glad we were able to meet her. You should come back again sometime. Maybe bring her dad if he can get off work."

A sad smile passes over her face. "I'm not sure when she'll be well enough again. We weren't sure whether her doctor was going to clear her tonight. It's the first time she's been out in… well, a long time. You and the Yeti have really been a bright spot for us during her treatments." Her lower lip wobbles slightly as she pulls the corner of her lips into a forced smile. "We're—"

Lilly's loud yawn interrupts her mom.

"We're way past bedtime," Lilly's mom announces instead of whatever she'd been saying. "Thank you both so much for your time."

She and the woman from Wishes and Wings both thank us again before the group heads to the door.

Lilly follows her mom a few steps before yelling, "Wait!" and spinning back to face me.

"Can you please sign my jersey, too?" she asks.

"Me?" I ask. "But it's Kane's jersey."

"It'll be more special if it's both of you," Lilly says. "Especially when you win The Great Yeti Challenge."

Kane hands me the permanent marker. "Definitely more special."

I sign my name on the four on the sleeve, and with one last fist-bump for both of us, Lilly and her mom leave.

After waiting long enough to make sure they're gone, I leave the family room, blinking fast as I force myself to maintain my composure. Kane catches up to me as I go.

"So, I guess we know which nonprofit we're going to pick, huh?" he asks.

I look toward him to agree, but he interrupts me, "Oh, shit." He reaches out to stop me, his touch sending shockwaves where it brushes against my arm. "You all right, Queenie?" His voice is so soft as he asks that it's even harder for me to hold on to my emotions.

I swallow hard. Where's my dad's gruff "you're fine" when I need it? *Never let them see you cry.* It's literally the first rule of being a woman in a man's field. As soon as they see you cry, you're done. You've lost.

"Of course," I reply, forcing myself to ignore both the puddle building in my lower right eyelid and Kane's warm hand that's now rubbing circles on my upper arm. "We should definitely go with Wishes and Wings for our pick."

"Good." Kane steps back with one last long look at me. "I agree."

Chapter 10

Beckett

"Did you see the email from Sabrina that just came through?" Li asks from the locker next to mine.

"No." I keep my attention wholly on the stick I'm retaping.

"It's a reminder about The Great Yeti Challenge. The second event is coming up."

"What are you and Coach going to do for your talent?" Larsen asks from a few lockers over, a slightly evil tug to his smile.

"Do you think arguing about who the greatest defenseman of all time is will do the trick?" I ask, remembering the conversation Coach Blake and I had after the Vancouver game a few days ago. It hadn't started as anything. Just the two open seats in the team dining area, celebrating a win against a good Stormriders team.

We were deep into a discussion about the best players. She'd been halfway through a bite when I'd said Stevens was the greatest. She'd stopped chewing and set her fork down like I'd just insulted her grandma. "Absolutely not," she'd said, arguing that he was aggressive, not elite. "Sacrifice doesn't win games. Decision-making does. Positioning. Discipline."

"I'm fucked, then," I'd joked, thinking about the way I'd sacrificed my body over and over again during that game to make sure we walked away with the victory. She'd laughed, and so had I. Then there'd been this pause, just a beat too long, and it hit me that I liked the way she got animated when she cared. It was fun, and I was relaxed in a way that I hadn't been in a very long time. But then, when the staff stopped by and asked whether we needed anything before they left, the room around us now empty, the feeling had, thankfully, vanished.

There are two quick raps on the locker room door and a long pause—the signal Queenie uses to let us know she's about to come in, so we should throw whatever we can over any exposed penises. Or at least that's how Larsen explained it to me when it happened on my first day, when I'd looked with confusion at the door. According to Larsen, she "doesn't need her eyes burned by the sight of our flaccid dicks."

"Ah, hey, Coach," Larsen greets when she opens the door, and I'm suddenly very aware of the fact that I don't have a shirt on. And, inexplicably, of the fact that Larsen is only in compression shorts.

Damn it. No. She's just another coach. Coaches walk into locker rooms all the time. She has seen *all* the things. And just like every coach I've had before her, she has zero interest in seeing anyone here naked.

"Larsen." Coach nods at the rookie. "How's the rib?"

The rookie took a nasty hit during our game against the Seattle Tempest and almost had to sit out the Vancouver game. Luckily, he has the recovery benefits of essentially being a child, so he was cleared to play.

"Looking real pretty these days." He shows her his left side, where the bruise is starting to yellow.

"Well, I'm glad there's finally something pretty about you."

Larsen laughs before saying, "We were just talking about what talent you and Kane are going to do. My guess is singing."

Queenie's eyebrows pull together in a way that makes it *very* clear that she will not be singing. "It's so hard to pick just one talent when you're amazing at everything," she deadpans, causing Li and Larsen to both let out chuckles. "Unfortunately, we have to filter out the things Kane can't do, so we're quite limited in our options."

Now, the two dumbasses are practically rolling around on the floor, and Coach is looking quite pleased with herself. I'm apparently suffering from a minor heart attack because it seems to be beating about four times its normal speed.

"I have to go to a community event this afternoon, Kane. Do you want to stop by my place once you finish up here?"

I nod. "Sure, it'll be around—"

"Six fifteen."

"Are you stalking me, Coach?" I ask, feeling pleasantly surprised that she knows my routine.

"In the sense that I know what each and every one of my players is doing at almost any given moment when they're in the barn, yes."

"Yessss," Larsen whispers. "I *knew* she was obsessed with me."

"Dude," I bark at him.

"What?" he asks, holding his hands up. "My farm team coach was obsessed with me, too, and he was even bigger than you are, Kane."

"Sounds good," I respond to Queenie, completely ignoring the rookie. "Though, let's meet at my place. I can have my chef leave meals for two. I've seen firsthand what your culinary skills are."

"I wasn't offering to feed you, Kane," she clarifies. I swear Larsen and Li look like they're in a movie theater with a bowl of popcorn. "And even if I was, I assure you I can cook steak and broccoli just fine."

"Um, if you're offering, Coach—"

"Certainly not, Larsen."

"We're better chefs, anyway." Li is slightly less confident than Larsen but still willing to jump in on the chirping. "Three unbiased judges said so."

I catch the slight smirk at the corner of his lips and let out a laugh. "I think you two might have paid off the judges."

"Never!" Larsen boasts, chest puffed and ready to defend his honor.

"Mm 'kay, boys. Well, this has been fun," Queenie says, turning her attention to our captain, who has been quietly gearing up by his locker. "J.D., when you get a chance, can you come to my office? I'm worried idiot-itis might be contagious, and I can't risk catching it in here."

She leaves, and for the next five hours, all I can think about is having dinner with her. During drills with Rob, I push myself and Li hard to make sure we don't have to stay late. I practically run to the first available physical therapist, not caring that I had to shove Dom out of the way. He's the backup goalie, anyway.

Finally, I'm showered and changed, and following my chef's directions to heat up the miso-cod-and-asparagus meal for us.

At exactly six fifteen, there is a knock, and with one last glance around the apartment, I pull the door open.

Fuck. Queenie—she would hate it if she knew how often I refer to her as that in my head—has changed out of the pantsuit she was in earlier today and is now in joggers and a long-sleeved Yeti tee. Her hair is pulled on top of her head in a messy bun. It's the least put together I've ever seen her.

"Kane," she says, stepping in. Her tone is professional—almost cold—and I miss the banter from the locker room. She takes in the room around me, and I do the same, suddenly realizing just how cookie-cutter the place is. Besides my gym bag taking up a corner of the living room, I haven't changed a single thing since I moved in. No pictures on the walls. No blankets thrown over the couch. No game console hooked up to the TV.

"It's the flipped version of mine," she observes.

I pull on the back of my neck. "I'm sure yours has a few more touches of home," I offer, not sure why I'm embarrassed. It's been over a month since I was traded to Denver, and we've had seven away games since then. Though I never got around to decorating my place in Florida, either.

She considers it. "I don't really think so. I guess I have a picture of my dad and me on that little table between the couch and the window, but otherwise..." She squints. "No. I think they're exactly the same."

"Do you want it to feel more like... home?" I ask before I can stop myself. I know I shouldn't, but there's a part of me that wants to learn every detail about Finley.

Her gaze flicks to mine, quick and guarded. "I'm not even sure what that means at this point."

It's the way her jaw clenches that tells me she wishes she hadn't answered at all. "I didn't mean to pry," I mutter. "Just... curious, I guess."

"It's fine."

"Plus, the apartments are nice as they are," I state, wondering where the funny woman who argued that Stevens wasn't the best defenseman of all time at dinner the other night went to. The one who poked fun at Larsen today.

The timer beeps, and I pull the food from the oven, plating a piece of cod and a healthy scoop of asparagus for each of us.

"You didn't have to feed me," she says.

"Might as well. We both have to eat."

"Well, thank you."

We eat in a silence that isn't quite uncomfortable, but it's not natural, either. I just… don't know what to say. She's in full coach mode, and for some reason, all I want is for her to be able to be herself around me. To not wear the fake smile she puts on when she's trying to be the perfect version of herself that people expect. The one that makes it impossible to get to know the real her.

"I've been working on that whole leadership thing we talked about the other day," I offer when I can't handle the silence any longer. Wanting to offer up something more, I continue, "Seeing it from your point of view, I understand why I've been overlooked as captain for so long."

"I'm glad I could help." Her shoulders lower just slightly.

"So, since you're clearly all-knowing." I send a grin her way. "Any thoughts on what you want to do for the talent show?"

She lets out a small groan, and fuck—I feel that a little too deeply. "Look, I know that after meeting Lilly, you and I are both totally in on winning the Challenge, but can we please acknowledge how ridiculous it is to have a talent show? You are literally professional athletes. Playing hockey *is* your talent. People watch you do it multiple times a week."

"I don't think you coaching me while I play hockey is going to win us this one," I say.

She lets out a soft chuckle, and I catch myself staring at her lips for a fraction too long.

"I can still do a few hockey tricks," she replies, tucking a loose strand of hair behind her ear, and pulling my gaze back to hers. "We could put up one of our opponents' mascots and break it. Show off the slap shots."

She's out on the ice with us regularly, so I know she's not just volunteering me. I have no doubt her slap shot is worthy of the talent show.

"God, that would be..." Hot. It would be fucking hot. Though I obviously can't say that. "Good. Yeah. But we aren't on the ice," I remind her instead. "Sabrina's email said we're performing in the team theater."

I was honestly surprised when the HR woman showed me that room on my tour on the first day. Turns out, playing for a team that just built a new practice arena and office space has definite perks.

"Well, shit," Queenie curses, leaning back in her chair. "I have no non-hockey-based talents."

I snort. "That's a lie."

She doesn't smile this time. Her fingers tap against her plate once, controlled but still noticeable.

"Well, I sure as fuck can't sing," she says after a beat, and I grin, pleased that her snarky side is making itself known again. She pauses, her jaw clenching. "It's not that I don't want other talents or interests, or maybe it is. But it's more that I just don't have... room in my life for them."

Her words hit me in the chest. It's exactly the way *I* feel. Yet, I've never met a woman who understood the space this sport takes up. The way that curiosity for something more will occasionally poke its head up, only to be whacked back down again by training or games or just the headspace of staying on top of everything. "I know a thing or two about not having enough room in your life for anything but hockey."

She lets out an exhale that might've been a sigh or a laugh. "I'm sure you do. It's pretty hard to make it this far without it taking over your entire life."

We both sit in a charged silence, and finally I moan, "God, I bet Larsen has a million ideas for things to do."

She chuckles. "Yeah, to make a complete fool of himself."

"True."

"It's also..." she starts before trailing off.

"What?" I ask.

"Well, it's just that—it's challenging, doing something like this. In my position, I mean. If Larsen does something stupid, it's funny. If I do, it somehow becomes a meme about why women shouldn't be allowed to coach men."

"I don't know if that's true. You're a person like the rest of us. You're allowed to be silly."

A smile flits across her face, but then she swallows whatever she's about to say. Finally, she shakes her head. "I'm not like the rest of you. I mean, you literally call me Coach Blake rather than Blake."

I shrug. "I call you Queenie most of the time. At least, in my head."

She glares at me, and I can't seem to help the smile that spreads across my face. There's something about riling her up that makes me feel like I just won a fight on the ice.

"I mean, I'm not going to stop calling you that—you are the Ice Queen—but I think I get it. I've felt the need to succeed, to be perfect," I say. "It might not be the same pressures, but the results are the same."

"It's not just about succeeding. It's about paving the way for the women and girls who come after me. About making sure that nothing I do looks bad for women."

I study her. "That sounds really hard. To feel like the success of your entire gender is on your shoulders." I reach out and place my hand over hers. Electricity sparks between us, and we both jump, jerking away from each other.

"Sorry," I apologize. "I just mean I could see how it would be hard. I can't imagine the expectations." I stare at her as she picks at her food. "Would you feel less like you're in coach mode if I call you Finley?"

The name feels weird rolling off my tongue.

"That's the problem, I don't think I *can* come out of coach mode for this. I'm only here because someone decided it falls under 'other duties as assigned' in my job description. So yeah... I *always* have to be in coach mode."

"Not when it's just us. You can just be... you."

She considers it, her gaze scanning me as if looking for signs that I'm not being sincere. "That would be... nice. But only when it's us." Her eyes gleam, amused. "The first time you call me Finley in front of anyone, I'm forcing you to do sprints until you puke, and then I am benching you for the next game."

I chuckle. She drives a hard bargain. "I can agree to that... Finley."

"Well, thanks... Beckett."

The conversation turns lighter then, as we talk about growing up playing hockey. The injuries and experiences. Finley shares a little about what it was like growing up with a Hall of Fame coach for a dad. I tell her my dad played hockey, too, though she clearly already knew that from my bio. My ribs hurt from laughing when she tells me about having to do sprints for showing up late during her first few weeks of college. Her roommate had hidden her skates in retaliation after Finley punched the girl's boyfriend when he snuck into their room in the middle of the night.

"So you were fun in college?" I tease. Finley might just be more fun than Coach Blake.

She smiles. "Not as 'fun' as I'm sure you were. I saw the puck bunnies who lingered outside the rink for the men's hockey team."

There's a tug in my chest, a feeling like we've actually made some kind of breakthrough here.

Except not the one we actually needed, which was figuring out what our talents are. I know I disagreed with Finley's assertion that she only had hockey-based talents, but I have no idea what else we can *do*. The only time I've tried anything else was... college.

"Oh! Maybe I do have an idea for the talent show. So, in college," I start hesitantly.

Finley quirks her eyebrow, her expression suggesting she's following that train of thought down the puck-bunny path from earlier.

I lift my own eyebrows suggestively, willing to go along with her teasing.

"I don't think they'll let us do *that* in the theater," she says, a belly laugh chasing out the words. And fuck. Now all I can imagine is laying her out on a stage and giving her the show of a lifetime. Though not with the entire team watching and cameras rolling. I'm very fucking possessive and do not share well.

"Beckett." Finley snaps in front of my face.

I jolt, my mind returning to the conversation. "Right. Anyway. So, in college." I pause, daring her to make it sexual again. "I needed an elective, and my only option for the timeslot I had available was dance."

Finley laughs again. "No way."

"Yeah, I mean, it's supposed to help with coordination and—"

She holds up her hands. "I wasn't judging. I took dance in college, too."

I stare at her. She stares at me.

Damn her eyes for looking like that.

"So we're dancing?" I finally suggest, pulling my gaze from hers.

She shakes her head. "Only if you did something other than ballet, because I can assure you, I *will not* be getting up on any stage in a tutu."

"They'd be able to add a Yeti tutu to the team store, though," I joke. "Think of how much Sabrina would love that."

"I'm going to make you room with Larsen on the next away trip. One king bed. Snuggling," Finley deadpans, and I can't help but laugh.

It feels good to let go, just a little, and the laughter just keeps coming, pouring out of me until my cheeks hurt.

Finally, when I'm able to catch my breath, I hold up my hands.

"No, mine was a contemporary class. And it just so happens that the dance I was assigned was the one from *Dirty Dancing*."

She leans forward slightly. "Because you could do the lift?"

"Oh, certainly. And I look damn good in all black."

"Were you also paired with some cute petite blonde?" she asks. "Because I have to tell you, I'm none of those things."

I want to argue with her about the cute portion, but decide on a different tactic. "You're petite compared to me."

"I'm petite compared to no one. I'm not a light human. I'm made of a lot of muscle. Skater's muscle, not runner's muscle. It's big and bulky."

Lies. I mean, not that she's not made of muscle, but she's not bulky. She's strong.

"I can do it," I assert. "If you can do the steps, I guarantee I can do the lift."

It's a challenge, and we both know it.

We also both know she won't say no. Coach Blake doesn't back down from a challenge, and based on the gleam in her eye, I don't think her less professional counterpart, Finley, does, either.

"Prove it."

"Now?" I ask, looking around the room. Okay, this may have backfired. I know I can do it, but I should certainly warm up beforehand. Fuck.

"Yeah," she says, sending the challenge right back at me. "We'll go out in the hall. I'll run; you catch me."

I nod. "I'll always catch you. And you better get your pink dress ready, because if we're doing this, we're fucking doing this all the way."

Chapter 11

Finley

I start the video on my screen again, watching Jennifer Grey's feet as if she's a center on the team we're playing for the championship.

One, two, three, four, I count in my head, questioning every life decision I made that got me here.

Shit. Left, not right.

I run through it a few times before my watch buzzes, letting me know it's time to head to Kane's—Beckett's. I'm not sure I'll ever get used to calling him that, even if it seems strangely natural to have him call me Finley instead of Coach Blake.

"Come in!" he hollers in response to my knock.

I open the door, slowly moving into his space. "Beckett?" I call.

"Here," he says, walking out of his bedroom. "Sorry. Needed to take a shower before standing too close to anyone."

His dark hair is still wet, clinging together as he runs his fingers through it. I forcibly pull my gaze to his face, reminding myself *again* that he is my player and ogling is out of the question.

"Cleanliness is always appreciated."

He quirks an eyebrow, and I bite the inside of my cheek to stop myself from taking back the inane comment. "Noted."

I hold up my laptop. "I've got the video, so we can practice with the movie, at least for the first few attempts."

"Perfect."

I pull the video up as Beckett shoves his coffee table to the side. As soon as I hit play, I move to the center of the room as the opening strains of "(I've Had) The Time of My Life" start playing.

Beckett walks toward me, and my body buzzes in anticipation. This performance is making me more nervous than I'd like. Wrapping his arms around me, we both do our best to maintain an appropriate distance, nothing like the embrace on the screen in front of us.

We move cautiously at first, finding our footing together. He gracefully spins me out, and I laugh at the sudden movement, a giddy feeling like when you lose your stomach on a roller coaster bubbling up within me. Beckett's hand tightens on my waist, almost as if he's going to pull me in close.

Beckett steps on my foot, and he curses.

"My bad," I mumble, my gaze laser-focused on my laptop. I can't ever seem to remember these steps, which frustrates me to no end.

We muddle through the part with the quick steps, finding our groove as he spins me again before pulling me close once more. Our gazes land anywhere but on each other.

"Where's the hair flip?" he asks, as I move side to side, his hands two hot irons on my waist.

Beckett twirls me around as I mumble, "It'll be a cold day... in hell... when I do that. "

"Ah, come on, Queenie."

"So many sprints," I threaten, as I place my hand back down on his shoulder, and he laughs like he knows I'm joking.

We move through the more traditional dance portion, our movements more rigid, less... thrust-y, than the couple on screen. We both pause, not sure what to do as the couple on the screen stares lovingly into each other's eyes. Thankfully, it's only moments before we're dancing again, our bodies slowly finding the rhythm.

Finally, Beckett lets go of me, and I quickly say, "No hand kiss." He shrugs before turning away, and I'm amused when he does a limited version of the male solo, hamming it up as he reaches the part where he's down on his knees.

"You're supposed to be laughing at me adoringly," he teases.

"Is *this* not an adoring look?" I ask, careful to keep my expression blank.

"I think we might've discovered why you're single," Beckett teases without missing a step.

"And here I was thinking it was the fact I'm already married to my job," I banter. We get to the section where I'm supposed to hop off the stage, preparing for the big lift, so I press pause on the laptop. We'll have to go out to the hall for that.

"Is that why?" Beckett asks, not even breathing heavily.

I shrug. "I don't honestly know at this point. There aren't a lot of men interested in dating me, and the ones who are... tend to like a strong woman in theory, not practice. My last boyfriend said he loved my drive, until I worked enough late nights in a row that he started calling me cold. It's probably for the best, anyway. My schedule is a lot for anyone to have to put up with."

"I don't believe that. Any man would be lucky to have you," Beckett says softly, his right hand tightening into a fist by his side.

"The only one who ever might've agreed got scared off the first time he met my dad. Apparently, Hal Blake is too much, even for those who worship him as a coach."

"It must be hard having him for a dad."

I consider my answer. "He's the reason I am who I am today. Some people think he puts too much pressure on me, but he just wants to make sure I achieve my goals."

"I get that."

"Did your dad pressure you to play hockey like him?" I ask, though I immediately regret the decision, remembering the sentence that always follows that one in the articles. Beckett's dad played AAA hockey until he died in a car wreck.

"He did. And yeah, he's a big reason I've pushed myself as hard as I have."

There's a pause, just a second or two, where neither of us says anything. He opens his mouth as if to say something else, but closes it, his gaze snapping away from my face.

Regret twists low in my belly. I shouldn't have said anything. Shouldn't have opened up like that with a player, shouldn't have tried to connect—especially not *him*. I bite the inside of my cheek, holding the emotions threatening to spill over at bay. I want to take it back, but instead, I turn my attention to the laptop screen, hoping we can move on.

Beckett nods, his gaze seeming to pick up everything I'm not saying, though I know my face is expressionless. "Well, that was good for a first try."

"*You* were good," I say, forcing myself back to the light banter we'd fallen into earlier. "I can't believe you remember that much from college. That was ages ago."

"Ouch." He clutches his chest as he moves into the kitchen. "It wasn't *that* long ago. And I practiced. I told you I would."

"I believe you. But I also practiced, and I messed up about twenty times more than you."

"You did not." He hands me a glass of water as he takes a sip of his own. "Plus, this is our first practice. We have time to get it right."

I nod. "Right." Though it doesn't feel that way now, I have no doubt we'll get there, even if it means I'll have to spend every day with Beckett. Practicing.

"You can count on me," he says, before winking. It was so nonchalant, I'm not even sure he noticed he was doing it.

A laugh bursts out of me. "Did you just wink at me?"

"Maybe?" But the smirk dancing at the corner of his lips tells me he most certainly did.

"Get it together, Beckett." I push his arm before immediately breaking the contact. What the hell am I doing? Am I... flirting with my player?

Beckett just chuckles. "Should we try again?"

"Yes." I force myself to be professional. I get into position, while Beckett restarts the video.

We run through the beginning of the dance three more times, getting to know each other during the breaks, before finally deciding we need to work on the lift. I almost want to say no, to stay in his apartment where we get to be the versions of ourselves who laugh together and tell stories about painful middle school dances and a packed auditorium for a college dance performance.

When we get into the hall, we both walk to our respective ends, and I silently pray none of our neighbors choose this moment to leave their apartments.

"Ready?" Beckett asks, humor lacing his tone.

I push onto the balls of my feet a few times. "Just psyching myself up. I'm not meant for flying."

"I didn't drop you last time."

No, he didn't. But that was half the problem. Having his hands on my hips, lifting me like I weighed nothing, was a shock to my system that I'm not sure I can survive again. The way his warmth seeped into me. The strong, reassuring strength of him.

I'm embarrassed to admit I've found myself daydreaming about it multiple times.

"I've added some muscle weight since then," I say. The side effect of choosing to try to work out my pent-up energy by lifting weights.

"You are in the weight room almost as much as the guys," Beckett notes, something about his grin telling me he finds this whole situation funny.

"I hold myself to the same standards as my team. Culture of accountability and all." I fall back on my usual answer. And I do. I would never expect a player or staff member to do something I'm not willing to do myself.

"And from everything I've seen about you, that seems true." He tilts his head. "Come on, Finley, I've got you."

I nod, believing him. Hell, that's not my problem. I *know* he's got me. I'm just not sure if I'm ready. Forcing myself into action, I move, the toes of my shoes dig into the floor as I run toward him, the tingling in my chest amplifying with each step. I spread my arms as wide as I can in the hallway as Beckett bends his knees.

Then, I jump.

His hands hit me low on the hips, his thumb pressing the inside of my hip bone, and a small gasp slips out of me as I tighten every muscle in my body. Holding myself straight is my one job.

Beckett straightens, lifting me overhead, and we both hold there as he counts out loud.

Heat zips through me like overtime levels of adrenaline, my body betraying my careful control. My gut tangles into a deep knot, begging me to do something.

When he gets to four, he lowers me, keeping my body close to his, his touch lingering half a beat too long.

"Okay, well, that was..." Beckett lets me go, stepping back as he runs his hand through the dark strands of his hair.

"Yeah, totally," I agree, forcing my gaze away from the muscles bunching along his forearm. The ones that just lifted me over his head like I wasn't too much for him.

"So—"

"I guess—"

We both start speaking at the same time and then chuckle.

"I should probably—" he starts again, just as I say, "Well, I'd better—"

"Go." We say the final word at the same time, and an uncomfortable laugh sneaks out of my throat.

"Right." I nod. "I'll see you at practice, then."

A tight smile pulls on Beckett's face. "See you tomorrow."

Chapter 12

Beckett

I've been in the PT room for almost fifteen minutes, too nervous to focus on hockey. I wasn't this nervous before my first pro game.

It's not the dancing; I can handle performing in high-pressure situations. I've already had to do this dance in front of people once. What's another time?

Plus, we've practiced. We've practiced the shit out of this dance.

In my apartment when we're in town, and once each in Arizona and Texas. Turns out, hotel staff are almost scarily willing to open up an empty ballroom when two grown adults tell them they have to practice a dance for their charity competition. Dallas might've been because the woman knew Finley, based on the double take she did when we asked. Though she did call her *Blane*, so maybe not a huge fan.

We've got this from a dance perspective.

So, the nerves I'm feeling? That's all Coach Finley Blake. The woman I can't seem to stop fucking thinking about. The one whose eyes have to be the same damn color as Yeti blue, so I swear I see them everywhere I look. I'm afraid I'm losing control, and this final dance might be too much. Or maybe not enough. And it's the fact that I can't tell that has me questioning everything.

"I can't believe we have to do this," Finley says as she walks into the room, her long dark hair bouncing in her ponytail with each step. She's wearing a pink Yeti shirt with black yoga pants, showing every single muscle in her legs. They weave up her body and around her hips. The hips I'm going to have my hands on very soon.

We've watched *Dirty Dancing* about five hundred times now, and the pink shirt from the team store was as close as she was willing to get to the dress in the movie. The amount of thought that woman puts into her attire to make sure she's both feminine enough but not too feminine to be a head coach is... disgusting, frankly. Society should really get its shit together.

I continue stretching, making sure my body is warm and ready for this. I can't be off my game, and damn it, if Coach Blake doesn't knock me off-balance more than any woman I've ever met.

"I can't believe it's been two days since we've been able to practice together," I gripe. Sure, I would've liked to practice together a few more times, but really, I just miss spending time with her... as a friend.

"Turns out, having highly demanding jobs doesn't mix well with participating in silly competitions."

I nod. "Li and Larsen resorted to practicing in Li's room when we were in Dallas. I tried to get Larsen to spill what they're doing, but they're being secretive shits about the whole thing."

Finley bounces on her toes a few times. "I'm ready for this whole thing to be over with."

"Same," I agree, though it's not entirely true. I may not want to be doing these events all the time, but I'm not ready for our time together to be over.

"Hey!" a petite woman I don't think I've ever seen before calls as she walks into the PT room. "Sabrina asked me to get you both. It's time."

"Oh my gosh, Charlotte, how do you always know to turn up for these things?" Finley asks.

"Besides the fact that knowing what's going on in Denver is literally my job?" Charlotte replies as we all walk down the hall together. "I also got a text from Lefevre."

"Sit with us?" Finley asks as we walk in, and I realize this petite woman, who looks like her entire outfit was designed specifically for her, must actually mean something to Finley. She's never mentioned her before, but she must be a friend.

We're last to perform, as requested, so we settle into a row in the back, as far as possible from the hoard of PR team members holding cameras.

Sabrina doesn't take long getting everything going, and she quickly hands the microphone to the owner to say a few words. I appreciate this man's dedication, when the majority of owners would just let their team run everything and only show up for the most important moments.

Once Ken is done with his remarks, Li and Larsen start us off, running onto the stage like they've just won a championship. They start dancing a mashup, according to Charlotte, of the most popular dances on social media. The speakers are blaring, and Larsen has hip-thrusted more times than I ever needed to see.

"Ouch." Finley curls toward me to cover her face as the two collide mid-jump.

J.D. and Rob are next, doing a comedy sketch where they each pretend to be the other one giving pre-game locker-room speeches. J.D. does a monotone, Santa-coded version of Rob, and Rob absolutely kills it with a wild motivational rant. I'm not sure the fans will get the "synergy" references, but the team is here for it.

Lefevre and Doctor Pearce do something that's half magic, half chemistry, and completely impressive, especially when they make a puck levitate with magnets.

They leave the stage to be replaced by Björk and Volkov, rocking cutoff jean shorts with jean vests and their long blonde hair hanging in their eyes. Loud rock music blares, and they start to sing in both Swedish and Russian.

"Well, how 'bout that!" Finley says. "Did you know those two could sing?"

It's so cute when her midwestern comes out that I can't help but smile. "Yeah, we sit around the locker room doing sing-alongs all the time," I reply, chuckling when she elbows me.

Everly and John take to the stage next and pull out four huge stacks of cups with the Yeti mascot on them. On beat with their pop music, they start stacking the cups.

There's an awkward silence in the place until Finley lets out a loud whistle and yells, "Yeah, John!"

The team takes their coach's signal as an order to cheer and ups their noise game—starting an "Everly" chant when she almost knocks a cup over. As their song comes to an end, they slide the cups down, collapsing the massive pyramid they created in just a few movements.

Well, shit, that's everyone but us.

***

"(I've Had) The Time of My Life" starts, and the crowd goes wild as the lights dim. My eyes meet Finley's as she stands in the center of the stage, shoulders thrown back. I slowly walk toward her, even doing the little finger quirk before I reach her. Her eyes meet mine, something sparking in them.

I pull her close before dipping her low. Her back bends until her long ponytail sweeps across the floor.

The boys in the seats lose their ever-loving minds, and the pleased smile that crosses Finley's face is a real one.

We don't do the forehead part, the one where our gazes are supposed to connect with fire and passion—my dance instructor's words, not mine. We're walking a fine line when it comes to professionalism, but I know it's going to bring home a victory.

I twirl her out of my arms and quickly pull her back in, in a reflection of the dance we've been doing lately, the one where we get one step closer before quickly taking two steps back.

Watching her eyes as we cha-cha, I do my best not to mess this up. It's where I'm most likely to stomp on one of her toes. Her smile softens slightly as our eyes meet, and warmth grows in my chest—fuck. What am I doing? She's my fucking coach.

We turn, her left arm coming to rest on my shoulder as we shift into that portion of the dance. When we come back together, Finley scans my face before quirking an eyebrow. Knowing I can't explain the sudden unease curling around my core, I subtly shake my head. I don't know what's happening to me right now.

She squeezes my bicep with her left hand, holding on long enough to tell me she's there. That maybe, just maybe, she understands.

As we dance across the stage, she dips her head back and then flings her hair up, the move I teased her about relentlessly for not even trying.

I know she did it just for me.

It's going well, we're making our way through the middle, our steps perfect, everything aligned. Her giving a step, then me giving a step. The excitement in the room is building. They know what's coming. But they've forgotten the best part isn't the big lift at the very end. It's the little hip thrust section that's as close as I'll ever get to *more* with Coach Finley Blake.

She looks completely put out during the whole section, but she does it, even going so far as to yell out, "Sprints until you puke to anyone who ever mentions this again!" midway through.

I'm surprised Larsen didn't catch fire the way her eyes were laser-focused on him as she said it.

Our first lift happens, the one where she kicks her legs into a split and holds them at waist height while I spin her around, and—shit. She jumps a little higher than usual, and her warm breath hits my neck, causing every ounce of blood in my body to flow south. Sexy dances and even sexier coaches do not mix. *Should* not mix.

I get myself under control enough to set her down, sneaking in the hand kiss from the movie that she vetoed in practice.

And then I jump my ass off the stage, knees up in a full cannonball pose, desperate for the distance between our bodies, yet missing her touch the moment I leave her.

Instead of dancing around the auditorium like Patrick Swayze does, I pull Larsen up, twirling him around just like I did to Finley.

The room loses it.

Coach does her part, smiling and dancing on the stage, and I hate that I want her smile back to being only for me.

After dancing with all the players in the front row, I jump back onto the stage and nod once. Finley returns the gesture before running to me, nothing but calm determination on her face.

Then, she jumps.

My hands find her hips. I power out of my squat, my arms extending overhead as I press her to the sky. I hold her there, her weight nothing compared to the heat of her body pressing into my palms, and it feels right.

Her arms go out, the overhead light illuminating a halo around her head as I stare up at her. She looks like an angel, and for one second, I let myself feel it: the longing that has been growing since the day I set my eyes on Coach Finley Blake.

And, fuck. I am so screwed.

I know we finish the dance, but I couldn't tell you a single thing that happened after the lift. Not a single one.

Chapter 13

Finley

"You can go in," Paige says from outside my office.

Sabrina walks through my door, smiling widely, and I try not to be annoyed that the competition is taking up so much of my time.

"I have great news, Finley," Sabrina announces, taking a seat across the desk from me.

"We've had such a great response to the first two challenges that we're calling it and announcing Kane and me as the winners?"

Sabrina chuckles like I'm joking. "Definitely not. The better the response, the more I want to add an additional challenge! But the internet's response to the talent show is what I'm here to talk about," Sabrina explains.

Oh no. That can't be good.

"What do you mean?"

"Have you been on any social media today?" Sabrina asks.

"You know I haven't. I let your team handle my professional account for a reason. I don't need to see what people say about me online. All it does is distract me from what I should be doing: coaching."

"Yes, yes. I know. Are you at least aware of the fact you're trending?"

I shake my head. "No—actually wait. Larsen mentioned something about it after the first challenge. Something about L-squared."

"I think it's double L. The hashtag is just a two and then the letter L." Sabrina waves her manicured hand. "But that's not why I'm here. Though, if you wanted to consider changing your defensive pairs, so Li and Larsen—"

"No," I interrupt. I draw the fucking line at changing my game plan to play into media attention.

She shrugs. "I just thought I'd ask."

"Well, the answer is no," I reply, straightening my back.

"Anyway," Sabrina continues, her voice just as cheerful as ever. "The real reason I'm here today is to talk about *your* name. Or, more specifically, your and Kane's. TeamBlane is viral."

My chest tightens. Team Blane? Like... a couple name? There's no way the audience saw anything between us, right? Of course not. Because there *isn't* anything. And I made sure I buried my feelings down deep—even if I did catch myself smiling at Beckett. But it was just a friendly smile.

And shit. That's what the woman called me in Dallas. It wasn't a slip-up. She *knew*.

Sabrina continues, "They *love* you two. Particularly, the clip where you tell the team they're going to have to do sprints. Over five million views already on that one. Truly, it's gold. It's the most successful community-engagement content we've had in years."

Oh, thank goodness. It's not *us* they like. It's our team they like. It might be a fine distinction, but it's a very fucking important one.

"Okay, well, thanks for letting me know," I say, turning back to my work.

"This isn't just a heads-up," Sabrina replies. "We're going to need to lean into this one. Have the two of you do a few additional videos together, teasing the next challenge, talking about the team, that sort of thing. Maybe even an interview or two for some of the local networks."

"Sabrina, I'm already spending a lot of time away from my actual job to make this happen. Can't you get Li and Larsen to do it?"

"Knock, knock," Mr. Peterson calls as he stands outside my office door.

Great. I guess everyone is just turning up today. Why not the team owner, too?

I gesture toward the other chair in front of my desk. "Come on in."

"I was just giving Finley the good news about the success of the last competition," Sabrina tells Ken with a smile.

"Well, great minds must think alike," he replies. "I came to offer my congratulations as well. You know, Coach Blake, I wanted to see how you'd handle being the face of the team when the pressure is on, and it sure is convenient I get to before we're in the playoffs."

"Well, thank you," I say, not sure how else to respond to his comment. Was being named interim coach after my boss had a heart attack on the bench, and then becoming the first ever female head coach at the ripe age of thirty-one, *not* enough pressure?

"Of course. This really is a great opportunity to cement you as the head of this team."

I give him my media smile because, what the actual fuck? Am I not cemented as the head of this team? Interim has been gone from my title all season.

After promising to do whatever Sabrina needs from me, I tell them I have to leave, grabbing my skates to get a bit of ice time in before our game against the Archers tonight.

I skate laps, trying to burn off the angry energy flowing through my veins at the fact that the external optics matter so much. That so little of what I'm evaluated on is the way the team plays on the ice. That I've heard more about The Great Yeti Challenge than Pike's recovery.

My watch buzzes, letting me know a call is coming in. Seeing it's from my dad, I skate over to where I left my phone sitting by the bench.

"Dad," I answer, stepping onto the rubber matting as I hastily make my way to the coaches' suite. "Give me just a second."

He remains silent while I walk down the tunnel, and I wait until I'm in the coaches' room with the door closed before I put him on speakerphone.

"How are you?" I ask, untying my laces.

"I've been better, Finley. What is this I hear about you going viral for a dance? With a player?"

He says *player* like it's a bad word, and I know it is in this situation, but at the same time, Beckett isn't just some player. He's the man who understands what it's like to be fully committed to the job. The one I've laughed with in the last few weeks more times than I have in the years before he moved here with *anyone*. The one who lifted me like I wasn't a burden and never once let me fall.

I force myself to take a deep breath, to think rationally. I did what I was told to do. Nothing more. The slight warmth in my chest when Beckett's around? It's nothing. Heartburn at most. The butterflies that seem to find me when Beckett is around were nothing when I was sixteen, and they're less than nothing now.

"I told you about the social media thing Ken is pushing. You know how these things are," I reply.

"But dancing, Finley? That's a reckless reminder to the world that you're a woman."

"We weren't the only team who danced, Dad."

"You're the only one who doesn't get to blur the lines, though," he practically barks at me. "*You* can't afford to have people question your professionalism, Finley. *You*. Not Kane, not Li, certainly not Larsen. Damn it. I knew you weren't ready for this. When you're fifty? Sixty? Sure. But a thirty-one-year-old coach? It's really fucking rare. I don't care how forward-thinking Ken Peterson is, or how much of a push there is for younger coaches. It was bold if you were a man, but it's just plain stupid to put a young woman in charge of a team of men."

"Dad," I cut him off, knowing it's the only way to end his rants. I know I can do this job better than *any* man, but I also know that he's right. I wouldn't have put myself in charge right now, based on the optics alone. But I *am* in charge, and I don't plan on doing anything to mess it up.

"Just don't give them a reason to question you." He sighs.

Don't mess up is the real message. One I know well.

"I know," I say. "But I have to do this. Even if I don't like it."

Though that's not necessarily accurate. I liked dancing with Beckett. I liked practicing with him. I liked the way the warmth of his body seeped into my own through every point of contact.

Dancing with him felt easy. If I missed a step, he'd cover for us. And when he held me above his head, there was no doubt in my mind that he had me. It was... fun.

And something else. Something that felt soft and new. A sign that maybe those butterflies from all those years ago aren't as meaningless as I need them to be.

But, no. This can't happen.

I hang up with my dad in time to see an email from Sabrina come through, one with details of the next challenge that explains how we'll be paired with other professional athletes from Colorado. It also reminds us that the fourth challenge will test our knowledge of each other. It legitimately tells us to spend time "getting to know one another."

And, damn it, why am I smiling at that directive?

Okay, yes. Beckett and I will need to spend time together to practice. But that's all it will be. Hockey practice or preparing for The Great Yeti Challenge.

A second email from Sabrina hits my inbox, this one with a short list of additional filming she wants Beckett and me to do, including a request for me to wear the pink Yeti shirt again. Turns out, it's sold out at the team store in the twenty-two hours since the last competition.

I reply, agreeing to the filming times.

And that little flutter in my chest? It's not because I'm irritated at the additional time away from my job, like it should be. No, it's because I just got told to spend more time with Beckett Kane. And that's a real problem.

Chapter 14

Beckett

The puck rattles free, and my body is already moving before I realize that my legs feel heavier than they normally do at this point in a game. I angle my hips, cut off the lane, and shoulder their winger just enough to separate him from the puck without drawing a whistle.

Clean. Controlled.

The crowd surges as I pivot toward the blue line, tracking the play. Chicago's pushing harder now, desperation bleeding into every move. They're getting sloppy. And dangerous.

The puck snaps cross-ice, and I close the gap fast. The winger tries to dangle inside. Bad choice. I step into him, timing it perfectly. Chest to shoulder, weight through the hit. He goes down, and the puck slides loose.

I barely register the roar of the crowd. I glance toward the bench on the backcheck—just a quick scan out of habit—and that's when I see her. Coach Blake stands behind the boards, arms crossed, expression unreadable. Her eyes are locked on the ice.

On me.

Something in my chest tightens. Not nerves, but something sharper. Cleaner.

I dig deeper into my edges.

The next shift, I play more aggressively.

When one of their forwards takes a run at our goalie, I'm there in half a second, dropping gloves and getting in just enough to make my point.

When I skate to the box for my two minutes, I don't look at the bench. I don't need to. I can feel her attention like a lightning rod between my shoulder blades.

Ten years ago, I played like this because I was trying to prove something about who I could be.

Tonight, I'm playing like this because I know exactly who I am.

And I want Finley to see it.

***

"You were on fire out there." Li slaps my shoulder as we make our way into the locker room after a hard-fought win on our home ice. "The hit you threw after that asshole ran the goalie? I don't care how long you sat; it was absolute perfection."

Down by two at the start of the third period, Chicago sent their enforcers out more than usual, and I met them hit for fucking hit. You can always tell when a team's getting desperate—their big guys start leading the rush like they're goons in a street fight.

For the first time in a long time, I felt *good*. Like I did five years ago, when I was on top of the hockey world.

"Yeah, man, what's gotten into you?" Larsen asks. "I thought you were going to break a hip or something out there the way you weren't even trying to avoid those assholes."

I shove him hard into the wall, but he bounces right back. "I'm not that fucking old."

"I know what this is about," Larsen chirps as we make our way into the locker room.

It's about me being a damn good hockey player. I refuse to admit it could have anything to do with the woman standing behind the bench. And since I'm not admitting it, there's no way Larsen knows about it.

"Now that you're a big celebrity, you wanted to make sure you didn't let your fans down."

I pull my helmet off, placing it on the top shelf of my locker. My gloves go on the shelf below before I drop onto the cushioned seat, my eyes drifting up to the image of the yeti mascot on the ceiling.

"I never let down my fans," I retort, hoping if I don't mention TeamBlane, he won't, either. I pull my jersey over my head and throw it onto the pile, careful to avoid the logo in the middle of the room.

"But these are not just your fans, yeah? Coach is the one they're all watching," Volkov says, from across the room.

"Really, Volkov? You pay attention to this shit, too?"

"I find Americans' obsession with silly little videos very interesting. Plus, I looked damn good up there. The judges were obviously biased toward English music."

"Oh, please," Larsen starts, but we all quiet as Coach's double knock comes, followed by her assistant coaches walking into the room. Finley enters last. She's in complete coach mode, with her black suit and heels on.

"Good game tonight, fellas. They hit hard, but we hit harder. It's exactly the type of play we need to get us to May. Focus on recovery tonight. Hydrate. Fuel. Hit the cold tubs. We've got Winnipeg in two days. They play heavy. Optional skate tomorrow. Mandatory treatment. We'll dial in systems and matchups then."

It's the exact speech we need. Short, sweet, and to the point. This isn't about getting us fired up. It's about letting us move forward without needing to be the loudest voice in the locker room.

"Anything else?" she asks her assistant coaches.

When they have nothing, she nods at the team. "Good work out there. J.D. and Lefevre, you're on for press."

"You know," Larsen says thoughtfully as he works his pads off, "if I weren't competing in The Great Yeti Challenge, I'd totally be cheering for Coach. She's a fucking badass. Even if she could lighten up a little."

"She is pretty great," I agree. "But I totally disagree. She's funny. I think you just can't tell when she's being sarcastic, Rookie."

The room goes quiet.

"Oh, shit," Lefevre whispers, and I catch J.D.'s slightly downturned mouth.

"What?" I ask, looking around.

When no one answers, I bark it again, "What?!"

Volkov stares at me, his blue eyes piercing my soul. "You know you can't actually like her, right?"

"He likes Coach," Larsen groans, like he just found out why everyone is being weird, too. "You can't *like* Coach."

"You literally just said you like her."

Larsen widens his eyes like I'm the slow one here. "Yeah, as a coach."

"I *agreed* with you." I rub my hand through my sweat-slicked hair. "It was the exact same."

"It wasn't," Volkov states.

"We're... partners. In this stupid competition. I like her as a partner."

Hearing what I said, I shake my head.

"I mean, like a colleague. A person I don't hate spending time with. A work friend."

It's okay, I can *like* her. I mean, it's impossible to spend any amount of time with the woman and not like her. I just can't *do* anything about it. Which is fine.

"A friend... who's a girl?" Larsen teases. "So, a girlfriend."

"Larsen," Volkov chastises. "Enough."

"*I've* been friends with women before," I say. Probably.

"Dude, no, you haven't," Larsen disagrees.

Li shoves his friend. "Give it a rest, man. Sometimes, men and women are friends. It doesn't have to be anything more."

"I'm not saying it *is* more," Larsen protests. "I'm saying, Kane wants it to be, with Coach, which is a recipe to have your ass traded twice in one season. Which would essentially be the death of his old-ass career."

There are snickers around the room, and I roll my eyes. "Yeah, yeah. I'm old. Got it."

Volkov stands, only partially undressed. Even without his goalie gear, he's a huge motherfucker, and now he looks like he wants to pummel every single one of us. "She's a damn good coach. We all know she's what our team needs. But she will be gone if they think the fact she's a woman is distracting to *any* of us." He looks me dead in the eyes. "You weren't here last season, Kane, but she got interim not because of her last name and who her dad is, like the press says."

As much as I want to do something, to argue that *I just agreed she was a badass*, I don't. Because this is the first time I've heard anything about *how* Queenie got her position. I need to know what the Russian has to say.

"We, as a team, went to White and Peterson and said we wanted Coach Blake. They were going to get someone external, but we said no. That Blake was who we wanted—who we *need-*

ed. She had helped every one of us while she was an assistant, and we knew she was the right person for the job. They warned us of the optics. Of a young woman coaching men. We said we didn't care. She was too good a coach to pass over. And just like they said there would be, there was chaos in the media. A lot of hate."

He looks around the room, and the players who were on the team last year all nod gravely.

"But not in our fucking house. We did everything she said. She was nothing more than a coach to us. *Nothing*. We are better because of her as our coach, and *no one* is going to fuck that up."

He looks at me, and I give a subtle dip of my chin.

"Good." The large Russian sits back down after what is certainly the most words I've ever heard him say at one time, maybe in total.

"Yeah, what he said," Larsen says, already bobbing away from the jab I throw half-heartedly at his chest.

I drop my head into my hands. "I just agreed with Larsen that she's a badass. I didn't ask him to officiate our wedding."

An image pops into my head uninvited, one of Finley walking toward me in a long white dress, her dark hair curling gracefully past her shoulders.

Volkov groans. "No wedding."

"I said *not* a wedding!"

"Leave the old man alone," J.D. cuts in on my behalf. "He had a hell of a game tonight, and I'm sure he has about an hour's worth of cooldown still to do. Let the man get home to his..." He trails off, clearly trying to figure out what I have waiting for me at home.

Nothing.

Now that my dance practices with Coach are done, the answer is nothing. And I refuse to acknowledge the sinking sensation that causes behind my rib cage.

"Plants?" he finally asks.

I shake my head, and J.D. lets out a little grumble. "I'm getting you a dog for your birthday. It's just too sad."

"So they can spend half their life in doggy daycare?" I ask. "No, thank you."

I slowly undress, my adrenaline from the game completely gone after the roller coaster Larsen just took me on.

Li is the last one in the locker room with me, and just before he reaches the door to leave, he turns back to look at me like he has finally made up his mind to say something. "Larsen's an idiot, but he's not wrong. You can't treat Coach like you would any other coach, because, to the rest of the world, she's not. And she's finally getting the respect she deserves," he says. "I know you two are just friends, but it doesn't matter. If people have any reason to think there's something more, it could mess up her entire career."

Li and I have slipped into an easy pairing since I joined the team. He's easy to read and is learning how to trust his gut a little more when he's on the ice with me. Besides Finley, he's the closest thing I have to a friend, well, him and Larsen, I guess.

And, based on the way I've seen him around Doctor Pearce, I know he's spent more time thinking about the ramifications of having feelings for a coach than anyone else on this team.

"I'm her partner in the competition," I remind him. "What would you do?"

Li looks at me, his gaze finding that kernel of something in my soul. The roots of something more that I can't seem to kill. "I don't know. But I would do everything in my power to make sure my feelings didn't fuck things up for her."

Fuck.

"And maybe don't dance with her anymore," Li suggests before walking out the door, leaving me alone with my thoughts.

They didn't say anything I don't already know. This *can't* be anything. I just don't know why it suddenly feels like it already is.

Chapter 15

Finley

He's been home for almost an hour.

Not that I'm stalking him. I just happened to be near my door around the time when he got back from the arena.

So, I heard him walking down the hall. And his door close.

It's not a big deal. We just need to practice. Not for the next competition, which is going to be some sort of maze or skills event with other professional athletes from the area, but for the one after that. The one where we're tested on how well we know each other.

It's our duty, to the team, to practice. Sabrina said so. More or less.

I pull out my phone and type a quick text, asking Beckett to come over. I stare at it for a minute before deleting the whole thing. Too formal. I try a few more times before finally giving up. I have no idea how to casually text. Plus, putting anything in writing makes it seem official.

It's fine. I'll just go over. Knock on the door. He's probably watching game film tonight, anyway. It's what I should be doing. We could watch it together. While we chat. Two hockey team–based things that must be done.

It's the only efficient solution, really.

Knowing it's what any respectable coach would do, I slip on my tennis shoes and grab my laptop. Laptops are the height of professionalism.

I walk across the hall and knock twice. *Fuck.* That's how I announce myself at the locker room. Making a snap decision, I lift my fist and knock a third time.

"I said I was fucking busy tonight, Larsen!" Kane yells, pulling the door open as he finishes his sentence.

He looks good. And, holy mother above, what is that smell? Is that him? I scan his fresh-from-the-shower hair, past his navy suit jacket, down the seams of his tailored pants, to his expensive-looking leather shoes before bouncing up to his face, where his gaze meets mine.

Smile, Finley. I squeeze my short nails into my palm, determined not to feel anything about the fact that Beckett is *clearly* about to go out on a date.

"We can do this another day." I nod toward my laptop. "Should've texted first."

"Finley." Beckett's eyebrows draw together in confusion. "Want to come in?"

I shake my head. Definitely not. I can't stay this close to date-ready Beckett for one minute longer. I might cry... or institute a no-dating policy for the team. Neither of which is acceptable. "You're busy. No worries. I wouldn't want you to be late for"—I gesture sporadically at his various limbs—"your thing."

He quirks his head to the side before looking down at himself. "Oh, it's okay. No thing."

"You just said you were busy. And you're wearing a suit."

Boy, is that an understatement. Like he's somehow in the same league as the accountant who has to put on a suit to go sit in a cubicle all day. He is fucking *wearing* a suit that is hugging every single inch of his immaculately toned body like it was made for him.

Beckett chuckles. "I'm only busy if it's Larsen asking."

"And the suit?"

"I just got a delivery of game-day suits from a designer I like to work with. Since I was freshly showered, I figured I should try them on." He holds his arms wide. "What do you think?"

Good. *Sooo* good. "Not bad," I say instead. "Do you always try your suits on with shoes?"

He looks at me like I'm an idiot. "Of course, Finley. Do you know nothing about trying on suits? The shoes tie the whole outfit together. They can make or break an entire ensemble."

"Oh, I know *all* the things about trying on suits," I tease. "I may not be Kim Mulkey, wearing sequins and feathers for my games, but I still know a thing or two about them."

He cocks his head to the side. "She's the..."

"Women's basketball coach, yeah."

"Right. I was getting there."

I nod like I totally believe him. "Sure you were."

"Now that we've established that we both know things about suits and that everyone watches women's sports, can you please come inside?" He steps back to hold the door open wider.

I let out a small laugh. "Well, since you're clearly desperate for my company."

"Right," he chuckles as he reaches up to rub the back of his neck. "Clearly."

I walk in and, suddenly, I'm uncomfortable. He's not watching film. He's trying on suits. What exactly am I doing here? Trying to get my Beckett time, not that I can tell him that. And maybe a bit of Finley time. The few minutes a day when I'm not Coach Blake, not the first female head coach, but just Finley, the woman.

"Water?" he asks. "I have sparkling and the kind out of the fridge."

"Fridge water?" I ask. "That's so fancy. In fact, I remember it being very tasty the last time you offered it to me. Who could turn that down?"

"No one. I've heard it's even kept people alive," Beckett replies, grabbing two glasses out of his cupboard and filling them both. He hands me one, his eyebrow raised as I stand in the middle of his kitchen.

Real smooth, Finley.

"So, um, with the trivia competition coming up, I thought it would be smart if we spent some time together. You know. For research."

Beckett doesn't say anything, just searches my face.

When the silence has gone on too long, I add, "For the kids, of course. So they don't lose out to the sea lions."

"For the kids," he replies, like it's an answer to a question he's been considering for a long time.

"Well, and Sabrina. And the team. Lots of people, really."

"It's almost a requirement," he says, nodding slowly. "No option."

"Right!" I agree. "It might actually be part of our contracts."

Beckett's smile pulls wide across his face as he leans his hip against the counter. "I'm in. What's with the computer, though?"

"Film," I answer with a nod. Because, yup. "I thought we could prep for Winnipeg together. Team things, you know?"

"Team things. I... I like that. Want to get it set up on my TV while I go get changed?"

"Not planning to wear your suit all night?" I ask. I could be convinced it's a good idea. I could also be convinced it is the world's worst idea and would end with me getting fired and letting down literally everyone.

Beckett smirks. "This is a game-day suit, Finley. Not a film suit. Don't be ridiculous."

When Beckett returns a few minutes later in gray sweatpants and a black T-shirt that's stretched across his chest and shoulders, I regret that he's changed. Even the suit was safer than this.

Why, oh why, must men look so good in sweatpants? Me in sweatpants? Homeless raccoon. Beckett? So fucking terrible. I mean, really, really yum—yucky. Gross. I definitely don't want to lick... anything.

"So." I force my gaze back to my computer screen. "Want to start with the Blizzard at the Guardians?" I ask, naming the team we are about to play and the one we just beat. "Or do you want to watch the Blizzard's most recent game against the Riptides?"

"What would you normally do?" he asks, like he might want to know because it's something about me, not because he can't decide.

"I'd start with the Guardians since we just saw them, and then move to their most recent game. Doctor Pearce also put together a file of specific plays I need to see, so I usually finish with those."

"Let's do that, then," he says.

I pull up the video, navigating Doctor Pearce's ridiculous folder-naming conventions, and mirror the game from my laptop to his large TV. Luckily, he kept the one that came with the place, so it's like mine and my adapter works.

He drops onto one end of the couch, clearly leaving the other side open for me.

"Okay," he starts as I sit as far from him as possible. "What's your usual night look like?"

We talk about our lives, sticking to topics that feel easy, ones that might come up in a trivia game about ourselves. Our routines. The food we like. Nothing about our pasts or how we got here. Nothing with potential landmines.

We're both, unsurprisingly, boring. Our routines are our lives. We don't have much time or make much time for people or activities outside of hockey. I survive on coffee. He's powered by protein and greens. It should be dull, but somehow, everything feels easy. Like, he understands why I spend every night watching game film without me having to explain myself. Like, he would enjoy curling up on a couch and spending hours dissecting a team's weaknesses and how my players could exploit them. If only he weren't one of those players.

But, no. We need him. The Yeti is a different team now that he's there. I need Beckett Kane on my roster. It's just too bad that I also appear to want him in my life.

"Rewind that," I say, my eyes following the Blizzard's center as he delays on the zone entry and drags the winger out of position.

We both lean toward the laptop at the same time, and our shoulders touch when we reach for the trackpad.

My breath catches. I can smell his soap, feel the warmth of his skin where it touches my bare arm.

"Sorry," I apologize, and he quickly pulls back. I clear my throat, rewinding to the start of the play.

When I lean away, I realize we're closer than we were before, our shoulders almost touching. It's close enough to feel like something without it being anything.

I don't move away.

Neither does he.

"Do you see it?" I ask, taking in his profile as he tracks the center again.

Beckett exhales slowly before reaching out and tapping the space bar to pause the film. "He likes to bait the D-men. Slows up just enough to make them bite and pull them out of their gap."

I nod. "He runs *every* entry through that hesitation move. We can pick it apart if you guys see it early enough."

"I can't believe I didn't catch it until now," Beckett comments, the look on his face something close to admiration.

I grin. "Well, to be fair, it is my job to catch it. Not yours."

This—*us*—feels easy. Too easy.

Beckett pauses, a soft smile pulls at the corners of his mouth. "You should do that more."

"What?"

"Smile," he answers, and his thumb, as if controlled by an entirely different being, slowly traces a line down my cheek, leaving a trail of tingling flesh in its wake.

He quickly removes his hand, a look of horror flashes across his features, and the sudden loss of contact hits me in my chest—a place I hadn't known was hollow until he momentarily filled it with his touch.

I reach out and hit the space bar, restarting the film and unnecessarily pointing out the way their goalie drops too early.

We fall into an easy analysis of the play, discussing their team in a way that feels much more enjoyable than any other strategy session I've been in with my coaches.

Finally, we make it through all the film, and, unable to put it off any longer, I start to gather my things.

"You know," Beckett says, massaging the back of his neck, "this has been a lot of fun. I didn't... Well, I didn't realize how lonely I'd been."

It feels like an echo clanging through me, so I offer him the only thing I can—my truth.

"Me, too."

We're both silent as I close the laptop, and I wonder whether he's regretting confessing that to me. If he thinks he said too much, or if it feels like someone understands him for the first time in a long time. Maybe forever.

"We should do this again sometime," I offer, turning back from the door I just opened.

Beckett nods, and I swear he's fighting a smile. "Whenever you want, Finley."

Once I'm in my apartment, I lean against the door, my heart racing like I just sprinted two miles rather than slowly crossed the few feet between our apartments. And as I stand there, all I can think about is when I'll get to do it again.

Chapter 16

Beckett

I touched Finley Blake.

And it did something to me.

It took all my effort to make myself remove my hand from the soft, heated skin of her face. And after that, I have no idea what happened. All I knew was that I wanted to touch her again.

God, did I really confess to being lonely while in a hormone-induced blackout? Fuck, my brain needs all the help it can get—I can't be sending all that blood south.

Now, I've been lying in my bed, trying to sleep for the last hour.

Unfortunately, every time I close my eyes, she's there. Beautiful and strong with a piercingly intelligent glint in her eyes.

I can't stop thinking about her in the exact way I swore I wouldn't.

My mind has a different idea, though. One that involves significantly fewer clothes.

I squeeze my eyes shut, sliding my hands under my ass to keep myself from giving in to the fantasy that keeps playing through my mind.

"Such a good boy."

Fuck. Now she's talking to me. And, turns out, I've got a praise kink when it comes to Finley Blake. Great. Usually, *I'm* the one who likes to give praise in bed.

"What's the harm in touching yourself?" Finley asks in my mind as she crosses her arms, daring me to disobey.

I will not be reflecting on the fact that my fantasy version *of my hockey coach* involves her wearing her game-day suit, tall black heels, and no fucking shirt under her jacket.

"This is so messed up," I mutter before slowly sliding my right hand out from under me.

Just this once. I'll give in to the temptation this once, and then I'll move on. We'll get through this competition. And then, to fill the fucking void not spending time with her will cause, I'll go on some dates. Go out to a few bars with the other guys, maybe a club or two.

But, for now, I need release. I'm not sure it's even healthy to have an erection for this long.

I search the nightstand next to me, digging through the drawer until I find the small bottle of lotion I keep there, though, with the way my dick has been weeping, I'm not sure it's needed.

Closing my eyes, I conjure Finley again. Now, she's in nothing but one of my T-shirts with her hair in a messy bun on top of her head. And a real fucking smile. The one that accompanies the laugh that makes me wish I could bottle it.

In my mind, Finley pushes me onto the rumpled comforter, a playful glint in her eye as she climbs over me, her hands smoothing up my thighs as she goes.

Her mouth wraps around my cock as my hand acts as the poor substitute in real life. She works my length, using her hand to help with all of me. I let out a moan, and Finley laughs. The sound, combined with the imagined vibrations, brings me straight to the fucking edge. I'm not sure whether I'm glad she's not really here to see me come like a two-pump chump, or if I would give my left nut to have the chance to feel the tip of my cock hit the back of her throat. To hear her breathless choke. To gasp when she grips my balls a little too tight, reminding me exactly who is in charge here.

I work my hand faster, knowing if I stay in this dreamscape any longer, I won't be able to get back out. That I'll do whatever it takes to turn this dream into reality.

Squeezing slightly tighter around my bursting cock, I pump once, twice, three times, before coming with a grunt all over my hand and stomach.

"Fuck," I mutter, using my briefs to wipe the cum off my body.

As I drift off to sleep in a post-orgasm haze, I realize I'm already looking forward to tomorrow—not because of hockey, not because of my real life, but because I'll be able to spend a few minutes with the version of Finley I so desperately want again tomorrow night. The one who's only allowed to exist in my dreams.

Chapter 17

Finley

Boston is loud. Their fans are hostile, and their boys are out for blood. As we near the end of February, teams are playing like their season is on the line—because in most cases, like ours, it is.

Our team moves the puck, J.D. pushing forward as our wingers fly to beat him into position. Murmuring to Shaw, I make a suggestion about a tweak before turning my attention back to the play.

Kane racing along the boards catches my attention, and I remain transfixed, hyperaware of what he's doing. He's the anchor of our D, and I need him. That's why I can't look away.

Boston plays a fast transition game, and our defense has been in chaos more than I'd like. I watch, transfixed, as Kane slams into number eight. They battle against the boards, large bodies knocking into each other. Björk digs the puck loose and slaps it to point. Kane collapses onto the front of the net and ties up a stick to clear the rebound into the corner. He's barely had time to recover before their left winger is there, firing a shot through traffic. Kane's stick darts out, meeting the puck just in time to block the shot.

There's something about the way Kane is moving that isn't quite right. I can't quite put my finger on it, but it's something in the way he accelerates. Or changes speed, maybe. Like he's not at full strength. Maybe his—

"Coach Blake?"

"Huh?" I ask Rob.

"I said, did you see that hole Lefevre just found?"

"Yes." My eyes dart to the other side of the rink, and I wonder what I missed when I was unable to tear my eyes away from our defense. From Beckett.

It's exactly the type of distraction I cannot let happen, though this time it might've been warranted.

The game is another brutal one, and the men give it their all. With less than thirty seconds left, Kane jumps a zone and forces a turnover. J.D. takes the puck, flying across the ice to drill a shot through the five hole before the goalie can seal it with fourteen seconds left on the clock.

Boston wastes no time pulling their goalie for one final push. The seconds tick down as Boston fires shot after shot at our goal, my players always there to get in the way.

Finally, the buzzer sounds, and there is a mass of black Yeti jerseys as they all dogpile on J.D. Beckett extracts himself early, and as he skates toward the bench, our eyes lock in the chaos. A warmth spreads inside me as I return his smile with one of my own.

I'm proud of him. In a way I shouldn't be. The thought hits me like a punch to the gut.

And when he dips his chin in a slight semblance of a nod, it doesn't feel like a player acknowledging his coach. It feels like more.

***

Josie hands me an envelope with my name on it as I climb off our charter plane and onto the bus four hours and ten minutes later. I make my way to my second-row seat, the same place I always sit on the team bus, confirming my room key for our stay in Philadelphia and a schedule for the next thirty-six hours are safely in the envelope.

Beckett is a few people behind me. As he passes, his hand lightly grazes my arm. My gaze flicks upward, catching the slight smile on his face as he continues, acting as if he didn't just light my entire right side on fire. It's late, well past the time when good decisions are made, and the need I normally keep locked deep down inside is surfacing.

"Let's talk systems and adjustments, so we can go straight to sleep, eh?" Rob says as he sits in the row across from me. My feelings are too all over the place to expect any kind of decent rest, but if it helps Rob get his beauty sleep, I'm fine to run through what we need to here, rather than waiting until we get to the hotel.

We discuss options for our game tomorrow—technically, tonight now—against the Hawks as the bus winds through the deserted streets of Philadelphia. A few guys look half-asleep in the back, but most are still riding the post-game adrenaline, trying to cool down enough after the game to be able to sleep when we get to the hotel. I've already let them know there wouldn't be a morning skate after the pounding their bodies took this evening, so they'll likely rest as late as they physically can.

When we get to the hotel, the players all bump and push to try to get into the elevators, everyone tired and grumpy and ready to get to their rooms. I let the first elevator go, but the second is just as full, and I end up smashed against Beckett, his arm almost wrapped around me as we test the equipment's maximum weight capacity.

"Good game tonight, Coach," Beckett says softly. It's not intimate—just a congratulations between colleagues, but the way his warm breath tickles across my ear and neck makes it feel far too private for the number of players and coaches surrounding us.

I swallow hard, begging my hormones to stop their nonsense.

"Thank you. You as well." I tilt my head up enough to catch the glint of amusement in his eyes.

"Yeah, I heard the end of your interview tonight. You said some nice things about me to the press."

I shrug, though his comment sends my worry into overdrive. Was I too positive about his play at the end? It would've been weird if I hadn't mentioned him, but now, maybe I said too much. Was it what I would've said about any other player?

We all pour out of the elevator on the twelfth floor, a flurry of motion as we all make our way to our rooms. Beckett and I both look at the room numbers on the wall before heading in the opposite direction from the rest of the team.

"Looks like they stuck you on the staff side of the floor," I tease. "Is it because you're too old to room next to Larsen?"

Beckett's laugh is a short chuckle, almost a wheeze, as his hand flies up and lightly wraps around his ribs.

"Are you okay?" I ask. "Did the trainer see you? Do you have an ice pack?"

"Yes, dear," Beckett replies, walking down the hall.

"Dear?" I ask, hoping my amusement isn't obvious to anyone else who might be in the hall.

He gapes at me, his eyes immediately widening when he realizes what he's said. He clears his throat. "I mean, yes, Coach. I did all the things I was supposed to. I iced on the flight, and I have new packs in my bag to strap on once I'm in bed."

"Did they just look at your ribs? Or did you get a full exam?" My curiosity about his acceleration from earlier resurfaces. "You seemed like you were a bit less explosive than usual, even before you took that hit."

Kane's gaze darts away before snapping back to mine. "I'm fine. Just a little sore. You know how it is when you reach my age."

"Are you sure?" I ask. "Because if something is bothering you, even if it seems inconsequential, you need to tell someone. Culture of accountability."

"I'm fine, Coach," he says before coming to a stop. "Well, this is me."

I stop as well, our rooms, evidently, across the hall tonight.

"Neighbors for life," I joke, wanting to cut through the chill that's lingered between us since I asked him about his injury.

Beckett scans his card, turning to face me as he pushes into his room. "Lucky you."

If Tantalus was lucky to be constantly surrounded by fruit and water without ever being able to eat or drink, then sure, I'm lucky, too.

I wash my face and get ready for bed, my mind on what's happening across the hall. Is he tucked in bed for the night? Watching film for the upcoming game? Was he able to get his ribs wrapped so the ice stays on? Did he have to call a trainer?

After spending the last few nights together watching film and answering random questions about ourselves in what has become an unofficial ritual, it feels weird not to be with Beckett. I roll through a list of excuses I could make to visit him, like checking on his injury, practicing for the competition, or needing to talk to him about matchups for tomorrow. But they all feel flimsy. Especially for this time of night.

If I ran into Rob in the hallway, would he really believe I was headed to a player's room in the middle of the night to talk matchups? Well, Rob might believe it of me since he's been on the receiving end of many a late-night strategy call, but I don't think it would fly with literally anyone else from the team.

Though, it is just across the hall. How likely is it that I'd run into someone in the seconds I would be exposed?

I drop heavily onto the bed. I shouldn't do it. For all I know, Beckett has his own rituals for decompressing after a game, and if it happens to be of the female variety, I'd rather not know.

As his coach.

Even if I haven't heard any evidence of that since he moved in across the hall.

There's a soft tapping from the hall, and after a moment, a deep voice whispers, "Queenie."

I jump from my bed, and when the comforter catches on my foot, I'm thankful for all the agility drills I've done over the years that allow me to perform a spin in the air to free myself before rushing to the door.

"Hey," I gasp, swiping strands of hair out of my face.

He's here. Beckett is here.

"Hey," he replies, his voice low, his gaze penetrating. "Can I come in? I had a film question about tomorrow."

I don't even try to hide my skepticism as I pull the door open wide, gesturing him in. He passes by so close that his sweat-shirt-covered chest almost touches mine, and every last one of my nerve endings snaps to attention.

I close the door before asking, "Film question, huh?" I force myself to face the man I can't seem to ignore.

"Yeah. Do you want to watch film together?"

I let out a laugh. "*That's* your question?"

"It is a film question, Queenie."

I roll my eyes at the nickname's reappearance. "What kind of coach would I be if I supported you watching film at four in the morning?"

"The kind who knows I'm not going to bed for at least another hour anyway."

I glance around my room, knowing I should say no and turn him away, but also wanting nothing more than to slip into our comfortable routine.

"Fine," I say. "But we're watching forty-five minutes of Sutton's highlight reel for Philadelphia. No game film or you'll be here way past your bedtime."

My room is a standard king room, so there are limited seating options. "Shoes off before you get on my bed, though," I demand, claiming the spot on the far side from the door.

Beckett takes in the bed and then scans the rest of the room before giving a subtle shrug. He toes off his shoes before fluffing the other pillows and sitting down in the spot next to me. It's a king-sized bed, so there's plenty of room between us, but somehow, it feels like we're getting very close to crossing a line.

I pull up the footage on my laptop, setting it between us as a physical reminder that hockey might bring us together, but it's also the reason we have to stay apart.

We watch for a few minutes in companionable silence.

"Okay, what was the worst date you've ever been on?" Beckett asks, easily switching to our normal routine. We're committed to winning The Great Yeti Challenge, which means we need to know everything there is to know about each other.

The unfortunate side effect is that the more I find out about Beckett, the more I like him as a person.

If only he was a shittier human.

"When I first started working with the Yeti, I went out with this guy to a place downtown that's like a six-story acid trip, and he was committed to figuring out the story... or puzzle... that's hidden throughout the place. Honestly, I'm not sure. After an hour in one room, I faked intestinal distress and left."

"Couldn't come up with a better excuse, huh?"

"Impossible. No one questions the shits. Though, I'm pretty sure he wouldn't have noticed if I just left. He was obsessed with the place."

Beckett chuckles, and we both fall silent as a Philadelphia player performs a textbook deke on the computer screen in between us.

"What about you?" I ask.

I wonder if Beckett craves these little glimpses into each other's lives like I do, or if he truly is just here so kids like Lilly can have a few more of their wishes come true.

Or maybe he hates sea lions.

"I haven't *dated* much," Beckett says, his eyes glued on the screen. I take from the specific emphasis that he may not have dated, but that doesn't mean he didn't spend some quality time with women over the years.

I uncurl my fist where it's wrapped tightly in the sheets next to me. Of course Beckett has hooked up with a plethora of women. He's been a professional hockey player for over a decade, and he was one of the most elite college players before that.

You throw millions of dollars at men in their twenties, and what do you expect to happen? They live hard and fast.

Swallowing thickly, I force out a laugh. "Well, sure, but you had to at least go to dinner before or something, right?"

He tilts his head to the side, considering. "I hooked up with a girl in New Orleans once, and afterward, she asked for a grand."

Okay, well, I guess we're getting *real* personal. I don't know why I'm so pleasantly surprised to get a glimpse of the messy part of his life.

"And that was... more than you were expecting?" I ask.

"I"—he runs a hand through his hair—"was not aware payment was expected."

"You accidentally slept with a hooker?" I ask, a cackle bursting from me. I slap my hand over my mouth, suddenly worried about who's in the rooms next to me.

"We did not, in fact, sleep together," Beckett admits sheepishly.

My eyes are practically bugging out of my head as I slam my fingers down on the space bar and give Beckett my full attention. "I need *all* the details."

"I think you have enough information."

"Oh, I certainly do not."

He shakes his head, restarting the film. "Well, that's all you're getting."

"Beckett Kane, you tell me right now how you accidentally ended up paying a woman a grand for... something." I poke him in the ribs, making sure to avoid the ice packs.

He traps my finger against his side, and it pulls me into him slightly as I let out a laugh.

"Come on," I urge. "It can be our secret."

Our eyes meet, and it's like all the air is gone from the room.

His gaze drops to my lips, and I can't help but pull the bottom one in slightly. It feels like we're talking about more than just his escapades in New Orleans.

"Yeah, our secret," he says. He shifts slightly forward, his sleepy eyes glued to my mouth.

I can't look away from his mouth. They're the most masculine lips I've ever seen. They're thick and flat, just a slight bow on the top.

He's slowly moving toward me, and I'm in a trance. There's no way I could move away even if I wanted to.

And I don't want to.

I can almost feel the soft pressure when, suddenly, the game film is playing again.

I lean back, shaking my head slightly.

What the fuck was that?

He looks as alarmed as I feel—clearly neither of us is thinking correctly this late. Nothing good happens after two in the morning.

But I also don't want him to leave—*can't* let him leave with that hanging between us.

But I also can't talk about it with him.

A moment passes before I cough and say, "So, I think you have to tell me, what service costs a grand?"

"She stuck her finger in my butthole," he answers quickly, like I'm just going to let *that* go.

I stare at him, biting my lips to keep from laughing. "And were you aware that's what you were getting, or did she just peg you for a butthole guy?" I ask, and it's like a dam breaks inside me, the laughter surging forth. It appears I've hit the level of tired that is roughly the same as being intoxicated.

"Oh, God." I wipe the tears from my eyes. "Pun not even intended."

"I guess I just have that look about me." Embarrassment and amusement war with one another on his face.

I don't know how many people get to see this side of him, but I know it's been a very long time since I joked like this with anyone.

We watch the last few minutes of the film, Beckett's smile never quite leaving his face.

When the video reel Sutton put together fades to black, I stare at the screen, my gaze flitting away when I realize Beckett is slowly getting to his feet on the other side of me.

"Thanks for watching with me, Queenie."

"And I won't even charge you a grand for it."

I can't be sure, but I swear as he leaves, he mumbles, "I'd pay way more than a grand for this."

Chapter 18

Beckett

"Thanks for the ride," Finley says, her long legs reaching the ground as she slips out of my pickup truck and onto the mostly empty parking lot outside the practice football field for the Colorado Stallions.

"We were headed to the same place. It made sense. Plus, that's what's best for the environment."

"The only reason we'd bring Larsen with us." A pretty smile pulling across her face as she points her thumb toward the back-seat.

"Yeah, thanks for the ride, Dad," Larsen agrees as he and Li both climb out of the back.

Right. I'm just a really big fan of the environment. I mean, I *am*. But also, after I almost kissed my fucking coach the other day, it seems prudent to have a chaperone. And nothing kills the mood quite like Larsen yapping for twenty minutes about how many bananas are too many for one smoothie as we drove through rush-hour traffic.

Which is why I panic-invited him and Li after I offered Finley a ride last night during our standard dinner-and-trivia-practice session.

Li holds back, waiting for me to head in. "You okay?"

Li is a genuinely good guy and one of the best players I've ever been paired with. He also has the patience of a saint, which explains how he can spend as much time as he does with Larsen. That said, he's made his opinions on me and Coach Blake very clear.

Not that I disagree—I'm just doing a poor job of staying away.

"I'm ready for this competition to be done. We've got actual games to worry about. We shouldn't be wasting our time with this."

"I thought you were enjoying it."

"Enjoying something and it being a good idea are two very different things," I reply. "In fact, I've found I rarely enjoy the things that are best for me. Take sprints and ice baths, for example."

"Yeah," Li agrees, though his voice is low. "Sometimes, I just wish there was a way to get what I want without it being a bad decision."

"Don't we all."

Sabrina welcomes us as we head into the media room of the football team's practice facility, and a few minutes later, she calls the whole group together. Much like last time, she says a few words before handing it over to Mr. Peterson. This time, though, the owners of the Stallions and the Mountaineers are with him, welcoming fans from three of Colorado's professional teams.

"That's Charlotte's dad," Finley whispers, sliding up next to me as the owner of the Stallions thanks his players and the fans for a great season.

"No shit?" I ask. "I didn't realize she was a Langford."

"Yeah. She and her twin brother have spent their entire lives in the spotlight."

Sabrina takes over again, explaining the Mile-High Matchup event, where our existing teams are paired with two other pro athletes to compete in an obstacle course relay, a reaction drill, Colorado trivia, and a coordination task. After announcing the teams, she directs us to get to know one another while we put on the provided team jerseys.

Finley and I walk toward the black mesh jerseys, each grabbing one.

"Beckett Kane, how the hell are you?" Callan Devine, one of the top quarterbacks in pro football, asks as he joins Finley and me.

"Good. I can't believe we're on the same team. What's it been, six years?" I ask, shaking his hand and pulling him in for a hug.

"Seven," he answers with a smile. "If you can believe that."

"Damn, we're getting old," I reply.

Callan and I were in Florida at the same time for a few years, and as top players in our respective sports, we ran in the same circles. It'll be fun to be back in the same state as him.

"Hey," the man I assume is our fourth says. "I'm Jameson."

He's almost my height, and he's here, so he's clearly an athlete in Colorado, but I don't recognize him.

"Good to see you again." Callan gives him a handshake and a hug as well. "I saw you won your tournament last weekend in California, congrats."

Noticing Finley is passively watching this exchange, I nudge her forward. "I'm sure you both know Coach Finley Blake."

"Oh, yes, I'm just *so* famous." Finley shoots me a smirk as she shakes their hands. "Nice to meet you."

"I think my wife might've bribed your media person to put me on your team," Jameson confesses. "She's a huge fan after that dance routine you put on."

"You'll have to bring her to a game someday. I love meeting fans." Finley is clearly in full professional mode. She tilts her head, taking him in, and I have to shove the feelings welling inside me down. I will not be jealous of a married man because Finley is looking at him.

"You're one of the professional golfers here, right?" Finley asks.

"That's me. JT Johnson"—he points to a tall blond man slapping hands with Li and Larsen—"is the other golfer they called in. Oh, God. I think they're practicing a team cheer."

"No team cheer," I say, and Jameson agrees.

"Come on, Coach." Callan nudges Finley. "You and I can have our own secret handshake."

She lets out a short laugh. "I'm on Team Grump, I'm afraid."

"Oh, come on. A chest bump? Knuckles. A quick elbow tap?"

She laughs again, and fuck. He's flirting with her. Callan is decidedly *not* married. But the two of them are, well, they'd be pretty fucking perfect. There's nothing against dating players from entirely different sports, and no one understands the craziness of a professional sports schedule better than someone who's in it.

Though, maybe that would be the worst pairing.

Sabrina tells us all to make our way outside for the first event, and I follow slightly behind, watching every interaction between Finley and Callan, convincing myself that navigating two professional schedules would actually be terrible and they'd break up within days.

I'm feeling much better by the time we reach the field, only to be pulled up short as I almost run into the group in front of me.

"Wha—" I start, only to realize what has everyone's attention. There is a giant-ass inflatable snow mountain in front of us, taking up almost half of the field. Where did they even find one that big? And, wait, is that—

"It's a fucking Wipe-Out course," Jameson groans next to me, as Larsen starts doing a dance.

"Yes! I've always wanted to try this game! Sabrina, you sweet angel. Making all my dreams come true today!" Larsen says, bouncing on his toes.

Sabrina whistles, catching our attention, and as a group, we make our way to the base of the structure.

Once we're all there, Sabrina explains the game. "It's not hard, folks. It's a relay. One person starts. The next competitor can't go until the one before them has successfully made it to the other end, run back, and hit their teammate's hand. You have five minutes to strategize."

As soon as we're in our huddle, Finley takes control. She walks us through the plan, intentionally putting herself and Jameson first and second, so Callan and I can make up time if we need to. It's exactly how she is in practice. She's six steps ahead, talking us through the obstacles we can see and what might be the best way to approach them.

"Definitely pay attention to everyone else as they go. Likely, the people who play the same sport as you will be the most useful because your specific strength will get you past each obstacle. Going back will always take longer than waiting a few more seconds until you've decided the best way to get through one of the obstacles."

We all nod. We know how to take direction in a competitive environment.

"If we need to tell each other something as we're going through, I'll yell. My voice will be the most distinct in the crowd. While I'm going through—"

"I'll do it," I announce. "You'll know my voice best."

They all look at me, and Finley quirks her eyebrow.

"Because you met me before today," I say. This has nothing to do with anything other than winning.

"Sounds good to me," Finley replies, and there's a small piece of me that wonders if maybe it does mean something more. The sound of her voice is imprinted on my soul, not from her yelling at me while I'm out on the ice, but from the soft way we've connected over the last few weeks.

We finalize our game plan, and with a bob of her head, Finley heads to the starting line. It doesn't matter that we'll be scaling an inflatable mountain, bouncing across fake snow boulders, or climbing a rope ladder to the top of a second peak before coming back down on a large slide—everyone on that field is zoned the fuck in.

The Colorado Stallions' mascot pretend fights with the Yeti, and finally, Sabrina lets out a loud whistle to start the race.

I can't take my eyes off Finley. Every movement she makes is efficient. She's not the fastest out there; the taller men are able to reach the higher handholds, but she's strong. And she's beating Everly and Dr. Pearce.

Larsen is going first, too, and he's taunting Finley when he reaches the top before her. With one last effort, she pulls herself up next to him, not hesitating before pushing him to the bottom of the mountain.

Fuck, she's amazing.

Without a backward glance at Larsen, who is aggressively climbing up again, Finley stares at the four white balls in front of her before quickly leaping onto them, one foot barely touching each as she passes.

Two rows down, Rob does the same after watching her.

Jameson, Callan, and I discuss our strategy as she climbs the rope at the end. She dives headfirst down the slide and sprints to the end, giving Jameson's hand a hard slap as she reaches him.

"Hell, yes, Coach Blake," Callan says, picking her up and giving her a hug while spinning her around. "The kid's face when you pushed him off was epic."

I blast up the mountain when it's my turn, doing my best to close the distance between me and Volkov. Li is coming up behind me quickly, and despite the overly bouncy nature of the ground beneath me, I'm confident I can win this. Callan took the third leg and managed to get ahead of everyone but Volkov's team. I'm not sure who decided these teams, but two football players and two hockey players versus two interns, a football player, and a pitcher seems unfair. Especially since the pitcher is even older than Callan and me.

I dive down the slide and roll off the end, landing on my feet and immediately turning to run back to my team. As I sprint past Volkov, I swear Finley's face lights up. And that, alone, makes this whole thing worth it.

***

We've got to win the last event. It's a three-way tie for first place after we won the obstacle course, the interns destroyed us in the Colorado trivia game, and Volkov and Björk barely won the tech-based reaction game. Larsen almost threw a temper tantrum when he realized how bad their fourth teammate's hand-eye coordination was. To be fair to him, he is the Stallions' kicker.

"Okay, everyone!" Sabrina calls. I'm not sure where she got a megaphone, but she's letting the power go to her head. "This last challenge is all about teamwork. You'll break up into pairs. One of you will be blindfolded; the other will not. If you're blindfolded, your job is to navigate through the maze in front of you. Your teammate's job is to guide you through verbally."

I'm not sure where they got enough blocks or people to make it happen, but while we were inside for the last two rounds, four different mazes were built. Together, they take up half of the field. The walls are only about two feet tall, so you can see the way to the center.

"Your first pair has to get to the center before your second group can come back out. Okay!" Sabrina claps. "Pair up and then send your second group to the center."

"Coach—" I start, but she's not next to me anymore. She and Callan are high-fiving, clearly going to pair up for this one.

I squeeze my fists, forcing air through my lungs.

I will not punch a wall. I will not punch Callan. I will not—

"Looks like you're stuck with me." Something crossing Jameson's face that's a mix between a smile and a grimace. "I know I wasn't your first choice, but I'm willing to be blindfolded or the directions guy."

I run my hand through my hair. "Sorry. I'm just..."

I don't know. I don't know what the answer is. Callan is a good guy. Someone I could see myself calling a friend.

"It's okay. I've been there before," Jameson offers.

I squint, not quite sure what he means. Finley and Callan join us, and we decide we'll be team two, so Jameson and I head to the center of the maze to wait.

As we walk, I ask, "What do you mean you've been there before?"

He shrugs. "When I met my wife, I was dead set against ever dating someone seriously again. I convinced myself we were just hanging out. And then, yeah—I guess I'm reading way too much into it, but it seems like maybe you're in that spot: where you know you shouldn't be anything more than friends, but you... want more."

"I don't want more. She's my coach."

Jameson holds up his hands in a placating gesture. "Right. Of course. I didn't mean you did. I shouldn't have said anything. I think my wife's meddling sisters are wearing off on me."

"We would both lose our jobs if anyone thought we were anything other than a player and a coach," I remind him. He needs to know he can't go around saying shit like that.

"I would never say anything to anyone else. I just thought maybe you could use a friend who's been there."

I shake my head; my gaze locked on Finley as she helps Callan get the blindfold on.

"I appreciate it, but there's nothing. Really."

We both watch in silence as Finley leads Callan through the maze. Finley is sure of her directions, and Callan follows them perfectly. They're so coordinated, I know Finley is going to be trending again this week. Unfortunately, it's not going to be my name combined with hers; it's going to be Callan's. Something like Finlan.

Fuck, his last name is Devine. It'll be Devinely. It's a great couple name.

Might as well buy them an ultra-expensive Crock-Pot as a wedding gift and call it a day.

Though if they got together, it would actually be for the best. We both know nothing can come of this.

Hell, besides that almost kiss in her hotel room, I'm not even sure she's interested in me like that. And I might be the kind of asshole who has a crush on his coach—not that I'm saying I do—but I'm not the kind of guy who has feelings for women who are taken.

So really, it'd be helpful if they decide to date.

Jameson starts to pull his blindfold on as Callan gets close to the center of the maze but stops himself. "If you ever reach a point where it's not nothing and need a friend who isn't on your team, I'm around. And Bryn loves an excuse to get out of Wild Bluffs and have date night in the city."

With that, he tugs on his mask, giving a thumbs up once he confirms it's in place.

We give it a valiant effort, but apparently, Larsen and Li are so in sync that they practically danced through the maze. The social media team showed us some video clips of Li meticulously guiding Larsen through each twist of their challenge, and honestly, they should've won.

With this competition a wash, Finley and I have to win these next rounds if we're going to guarantee the funding goes to Lilly and the Wishes and Wings program.

I head out as soon as Sabrina wraps everything up, knowing the rest of the crew I drove in will find me at my vehicle. Or they can take a rideshare back, for all I care.

"Hey, Beckett," Callan calls, catching me halfway through the parking lot. "I have a poker night with some of the other old pros in the area every now and then. You should come."

Right. Like I'm going to hang out with a bunch of other old, almost washed-up athletes. Does anything sound more depressing than that?

"I don't know," I say. "Things are crazy this time of year."

"I get it," Callan replies. "Honestly. But I also know how isolating this life can be. Especially when you're older and out of the party scene. It's a good, low-key time. Just think about it."

"I will." There. Done. Thought about it. Still no.

"Oh, and how cool is Finley?" Callan asks, turning as he walks away. "God, she reminds me so much of my little sister. I swear it made me want to give her a noogie."

I smile and wave. "So cool."

Maybe I will make his next poker night.

Chapter 19

Finley

"Queenie?" Beckett calls, knocking on my door a second time.

I glance at the clock. Shit. I'm so late. Usually, I've already been at his place for twenty minutes by now, eating the meals he insists his chef makes for me and chatting about our day. Or the upcoming game. Or practicing for the next challenge—which is really just trying to learn everything about each other.

Except, not tonight.

Because tonight, after a long conversation where my dad reminded me of the very fine line I walk every day, I made the mistake of opening the comments section of one of the Challenge videos. It's of Beckett giving me pointers as I crossed the obstacle course, and it looks like we're in perfect sync. Of course, someone had to make a benign comment about how great a couple we'd make. The responses have been brutal. Disparaging. Unsurprisingly, way more judgmental of me than him.

Though in this situation, I *would* be the one in the wrong.

Yay me, for finally being in a position where I can abuse my power.

I use the knuckles of my pointer fingers to wipe under my eyes as I make my way to the door.

"Hey." I clear my throat, hoping he won't notice the hitch in my voice.

"Hey, I brought dinner over here since you were taking forever," Beckett says, focused on the two plates of food in his hands.

I step back to let him in. "Thanks."

"You're wel—wait. Fin, have you been crying?"

After wiping my eyes again, as if it will hide the truth, I shake my head. "I'm fine."

Beckett sets the plates on my table before walking toward me. He dips his head slightly, so his eyes are directly in line with mine. His thumbs gently stroke beneath my eyes, swiping more tears from my face. "You're not fine. Tell me what happened."

My breath hitches. Oh my goodness. He is inches from me. He's touching my face. Suddenly, I don't care about the comments. It's taking every ounce of my concentration not to look at his lips. Because I know if I do, I won't be held responsible for what happens next.

And that would be terrible. Horrible. The worst. Beckett Kane's lips pressed to mine would be catastrophic.

"I made the mistake of reading some comments online," I say instead.

Beckett exhales a sigh of relief. "Internet trolls. I'm sorry, Finley. Though I'm happy it's not like you're dying or they fired you or something."

I let out a snotty chuckle. "Why would they be firing me in this fake scenario of yours?"

"I take it back." He dodges as I try to punch his arm. "You had a hair in your eye. It was nothing!"

"Rude, Beckett. Really fucking rude." But he has me smiling again, which, judging by the pleased look on his face, is what he was going for.

"Come on." He pulls out a seat at the table before dropping into it. "Let's eat before this chicken and asparagus gets cold. There is literally nothing worse than cold asparagus."

We eat in silence for a few moments before Beckett asks around a mouthful of chicken breast, "What comment got to you?"

I shrug. I don't need to get into this. I shouldn't have been looking. I learned long ago that reading comments, hell, going on social media, is a recipe for disaster. I just... wanted to see the videos of us.

"I almost got in a fistfight with an eighty-five-year-old grandmother once—not that I knew that about her at the time," Beckett offers.

"What?" I ask, my attention still on my food.

"It was my first year in the league, and she called me a limp dick on every video of me the team posted. Supposedly, I was hitting too soft for her liking."

A laugh escapes me. "How did you find out who it was?"

"She showed up at a game. Had a sign telling the coach to 'bench the limp dick.'"

I sputter; the drink I was taking shooting up my nose instead of following its normal path. "No."

"Yes," he admits solemnly.

"What happened?"

"Honestly, nothing. I noticed it, and it threw me off my game a bit, but then I realized I'd been all bent out of sorts about what a stranger thought."

Our pinkies touch on the table, and a jolt of electricity passes through them. A reaction I'm beginning to realize happens anytime we come in contact.

I smile. "I need you to know I will, without a doubt, bench you if she shows up with one of those signs to one of our games."

He looks at me, his eyes wide. "Don't let Mildred know she has that kind of power over you. She'll fly to every one of our games."

I snicker, the earlier hurt and anxiety from the comments melting away after a few minutes with Beckett. "Oh my God, you know her name," I say on a gasp.

I didn't realize how much I needed a friend in my life.

Beckett watches me laugh while finishing up the food on his plate. Finally, when I'm back under control, he grabs my plate and takes it to the sink. He quickly rinses both and puts them in the dishwasher. We're normally at his place, but he stops by mine every now and then.

"Are we watching the Thunderbirds for tomorrow, or re-hashing the Riveters game last night?" Beckett asks as he sits on my couch.

"Prepping for tomorrow. I think we spent enough time with the team rehashing how we managed to drop the game to Detroit." I pull up the Thunderbirds' highlight reel, courtesy of Dr. Pearce.

Beckett scoffs, draping his arm over the back of the couch. "Sure. Like you're not going to watch it again once I leave."

I lean back, shifting until the cushions are in the right place. He's not wrong—and I both hate and love how well he knows me. How willing he is to simply accept me.

I also hate that, after the day I had, all I want is to cuddle into him and let him hold me. I can almost feel the heat of his body seeping into mine. The slow caress of his fingertips as he absentmindedly strokes up and down my arm. A gentle forehead kiss that magically absorbs all my stress and puts an immediate stop to my overthinking.

And if he happened to miss my forehead and kissed my lips instead... I bite the inside of my cheek. Hard. Those thoughts are not allowed.

"Ready to tell me what comment got under your skin today?" Beckett asks, his gaze still locked on the television. I know it's how he gives people space, and I appreciate that it takes off the pressure of having to look him in the eye as I admit what I was doing.

"I wanted to see some of the videos the team has been posting from the Challenge, so I was on socials."

Beckett's face darkens, his jaw clenching. "Wanted to see how good a team you and Callan were last event?"

I shrug. "I just wanted to see the funny ones. I had a shitty day at work, and I was looking for something to entertain me. To distract me from the fact that we might not make the playoffs. That my job will certainly be on the line, or if it isn't, it's literally only because I'm a woman. Which is its own level of drama." I sigh. "It was just one of those days, and I was looking for an escape."

Beckett lightly rubs my shoulder with the hand along the top of the couch. "Fin, we're making the playoffs. You're a great coach. We're a good team. And even if we don't, they're not going to fire you—and not because you're a woman. Because you're good. The team loves you. I think Larsen would organize a full team walkout if they let you go, and that's saying nothing of the veterans who are remarkably loyal to you."

It's easy for him to say. He had to give up a lot of other things to get to where he is; he had to push himself harder than anyone else around him to make it to the pros. He had to want it more than almost anyone. I had to do that while also carrying the weight of knowing I was paving the way for women everywhere.

I didn't have to be the best; I had to be perfect. And as head coach, it's impossible to be perfect. I'm destined to fail.

"I know," I say in response to Beckett's comments. There's no use arguing.

I tuck my feet under me, forcing my back a little straighter. "So, what does your ideal vacation look like?" I ask, distracting him with our game.

The side-eye directed my way at the topic change would put even the sassiest of middle school girls to shame, but he lets me have it, anyway. "A month in a cabin. Cool mornings. Lots of hiking. Peace. What about you?"

"I'd join you in the cabin. But I want to spend my days doing those fancy puzzles. You know the ones from really nice wood instead of whatever normal ones are. And instead of being cut into normal shapes, they're like ice-skaters that you're trying to fit together. My grandma sent them to me for Christmas, and I always loved spending hours just zoned in on completing it."

He tilts his head. "I guess I wasn't a big enough nerd to get the fancy puzzles."

I lightly shove him. "Rude."

Getting serious again, Beckett leans forward, clasping his hands together as he places his elbows on his knees. "Why did the comments get to you this time, Queenie?"

I want to tell him. I do. But the problem is, it's not just about what they were saying; it's the fact that they were right. And I don't know how to give him that truth without giving up too much of myself. Though, if there is anyone I'd be willing to give that much of myself to, it's Beckett.

"It's fine if you don't want to tell me." I swear there's a note of sadness in his voice. Like he's upset that I'm not willing to share my burdens with him.

"It's embarrassing, is all," I admit before taking a deep breath. "They were talking about us—together."

I pause, waiting for some reaction, but Beckett just nods.

"And, I guess, I realized that maybe what we have is... inappropriate."

I have his full attention now, his dark brown eyes piercing into mine. It feels like too much. "What do you mean?" he asks.

I shrug. If I knew what I meant, I wouldn't have this problem. I'd be making a change. "I guess, it's just—do you remember when we met?"

"In the hallway?" he asks.

The hollow feeling in my chest isn't fair to him. There was no way those ten, maybe twenty, minutes he spent with me when I was sixteen meant anything to him. Even if it was everything to me. Even if it started as a crush that lasted *way* past an acceptable amount of time.

"We actually met when I was sixteen."

His eyes go wide. "What?"

"You were in my high school's rink practicing when you were home for Christmas break. I was working on my slap shot."

"That was *you*!" Beckett exclaims. "I never put that together. I mean, I don't think you even took your helmet off. Though I suppose I should've put two and two together. I knew your dad lived around there, and how many girls are at the rink by themselves the day after Christmas?"

I shrug. "It's not a big deal. You helped me. Gave me a few pointers."

He's into the story now. "Yeah. I remember that. I was impressed."

"Right," I say with a small eye roll. "I'm sure."

"I was. But what does that have to do with the comments about us now? Did someone put it together that our paths crossed when we were kids?"

I shake my head. "Not yet. But I'm a little worried they will." I glance at the TV, unable to hold his eye contact any longer. "I may have had a crush on you after you helped me. I mean, I got a starting spot because of your help—and well, it was not a well-kept secret."

Beckett's face is a mask of cocky pleasure when I finally force myself to meet his gaze. "You liked me?"

"Oh, please. You were"—I wave my hand to encompass his whole body—"all of this, and I was sixteen."

He reaches out, grabbing my hand and pulling it toward the center of his chest. The sound that comes from me is most definitely a grunt of surprise—not a sound of pleasure.

"All of this, huh?" he teases, a cocky grin on his face. "Sixteen-year-old you had such great taste."

Such great taste. Unfortunately, thirty-one-year-old me has similar taste, and that's the fucking problem.

Instead of telling him that, though, I roll my eyes and pull my hand back. "I'm worried someone from high school will start saying shit. Tell people how I had a crush on you when I was younger. It was a standing joke on my teams in high school and college that you were the only person I'd give up my no-dating rule for."

"No-dating rule, huh?" Beckett asks before turning serious. "A high school crush is nothing, Fin. I know it seems like a big deal, but even if they did say something, no one would care."

I wish I agreed. But this wasn't just your standard starry-eyed teen who then forgot all about the boy when they left home. I was slightly obsessed with the man. And I'm his coach now. And that crush might be coming back with a vengeance.

Fuck, who am I kidding? It's all the way back.

"People would care. You're my player, Beckett. I'm your coach. We're... We probably shouldn't even be hanging out as much as we are now."

Beckett's eyes meet mine, and there's pain there, even as he asks, "Do you want to stop?"

I shake my head. "No."

"Then fuck what people think. We aren't doing anything wrong."

Maybe *he's* not. But he's never liked me as anything more than his coach. Maybe a friend. A friend he occasionally wants to kiss when it's late at night and he's on an adrenaline high from his game. I'm the one who has gone and made it inappropriate. It's my feelings that aren't okay.

I fucking told White not to trade for Kane. I told him. If he'd just gone off my damn list, I wouldn't be in this situation. I'd be—alone. Watching film by myself as I eat yet another steak and bagged salad for my dinner. And my job would be... well, still on the line because Beckett has been instrumental in turning our season around. But I wouldn't be conflicted.

And I sure as hell wouldn't be considering throwing my career down the garbage disposal just to feel his lips pressed against mine.

"I know," I say finally. "But I'm not sure where that line is, so how do we know when we've crossed it?"

Chapter 20

Beckett

"It's not about getting the puck, Li," Finley—Coach Blake—yells from where she's skating at the center of the ice. "You can't give up your defensive positioning. Do it again!"

"Yeah, Li! Culture of accountability!" Larsen chirps from where he's standing off to the side, waiting for his turn. "Your mistake. Now, fix it."

We run through the drill once more, the defense working through PK scenarios while our offensive team focuses on exploiting the extra manpower to score.

Skill-work practices used to bore me, but now that I'm with the Yeti, I'm starting to appreciate them. I'm sure it has nothing to do with these practices being the ones that Finley is most likely to join.

Almost everything I do with the Yeti feels more enjoyable than when I was in Florida. It's like I have my old spark back. The one that told me I was one of the luckiest motherfuckers in the world, getting to play hockey for my career rather than work some boring desk job.

If it weren't for my damn body reminding me how old I am, I would swear I have another decade left to play. I'm excited to come to the gym each morning. It's no longer solely about my routine and making sure I make it through the next game. I'm excited about the future and the things I can achieve here. Unfortunately, during the game last week, I took a hit that has made my hip a constant reminder of my age.

When practice is over, we make our way into the locker room, the team surprisingly quiet as they shuffle in. Too quiet. I glance around, taking in the way the guys seem to be watching me out of the corner of their eyes. Except Larsen. He's just staring at me and my locker.

Crap on a cracker. What does this buffoon have planned?

Not willing to ruin his fun, I cautiously approach my locker. I snort out a laugh when I see what's inside.

"Rookie, did you get this made just for me?" I ask, holding up the apron with a female yeti body clad in a black-and-blue Yeti bikini.

The room breaks out into raucous laughter, Larsen the loudest of all.

"Just a reminder, you might want to practice before the next competition," he gets out through gasps of laughter.

I slip the apron over my head, letting it hang instead of trying to tie it around my pads. I look down. "Is it just me, or do I look damn good as a yeti?"

The men laugh again, some catcalling as I put my hands on my hips, jutting one to the side in my best impression of a runway model.

"Get it, Kane!" Lefevre hollers.

"Show him the best part," Li encourages Larsen.

"Oh, you're right!" Larsen exclaims, scrambling to pull off his gear so he can dig through his bag. With a flair of drama that only Larsen can pull off, he unfurls another apron, this one with a male yeti in Yeti swim trunks. "For Coach Blake."

The boys are at it again, laughing and causing a scene.

"I can't wait for you to give it to her," I say, one eyebrow raised.

Larsen shakes his head as he sits down to start working on his skates. "Nope. I'm just going to sneak it into her office. She'll never know it was me."

I snort. "She'll know it was from you the second she opens it."

Larsen glances from me to the apron and back before nodding once. "Worth it."

I can imagine Finley's face. She'll pretend to be annoyed, but there will be a little crinkle at the corner of her eye that means she secretly finds it hilarious.

I'm going to miss that crinkle when this competition is over. It's been nice having a friend I can spend time with who gets it... gets *me*. She wants to watch film. Wants to talk hockey. Is on the road with me rather than complaining I can't join some activity or another.

But I also know she thinks it's crossing a line to be friends with her players—and maybe it is. This competition gives us a team-mandated reason to spend time together, but once that's done... I know she's going to put a stop to it.

Even if she doesn't want to.

Finley lives by a rigid moral code, and I know she won't break it. Asking her to would only make it worse. And I care about her way too much to ever ask that of her.

"Team dinner at my place tonight!" J.D. yells as the first wave of guys start to leave the locker room. "Gloria will be pissed if she cooks all this food and no one is there to eat it."

"You going to be able to make it tonight, Kane?" J.D. asks. "Gloria mentioned you haven't made it to one of our dinners yet, and she'd really like to meet you."

Luckily, having a wife or girlfriend committed to the team is not a prerequisite for being the team captain, but there is a strong correlation between the two.

I consider telling him no. Giving my usual excuse of needing to cool down. To stretch. To eat my dietitian-approved meal. But, at the same time, I know I should go. Hell, I *want* to go.

"Yeah. I'm going to try to make it," I say, hoping that will be enough of a commitment for him.

The double knock at the door announces Coach's arrival. "Larsen!" she yells, striding in, a small smile on her face when she realizes it's only J.D. and me. "Did you all see my new apron?" she asks, holding it out.

I grab mine out of my locker. "Matches mine."

She laughs, her eyes sparkling with mirth.

J.D. looks between us before knocking once on the locker next to mine. "Well, I'm going to head out. I'll text you the address, okay?"

"Thanks, man." I give him a fist bump.

"Team dinner?" Finley asks as soon as J.D. is gone. "That's new for you. Did you confirm there will be steamed broccoli?"

"Haha. You're so funny," I grumble. "I'm sure Gloria will have something that fits my diet. She docs know she's feeding a team of professional athletes, right?"

Finley shrugs. "I'd assume so."

"You've never been to a team dinner?" I ask, not really that surprised.

"No."

"Want to come with me?"

Finley considers it before shaking her head. "No. Team dinners are for the team."

"And you're not part of the team?"

"I am, but also, I'm not."

"Sounds tough," I say, truly meaning my words. Being Finley sounds hard. The pressure of being the first female head coach is nothing compared to the pressure she puts on herself. And she's right. She's not a part of the team. But she also *is* part of the team. "Do you and the other coaches ever do dinners?"

"We eat together when we're on the road," she replies, her head tilted slightly. "Sometimes when we're working late, we'll call in food. So we end up eating together at least a couple of times a week. But, no. We don't go out to a restaurant or each other's houses."

"Not really friends?" I ask, sitting down to pull on my shoes.

"Rob is almost a father figure to me, if that makes any sense. He's the only one I talk to about anything remotely personal. Sutton and I have worked together since I came to the Yeti, so we're work friends. Nyquist is, well, Nyquist. Goalie coaches are just as isolated as goalies tend to be. And Shaw... wants my job. He's never hidden the fact he's waiting in the wings for me to fail. He's a great coach, but not a candidate for friendship."

I place my elbows on my knees, not interested in ending our conversation, even though I'm done changing. "Do you use an application process to sort through all your friend candidates?" I ask.

"Oh yes. It's very rigorous. Double blind and everything. Cuts down on bias."

"I'd expect no less from you. I can't imagine when you find the time to sort through the hundreds of applications you must get each week."

A wistful smile crosses Finley's face. "I think Charlotte is the only one who has ever stuck around long enough to make it through the process. And I'm pretty sure that's because she's too stubborn to quit."

"I'd be interested in applying, you know," I say solemnly. "If you should ever open the pool again."

Finley blinks slowly. Once. Twice. "I... I, unfortunately, can't accept applications from players."

"Maybe in a few years, then." I slowly get to my feet.

Finley's eyes flash with interest as she watches me stand, but I hide the slight pain in my hip well because she doesn't say anything as I make my way past her.

"I'm going to miss spending time with you when the Challenge is over," I admit softly.

I rub my chest gently to try to dispel the ache at the thought of not spending time with this interesting, intelligent woman. Of knowing she's just across the hall but might as well be miles away.

"Me, too," she replies, almost so quiet I don't hear it.

But I do.

Chapter 21

Finley

"You've been such wonderful sports about all of this, and, as of our game last night, we've increased attendance by over twenty percent. I'm so appreciative of all the participants and the PR team for making this happen," Mr. Peterson announces from his place at the front of the room. "And a special thank-you to the social media team, who have been working on overdrive since February, producing content and handling the increase in activity on our accounts. Sabrina, I'll hand it over to you to tell us what today's event looks like."

We're back in our practice facility for this one; the players' lounge has been reconfigured to have six pairs of seats spread in a semicircle in the middle of the room.

"Thanks, Ken," Sabrina says, taking the microphone from Mr. Peterson. "Today's event is a Yeti-tastic version of *The New-lywed Game*! You might not be real couples, but, heck, you spend more time together than you spend with your actual spouses."

She pauses for laughter, but no one seems to think it's that funny. It's not untrue, but the married guys don't like to be reminded of the fact they're closer to their teammates than they are to the loves of their lives. Or, at least, they spend way more time with them.

J.D. is glaring at the head of PR, the angriest I've ever seen the team captain, but Rob gives him a consoling pat on the arm. Larsen takes the opportunity to plant a wet kiss on Li's cheek, giving a saucy wink to the phone that was shoved in his face to capture the moment. The social media team can't get enough of that guy. He *does* have a knack for forcing his way into your heart.

"Anyway," Sabrina continues. "We'll ask a question, and one person from each pair will write down what they think their partner will answer on the dry-erase board. After the answers are locked in, the other partner will reveal their answer out loud. Points are awarded based on how well the answers match! So, decide who will write the answers first for your team. Have those people sit in the seat with the boards on them. Other partners, you'll be in the chairs across from them."

"Want to write first?" Beckett asks, his arm brushing against mine just enough to send a shockwave of adrenaline through me.

"Yes."

"Great." I can feel his gaze as it roams across my face and down my body. I'm not sure what he sees, but he says, "We've got this."

Nodding, I watch Li and Larsen do an elaborate handshake and try to hold in a grimace. "I'm not sure whether we can beat them. I'm pretty sure they spend all their time together. Also, was that the handshake from *Parent Trap*?"

Beckett tilts his head slightly, considering his teammates. "I don't know why this is only just occurring to me, but do they share an apartment?"

I shake my head. "They have their own... right?" I ask. "They definitely don't live together... do they?" I'm truly not sure now that he mentions it, but I can't imagine two grown men choosing to live with each other.

He shrugs. "Some guys just don't like to be alone. Though I'm pretty sure they told me they live separately."

"It's alarming that neither of us knows the answer to that," I murmur.

Beckett nods as we make our way to our seats. "I'm offended now that I think of it. They've been over to my place for dinner like four times since I moved in, and they've never invited me to theirs."

"Maybe because it's the equivalent of a college dorm," I suggest as I pick up the board and slip into my seat.

"Good luck, Queenie," Beckett says as the host of the event walks out. She's the friend Charlotte mentioned a while ago, and, according to Charlotte, she's willing to do anything to turn the Denver Miners into a winning baseball team. Unfortunately, no one wants to pitch at a mile high, so it's an uphill battle.

"Hi, everyone," she says with a smile. "I'm Sage Sinclair, the GM for the Denver Miners, Colorado's professional baseball team. I'm so excited to be here with you all today. Before we get started, I wanted to invite everyone tuning in to join us on March 26 for Opening Day."

Sage looks like she's barely a day over twenty-five, with her sun-streaked blonde hair and loose beach weaves. She's stunning, and I subtly look over at Beckett to see if he notices how pretty she is. He's staring at her, but rather than desire in his eyes, all I see is polite interest.

Not that it would matter. They'd probably make a great couple.

"All right. Everybody ready to get started?" Sage asks, her voice clear and strong.

Noises of confirmation come from around the room.

"Okay. First question: If your partner could have any pet, what would it be?"

I think about it for a moment, remembering how Beckett had a dog as a kid, but that doesn't feel quite right. Realizing I do know the answer, I quickly write it down on my board.

Sage starts with Rob and J.D., the team on the far end, and works her way around the circle, asking the question again and having each person verbally answer it. Once they've given their choice, the guesser shows their response. Unsurprisingly, J.D. is a dog man. Very surprisingly, Volkov wants a pet sugar glider.

"Kane, what pet would you have?" she asks when it's our turn.

"Cat," he answers with a definitive nod. "A black cat, if possible."

"Coach?"

I turn my board around slowly to show: Black cat.

The shy smile Beckett offers is like a candle, warming me from my toes to the tip of my head. It's like he's surprised I was paying attention these past few weeks, or I might've forgotten or something. Like that's possible.

Sage keeps us moving quickly, running us through questions like:

"Which app do they use the most on their phone?" Easy. Health.

"What's the best vacation they've ever been on?" Fishing in Canada during college.

"What's their go-to karaoke song?" The Killers' "Mr. Brightside." I died laughing when he told me that.

When Sage asks, "What is their favorite city to travel to for work?" a slow, evil grin threatens to spread across my face as I quickly scrawl down my answer. It's almost unbearable, waiting for Sage to ask the three teams before us. Finally, when she asks

Beckett, his eyes meet mine. He closes them as if he can't believe what he's about to say, but he does it anyway. "New Orleans."

"Yes!" I practically yell, turning my board around to show off *New Orleans* written in the center.

Beckett shakes his head slowly, mouthing, "You're dead to me."

I laugh as I grab the eraser, ready for the rest of the questions.

We're tied with Li and Larsen once again when we successfully get all ten of the first group of questions. Beckett grabs the board and marker from me as I hand them over the gap between us. His fingers brush mine, and I swear he holds on a millisecond longer than necessary. It's probably wishful thinking, but I swear he does it just to touch me.

I thought it was nerve-wracking being the one to answer, but being on this side of the question is even worse: What if I forget my answer? How does Beckett know that I'd pick a photographic memory if I could have one superpower, when I ran through five options before settling on that one?

I'm not surprised when Beckett correctly answers, "What's your colleague's favorite coffee order?" Larsen is so annoyed by how easy the question is that he actually yells the answer from across the room before I do.

We're still tied with Li and Larsen when Sage asks, "Which fictional character best represents them at work?"

Beckett looks at me, raising his eyes from the board, and it's impossible to miss the unfiltered joy dancing through them. *Jesus Christ.* Did he pay someone to get this question in there? Actually, from the way Larsen is cackling, if anyone bribed the social media team to include it, he's at the top of the list.

"Elsa," I reply begrudgingly when Sage gets to us, and Larsen loses it. He's practically falling out of his seat, the whole room staring at the spectacle. Except me. I'm staring at Beckett, who looks... genuinely happy, his head dropped back, laughter pouring from him as his shoulders shake.

It's a goddamn sight to behold, and it does something to my heart that I fear may be irreversible.

***

It's a tie.

"Li and Larsen—"

"Double L!" Larsen yells from his place, whacking Li on the back enthusiastically.

"Won the cooking contest," Sabrina continues. "Coach Blake and Kane took the victory in the talent competition. It was a four-way tie last week, and this week Larsen and Li and Coach Blake and Kane tied again."

I know the summary is needed to catch up viewers who haven't been paying attention the whole time, but all it feels like is a reminder that I should've been trying harder from the beginning. Beckett and I should've worked with a chef to teach us how to cook. I should've been studying up on Colorado knowledge for the trivia portion of the last event.

During our weekly call, even my dad decided to comment on the Yeti Challenge, saying something along the lines of, "If you're going to do something, Finley, you'd better do it well. Every single thing you do is a reflection of your work, and losing to your players is not the image you want to present to the world."

He's right. I should've done more to prepare. I could've performed better. And I'm not just letting down my dad, I'm letting down kids like Lilly who need something to brighten up their weeks, months, or years of treatment.

The other contestants in the room start clapping as Sabrina hands Sage a yeti bobblehead as a thank-you for her time.

"We'll see you all the first week of April for the final contest," Sabrina says excitedly.

"Do we get to know what it is yet?" J.D. asks.

"Nope," Sabrina replies sweetly. "It's a surprise."

Larsen walks over to us. "Okay, admit it."

"Admit what?" Beckett asks, giving the rookie some serious side-eye.

Larsen points between us, and my whole body turns to ice. He can't know anything. There isn't anything to know.

Beckett looks my way and raises an eyebrow. "Do you know what he's talking about?"

"Just ignore him," J.D. suggests as he joins our group. "That's what I do."

Oh good. More people to witness whatever is about to come out of Larsen's mouth. Not that I'm worried. Because there's nothing to be worried about.

"Oh, come on, J.D. You know those two cheated! I mean, sure, Beckett got some softballs for Coach, but do you really think she knew all those things about him? I'm pretty sure she doesn't even know my first name."

"You have a first name?" I ask. "I always assumed you just had the one... like Prince or Cher."

Larsen scowls at me as the rest of the men laugh at his expense.

"Now that you mention it, I'm not entirely sure I know *any* of your first names," I joke.

Larsen crosses his arms. "I'm not letting you distract me. I want to know how you cheated."

I glance at Beckett, and he shrugs. "Don't tell him. Make him sweat it."

"So you did cheat?! I knew it. Li! I told you they cheated. They've just admitted it." He twirls around, trying to find his friend.

"Did we admit to that?" I ask him.

"I didn't hear you." J.D. smirks.

We all disperse, leaving behind an annoyed Larsen.

"Good work out there, Queenie," Beckett says as I turn to go to my office.

"You, too. I guess we make a pretty good team."

As I work that afternoon, my mind keeps drifting back to Beckett and the limited time we have left together, trying to convince myself that maybe we could still be friends. Maybe we could still hang out and watch film together a couple of days a week or something. Just when we're home. Just as friends. Maybe.

Chapter 22

Finley

"Okay," I muse, tapping my key against the door to my hotel room, "this is starting to get weird. Did you request to room on the coaches' floor or something?"

Beckett shakes his head. "No. And I'm wondering if I should be insulted."

"Worried they saw your age and assumed you were a coach?" I ask.

"You're kind of a bully, you know that, right?"

I smile. "I've been called worse."

"Oh, yeah?" he asks, leaning against the wall rather than scanning his card to go into his room.

"High school boys don't like to be outplayed by a girl. And not every man thinks a woman should be coaching a professional men's hockey team. I've been called a four-letter word or two."

"There are a lot of stupid people in this world."

"That there are," I agree.

We stand there, staring at each other for what is certainly an inappropriate length of time.

"I'm not sure how I feel about you being next to me, rather than across the hall," I say finally. "It's going to force me to reorient myself."

"Do you think about where I am often?" Beckett asks, a smug smile playing on his face.

Constantly. Even when I'm not thinking about it, I somehow know where he is. It's like he's magnetic north, and I'm a compass. My soul has shifted, so it's always trying to align with him.

It's terrible.

"I'm a hockey coach. It's my job to be aware of everything and everyone around me."

His smile grows, as if he's aware of the truth beneath my lies.

"If you want to discuss film later…" I know it's risky when we spend time together on away trips. But I also hate the idea of missing out on the time we get to be Finley and Beckett rather than Coach Blake and Kane.

He nods. "Right. That would work… to go over that play from tonight."

"Okay."

I'm not sure exactly when it started, but we always do this when we're outside the safety of one of our apartments. We act. Pretend we're not doing anything wrong. Even though we aren't.

Probably.

I'm still not sure where exactly the line is between coach and friend. And how will I know when I'm crossing it?

I walk into my room, and my heart leaps when I hear a knock. Glancing at the source of the sound, I realize there is a connecting door between our rooms. The way my heart speeds up is definitely crossing the line between coach and… more than friends.

Unfortunately, I don't seem to be able to control my reaction to the man anymore. I've never been as physically attracted to someone in my life, and now that I know how great he is as a person, it's starting to wear on me.

"Hey." I open the door to reveal Beckett, his dark eyes dancing with mirth.

"Hey right back," he replies. "What are the odds?"

"I didn't realize hotels like this even had rooms with connecting doors."

"Just lucky, I guess," he says on an exhale.

Standing here on either side of the doorway, my body responds to his nearness. We might sit by each other frequently, but I'm almost never looking at him from the front, and so have not built up my immunity to the sight that is Beckett Kane, in a hotel room, mere inches from me.

He's wearing a pair of gray sweatpants with a black Yeti shirt pulling across his broad chest. His dark hair is hidden under a black backward Yeti cap, and fuck. It's the exact same thing I've seen men wear for almost twenty years. But somehow, tonight, with him, it's setting me on fire.

I want to jump into his arms. To wrap my legs around his waist. To kiss him so deeply, it's impossible to tell where I end and he begins.

I don't know what he sees on my face, but his body reacts, going taut, as his pupils expand.

"You've got…" He leans forward to brush a strand of hair back behind my ear. The path his finger traces tingles at the sensation, and I have to bite my cheek to keep a purr from escaping.

He keeps his hand there, and I lean ever so slightly into his touch, my eyes closing of their own volition.

Pull away! Fuck. He is your player!

"Fin," Beckett murmurs, and I snap my gaze to his.

He's even closer now, the warmth of his body seeping through the inches of space between us.

"You look... so beautiful tonight." His breath hitches slightly, and he pulls his hand from my face like it's on fire. "I mean, just like, you know, good. In the way a friend would say to another friend. You look good, pal. Looking good, buddy."

A shiver flows down my body, leaving small shudders as aftershocks in its wake. I pull my lower lip into my mouth, fascinated by the way Beckett's gaze tracks it, not looking away.

I swallow hard. "Thank you."

Every inch of my body is desperate for him to touch me again. "You look... good... too, pal." I try to smile, but I'm not sure it's worked. My ability to convince myself this is a bad idea seems to be broken.

I don't know whether it's the adrenaline from the overtime win or the fact that I can move in and out of Beckett's room freely without anyone seeing us, but suddenly, I want nothing more than to see where this can go.

"I don't know if I've ever had a coach call me pal before," Beckett admits. His eyes are still on my lips, and he says it as if he's almost in a trance.

But the word coach is enough to pull me from mine.

What the fuck was I thinking?

I am his coach.

I can't do this.

"I've got to... bed," I manage to get out. "Super tired. Sorry. No film tonight."

I jump back, shutting the door, not waiting for him to say anything else.

Unfortunately, the closed door does nothing to help settle the need raging through me.

I force myself to get ready for bed, and instead of turning on film, like I normally do, I lie there, unable to think about anything except what would've happened if I hadn't shut that door. If Beckett had kept his beautiful mouth closed and had leaned in and kissed me instead.

Would I have stepped into him, closing those last breaths of space between us? Would he have tipped my chin up and run his thumb over my lip before kissing me?

I fight the desire to slip my hand into my sleep shorts, knowing I shouldn't get off to images of Beckett Kane.

A low sound comes from the other side of the wall, and I still. It was quiet, but something about the deep sound feels... needy. And what if he needs help? I slip from my bed and tiptoe to the wall, placing my ear against it.

There's a rhythmic sound I can't quite place, and after listening for another moment, I'm suddenly hit with the fact that it's sexual. Did Beckett pop down to the bar to pick up one of the puck bunnies loitering there after I slammed the door in his face?

My stomach twists into a knot as I bite the inside of my cheek. I know I should stop, but instead, I move a few paces forward, right where I imagine his bed would be.

I listen for a few seconds, jealousy and need warring within me, before I realize he's alone. That he must be fucking his own hand.

The jealous part of my brain now fully appeased, the need takes over, and I lean back against the wall, licking my index and middle fingers before sliding them into my shorts.

My fingers slide around my clit before dipping into the wetness between my legs. Listening to Beckett on the other side of the wall, I match his rhythm as I let my mind wander... What would it be like to be there with him?

The hunger in his eyes as he stared down at me, spread wide on his bed. The slow way he would prowl toward me before dropping to his knees, his hands sliding up my thighs before slipping a finger inside my pussy.

There's a low groan on the other side of the wall, and in my mind, it's the sound he makes the first time he tastes my core.

I increase my tempo as I imagine him feasting on me.

"Fuck, Beckett," I moan lightly, and the sound from his room stops.

Oh, shit. He heard me. Oh, God. Not only does he know I was fucking listening to him like some kind of pervert, but now he knows I was getting off to the sound of him masturbating.

I want to stop, but I can't. My body demands release.

Then, as if nothing happened, the sound of him stroking himself starts again. Possibly even slightly louder than before.

"Fin." The sound is low and anguished.

Oh fuck. He... We... We're doing this.

I slide my fingers across my clit again, and when a moan slips out, I don't even try to keep it quiet. "Mmmm. Yes," I whisper. Hoping he hears me. Praying he doesn't.

"Fin. God. Yes. So good." His deep voice is a rumble.

I work myself with my fingers, no longer imagining what could be, but instead, living in this moment. Knowing Beckett is on the other side of the wall, his hand wrapped tightly around his cock as he pumps to the image of me.

It's the most scandalous thing I've ever done, yet I can't stop myself.

The pressure builds, and my head drops against the wall, a dull thud echoing as I quietly chant, "Yes, yes, yes."

There's movement, and then a thud on the other side of the wall, right where I am, and I tell myself he's moved. He changed position, so he could be here, as close to me as possible, as I unravel.

"Fin," he chokes out, and the sound of his hand sliding over his dick slows, becoming inaudible over the blood pumping in my ears.

I don't know how long I stay there, leaning against the wall, but when I'm fully back inside my own body, I press my hand against the wall and say, "Goodnight, Beckett." I can barely hear it, so there's no way he can, but I needed to say something. To commemorate what just happened—what can never happen again.

"Goodnight, Fin," I swear I hear as I move back toward my bed.

Chapter 23

Finley

I take one last look in the mirror at my outfit, trying to refrain from rolling my eyes at the brown cowboy boots and slinky blue top Charlotte had delivered to my apartment. According to her, "You can't wear Yeti gear to a Jaxon Steele concert."

Trust me, as a huge Steelie, I'm well aware of that. I just don't happen to own anything other than Yeti gear and power suits.

I touch up my mascara one last time before determining I'm as ready as I'll ever be. Throwing on a coat—she can't protest a Yeti coat—I head out.

"Hey," I say, drawing up short as Beckett steps into the hall at the same time as I do. He's wearing blue jeans and a Henley, and damn. He looks good.

I shove the sound of him coming, my name slipping from his lips, from my mind.

I can feel the light flutter of his gaze as he takes me in as well. "Hey," he replies, sliding his hands into his pockets. "Where are you off to, all dressed up?"

His eyes are piercing as he waits for my answer, but all I can think about is whether he's going to tell me I look beautiful again.

"I'm going with Charlotte to the Jaxon Steele concert. I thought I told you?"

We've hung out—watched film a few times together since the incident I can only think of as masturgate, and things are surprisingly uncomplicated. Even if we both know what we did, we don't talk about it. And if God loves me at all, we never will.

He shakes his head, a pleased smile creeping across his face. "You didn't mention that. Just said you were busy tonight."

"Ah. Where are you going?" I ask. It could be a date. He sure smells like he's going on a date. Some clean and masculine cologne floats between us, trying to convince me to make bad decisions. I can guarantee it will be a feature in my fantasies this evening.

"The Jaxon Steele concert," Beckett replies, a twinkle in his eyes.

"Are you... You're not... What?"

"Jameson Walker invited Callan and me, plus a few other guys he knows in town, I guess."

I can feel confusion and amusement warring on my face. "Wow. Invited the whole Yeti Challenge team except me. Rude, Jameson." I'm teasing, but the old hurt of never quite being a part of the team comes back in full force. It was better in college, when I was playing on the women's team, but in high school, I was always an afterthought. The girl who changed in a closet down the hall. The one who didn't know the inside jokes.

I shake off the thought. I moved on from that a long time ago.

My phone buzzes in my hand, Charlotte letting me know she's here. "Well, I should..." I nod toward the elevator.

"Do you want a ride?" Beckett asks. "I was planning to drive."

I shake my head. "No, but you should jump in with Charlotte and me. No need to navigate traffic and parking."

"I mean, if you're sure it's okay?" Beckett asks.

"Definitely. You know Charlotte: more is always merrier with her."

The elevator arrives, and I catch the hint of a scowl on Kane's face as he walks in.

"You okay?" I ask, our arms brushing as I face the front of the elevator. Instead of letting myself sink into the warmth, I subtly shift so we aren't touching.

"What do you mean?"

"You grimaced when you started walking."

He crosses his arms, shooting me a quick smile. "I did? I think you're seeing things."

"Are you sure? You took a hard hit the other night."

"I'm fine," he says, not quite curt, but definitely leaving no room for further questions.

We ride in silence for a moment before I ask, "So, is Jameson a big Jaxon Steele fan or something?"

"According to Callan, Jameson's sister-in-law dates Steele, or is friends with him. Something like that."

"What?! That's so cool! Dang, you're so fancy," I tease.

The smile he gives me feels real this time, so I lean into it, continuing to joke with him as we make our way through the lobby. When we climb into the back of the black SUV with Charlotte, I squeeze into the middle, Beckett's side fully pressed into mine. It's glorious, and I can't decide whether I want to take this opportunity to lean into him further or to force myself to maintain an appropriate distance.

"Well, this is a fun surprise." Charlotte's eyes dance with undisguised glee as she takes in Beckett. "You're looking fine tonight, Kane. Must be getting good sleep lately."

I want to murder her. I knew I shouldn't have told Charlotte about the hotel room, but I was feeling so guilty about masturgate that I needed someone to talk to. Someone I knew would tell me I was overreacting. I still feel a deep need to confess that I overstepped a boundary, but Charlotte convinced me that what I do in the confines of my own mind can't be used against me. Her actual words were, "If players got in trouble every time they picked you from the ol' spank bank when they were alone in a hotel room, there wouldn't be anyone left on the team, so I think you're safe."

Unfortunately, I've always had what Charlotte calls an overactive guilt complex that causes me to confess to any minor infraction. Though I don't think it's overreacting. I just believe rules exist for a reason. That if you make a mistake, you need to confess and make amends. It's literally the backbone of my push for a culture of accountability.

But I can't disagree that masturbating, alone, in my hotel room, technically isn't against any policies.

Instead of commenting on the sleep comment, Beckett tips his head in acknowledgment. "And you look lovely as always."

"And we both know Finley looks like a snack," Charlotte says, clearly enjoying her ability to stir shit.

"Charlotte!" I exclaim, my cheeks starting to burn.

It feels like the vehicle has become an MRI machine, Beckett's gaze scanning me, millimeter by millimeter. Finally, in a voice deeper than I've ever heard from him in the day, he agrees. "We do."

Charlotte asks Beckett how he ended up with an invite tonight, and when she learns he's in a suite with Jameson Walker and his family, her excitement kicks up a notch. Apparently, Charlotte met Jameson's sister through work, and now they're the type of friends who get a drink whenever Lila happens to be in Denver.

"So, I guess you're stuck with us all night!" Charlotte exclaims.

"Wait, what?" I ask, as Beckett's arm tenses, his hard muscles a wall against mine.

"Lila asked me to join them," Charlotte says again, like she's not shaking my entire world, even though she totally knows she is. "Lila took the night off from work so she could hang out with us since I told her I wouldn't be working, either. It should be so much fun. Plus, everyone in the box will be a professional athlete, seriously dating one, or related to one in some way, so it should be pretty low stress."

I bite the inside of my cheek. "You have a different definition of low stress than I do." I had big plans to scream the lyrics at the top of my lungs for two hours straight from the safety of Charlotte's family's box.

We pull up to the side of the arena, one not open to the public, but it also isn't the player entrance we typically use, and I realize what this odd feeling in my gut must be—I'm never here when the floor isn't ice. The arena hosts all of Denver's professional hockey and basketball games as well as the big concerts and other events that Charlotte and her team put on, but if it's not a game day, I'm not in the main part of the building. Just the practice facility.

We climb out of the car, and Charlotte pulls a badge from her purse. She scans it to open a side door, and we make our way through what is apparently the most VIP entrance. Beckett's fingers brush mine as we walk, and instead of stepping further away, I just let myself have the moment; hope and excitement filling my chest as I anticipate the next swing of our arms, the next contact made.

The backs of our fingers meet again, and it's all I can do to keep my face straight, my steps unfaltering, because I know it means he *chose* not to move away. At the thought, my traitorous mind conjures images of what tonight could be, if only he weren't my player. Holding hands as we make this walk, our fingers intertwined. Laughing, his arm around my shoulders, as we mingle with our friends. Listening to love songs with

Beckett's arms wrapped around me from behind, engulfing me with his size and heat. I'd lean my head against his chest, singing along as we gently sway to the music of my absolute favorite singer.

"Here we are," Charlotte announces excitedly as she scans a ticket at the door before handing a second one to me. "In case you need to leave for anything."

I tuck it into my pocket as Beckett holds the door to the suite open for both of us. It's fairly crowded inside, and Charlotte pushes her way forward, quickly finding her friend and giving her a big hug.

"Callan is waving at you." I nod toward the man. Beckett looks around, finding the men who invited him here.

"Go," I say when he seems hesitant to leave. He looks between us again, so I reiterate, "Go. Really. I'm good. I'm at a Jaxon Steele concert! Literally nothing could stop this from being the best night of my life."

Beckett chuckles as he finally walks away, and I slip into the corner, content to watch the flow of people around me.

Beckett is talking to Callan and Jameson, and even though I can only see half of his face, it's clear he enjoys their company. There's a wide smile crossing his face, and his shoulders are relaxed. It's Night Beckett. The man I spend my time with on a couch watching game film, not the professional hockey player who is laser-focused on his goals.

I'm still staring at Beckett when Charlotte joins me, leaning against the wall in a mirror of my posture. Her gaze follows mine, and she lets out a sigh. "The online world is rooting for you two."

"That's because no one in Colorado cares about sea lions." I feel a smile break across my face as Beckett laughs.

"Sure," Charlotte agrees. "Well-known fact that the people of Colorado, really the whole Rocky Mountain region, are sea-lion haters."

"You know what I mean."

"I know you haven't taken your eyes off that very attractive man since he begrudgingly left your side."

The body parts in question snap to her face as if proving her point. "That's not true."

The look she gives me is one of utter disbelief. "Okay, Finley. If you say so."

"He's my player."

"Who you want to fuck."

"I... You... That's not..."

Charlotte nods like I'm making complete sense. "Right. That's what I thought. Masturgate was a one-time thing, and now it's out of your system. No fucking required."

"He's my player. I cannot want to... fuck... him."

"And yet you do. And even worse, you want more than just a quick fuck." She takes a casual sip of beer.

Like she's pulling back a curtain that's been closed, the reality of it all hits me. I know I want Beckett. I want his touch on my skin. His lips pressed against mine, his tongue exploring my mouth. His body above me, behind me, beneath me, pounding into me in a restless rhythm. But it's more than that, I want his evenings and his weekends and every spare minute of his time.

I want his happiness and his frustrations.

I want *him*.

"Fuck," I say, trying to keep the panic I feel from my face. "It's so bad."

"The whole world is secretly rooting for you two to fall in love. If nothing else, that's what the Yeti Challenge has accomplished."

It's the first time I've wished for something from social media to come true.

"Is there really not a way you can make it happen?" Charlotte asks, leaning close to me, so we're not overheard. The opening act is playing, and none of us is paying much attention.

"I'm in charge of him."

"Male bosses sleep with their employees all the time. Like people barely bat an eye."

"Just because it happens doesn't make it okay. Plus, as a woman, we both know I'm held to *very* different standards." I pause, deciding how much I want to get into it tonight, but finally say, "I may have spent some time googling it. The women usually get transferred to different departments or something, so they aren't in the boss' direct chain of command."

Charlotte considers it. "Can he still play for the Yeti and not be in your chain of command? Like, could Rob oversee all decisions related to Kane?"

"Ah, yes. I'm sure the organization—and the world at large—will be totally fine with me handing over decision-making control to my assistant. No one will question that or suggest I clearly don't have what it takes to be the head coach if I need to outsource the *actual coaching*."

"Sarcasm noted, but what if he gets injured or something? I mean, he's old, and he plays hockey. He could break a hip at any moment."

"I actually think he's hiding an injury from me," I respond, willing to be distracted by the other challenge between Beckett and me. He isn't playing at full strength—I've been questioning it since he started with the team—but it's gotten worse lately.

"Not the point, Finley."

I shrug. "He would still be my player."

"Would he, though?" Charlotte asks. "You know I try to avoid knowing anything about sports if possible—I leave that up to my brother—but when players are actually declared as injured, are they even considered part of the team?"

"Yes, Charlotte." I sigh. "Plus, I think if masturgate has taught us anything, it's that I desperately need a release. I'm not even sure this is about Beckett at all."

"Right," Charlotte says. "So we're going with the fact that you're horny and *that's* the reason you're interested in your player?"

"Yes," I agree, though clearly it isn't the case. I've been interested in him since I was sixteen.

Charlotte nods. "Okay. Sure. I'm positive it has nothing to do with the handsome man you have a ton in common with. Truly, I fully support your delusions."

I groan, dropping my head against the wall. Across the room, Beckett's eyes meet mine. He lifts an eyebrow, silently asking if everything's okay.

I force a smile in response. Out of the corner of my eye, Charlotte clocks the exchange. When I look back at her, she's grinning.

"Yep. Nothing real there. You should probably just sleep with him, get it out of your system, and move on."

"That is not the conclusion we just came to, Charlotte. I'm his coach. I do nothing," I suggest instead.

"Oh, sure. Let the lust fire you started grow until you end up fucking your star defenseman on the center of the ice. I see absolutely no flaws in that plan."

"That sounds so cold. In this scenario, are we naked? Or is it more of a drop-the-pants-a-few-inches, hurry-fuck kind of thing?"

"He obviously takes his jersey off and lays it down for you to lie on. Don't be ridiculous, Finley."

"Why am I friends with you again?" I ask.

Her serene smile is an act. She knows the seed she just planted. And damn it, if I don't want to let it grow and see what happens.

Chapter 24

Beckett

As I stand in a concert suite full of famous athletes, the musical notes of Jaxon Steele's opening act continuing to play in the background, I can only focus on one thing: *Finley Blake is amazing.*

When she walked out of her apartment, my first thought had been, "Thank God I don't have to spend my whole day with her looking like that. I wouldn't be able to handle it." Apparently, though, I've pissed off God, or karma, or some higher power because here I am—not just at the same concert as her, but in the exact same suite. We're mingling as if we're a married couple doing the rounds before we head home to fall into bed together—I force that thought out of my head before it can finish.

Because Finley Blake can never be more than my coach.

And yet, instead of focusing on the concert, or, hell, what I'm going to do about the fact that my hip is getting worse, my gaze keeps finding her, my soul soaking in every flash of happiness that crosses her face. I *want* her to be mine. And after hearing her come, my name on her lips, I *need* her to be mine.

She's talking and laughing with Charlotte, and it's like I'm finally getting to see all of her. I know I'm one of the fortunate few who sees behind her mask, but Finley Blake at a Jaxon Steele concert is another level. She's excited. Maybe a little tipsy. Chatting with Charlotte, making her laugh like we're at a stand-up comedy show.

She seems happy. And it makes my heart do funny things I likely shouldn't be feeling.

"Kane," Callan starts, handing me another beer. "I see you haven't gotten any friendlier since moving to Denver."

I take a long sip of my beer. "I'm friendly. I just don't see the point in making small talk with a bunch of people I'll never see again."

"Or you could consider seeing them again. We live in the area. Everyone I know here is a good person, who you'd like if you got to know them."

"This is the only time we all have off, so what, we hang out once a year? Seems like a lot of work."

Callan stares at me, his gaze penetrating and a little sad, before he seems to shake it off, his ever-present smile returning. "We get together for dinner or poker at least once a month. You should join us."

I shake my head. "I truly don't know how you do it. How do you stay on top of your game, make time to be friends with all the guys on your team, *and* still socialize with other people?"

Callan runs a hand through his hair, his eyes flitting around the room. "I was in a bad spot a few years ago. Constantly focused on making sure I was in peak physical condition, that I was ready for every game, but I was in a bad place mentally. I realized I needed to connect with someone. So I started with my team. And then I ran into some of the same guys at events and whatnot around town and realized there are a number of older athletes in town who are... alone."

A faint buzzing fills my ears as the truth of his statement hits home. I know that loneliness viscerally. Except, it's been missing lately. Since I started intentionally engaging with the other defensemen, probably. My mind flashes a montage of images of Finley and me in one of our apartments. Sitting on the couch. Eating dinner together. Briefly making eye contact at practice when Larsen says something dumb.

Right. My teammates.

My gaze flits across the room, the tension releasing from my shoulders as I chase a dark flash of hair to find Finley. She's dancing to the song, she and Charlotte both singing into the tops of their beer bottles.

With a sigh, I refocus on Callan, who is introducing me to another guy in the room. "Kane, let me introduce you to Nate Riley."

I take in the man, at least a few inches taller than me, though I have at least twenty pounds on him, and make an educated guess. "You play for the Mountaineers?" I ask, naming the professional basketball team in town.

"And you're the Yeti's new defenseman and resident social media star," he replies, as we shake hands.

I sigh. "Yes. I've spent years trying to *avoid* becoming an internet sensation, and yet, somehow, here I am."

"It's not a bad place to be. There are worse things than the world trying to 'ship you with Finley Blake."

A part of me, the one that feels like it's coming home anytime I'm with Finley, could not agree more. And yet, there's also nothing worse than *the world* trying to 'ship *me* with Finley.

"Really? Is that how you'd feel if people were trying to set you up with your coach?" I ask.

Nate laughs. "Coach Mac has kept it tight for a sixty-year-old man, but he's not quite the same as Coach Blake."

There is nothing disrespectful about the way he says it, and yet, something inside me darkens at the thought of him dating Finley.

I fight against the need to ball my hands into fists, to send one flying through his face. Instead, I say, "Well, if you ever decide to date the person in charge of your career, you let me know. Maybe I'll start making dumb decisions, too, and we can all double-date."

"Deal," Nate agrees. "It sounds like the perfect evening."

Callan watches our exchange, amusement coloring his features. "I think you're both outkicking your coverage in that plan."

"Offensive," Nate jokes. "I'm obviously the one who would be settling."

I stay quiet. *Finley* is the one who would be settling if we were ever to get together. I might be a pro hockey player, but she's the first female coach in professional men's hockey's history. And more than that, she's smart. And so sarcastic, most people mistake it for bitchy, but I know the truth.

"We really shouldn't be talking about it." I know how much she would hate that this conversation is happening. How it wouldn't be happening about *any* other coach. "Coach Blake has enough to deal with without worrying about one of her players wanting to date her."

"And do you?" Callan tips his head slightly. "Want to date her?"

Shit. "That's not what I meant."

"So you don't?"

I consider telling him. Confessing the feelings that have been plaguing me. The need to be with her, but what good would it do? Instead, I offer another truth.

"We've become friends because of this competition. Am I a little bummed that once it's over, we'll have to go back to being strictly professional? Sure. But I would never do anything to damage her career. I thought I knew what dedication looks like after what it took to get to where I am, but it's nothing compared to what Coach Blake has had to do."

The opening act finally finishes, and after chatting for a few more minutes, Nate moves to catch up with another friend of his. As Jaxon Steele walks on stage to a cacophony of cheers, Callan says, "Come on, let's go listen to the concert of the year." Nodding toward Finley and Charlotte, he adds, "We can sit with *your friend*. I need to talk to Princess anyway."

"Princess?" I ask. Christ on a cracker. I do not love that he has a nickname for Finley. I force the jealousy threatening to explode from my sternum back down again. What is going on with me tonight?

"Charlotte Langford. Her dad owns half this town, including the Stallions. Yet, I swear she forgets my name every time we run into each other."

I let out a laugh. "First time that's happened to you?" I ask. Callan had a reputation for being vain when I knew him and, in typical quarterback fashion, would be highly offended by someone not knowing who he was. It appears he hasn't grown out of that particular trait.

Finley and Charlotte both turn toward us as we approach. My gaze meets Finley's as Jaxon Steele sings about lost love.

"Hey, Cameron," Charlotte says, as everyone shuffles to make enough room for us to join the group. "Great catch last weekend."

"It's Callan. And the season ended two months ago," Callan mutters, exasperation written all over his face. "And I'm the quarterback."

Finley laughs at the smile her friend gives the football player. I'm not sure whether she does it on purpose or not, but Finley leans into me slightly as her rich laughter pours out, and her touch is a lightning bolt through my system. She moves back, and the contact is gone too soon.

"Sorry," she apologizes, an embarrassed grin flashing at me.

I nudge her with my shoulder, refusing to pull away. "Never be sorry about that."

She nods, and we stay connected as we turn our attention to the performance, Callan and Charlotte bickering next to us.

When that song ends, I can't help it anymore; I look down at Finley. My stomach flutters: she's already looking at me. The small grin she gives me when our gazes meet is sweet and says things our mouths will never be able to. As much as I know I should, I can't look away.

And then it hits me: I certainly more than like my coach as a friend. *Fuck*.

On stage, the band moves into a slow song, and a few of the couples in the room kiss or start slowly swaying, their arms around each other.

Finley sings along, gently rocking side to side as she does.

A smile spreads across my face as I realize she knows every word. It's a perfect moment, and I want to wrap my arms around her so badly. To pull her into me. To rest my chin on the top of her head. Instead, I sway with her, my upper arm never breaking contact with her shoulder. The words of the song wash over me, and I let myself fall into whatever this is: this feeling where everything is right in the world.

Chapter 25

Beckett

"What's going on with your hip, Kane?" Finley asks when she walks into the recovery room after our game against the Thunderbirds.

I sink a little lower in the ice bath as she stops a respectable distance away. While our staff is male-dominated, Finley isn't the only woman around when we're naked. We've got PTs and visiting docs who are women. You reach a certain level when your body isn't even *your body* anymore, it's just a piece of equipment for the team to look after.

"What do you mean?" I ask, though I know exactly what she means. My hip has gotten worse since that hit last week, and I was slow tonight. Even if I thought no one else noticed, I was fighting pain with every push of my right leg.

"Well, I'm going to—" Lefevre says, jerking a thumb over his shoulder as he hastily exits the hot tub next to me.

Finley crosses her arms, but I don't miss the plea in her eyes. The one asking me to tell her the truth. "You've been babying it since you got here. I thought it was just a tweak, but it's not getting better. It was the worst it's been tonight. Did Florida know about it before the trade? Did they tell you to play injured? That's such a stupid, irresponsible thing—"

"Fi—Coach," I say, trying to stop her rant before she gets on the phone to yell at the Cyclones' GM. "They didn't know. There's barely anything *to* know."

She blinks at me, her calm demeanor more frustrating than if she were angry. "I don't believe that. It's obvious to anyone who has seen you play before that you're favoring your right hip."

"No, I'm not."

"Your starts are slower, and you shied away from hits on your right side all night. No one could miss that."

"No." I shake my head. "Everyone *has* missed that. You are the only one who has asked me about my hip since I got here. And I told you it's fine. Nothing I can't handle."

I should've been prepared for this. Should've seen it coming. She's going to bench me—hell, they might even trade me again—and then I'm going to lose my last chance at getting to be captain. Of fulfilling my dad's dream.

"You're telling me *no one* has talked to you about it?" Finley asks.

"No one," I reply as the timer on my phone goes off, telling me it's time to get out of this torture chamber. Ice baths are a necessary evil, but they are evil, nonetheless.

I stand, and Finley's breath hitches, even as her icy gaze stays locked on mine. Good thing I'm half frozen down there, or I'm not sure my reaction to her seeing my naked body would've been quite as benign. Wrapping my towel around my hips, I return her stare. "I'm fine, Coach."

"You're hurt and didn't tell anyone, Kane. I thought I made it very clear that's not how we do things on my team."

She follows me over to the PT bed, where Glenn is waiting to help me with a deep tissue massage and some stretching.

"Did *you* know about his hip, Glenn?" she asks, turning her focus to him.

"What hip?" Glenn responds.

She crosses her arms—an intimidating sight made more aggressive by her game-day suit. "The right one. The one that is *hurt*."

"It's not hurt," I say, turning over and lying on my stomach as Glenn gets to work. I don't know why she won't trust me. Sure, it's getting worse, but I can manage it. I *have* to manage it. I've told her before to drop it, and I need her to listen to me.

"I need his hip tested," Coach tells Glenn.

I feel his hands release me before she sighs, "Not now, Glenn. Tomorrow. Bring in Doctor Lowell."

"Coach, that's not necessary." I've told her it's fine. Why can't she just let it go?

"I can give you a minute." Glenn tries to leave.

"No. You stay. I have to go anyway," Coach says. "But I expect you in my office before you leave tonight, Kane. And, Glenn, make sure he sees Lowell first thing tomorrow. He doesn't touch the ice until the doctor signs off on it. I don't know how they do things in Florida, but we don't play our guys when they're hurt."

I say nothing, staring at the tips of her shiny black shoes through the hole in the table as Glenn starts to work my hamstrings. His hands dig in, thumbs pressing on a muscle that shouldn't be this painful. I bite down, refusing to react to the discomfort.

Because I've felt it.

The discomfort that has turned into pain. The ache that is lingering far longer than it used to. The mental math I do every shift to make sure I'm not favoring that leg, so no one will see it. It's manageable, barely, but I'm *managing it*.

But, of course, making it work isn't good enough for the woman who thrives on being perfect. She asked me about it, and I told her it wasn't a big deal. She should've listened. Because that's what *friends* do. They trust each other. And she should trust me to know what's best for my body.

Every press of Glenn's hands is like a drum beating it home. She should've listened to me.

She should've listened to me.

She should've listened to me.

By the time I'm ready to go home, I'm borderline livid. Who the fuck does Finley Blake think she is?

No one else noticed my hip. *No one.* Not the coaches nor the medical staff at Florida, and not the ones here. Shit. Even this week, she's been the only person to say anything. Because despite the pain, I'm still doing my job. Even if it hurts.

How dare she not take me at my word? How dare she tell me she knows I'm hurt, her eyes locked on mine, not giving me an out like everyone else does? Just clocked the lie I've been telling with every stride and brought it into the light without ever considering what it would mean *for me*.

Because a hip-specific exam by the team doc is the beginning of the end for my career. Once the injury door cracks open, I won't be able to close it again. The doctors are going to look harder now. Management will know. The league. And I can't afford that. Not now. Not ever.

The anger inside me grows with each step I take, sharp and desperate and clawing its way up my throat as I barge into her office sometime around midnight, not bothering to knock. Because if I don't shut this down now, it will be the end of my career. I can feel it.

"You can't bench me."

"Sit down, Kane," she says, her icy tone the opposite to my fire.

I widen my stance, crossing my arms. Like fuck I'll sit down.

She clicks her mouse a few times, like she's deleting emails or something equally as mundane and unimportant. As the silence swirls around us, my temper starts to cool enough for me to feel slightly ridiculous for refusing to even sit down. This is rookie hotheaded shit. Not what you'd expect from a veteran. From me.

But my pride won't let me listen to her when she won't do the same for me.

"Fine," she sighs. She stands, sliding her laptop into her black backpack. "We can try this again another day. But until then, you can't do anything until it's approved by medical, Kane."

"No," I explode, the flames roaring back into my veins.

"I've already let the team know you're hurt. You will report to PT and the medical staff tomorrow for an evaluation. You are not to be on the ice or do any training until it has been approved by Lowell. You will be listed as questionable." She stops in front of me, mimicking my gesture, and my vision goes red at the news that she's set this in motion. She didn't even wait for us to meet.

She continues, "If you do not walk your ass in here and coolly sit down tomorrow morning at eight so we can have a real, adult conversation about this, I will move you to IR. You will take the mandatory week. I will call up a replacement."

No. Fuck her. No.

"I thought we were friends, *Finley*." I spit out her name, and she flinches.

Then, as if summoned by the gods to take on an unwinnable quest, she squares her shoulders, turning into the fighter she had to be to get herself here. "I am your *coach*, Kane. This is what I'm paid to do. I make the hard calls."

I lean toward her. "Well, congratulations, you're making the wrong fucking one."

She looks me up and down, taking me in from my still slightly damp hair to my sneaker-clad feet. "Fortunately for me, your opinion doesn't matter here."

With that, she turns, walking out of her office without a backward glance.

Chapter 26

Beckett

Knocking on my coach's door at five in the morning is a terrible idea, particularly after getting approximately six minutes of sleep. But I have to be here. I have to apologize to my friend, the one I hurt. She didn't deserve that, especially not after she was the only one who noticed I've been compensating.

It took me a while to calm down enough to realize I'm not mad at Finley, and about that time, overwhelming regret hit me. I can still see it: her shoulders squaring. Her face freezing into professional coach mode. A wall sliding up between us.

And I deserved it. I treated her like a complete and total ass. It was unprofessional, and it was uncalled for. But what I realized at about three this morning is that I'm not even mad—I'm *scared*. Of what is going to happen, what the doctors might find. Because the truth is, the pain in my hip has gotten worse. And I'm not sure how much longer I can play through it. It's slowing me down when I'm on the ice, and I'm terrified of what that means for my future and my ability to play the game I love so much.

And I took that fear out on Finley when she was just doing her job.

At eight, I'll apologize to my coach for being a hothead. But it's two very different apologies.

The breakfast burrito and coffee from the shop four miles from here—the only one open at this time—are just so I have something to do with my hands. I know food and a warm beverage aren't going to dig me out of this hole, and I feel like shit about it.

About thirty minutes after leaving Finley's office, the full weight of what I'd done hit me square in the chest, knocking all air from my lungs. It was inexcusable behavior. It wouldn't have been okay with *any* coach, even if they deal with dumbass outbursts on a regular basis. But throwing our friendship into the mix, like it gave me the right to speak to her like that?

I'm fully prepared for her to slam the door in my face.

My heart aches at the thought, and I use my hand holding the sandwich to rub the ache.

"Do you have a heart problem I need to know about, too?" Finley's voice comes from behind me, and I startle, whirling toward her as hot coffee splatters across my hand and shoes.

"Fuck. If I didn't have heart issues before, I sure as shit do now," I say, wiping my coffee-covered hand across my shirt.

I stare at Finley, clad in running shorts and a T-shirt, sweat beading along her brow. Her long legs are slightly red, her cheeks rosy.

"Were you running outside, Fin?"

She crosses her arms. "Why are you here, Kane?" The way she emphasizes my last name, as if telling me that we're not on a first-name basis anymore, burns a hole in my stomach.

"I'm here to apologize."

"You can come to my office at eight, like we planned."

"No. I can't. I mean, I can. I will be there. I will be there early, and I will say I'm sorry, and I will do what you tell me to, even if I don't want to. But I need to apologize before that."

She hasn't moved, her stony glare making it impossible to guess what she might be thinking.

I try not to flinch when she finally moves, simply stepping past me to unlock her door. "Go home, Kane."

"Fin—" The glare she sends over her shoulder stops me. "Queenie." I refuse to call her Coach Blake right now. We're not at the gym. She might always be Coach Blake to me, but when we're here, in this space, she's also something else. Something *more*.

It's still less than I want, but I will be damned if I lose our friendship.

"Just let me come in. Please?"

"No."

I sigh. "Fine. I guess the hallway works." I take a deep breath, the words I've been mulling over and practicing since I last saw her suddenly fleeing, leaving me completely alone with a blank mind. "I, uh…"

"Wow. Thanks for that. All good, then." Finley plucks the coffee cup from my hand. "See you at eight, Kane."

Oh God. She's going to leave. I'm not going to get to apologize. My chest tightens.

"I'm sorry!" I shout.

"Shhh. Jesus," Finley chides, quickly scanning the hallway to make sure my sudden outburst hasn't pulled any of our neighbors from their apartments. I haven't met any of them yet, but I give zero fucks whether they hear me or not.

"Go home."

I shake my head. "Not until you let me apologize. Can I please come in?" I was going for apologetic, but somehow the question came out desperate.

Hell. I *am* desperate for her to forgive me. Nothing else could've kept me up all night, tossing and turning like I was. Not even the anxiety about what the doctors are going to find when they start probing my hip was enough to push the worry from my mind that I have somehow, irrevocably, damaged what I had with her.

She purses her lips, considering.

"Please?" It's so quiet I wonder if she heard it.

Her gaze continues to scan me before finally, she steps to the side, holding the door open. "Fine."

I walk into her space, and my mind assaults me with memories here. Of us watching film together. Learning that her favorite ice cream flavor is strawberry. Laughing as she talks about what it was like playing on the boys' hockey team in high school.

I can't lose this.

"I'm sorry, Finley. I…" I pause. She doesn't need a generic apology. She deserves the truth. And there's nothing I wouldn't give to keep her in my life.

"I told you how my dad played in the minors when I was growing up. He and my mom were high school sweethearts, and she wasn't even twenty when she had me. We lived close to my mom's parents so she could have some support, and my dad would move around all the time as he got traded from team to team. I'd see him when he could make it home. We'd talk on the phone once or twice a week, but you know how schedules are." I shrug, focusing my attention on the photo of Finley and her dad.

"By the time I was seven, Dad and I only talked about one thing—hockey. He'd run through what I should be working on, where I should be at with various skills. He ended every call telling me he was sure I'd make it pro someday, just like he would. That I'd get called up, and I'd wear a captain's patch as I held the Cup over my head." I pause and run my hand through my hair.

"I'm not sure about the details, but I think he got into drugs. I didn't know it then, but I think by that time, he'd realized he wasn't ever going to get the tap to move up. He crashed his car one night. Wrapped it around a light pole. It'd been six months since we last saw him." I scratch my fingers through my hair, remembering the stream of tears that had poured down my mom's face for the first month after we got the call. The itchy suit I'd worn to his funeral.

"My mom was devastated. But she took over his dream. Hockey *was* life. For both of us. She would work all the time to afford to send me to all the camps and to replace my gear when I outgrew it every year. She passed away two years ago."

I turn and meet Finley's gaze. "If I'm not wearing the captain's badge and holding the Cup, I've let them both down. And I'm old, Fin. We both know I have one season, two at most left, and that's if I'm lucky. I *have* to get it next year."

Her gaze searches my face like she's trying to put it all together. "And you think if you admit you might be injured, you'll get benched?"

I scoff. "Getting benched would literally be the least of my concerns. I'd be on IR. You'd bring up a young guy. You'd end up trading me because you don't need an old, hurt player on your bench, taking up salary you could be deploying elsewhere. Even if you don't, you're not taking the captain's badge away from J.D. for someone who didn't play half the season."

"You won the Cup with Nashville," she says, like she's confused.

I agree, warmth spreading through me as I tell myself she knows my career history because she was following it—*me*—closely. "Yeah. My sophomore season."

"So, haven't you achieved your dream?"

"Have you achieved yours?" I ask, knowing there's always another piece of the dream to reach for. I shake my head, not waiting for an answer. "My dad was so proud of being the captain of his team. More than winning the championship, at least toward the end, he was just so certain I was going to follow in his footsteps and captain my team. When I finally earned it in high school, it felt good. In college, when they gave me the patch, it felt great. But I haven't earned it at this level yet. And I can't be done until I do." I roll my shoulders back. "I *won't* be done until I do."

"Sometimes, we don't get a say in when one dream ends and another begins," Finley replies softly as she stands in her kitchen, leaning against the countertop.

I shrug. "Maybe. But this, this I have a say in." Rubbing my eyes with my pointer and forefinger, I realize I've veered off course. "Look, this isn't about me and my future. You are the coach, and you have to do what you have to do. But, you're also—" I pause, not sure how to put into words what she is to me. Sure, she's my friend. Fuck, my best friend at the point. But, she's also... "More."

She quirks her eyebrow.

"And you don't deserve to be treated that way. So, I wanted to tell you I'm so sorry for the way I behaved and for questioning our friendship when I got angry. It was inexcusable, but I saw my dad's dream slipping away. I heard my mom's voice reminding me of it, telling me to do whatever it takes to make it happen." I take a deep breath. "I was scared. And I took it out on you. And I'm sorry."

"You're not the first hockey player I've dealt with who was mad because I told him he had to be checked out by medical."

Her right cheek moves just slightly, and I realize she's biting it. It's her tell—one that's too damn easy to miss.

"You're not just *some* hockey coach. You know you mean so much more to me. And I'm sorry I turned our friendship against you. It was wrong, and even if I don't deserve it, I hope you forgive me."

She nods once. "You're forgiven."

Relief floods through me, and I take three long strides to her, sweeping her into a tight bear hug. I pull her against me, breathing in her forgiveness.

Everything feels right.

After a moment, I realize what I've done. Oh, fucking shit. I'm hugging Finley. Aggressively hugging her. But I also can't seem to let go.

Chapter 27
Finley

I tap my fingers on the table, wondering how long this day can last. It's hard to believe it hasn't even been twenty-four hours since I confronted Beckett in the ice bath. The ice bath he was very naked in. Not that I noticed.

And after not sleeping well last night, my brain constantly replaying Beckett throwing our friendship in my face again and again, I'm tired. I understand being mad about being benched, but he made it personal. Like it's my fault for noticing he's hurt. Or maybe I'm feeling the mental exhaustion of having to maintain my coach façade during not one but four professional meetings with Beckett in that same timeframe. At least we got the few minutes together this morning to address this as us, not as who we have to be at the arena.

I know why he reacted the way he did. And even if it hurt, I meant what I said: he is forgiven.

"Thanks for coming in today, Dr. Lowell," I say as he sits at the conference table. He and his team ran Beckett through a variety of scans and tests this morning. Rob, White, and I have been waiting for the doctor to arrive with his final recommendations.

I saw the fear in Beckett's eyes when he told me his truth this morning, and I know that waiting for these results is killing him. Hell, it's been painful for me, too.

Unfortunately, I don't think the results will be what any of us want. I stopped by earlier when they were running some of the tests. Lowell asked Beckett to take three steps after sprinting on the ice, and he did it, but the hitch was there. More aggressive than I've seen from him.

"Of course. I know how anxious everyone is to get these results back," Lowell says in the understatement of the year. My stomach has been in knots all day. Even Larsen knew not to push me during practice. "Which is why I went with a clinical exam, functional testing with the trainers, and then an ultrasound."

"What's the verdict?" White asks as Lowell navigates his tablet, sending an image to the large screen in the conference room.

"It's not great."

My stomach drops.

He points to the screen. "This is a screen capture from the ultrasound on Kane's right iliopsoas," he explains, zooming in. "See this here? That's edema and fiber disruption at the hip flexor. In other words, inflammation consistent with a strain. Given his exam and the functional testing, I feel the ultrasound gives us what we need right now, but if he doesn't improve on schedule, or if the pain increases, we'll get an MRI to rule out anything deeper.

"How bad is it?" Rob asks.

Lowell tips his head from side to side. "It's not a full tear, which is good news. The bad news is that if he keeps skating on it at game intensity, he'll likely turn a short-term strain into something that lingers, or he'll compensate and blow up something else."

"So he could keep playing?" I ask, knowing that strains and sprains are a gray area in professional sports. Sometimes, they can play through them without too much risk. Sometimes they're out for months. I would never want to put someone on the ice who needs to rest, but I'd also never want to rest someone if they would be fine pushing through it. It's a hard balance, especially when there isn't always a right answer. Just the best answer at a time. Which is why I'm glad the decision isn't up to me.

"It's not my recommendation," Lowell says.

"So, what is your final determination?" White asks.

"IR. Three weeks." Once medical staff calls IR, that's it. None of us gets to argue. It's league policy.

I bite the inside of my cheek, making sure to keep my face impassive. I can't let them know that my heart is breaking for Beckett. I know it's just a strain, but Beckett isn't going to see it that way. An IR determination is a bad omen for a player his age. And after everything he told me, I know he's going to see it as a huge setback, if not the end.

At that moment, Paige knocks on the door. "Beckett Kane is here to meet with you all. Are you ready for him?"

White looks at Dr. Lowell. "Are you sure? Three weeks?"

"I'm sure," the doctor replies.

White nods at Paige. "Send him in."

Beckett walks in, his gaze darting to mine before taking in the rest of the room. I'm not sure what he sees behind the icy exterior I know I have up, but apparently, it is enough to kill whatever strands of hope he was holding on to.

He sits at the empty seat next to me, his face set in grim resignation. It takes all my self-control not to offer him some sort of comfort. I want to hug him. To take his hand. But I fight that urge.

"Kane, thanks for joining us," White says, taking charge of the meeting. The doctor makes the determination, but the GM is the one who puts it into action. I, as head coach, actually have very little to do with a player's trajectory once they're injured. It used to drive me crazy to have my roster controlled by others, but now? Now I see the very real benefit of not having to make the call.

"Dr. Lowell, want to kick us off?" White asks.

The doctor nods. "Kane, I don't think this will come as a surprise to you after the tests we ran today, but you've got a strain in your right hip flexor. My determination is that you go onto IR for three weeks. I want to be clear, I know you've been playing through this for a while, and playing well, but it's getting worse, and you're compensating, and that's how short injuries become long ones."

Beckett swallows hard, his gaze dropping as he asks, "That's the official decision?"

"Yes," White confirms. "I'll submit the paperwork directly after this meeting."

The corners of Beckett's lips twitch, like he might argue, but then he doesn't, letting out a slow breath instead.

"I'll leave directions with the medical staff," Dr. Lowell says, "but in general, no games. Modified training. Rehab starts today, re-eval at the end of week two. Just so you know what you're working toward, you don't return until you can sprint and cut without that hitch. That's the goal if we want this to actually heal."

The silence that follows is heavy. The decision has already been made, and even though none of us like it, it's what we're going to do.

"Come on, Kane," Dr. Lowell says. "I'll walk you down to PT, so we can go over things. I'm sure you have questions I can answer as well."

No. My gaze snaps to Beckett, but he's focused on the doctor. I wanted to have a minute or two to talk to him. To make sure he's okay. To be the friend he needs right now, even if just in a small smile or manly-pat-on-his-shoulder kind of way.

But I can't do that, and it's for the best... for my career, at least.

Chapter 28

Finley

"I think you're a witch," I say to Charlotte when she answers the phone.

I'm lying on my bed in a hotel room in Chicago. At midnight, she was the only person I knew would still be awake. She's also the only person I can possibly talk to about this.

"Like Ursula in *Little Mermaid* or Sarah Jessica Parker in *Hocus Pocus*?" she asks.

"The latter," I reply. "Obviously."

"While I can't help but agree, what did I do to earn such a title?" Charlotte asks. "And does it have anything to do with the fact that you were basically dancing with Kane all night at the Jaxon Steele concert a few days ago?"

I shake my head. Fuck. That concert feels like a lifetime ago. Which is part of the reason I called. Even though I should be prepping for our last push toward the playoffs. It's the middle of March, which means I have less than one month to make sure the Yeti are moving on to post-season play.

And yet, here I am. On the phone with a friend because of a boy. I'm so fucked.

"Kane is on IR," I announce.

There's a pause. "What's IR again?"

I roll my eyes. "Injured reserve. It means he's hurt badly enough that we need to open up his spot on the roster. We called up one of the defensemen from the minors tonight. He did fine."

"So, ignoring all the sportsy things you just said: Kane's off the team?" Charlotte asks, and even through the phone, I can tell she's grinning.

"Are you smiling?" I ask. "The man is hurt, Charlotte! You can't smile about a professional athlete getting benched for three weeks. It's literally a nightmare for him."

"Yeah, but doesn't it mean he isn't your player anymore?"

"That's not exactly how it works," I hedge. But that "exactly" is why I'm on the phone with Charlotte.

"Oh shit," Charlotte says. "Video call me right now. I need to see your face when you tell me this."

I do as she requests, unsurprised to see that Charlotte is all done up with a full face of makeup, her hair in curly waves hanging around her face.

"Are you considering doing something with Kane, Finley Blake?" she asks as soon as she answers.

"No," I lie.

Her eyes go wide. "You are!"

"I *am* still his coach," I remind her.

"But..."

"But I can't make the decision to put him back on the roster."

"So, he's not in your chain of command!" Charlotte all but yells.

I hit the volume-down button a few times before saying, "I'm not sure if that's how the legal team would see it, but Doctor Lowell has to sign off, and then White has to decide to put him back on the roster."

"Oh shit," Charlotte says. "So, what are you going to do?"

"I don't know."

"That's not very Coach Blake of you."

"Things have been weird between us. I was the one who made the doctors check him over," I admit, a pang of guilt hitting my ribs.

"So go talk to him."

"We're at a hotel."

"And he doesn't get to travel anymore?"

"No, he still came with the team."

She squints. "Then I don't see what the problem is."

"People could see me."

"Be sneaky. And if caught, lie."

"I just... What if it's a bad idea?"

"What if it's not?" she counters.

I bite the inside of my cheek before responding, "I don't know."

"Only one way to find out. And just pretend you're going to talk about some hockey thing if someone sees you."

My pulse kicks up, and I'm not sure whether it's nerves or excitement. "I could do that."

"Then why are we still on the phone?" Charlotte asks.

I stand up. "I'm still not sure if I can get past the fact that he's my player. It *is* wrong."

"You don't have to make any decisions right now. Just go talk to him. At least clear the air. You can go from there."

***

Three minutes later, I've figured out which room is Beckett's and am standing outside of it, knocking like I'm about to enter the locker room. Just a coach doing coach things. Nothing to see here.

The door flies open, and I try to contain my smile. "Kane. Do you have a minute to talk—" *Fuck. What was I going to pretend to talk to him about?* "Matchups?"

"Of course, Coach. Come on in," Kane says.

He smiles, and my heart melts. I wasn't lying when I told Charlotte things have been weird between us. As a coach, the kind of outburst he had is completely expected. Players hate being benched. It's justified, too. One injury, one stint on IR means a chance for them to be replaced. To lose their spot. To slowly become unnecessary for the team. And for a veteran who knows he's nearing the end of his career? It's dangerous.

But it's also what's best for the team. We can't have players on the ice when they're injured. And it's what's best *for him* in the long run. He has to use that hip long after hockey is done.

And I happen to care about his life after hockey.

Which made it hurt so much more when he threw our friendship in my face. I have to be his coach first, a fact we're both very aware of, but even if I didn't, it was the right call.

I slide through the door, and it closes behind me with a judgmental snap.

Okay, maybe I shouldn't be here. Shouldn't be thinking about the way Beckett's arms felt around me yesterday morning. Or the way he came into my office later and made the formal coach/player apology, too. The sadness in his eyes when we told him he was on IR for the next three weeks.

Seeing him in the coaches' section in his team gear, rather than suited up and on the bench tonight, was hard, even if it's the job—for both of us.

But it also sucks to suffer through it alone.

So, here I am.

To... discuss matchups.

Even if what I really want to do is hold him. Have his arms wrapped around me again.

"Matchups, huh?" Beckett says with a knowing smile.

"I just wanted to make sure you're doing okay."

"As a coach or as a friend?"

I pause, even though we both know the answer. There is no real reason I'd be here as a coach. "A friend."

He sits on the edge of the bed. "Well, in that case, it's been a pretty brutal day."

"Want to talk about it?" I ask.

He shakes his head. "No."

My chest tightens. Of course he doesn't. At least not with me. "Want me to go?"

"No. I'm just not sure how to walk the coach/friend line right now." The uncertainty is evident in his eyes.

"If it's easier, I think this may be the one time you don't have to think of me as your coach."

"What do you mean?"

"It's not up to me whether or not you are back on the ice. Sure, I could still bench you once you're off IR, but I have no say over anything regarding you in the next three weeks. I'm as close to being just your friend as I'll ever be."

A smile spreads slowly across his face. "Well, in that case, let's watch a movie."

"Wait, is this what you'd normally be doing in the evenings if I wasn't monopolizing all your time?" I ask.

He looks at me, his dark brown eyes pulling me in. "Yeah, Fin. I spend all my time watching TV. It's how I'm a professional hockey player at thirty-four."

"You're a jerk."

Beckett shifts so he's sitting fully on the bed and pats the spot next to him. "Come on, friend. I'll even let you pick."

We scroll through the channels together, discussing the various options before deciding on an action film that came out a few years ago. Unsurprisingly, neither of us has seen it.

As we watch, we talk. The conversation starts where it normally does: hockey. But after we talk about the game tonight and what we need to do to clinch a playoff spot, we move to more personal things. Beckett tells me about his plans once the season ends. I admit I should probably go see my dad, but it's like a three-day job interview anytime I'm with him.

"Larsen and Li were a good pair today," Beckett says after a loud action scene, where the supposed good guys caused about twelve different apartment buildings to be destroyed.

"They were," I agree.

"It was hard to watch."

"It was harder to watch them play without you than I anticipated, too."

"But I was also surprisingly proud of Larsen. He's really stepped up," Beckett adds.

I bump my shoulder into his again, but this time, I don't move away. He's warm and strong, and it just feels so nice to have someone by my side for once. "Are you becoming friends with the rookie?" I tease.

Beckett looks down, his eyes meeting mine. I'm practically resting my head on his shoulder, and from the way his eyes darken, I think he likes it. Maybe as much as I do.

He closes his eyes, his head tilting to rest gently against mine. "I'd prefer to think of it as more of a proud team leader situation."

My eyelids grow heavy as I watch the screen, but I blink hard, forcing myself to—

A loud explosion on the screen sounds, and I jerk awake, blinking a few times before my brain catches up with reality. I fell asleep on Beckett's shoulder. He blinks at me, like he, too, just came back to consciousness.

"Sorry," he mumbles. "Didn't mean to fall asleep on you."

"Never thought I'd sleep with a player," I joke.

"I'm doing all sorts of things these days I never thought I would," he says softly.

"Oh, yeah?" I ask. I know it's a dangerous question, but I can't help myself. The pull between us tonight is so strong. I can't seem to fight it.

"Can I kiss you?"

My heart stops, the room becoming too small. Kiss Beckett Kane? It's my high school dreams turned grown-up desires merging into one terrible, horrible, amazing possibility. And I desperately want to say yes. To lean into him. To press my lips gently against his. To slip my tongue into his mouth and dance with it as I swing my leg over him until I'm seated firmly on his lap. To let go and take exactly what I want, while knowing it's what he wants, too.

A small sound escapes me, and I'm mortified that it can only be described as a gasp.

Beckett's face morphs into one of alarm. "Oh, God. I'm sorry, Finley. I... Please forget I asked," he pleads, quickly shifting to climb out of bed. He holds his hands in front of him defensively. "I know we can't be anything more than we are now. Shit, I know that once this PR stunt is over, we can't even be what we are now, but there is this pull between us. It's... I've never felt anything like it. I'm hyper-aware of where you are and what you're doing." He runs his fingers through his hair. "I know we can't do this. Even if you're barely even my coach right now. I just..."

I stand, too, our gazes meeting in an awkward staring contest over the bed. "It's the same for me," I confess, needing him to know he isn't alone. "I catch myself watching you too much during practice. Focusing on you during games instead of the whole team. Noticing you in the damn hallway. I can't seem to stop."

My heart tightens painfully. "But we still... shouldn't do this," I say, knowing it's true, no matter how much I want to cling to Beckett's warmth. To feel his lips against mine. To fall into his embrace and let go for once in my life.

"I know, Finley. And I would never do something that could jeopardize everything you've worked for. I just... I wish I could." He rubs the back of his neck. "I... Can we just chalk this up to me waking up next to a beautiful woman and leave it at that?"

I nod, my mind too busy basking in the knowledge that Beckett thinks I'm beautiful to form any kind of real response.

Chapter 29

Finley

"Shit," I groan as I frantically move my takeout burrito bowl to my other hand so I'm able to dig through my bag. "No, no, no."

I drop to the floor, setting everything down so I can dig through my bag. Fuck. How could I have forgotten my keys at the arena today of all days?

"Finley?" Beckett's in his open doorway, a concerned look on his face. "Are you okay?"

"Yup," I say, dropping my attention back to my bag. "Totally fine."

"Oh, really? Is that why you keep mumbling curse words?"

I continue to rummage through my bag, my anxiety mounting with every second. "Yup. Very normal thing I do."

He raises an eyebrow. "Huh. Weird that I haven't noticed that quirk before. Maybe it's a new habit, though," he offers. "I haven't seen much of you in the last two weeks."

Because I have been actively avoiding him. Like "hide in a storage closet when I hear him walking down the halls" kind of avoiding him. Staying in my office until two or three in the morning.

I've never been so caught up on my work, even if today marks the first official day of April and the final sprint of our season.

I stand, pulling my backpack over my shoulders. I stare at the numbers on Kane's door rather than meet his eyes. Because I'm weak. "I've been really busy lately. You know how it is."

He nods slowly. "Sure. I know how it is."

The way he says it makes it very clear he knows I've been avoiding him, and he knows *why* I've been avoiding him. Because he asked to kiss me. And I wanted to say yes. And somehow, I said no.

And I'm terrified I won't have the willpower to say no again. Not that I think he'd ask again. But I might. And I *can't*.

"Well, I'm headed back to the office," I announce, turning to walk down the hall. "I'll see you tomorrow at the final event for The Great Yeti Challenge. Go us!" I throw a fist in the air, *Breakfast Club*-style, and am immediately thankful my back is turned, so he can't see the mortification on my face. What in the world was that?

"Finley," Beckett calls after me. "You can't go out in this."

Wrong. I *shouldn't* go out in this. It's a literal blizzard outside. But there is a distinct difference between can't and shouldn't. I grew up in ice rinks and surviving the Michigan winters. I can make it back to the arena to get my keys. If it's too bad, I'll sleep there.

"I'll be fine," I say, still not turning around while I wait for the elevator.

"They're calling for two feet of snow in the next twelve hours, plus it's freezing outside."

"I've got a coat," I reply.

"They shut down the roads. It's why you let us out of practice early."

"It's not that bad." I stare at my distorted reflection in the silver doors of the elevator.

"Finley."

"What are you doing?" I ask as Beckett comes to stand beside me.

"Convincing you not to get yourself killed."

"My keys are at the arena."

"Just stay with me."

My gaze snaps to his, and I can see the sincerity in his offer. But the surge of need that shoots through my body tells me it's a terrible idea. I shake my head.

"Queenie. Just... call the apartment manager and get them to let you in."

Yes. It's a great plan. I pull up their contact information, sighing in relief when a woman answers. Unfortunately, the news isn't great.

"They're on their way," I lie cheerfully.

He scowls at me. "I heard her say they sent their staff home early today, too. Because it's a blizzard, Fin! *You* said so yourself when you cancelled practice for tomorrow and told everyone to just work out with whatever they've got at home. We're in the final stretch of the season: we both know you never would've made that call if it wasn't serious."

"We don't live as far away as some of the team does," I argue, remembering the view from the building's window of the dark night and the way the streetlight illuminated the snow falling sideways. But there's at least a chance I'll make it to the arena. I know I won't make it through the night without making a bad decision with Beckett if I'm shut away with him while the world freezes into a winter wonderland.

"Fine," Kane says. "I'll go with you."

I whirl around, my chest squeezing at the thought of him going out in the howling wind. "No! You're injured. You can't be out there."

"If you can, I can. Just wait for me to go get my coat," he demands.

"No. I'm fine."

"You know it's not safe out there, Fin. Please, if you can't stay with me, let me go with you."

I drop my head back, staring at the ceiling as I consider my options. Finally, I say, "Fine."

Beckett stares at me long and hard before heading toward his door.

The elevator arrives while he's still inside, and I walk in, frantically hitting the close door button. I race to the front of the building when I get to the first floor, stopping just long enough to pull on my winter hat and stick my hands deep into my pockets. I'm blasted by snow when the revolving door opens to the elements, and I strongly contemplate taking it for a full circle and hiding somewhere. But I know that would lead me back to Beckett and the bad decisions I'm not sure I can avoid much longer.

Instead, I take a step out into the cold, pulling up my hood, tucking my chin, and squeezing my eyes to try to mitigate my skin exposure. I'm going to fucking freeze to death.

It's definitely worse than it was twenty minutes ago, when I made the short trek from the restaurant next door, where I'd been hanging out since I told everyone to go home hours ago. I thought if I waited long enough, Beckett would assume I wasn't coming home, and I could avoid him again tonight.

I've never been someone to run from my problems, but since he asked to kiss me over two weeks ago, I've become a master of avoidance.

Because I know what the alternative is.

Between the wind, the snow, and the darkness surrounding me, it's slow going. I've barely made it a block when I hear faint yelling behind me. I turn around, squeezing my hands to try to bring warmth to them as I blink against the onslaught of snowflakes attacking my eyes. Holding my hand up as a shield, I peer at the dark figure. The one that appears to be in a fucking T-shirt.

"What are you doing?!" I scream. I know I should be more concerned that I'm approaching a crazy man in the snow, but at the same time, I'm certain it's Beckett, coming after me after I left him behind.

I start to shout again, but a cold gust of wind blasts its way down my throat, causing all the air to leave my lungs. Gasping, I bend over, trying to escape the frigid air long enough to pull a lungful of oxygen into my body.

"Finley! Fuck. Finley! I'm coming!" I hear.

I make an *I'm fine* gesture with my hands, but it doesn't stop the giant of a man from continuing his hard push toward me.

He's going to fall over. He's going to hurt his hip and never recover. And, for what? Me? I'm not worth ruining his career.

I'm pulled against his chest, finally able to breathe as his large frame blocks the wind from reaching me. He's covered in snow, his eyelashes lined in white like a tree after a frost.

"What the fuck are you doing?" I ask, banging my fist against his chest. "You're going to die!"

"Then come back with me."

I look into his eyes and see the truth: He'll follow me if I keep going. But he knows it's a terrible idea.

"Come on!" I pull of my scarf and hat and hand them to him.

He shakes his head. "You need them!"

"You need them, you fool!" I shout back. "Put them on, or I'm going to the arena."

Beckett glares at me as if trying to decide how serious I am before grabbing the clothes from me. He shoves on the stocking cap and quickly wraps the scarf around his neck. "Happy now?"

I shake my head, then reach out and grab his hand, shoving my gloved one and his bare one into my pocket.

We trudge back in silence, the journey infinitely longer now that we're heading into the wind. I peek at Beckett as he walks, never complaining, just lumbering forward through the blizzard.

No one else would've come after me.

No one.

"Are you okay?" he asks as soon as we're in the lobby of our apartment building, dipping his head to look me in the eyes.

I nod before asking what I really need to know, "Why? Why did you come after me? And why don't you have a coat on? What were you thinking?"

A smile tugs at the corner of his now-blue lips, as a drop of melting snow falls from his eyelashes.

"No, don't tell me," I say. "We've got to get you warm first."

I rush to the elevator, and it opens immediately after I push the button. As soon as the doors close, I open my arms wide. "Come here."

Beckett doesn't hesitate, just slips his frozen hands under my coat, burying his face into my chest.

Even if it's just to keep him warm, something about the contact feels right. Like the first time I hit my slap shot the way he taught me, and suddenly the coaches started looking at me like I belonged. Like the moment I'm watching film, and suddenly I know just what to do.

It's clarity and comfort in the most terrifying way.

I reluctantly let go of him as the elevator reaches the twelfth floor and slowly follow him to his apartment.

He walks inside, holding the door open for me, but I can't seem to move my feet past the threshold.

"Come on, Queenie," Beckett teases despite the shivers wracking his body. "It's just one night."

Which is exactly what I'm excited about. And what I'm afraid of.

Taking a deep breath, I step into Beckett's apartment, knowing I'm not strong enough to keep whatever is about to happen from happening.

Chapter 30
Beckett

"Wait here. I'll be right back," I say, desperate to get out of my snow-covered clothes, but equally as concerned that Finley is about to bolt again. "Don't leave."

As I just witnessed, Finley Blake is not the type of woman to wait around when she's decided she's going to do something. Especially not when the man she's waiting for is someone she's been avoiding for weeks. The one she went out in a fucking whiteout in order to avoid.

It's truly astounding how royally I fucked things up with her.

All because I had to open my damn mouth.

That deep sense of need that I thought I couldn't bear any longer? Way less painful than having her dart from the room anytime I enter. Or the nights at home that were never a problem before but now are unbearably lonely.

I quickly change into a clean pair of sweats, throwing on the thickest Yeti hoodie I own before hustling out to the living room. Finley's sitting on the couch in her usual spot, a lost look on her face as she stares out my window.

"Here." I hand her the extra pair of sweats I grabbed. "You can change in the guest room. Or the bathroom. A hot shower might be nice. For you," I say, before forcing my mouth closed. Rambling is not helping this situation.

"Are you okay?" she asks quietly, and my heart aches at the worry in her tone.

"A little chilly, but otherwise totally fine." I spin in a circle. "See? The cold doesn't bother me."

"I think that's supposed to be my line." She stands slowly, her eyes scanning me. Stepping closer, she reaches out a hand, her warmth burning into my skin as she touches my cheek. "Why would you do that, Beckett?"

"It wasn't safe." I'm not sure what she doesn't get about this. I would follow her anywhere: a snowstorm, the desert, the fucking moon if it means I can keep her safe.

Her thumb gently caresses my cheek, and I can't help but lean into it. "You could've gotten hurt," she says.

"I know. But I couldn't force myself to care. I just needed to make sure you were okay. That's all that mattered to me."

We stand there for a moment, her fingers lightly brushing my face, our gazes locked.

Finally, I say the words I've been trying to say for the last two weeks. "I'm so sorry, Fin."

She cocks her head to the side slightly. "For what?"

"For ruining our friendship."

She lets out a breath that could be a sigh or a chuckle. "That's not at all what happened."

After dropping her hand, she takes the clothes from me. "You have nothing to be sorry for, Beckett. Truly. I'm the one who should apologize. So, I'm sorry I've acted like a child lately."

"You don't need to—"

She holds up a hand, cutting me off. "I do. Our friendship—*you*—means so much to me. And I acted like you didn't. It wasn't right."

I stare at her, not sure what to say, when all I want to do is confess that this is so much more than friendship. That I want more. That I want *everything* with her.

Instead, when she steps around me to head into the bathroom, I let her go. I won't put her in an awkward spot again, even if it means popping every thought of more as it bubbles to the surface.

"I put on the Phantoms game," I tell Finley when she exits the bathroom a few minutes later. "I also pulled the comforter off my bed. Turns out, I don't own a blanket."

When she walks over, I smile at the way my clothes fully engulf her smaller frame. "You look good, Fin."

She lightly punches my arm as she sits in her spot on the couch. I throw our makeshift blanket over her lap, taking the opportunity to cuddle slightly closer.

For the body heat, of course.

We watch the game in silence for a few minutes, falling into our old rhythm. These past few weeks have taught me that, even when we're not talking, just being with Finley is enough to make me feel whole in a way I'm not sure I have since I started playing hockey. Since I started chasing my dad's dreams and embracing them as my own.

"I wanted to say yes," Finley admits, her eyes still glued to the game on the television.

"What?" I ask.

"I've been avoiding you, not because you wanted to kiss me, but because *I* wanted to say yes." She finally looks at me, and I can see the uncertainty in her eyes.

"You... wanted me to kiss you?" I ask, a million butterflies taking off in my stomach at once.

She nods, her gaze dropping from mine to my lips.

This. It's everything I've wanted, and all the things I know I can't have. That I *shouldn't* have. But, if Finley wants it, too, who am I to resist? Hell, I haven't been able to resist her since we started spending time together. What would possibly make me think I could do it now, when she's looking at me like that?

"Do you want me to kiss you now?"

She nods again, just once, and as much as I want to crash my lips against hers, I can't risk a misunderstanding. Instead, I lean toward her, my hand finding her cheek. As I lightly stroke it with my thumb, I murmur, "I need to hear you say it, Queenie. Tell me I can kiss you."

Rather than responding, she leans toward me, her mouth pressing against mine as her arms wrap around my neck. I catch her, lowering us both, so she's lying on top of me as our lips explore each other.

The kiss isn't gentle. It's heated and rough, and I demand more, teasing my tongue along the entrance to her mouth. She opens for me, and suddenly our tongues are dancing, a sensual entwining that snaps every last thread of my control.

I pull her body into mine, my hips thrusting of their own accord when she grips my bicep to rock slightly against me. It's just one small movement, but it ignites a raging need inside me. The one that's been building for months.

"Can I—" I begin, but she cuts me off.

"Yes," she replies, her ice-blue eyes dark with lust.

I chuckle, the sound warm and deep between us. "You don't know what I was going to ask."

"It doesn't matter. The answer is yes. I fucking want this. I want it *all*."

A tiny voice in the back of my head tries to tell me this isn't a good idea, that she doesn't mean it, but I forcibly shut it down. Finley Blake is not someone who agrees to things she doesn't want.

I have her borrowed sweatshirt over her head seconds later and throw it as far from the couch as I possibly can. Making sure she's covered with the comforter, I start to explore.

My hands flow from her ass to the sides of her breasts, tracing and teasing every line as I continue to kiss her.

Needing more access, I wrap my arms around her and flip us both. Our lips break apart, and I drop my forehead to hers, breathing heavily.

"Fuck," I groan. "You're perfect."

A cocky smile plays across her lips. "Then why are you stopping? Make me come, Beckett."

I drop my mouth to her beautiful, dark pink nipple, nipping at it gently before sucking it into my mouth. She may be in charge most of the time, but not here.

She arches at the touch, letting out a sigh as her fingers rake through my hair. I suck harder, and her body jerks. I'm sure I could have her falling apart in minutes, me following close behind, no doubt, but now it's a challenge. And I plan on making this last as long as possible.

Before I make her come, of course.

"That's right, just like that," I murmur as she whimpers slightly.

I take my time, exploring, tasting, sucking. Moving from her neck to her perky tits to her hip bones and back up again.

She grinds against my erection, and I moan, "Good fucking girl."

I move against her, the friction like a trophy at the end of a hard-fought season, but when she gets too close, I pull back, keeping the tension at a point that's enough but not too much.

"Fuck, Beckett," she breathes. "Please."

I stop my ministrations, leaning close to her ear. "Since you asked so nicely."

She shudders as my breath caresses her ear, and I take that moment to slip my hand between us and into her oversized sweatpants.

"Fuck, baby, are you not wearing any underwear?"

She shakes her head, a wicked smile pulling across her face. "They were freezing."

I am never washing these pants again.

I work two fingers over her clit, dipping them into her wet pussy to get the slickness I need. She's tight and warm, and I barely hold back from stripping her naked and taking her hard and fast.

But I don't know if that works for her, and I need her to come before I take her the way I want to. Because once I'm in her tight heat, there's no way I'm going to have enough blood flow to my brain to make sure she comes first.

While stroking the inside of her channel with a finger, I work her clit with my thumb. She moves against me, soft moans slipping past her lips.

Her eyes lose focus, and her head drops back onto the couch as her body arches against me.

"Eyes on me," I say, a jolt of pleasure racing through me as her dazed icy blues meet my gaze.

"Please, Beckett. Please," she moans, her hips speeding up their search.

"That's right. Just like that. You're doing so good."

I keep talking to her, telling her how perfect she is, as I slip another finger inside her, finding that rough spot and pressing with the pads of both fingers. At the same time, I increase the pace on her clit slightly, and from the low "fuck" she releases, I know she's close.

With a sweeping press of my fingers inside her, she comes apart, squeezing me as her body pulses with pleasure.

As she comes down, I kiss her cheeks, her neck, her chest. "Look at you. You're amazing. I've never seen anything as perfect."

She takes a deep breath before meeting my eyes. "Fuck. That was... wow."

I slide my fingers out of the front of her sweatpants, holding her gaze as I suck them into my mouth.

"I couldn't agree more," I say before licking my lips to ensure I don't miss a drop.

Chapter 31
Finley

My star defenseman just made me come on his couch.

And somehow, that wasn't the best part.

Beckett Kane is a talker. And the way he offers praise constantly is like a balm to my frozen heart. I can barely come up with words to describe the out-of-body reaction I just experienced.

Now all I want to do is to take him into his bedroom and return the favor.

Beckett lightly presses his lips to mine, and it's like my soul is curling up in its favorite chair. It's the feeling I get when I'm skating on freshly Zamboni'd ice—smooth and clear, more like home than any dwelling ever has felt.

He shifts slightly, slipping between me and the couch, and wrapping his arms around me. His erection juts into my hip, a very prominent reminder that I was the only one who found my pleasure. Suddenly, I'm ready for round two.

I move, angling my body so there is enough space between us to allow my hand to slip inside his sweats.

"That was amazing," I say, stroking his long length.

"Fin," he groans. "Fuck."

"Let me," I plead, trying to wiggle my way lower on the couch.

"Nope," he replies, pulling me up. "I need to be inside you. Now."

"Don't threaten me with a good time."

He shakes his head before somehow managing to climb over me and stand without ever touching me. Such impressive control of his body. "Come on, Queenie. If we're doing this, we're doing it the right way." With his arms scooped under me, he lifts me and the comforter with ease.

I nuzzle into his neck as he walks me to his bedroom. "I like the sound of that."

"Okay, princess." He drops me onto the bed. "On your hands and knees."

I glare up at him from my spot on his bed. "Not only are you demoting me from queen, but you're also bossing me around?"

"Oh, Fin. You may be in charge elsewhere, but in my room, I'm the boss. Not to worry, though, I'll still treat you like a queen."

And damn, if that doesn't make me even wetter than I already am.

Beckett's eyes darken as I refuse to follow his order. "On. Your. Knees. Queenie."

I shake my head, a thrill shooting through me at the anticipation of what he'll do with my defiance.

The corner of his lip curls up. "Oh, baby. Wrong choice."

He grabs my ankles, pulling me to the edge of the bed. I let out an "oof" as my back hits the mattress, which quickly turns into a squeak as he easily pulls off the extra-large sweatpants he loaned me with a tug.

When he drops his face between my thighs, his tongue darts out, licking up my slit as his hands slide up the insides of my legs.

"I'm going to make you pay, Finley Blake," he whispers against me.

"Fuck, Beckett," I moan.

"This is what happens when you don't listen, Fin."

I grab his hair, getting him to look at me. "I don't think you understand how punishment works."

"Oh, trust me, you're going to be begging me to stop soon." He grins like a devil.

"Game on, handsome."

He lowers his head again, running his nose along the inside of my leg from my upper thigh to the junction, getting just close enough to make me sweat before dropping his nose back to my other knee.

"God, you smell good," he says as he works his way back up my leg, biting and licking as he nears the place I so desperately want him.

After only a few moments of teasing and praise, I'm starting to see how torturous this might be.

My hips thrust of their own accord as he nears my center for what has to be the hundredth time, and his low laugh sends a wave of warm heat against me.

I bite my lip, refusing to let out the moan that wants to escape. I play to win.

He takes a deep breath in as if I'm a fragrance people spend millions on and lets out a deep moan. "Maybe I'll torture you tomorrow."

With that, he spears his tongue into my center, his hand slipping between us to work my clit.

This was not what was supposed to be happening, but I can't seem to care that he's committed to worshipping my body. Hell, I'm not even surprised to learn that Beckett is a giver in bed.

"Fuck, fuck, fuck," I chant, quickly drawing near to the edge again.

Switching tactics, his tongue moves to my clit, and he slips two fingers inside of me, rubbing my inner wall how I like. I'm not sure whether he paid attention on the couch or if he's just that good, but I can't seem to care.

My pleasure builds, and as he continues to stroke me, he nibbles on my clit. "Come for me, Queenie."

My vision blurs, stars dancing in my eyes as my climax builds.

"You're doing so good. Now come, baby."

And I do with a moan, my fingers digging into his scalp as I pull his hair.

"Fuck," I pant. "Wow. You're so good at that."

Beckett presses a sweet kiss to the tip of my nose, his eyes desperate as he asks, "Will you please, with a cherry on top, get on your hands and knees so I can fuck the shit out of you?"

This time, I don't even pretend to put up a fight. "God, yes." I scramble onto all fours, swaying slightly as I move toward the head of the bed.

He climbs on behind me before palming my ass, his large hands stroking softly as he lets out a sigh. "Finally."

He turns my face to look at him. "You good with getting spanked, Queenie?"

"Aren't you just a consent king, Beckett Kane?" I reply with a smile.

"Always, gorgeous. Now, tell me that I can spank your ass while my dick is buried deep inside you."

"Wrap it up, and then you can do whatever you want to me," I say, almost panting in anticipation.

Beckett digs through the top drawer of the nightstand with his right hand, his left continuing to caress my ass cheek. I look over my shoulder to see him tear open the wrapper with his teeth. He holds my gaze as he rolls the condom on slowly, and I wonder how I've gotten this far in life without realizing that putting on protection can be sexy.

"You ready, baby?"

"Yes." God, yes. I'm more ready than I've ever been.

"Good."

He slides his hands lower, dipping a knuckle into me. "You're still so wet, Fin."

"That's because I'm so ready for you to fuck me, Beckett. Now, do it."

"Yes, ma'am," he agrees, notching the head of his cock against my entrance.

Not waiting for him, I push back slightly, my eyes closing with the pressure.

"Fuck, you're tight," he groans, slowly pushing forward. "God, this is the most perfect pussy. So tight. Warm. Wet."

I thrust backward again, and he reaches forward to give my nipple a light pinch.

"Do you like that, Fin? Do you like it when I squeeze your pretty little nipple?"

"Yes," I moan.

Beckett rubs my ass again before spanking it, the sting jumping directly to my clit.

He does it again, grunting as my inner walls tighten around him.

"That's so good, Fin. So damn good."

With that, he increases his speed, thrusting unrelentingly. His fingers dig into my hips as he maintains his hold on me. I'm completely at his mercy, and it's everything I didn't know I wanted.

I reach between my legs, searching for the bundle of nerves that is demanding my attention. Beckett whacks my hand away.

"Mine," he declares as he starts to move his fingers over me. "That's mine. Your perfect cunt is mine. All mine."

I arch my back, and—fuck. The angle changes, the stars returning to my vision as I near my peak.

"Ohhhh," I moan, my movements matching his as we both seek our release. "Oh, yes."

I come for the third time, and Beckett follows, his body collapsing on top of mine as he whispers his praise in my ear.

His cock is still buried in me as I all but fall into a coma.

After a moment, Beckett climbs off the bed and pads from the room. He returns moments later with a warm washcloth and, despite my protests that I can do it myself, proceeds to clean our combined releases from me.

"Thank you," I say when Beckett returns to bed and lies down next to me, pulling the comforter over us both.

His dark eyes find mine. "For what?"

I press my lips together. Part of me wants to joke and say for making me come three times, but I know it's so much more than that. It's for being my friend. For showing me that there are things other than hockey to look forward to. For keeping me from becoming a snowman when I decided to walk out into a blizzard.

But I'm not quite sure if I'm ready to tell him all of that yet.

Instead, I snuggle next to him and lay my head where his shoulder meets his chest. "For making sure I didn't die in the snow. And... for tonight."

"I'd do anything for you, Finley," he declares, tilting his face to place a kiss on my forehead.

A kiss that makes me want to grab on to Beckett and never let him go.

It's on the tip of my tongue to ask him about it. About *us*. But what good would it do? The only possible outcome is that it would ruin our snow day, and that's the last thing I want right now.

I just want to stay in this cocoon of happiness and warmth for as long as possible.

So, I snuggle into his chest and drift into a post-orgasmic sleep. Moments later, maybe minutes, maybe hours, when Beckett whispers, "Goodnight, Queenie," and kisses me gently, I let myself dream of a universe where this wasn't just a one-night thing but my life.

***

The next morning, I wake up early, jerking when I realize the warmth at my back is Beckett spooning me. It's been so long since I allowed myself to sleep with someone that I've forgotten what it feels like to be held by a man.

And Beckett Kane is not just any man, I realize as I slowly move my ass against his very noticeable morning wood.

Not wanting to wake him, I slip my hand out of the covers to check my phone. The snow is still falling heavily, according to the weather app. The only new email I have is one from Sabrina, saying the final event of The Great Yeti Challenge has been postponed until next week.

There's a thought trying to disrupt my peaceful morning about what it means that I crossed this line, but I forcibly shove it from my consciousness.

That's a problem for tomorrow's Finley. Or at least Finley who isn't actively being cuddled.

Beckett groans behind me, lightly thrusting his hips as he awakens.

I roll in his arms, bringing my face near his. "I've been waiting so long to do this," I admit, sliding beneath the blankets until I'm eye level with his dick.

"Fin," Beckett groans, running his hands through my hair. "Come back up here. I'll make you breakfast."

"Can't. My mouth is going to be very full soon."

I peek out of the blankets as he drops his head onto his pillow, his deep voice still raspy with sleep as he murmurs, "Fuck, Queenie, you're killing me, but if you want my cock for breakfast, I won't argue."

"Good boy," I say, hoping he likes praise as much as he seems to enjoy giving it.

Because, as it turns out, I really fucking like being told how amazing I am while someone brings me to completion.

Chapter 32

Beckett

As Finley lightly grips my cock, I know one thing for certain: this blowjob is going to be life-changing.

Waking up with my cock pressed into the deep groove of Finley's muscular ass was enough to make me ready to come, but my already erect dick somehow manages to get harder at her touch.

She slowly lowers her hot tongue to the head, licking what must be a drop of precum from the very tip.

"Mmm," she moans, the vibrations pulling me even closer to the edge. Fuck. It's been a while since I was this ready to go first thing in the morning.

I let out my own moan in reply, digging my fingers into her hair and pulling lightly. "Your mouth is the best fucking thing in this entire world," I tell her. Though it's not quite the truth. *She* is the best thing in this entire world.

She chuckles before dipping her head and taking me all the way to the back of her throat. Her right hand grips the base of my shaft, working in tandem with her mouth, as she moves up and down my length.

"Ohhh, fuck. You're killing me, Queenie. That's so fucking good. So good."

She runs her other hand over my balls, teasing me with barely there squeezes.

I'm already breathing hard, and I pull the comforter off her, needing to see the way she takes me into her mouth. "You look so good. Your pretty pink lips are amazing, wrapped around my dick like that."

The image of Finley Blake gazing at me, spit running down her chin as she deep throats my cock—it's going to get me through *a lot* of lonely nights in my future.

Finley moves up and down my shaft, her warm mouth sucking me as she cradles the underside of my dick with her tongue.

Heat builds at the base of my spine, and she pops off me with one final lick before sliding her hand up, stroking me.

She increases her pace slightly, and I want to tell her how fucking good her hands feel. How whatever little twist thing she's doing to my balls makes me want to hold her hostage so I can fuck her hand all day, every day. But all that comes out are animalistic sounds as she finds a steady rhythm of pumping and cupping that has my hips thrusting into her.

I'm so close to the edge, I'm not sure I can last much longer. I am completely at Fin's mercy, and my chest tightens as I realize there's nowhere else I'd rather be.

I need to be inside her, to fuck her until she's so confused that she never wants to leave, but I can't move. Can't do anything but seek that final release my body's building toward.

My fingers flex in her hair, and she drops her mouth to the tip of my cock, licking just enough for me to unravel.

"Going to come," I choke out, wanting to make sure she has time to pull off if she doesn't want to swallow my cum. She makes a humming noise of acknowledgment, and just as the pressure inside me reaches its breaking point, she sucks harder.

I can't look away as her eyes meet mine, widening slightly as my seed fills her mouth. She holds my gaze and swallows before slowly licking her lips, like she just tasted the world's best ice cream. My heart skips a beat, and I consider dropping to one knee and asking her to let me become Mr. Finley Blake.

As I lie there catching my breath, she climbs up my body and drops a kiss to my lips before rolling away. I try to grab her, but apparently, my almost thirty years of hockey training mean fuck all when I'm in a post-Finley-blowjob coma.

"Breakfast," I say, willing my body to get up and make something for the gorgeous woman who just gave me the best head of my life.

I walk into the kitchen after slipping on a pair of sweatpants.

Here's the problem with cooking breakfast for Finley: I don't actually cook for myself, and as this is the first time that I've had a woman stay over in Denver, I'm positive my chef didn't make extra breakfast. I pull open my fridge door, taking in the prepared meals stacked neatly on the top two shelves. Catching sight of the brightly colored fruit peeking out from the chef's jars, I realize I do have a couple of smoothie mixes I can whip up. That is just going to have to do.

"Hey," Finley says as she walks into the kitchen a few moments later. "What's for breakfast?"

I nod at the blender as I add four scoops of powder from the cupboard next to it. "Protein smoothies."

Finley smiles, though it disappears quickly. "Wow. Thank you."

I give a mocking bow. "Only the best for you."

I flip the blender on, letting it run until a purplish-brown mixture is ready for us. I pour it into a cup and hand it to Finley with a flourish. "Here you go, madam."

"You know, some women want to be fed pancakes the morning after," she says as if they like eating frog legs. "I'm glad you realized I'm the kind who wants a protein shake. Though, maybe it was obvious after the workout my mouth just did."

I choke as the cold smoothie slams into the laugh bursting out of my throat, and Finley gives me a good-natured pat on the back.

"You okay there, Kane?"

I nod, setting my drink down before wiping my mouth on the back of my hand.

"So," Finley asks, "I don't think I can go to get my keys yet. Do you have any plans for the day?"

"I have a few ideas." I run both hands up the insides of her thighs.

"Oh, really?"

"We could go back to bed," I suggest and kiss the side of her lips.

"Don't you need to get in a workout today?" she asks, and I'm not sure whether she's teasing or really asking me as my coach.

"Who needs weights when I can just throw you around all morning?"

She takes a long drink of her smoothie, almost finishing the thing.

"Or..." I start.

"Or? Or what?"

I look at her and consider. "I actually bought you a little gift a while ago, and because you have been avoiding me—"

"I have not been avoiding you," she cuts in.

"Okay," I say, not even trying to hide my disbelief. She has been avoiding me. "Then, before you mysteriously got super busy and couldn't be found by me, and only me, anywhere in the arena or your apartment... I bought you a gift."

She raises her eyebrows skeptically. "A gift?"

"Yep." I open the linen closet with exactly one spare towel in it, and pull out the dark blue box I got for her one night after we'd been practicing for the trivia portion of the Yeti Challenge. I look at the image on the top for one final time, questioning whether I made the right decision, but it's too late now.

"What is it?" she asks.

Rather than explaining, I hand it to her. She looks down, a wide smile pulling across her face when she realizes what it is. "You got me one of those fancy wood puzzles."

My chest tightens at the sight of Finley happy because of something I gave her. It's better than a penalty kill. Better than scoring a goal. I would do anything to earn that look from her again. And if I'm not careful, it might just become my newest obsession.

"Yeah," I reply softly. "After you told me how much you liked them growing up, I went online and found a place in Boulder that sells the fancy ones you like."

She gazes up at me with an almost confused look on her face. "You found a fancy puzzle store, just for me?"

I smile. "Yeah, Fin. Of course I did. I would do anything to make you happy. Don't you know that?"

I grab my smoothie and sit next to her on the couch as she dumps out the puzzle.

"So, where do we begin?"

"Edges, Beckett. Edges."

"Luckily," I say with a wink. "I'm good at edging."

Finley laughs, her attention fully on flipping the puzzle pieces so they're all right-side up. "If I remember correctly, you edged yourself so hard last night that you couldn't even finish edging me."

"I never said *who* I was good at edging. I obviously meant me. And puzzles, of course."

"You're not good at puzzles, are you?"

"No idea. I think I was six the last time I did one," I answer, snapping two pieces with pictures of two kids together.

"Beckett! That's an inside piece!"

"I know, but—"

She turns to glare at me, and it's only the slightest twinkle in her eye that reminds me she isn't my coach right now. Just a woman I care far too much about.

I lift my hands in a placating gesture. "Edging it is."

We spend the next couple of hours putting together the uniquely shaped pieces until, finally, the full picture appears. It's a winter landscape. The image of a frozen lake somewhere in the Midwest, a group of kids playing hockey in the middle.

"You're right," I say as we both stare at the completed puzzle on my coffee table. "The fancy pieces are much more fun. And I felt so classy while doing it."

"I told you so."

We sit there silently for a moment before Finley turns to me. "Thank you for this. I honestly can't remember the last gift anyone got me, and well, this was really special." She leans in and kisses me on the cheek as she says it. As soon as her lips make contact, she pulls away, straightening her back as she checks her phone.

"Oh, Paige just texted. She said she was able to make it to the arena from her apartment, so I should be good to make it."

"We don't need to go yet." I reach for her again.

She smiles at me, and something settles behind her eyes. Not regret, but something like resolve. Maybe a bit of sadness. "I... can't, Kane. I've got to get back to work. It's April. We've got to get ready for the playoffs."

Chapter 33

Finley

I crossed a line.

A thick, black line with a neon sign saying, "Do not, under any circumstances, cross."

And that version of me cannot survive as the head coach of the Denver Yeti.

I can't make mistakes, and clearly *that* was a big one.

I pace my office as I run through the damage control that must be done. I don't think anyone saw us, but we're both famous enough that cell phones are dangerous. He's on the IR now, but what happens when he gets back? How do I remain neutral when I feel anything but toward him?

Did I leave my underwear at his place?

I search through my backpack, letting out a sigh of relief when I find the thong rolled up in yesterday's sweatpants.

The thought of sweatpants allows my mind to wander to a memory of Beckett pulling them off me before his mouth was on me. It was good. *We* were good.

I forcibly shove that thought from my mind. That is exactly why I don't date.

I don't get to be the type of woman who sits around her office fantasizing about the man she made the mistake of wanting. I don't get to want things other women do. And I certainly don't get to date one of my players.

I am a coach.

The leader.

A professional.

Always.

"Finley, do you have a minute?" Sabrina asks as I prepare to leave my office that evening, keys in hand. I really wish this woman would just call me Coach Blake, like everyone else.

"Of course, Sabrina," I reply, ready to give the team whatever they need.

"Great," Sabrina says, shutting the door behind her. "There is some chatter online, and I want to flag it with you early."

"Okay." I sit down. "What's up?"

"I just wanted to let you know that we're seeing a change in some of the comments about you on recent posts."

Instead of panicking like I want to, I ask, "What do you mean?"

"The tone online is shifting: it's less about the team right now."

"Okay..." I say.

"More about *you*. Things like, 'The forbidden-romance vibes between Team Blane are better than *Bridgerton.*'"

My stomach sinks like a ship that was hit by a meteorite. Fuck. I knew there was some romantic speculation out there because of the Challenge, but I hadn't realized it'd become the main noise.

"Or, 'There's no way her players aren't into her. Looking at you, Kane.'"

Jesus. What would it take to get a rumor about Larsen having a crush on me? Shit, I'd take the whole team at this point. Calling out Kane makes it worse.

"Anyway," Sabrina continues like she's not blowing up my entire world, "that's the gist of it. Though there is one picture circulating where you're on the bench and Kane's on the ice. It looks like you two are sharing a moment, but the majority of comments are pushing back because it's clearly just a weird angle or something."

"I... I wouldn't—"

"Oh, I know," Sabrina thankfully cuts me off. "You've worked really hard to keep your focus where it belongs: the team. And I know we asked you and Kane to do The Great Yeti Challenge and give it your all. You know we all value how disciplined you are in putting the team first and always upholding the professional boundaries required of your position."

"Thank you," I reply slowly, despite my heart rate speeding up as she reminds me of all the ways I've drifted from who I was. Who I need to be.

"It's just that, as you saw last spring, when the narrative starts to shift, it can do so quite fast, and it's hard to get back. I'd hate to see the focus pulled from the Yeti team and back on the topics we finally moved away from." Sabrina wipes her hands on her legs, standing as she does it. "Anyway, if you and Kane can just limit your time together for the next few weeks until things cool down, we'll make sure The Great Yeti Challenge focuses primarily on the other teams. I know you'll do what you're supposed to—you always have."

Oh God. I didn't. For the first time in my life, I didn't do what I was supposed to.

"I... Yes. Yeti first," I agree. "Of course."

"And just so you know, I didn't escalate this at all, even if I maybe should've. I know how seriously you take your role."

My breath hitches as a lump forms in my throat.

If only she knew.

"Thanks, Sabrina."

"Of course. And good luck this week. It's showtime!"

And as I walk out the door, I know she's right. I cannot afford any more mistakes, especially not as we enter the most important two weeks of my life.

Chapter 34

Beckett

"You're back!" I yell, yanking open my door when I hear Finley coming down the hall later that afternoon.

I went to the arena to work with the PT team on my rehab today and then hung around for a few hours while the other guys practiced and got their workouts in, but I have been home for a few hours. And I've almost lost my mind.

How do people stay home and just... do nothing? I want to be skating. Lifting. Fucking Finley until she cries out my name.

I need to be moving. Staying still is how you get slammed into the boards. How you get left behind. How you miss your dreams when they go skating by at a sprint. Plus, when I'm forced to be inactive too long, I start to think about things best left unexplored.

Like my future... and my past.

I watched some film, but even that seems lonely now when I don't get to analyze it with Finley. Though, thoughts of her are what have anchored me during this injury recovery. Knowing I need to be ready to come back mentally and physically so I can help her get the wins she and the team need. I'm not sure what

I'll hold on to if the end of the Yeti Challenge is the end of... whatever this is between us.

"Hey, Kane," Finley replies, still moving toward her apartment.

The hair on the back of my neck stands at the way she uses my last name. I'm not sure what's going on here, but something doesn't feel quite right.

"Dinner at my place?"

Finley stares at her keys for a moment before moving her gaze to my apartment door as she considers my offer longer than I would've expected.

Like she can't decide whether she wants to come back to my place or not. Maybe two sleepovers in a row is too much too soon.

Maybe I really tired her out last night.

Or maybe she's envisioning all the fun ways we can get wrapped up in each other again tonight. I know I am.

"I think I need to be at my place tonight," she says finally.

I shrug. "Not a problem. Let me go grab the food out of the oven, and I'll be right over."

"That's—okay. Thank you."

"Sure thing."

I hustle inside, quickly plating the salmon and broccoli onto two plates.

Finley left the door to her apartment open, so I walk right in, setting the plates on her table before grabbing a couple of forks.

Finley walks out of her room, still in the clothes she must've changed into at the rink since it's definitely not what she was wearing when she left my place this morning. She takes me and the food in for a moment before walking over and sitting down.

"Did you get everything done at the office that you needed to?" I ask.

She nods. "I did, yeah."

"That's good."

After a long pause, Finley asks, "What did you do after you left the rink?"

"I watched some film. Then watched the Mountaineers game."

"Oh, how'd they do?" Finley asks.

"They won by three, I think. I've never been much of a basketball fan, so I wasn't really paying attention."

"Ah. I get that."

I've never had a more normal conversation feel so awkward. After multiple minutes go by with us eating in a strained silence, I finally ask, "Is everything okay, Fin?"

"Of course. Why wouldn't it be?" she asks. But she stands, taking her plate and turning her back to me as she walks to the kitchen to clean it.

"I don't know, things just seem... off."

"All normal over here." That seems untrue, but I can't exactly put my finger on what's wrong. I mean, we're still here spending time together. It just feels different.

Pushing the thought aside, I reply, "Great. Are we watching Vancouver tonight or Calgary? I watched our last game against the Stormriders already, so my vote is Calgary, but I'm fine either way."

"I'm fine with Calgary." Finley pulls the correct video up on her laptop.

"Have you seen the way their center likes to circle off the wall instead of getting inside body position?" I ask, as we sit down.

"Yeah. We'll have to make sure we take away middle ice," she notes, completely missing the easy jab she normally would've given about not everyone loving the boards as much as I do.

The game starts, and we watch in silence. There's no easy banter. No discussion. No arguing. We're just watching. Together. But separately. Like we're strangers.

"Their goalie favors his right side," Finley says finally, and it's like I can finally breathe again.

"Yeah. He drops early, too."

She's staring at the screen instead of making eye contact with me, but that's okay. This game is a big one for us, and I know she's worried about it. Or maybe I'm only interesting to watch film with when I'm actually going to be playing.

Finley points to the screen, where their goalie has dropped before the puck is even to him. "It's too bad we won't have you in the game. If you got a lane, your slap shot could beat him."

I smile. "Was that a compliment?"

"Just the truth."

She's deadpan, not even a hint of playful bickering today, but I banter back anyway.

"Sounded like a compliment to me."

Instead of responding, she turns her attention to the game, taking notes.

I guess the game is more interesting than I am tonight, and suddenly, I feel in the way. Just an annoying neighbor she has to work around rather than a partner.

The next hour passes slowly, broken up only occasionally by a comment from one of us about a player. When the film ends, my conversations have been shut down so many times, I'm worried I might've imagined last night happened at all.

I've rarely spent time with a woman socially after sleeping with her, so I'm not an expert on the norms, but I don't think this is normal behavior. And I'm not sure what to do about it.

"Should we carpool to the final Yeti event next week?" I ask, grasping at any straw I can at this point.

"I'll have to be at the arena early, so I'll get there on my own." The way she says it makes my chest ache. It's nice. And polite. And if I could force myself to look at her face, I know she'd be wearing her work smile.

"Okay. Well, dinner tomorrow?" I ask, throwing out one final Hail Mary.

"I'm going to be working late all week. But thanks for the offer."

What the hell? *Thanks for the offer?* Her mouth was wrapped around my cock this morning. We are so far past "thanks for the offer."

Or, at least, I thought we were. But maybe I was wrong.

"Sure," I say. "Well, I'd better head to bed."

I walk out of her apartment and back to mine in a trance, like I'm in an alternate universe. It's like I teleported back to the first few weeks I lived here. The solitude I felt then was normal—the independence to focus on exactly what I needed when I needed it—but looking back, it was lonely trying to navigate a new town, a new team, with no one to talk to.

Getting paired with Finley for the Challenge changed that. Suddenly, I wasn't a one-man show anymore. I was part of the larger group, and that was nice. Even if it was always supposed to be temporary.

Though, it hasn't felt temporary in a long time. Definitely not since that fateful away trip.

I don't know why, but the Finley from last night, the one who made me feel joy and happiness for the first time in a long time, is pulling away. And there's something hauntingly familiar about the loneliness starting to burn deep within my chest.

Chapter 35

Finley

"Welcome to the final event in The Great Yeti Challenge!" Ken Peterson's voice booms across the arena, from where he stands on a red carpet at center ice. Applause thunders in the space, almost louder than it is at hockey games. But the crowd today isn't your normal Yeti fans. It's an odd assortment including representatives from the nonprofits selected by the various teams as their choice for the partner for next year; new fans who came to us through The Great Yeti Challenge; and a few of the loyal Yeti supporters who want to know *everything* about the team, from the plays and the trades, to each player's stats, to what happens behind the scenes.

There are far more women in the room than men, not a ratio the arena sees often.

The teams have been split up since the event started. Which means I don't have to be around Beckett, which is for the best. Because if the last week has taught me anything, it's that remaining professional is much easier if I'm just not around him.

What we did was stupid and reckless. It was not okay. So it *has* to mean nothing. What we did. What I felt. Even if the constant weight in my belly, the guilt I'm trying to bury deep, reminds me that it, in fact, meant *everything*.

The arena goes quiet as Ken reviews the rules of the game and, with a dramatic pause, introduces the Yeti players who will be helping with this challenge.

It's a pretty simple game. One person from each Challenge pair is the hockey player, and they have to make sound hockey decisions. They'll run through drills and standard scenarios from both an offensive and defensive perspective. Power plays, two-on-one, three-on-one, that sort of thing. The other person from the Challenge pair is off the ice, sitting on the bench. Their job is to decide, before the player on the ice can move, what the textbook answer is to the scenario presented by the Yeti players.

Honestly? It's genius.

Teams get points if they agree on what should happen, and they get points if the player on the ice successfully does what they're supposed to do.

We are not allowed to watch the other teams, so after Mr. Peterson and Sabrina finish their introductions, I head back to my office. We're second to last, so I have plenty of time to listen to the crowd as I question all my life's decisions.

Like, how I could've done something so stupid as falling for one of my players.

Fortunately, after avoiding being alone with Beckett for the entire week, I think he's realized things have changed.

Laughter echoes from the arena, and I assume the intern team is on the ice. Everly boldly decided to be the one to skate since she claimed not to know the names of any hockey skills. She was, apparently, a figure skater at one point, but even so, it has to be hilarious. Knowing who they picked from the Yeti roster to be the challengers, there is no doubt in my mind they went out of their way to make her look good.

Rob and J.D. are the team before us, and there's a surprising amount of clapping.

It was smart of them to bring in a different audience—normal fans wouldn't be this engaged with basic drill work.

Finally, it's our turn.

I walk down the tunnel to a roaring crowd; it almost feels like it's game day. But there's something about it that feels hollow. Just like it has all week.

I step into my bench and sit down at the small table they have set up in front of me.

"Here are your cards, Coach," Joslyn, a woman from the social media team, says, handing me a stack of cards with various moves and strategies written on them.

I quickly look through them all, sorting them into offense and defense, so at least I won't have to search through the whole group every time. There's some strategy here. A large part of the player on the ice being successful is having enough time to move. Which means I can't take too long.

"Ready, Kane?" Joslyn asks, and I meet his gaze for the first time in a long time.

I swallow heavily when I see a hint of hunger in his eyes.

He looks good, back on the ice in his full uniform. White and Doctor Lowell considered not letting Kane do this final competition due to his injury, but the medical team cleared him this morning, so they decided to let him participate with limited contact. I'd been so happy for him when we met with Doc this morning, but all I could do was tell him that he'll be starting on the tenth against the Titans. It was exactly how I would act with any other player, but it didn't feel enough with Kane. Or maybe it was still too much somehow.

"As soon as you place the puck on top of your selection, I'll blow my whistle, and your teammate can move," Joslyn says to me.

I nod. I'm ready.

Beckett starts on defense, and even though he's been off the ice for three weeks, you can tell this is where he feels most comfortable. He skates to the center of the ice as Cruz and O'Connor break away from in front of the other net. It's a classic two-on-one.

I quickly scan my cards, slamming the puck down on the one that says, "Take away the pass."

The whistle sounds, and Beckett moves, skating backward, letting Herrera in the net know he's taking the pass. It's a textbook play, and both sides perform well, though Cruz lets Beckett force him to shoot from the exact area he wants: the one where Herrera has the best chance to make the save.

Two large green check marks light up the screen, and the crowd goes wild. Two points for us.

Everyone resets, and the team charges, sending three-on-one. It's a situation that rarely happens at professional levels, but it does happen. Particularly when you have an eager, young defenseman who ends up going too deep, and the forwards get lazy with their backchecking.

I slap down my puck, and Kane springs into motion at the first sound of the whistle, as if he could anticipate exactly how long it would take me to decide. He's a by-the-book defenseman, and everything he does makes it look like he's leading a clinic on fundamentals. I almost wish I had made the rest of the team come and take notes.

Another two check marks. Another roar from the crowd.

Eventually, the scenarios become less textbook and more subjective, but still, Kane and I are in sync. Whatever answer I give, that's what he does. It's unbelievable.

As the double check marks continue to light up the screen, a TeamBlane chant gets started in the crowd—exactly what we didn't need. But I force myself to stay focused on men skating against Beckett, never allowing my gaze to watch him too closely. To be anything but a coach sweeping the entirety of the play. Finally, our turn is done, and as Kane heads down the tunnel to change out of his skates, our gazes lock. He dips his head, lifting his gloved hand for a bump as he walks by. I tap my fist to his and say softly, "Good work out there, Kane."

He keeps walking, calling a simple, "Thanks, Coach, you, too," over his shoulder as he passes me.

I make my way to the stands, sitting next to Doctor Pearce.

"How did you two do?" I ask.

"Nothing like you and Kane," Lefevre says from the other side of Pearce.

She pushes his shoulder. "That's because you kept doing unexpected things!"

"You can't always go by the book, Sutty."

I startle at the nickname. "Sutty?" I ask.

"Lefevre, here, thinks we're friends now."

That is… interesting. That they're just openly friends. It doesn't sit entirely right, like a sweater with arms too tight, but I can't decide why. Shaw has gotten beers with the guys many times, and nothing seemed wrong with it then.

"And you… disagree about being friends?" I ask.

"We have friend-like tendencies. And I was an excellent wingwoman for him the other weekend when we grabbed a couple of beers at the hotel in Boston."

"Hell yeah, you were." Lefevre extends his hand for a fist bump. "Rachel wasn't even a bunny, and I still convinced her to come to my room."

Sutton begrudgingly bumps her fist against his, and I realize they might actually be friends. Not friends like Kane and me, but just… work friends. It's an alarmingly boring realization.

"Well, that's officially too much information for me," I say, turning my focus to where Larsen is taking the ice. I nod toward him. "You want to talk about doing unexpected things... I can't believe they didn't have Li skate. At least then, Larsen's answers would be confined to what's on the cards."

"He'll probably pull out a marker and write his own answers," Lefevre jokes.

"Li is clearly the better player of the two," Sutton says defensively, before letting out a bark of laughter. "But he definitely wouldn't be performing standing spins at center ice."

I look back out, and sure enough, Larsen is doing figure skating moves while he waits. The crowd absolutely loves it, and the place explodes in cheers.

As predicted, Larsen is a source of absolute chaos. And that's not to say that he doesn't succeed. He earns every single point for stopping or scoring. But he and Li, despite how much time they spend together, are almost never on the same page.

I'm not sure if Sandström, the defenseman Larsen is typically paired with, needs a medal or counseling after playing with Larsen all season because he's able to somehow make Larsen's madness appear choreographed.

At some point during their turn, Beckett exits the tunnel. We make eye contact before he goes and sits with Rob and J.D. I rub my palm over the catching feeling in my chest.

When Li and Larsen's turn ends, Sabrina and Ken once again take the center of the ice. "Thank you all so much for being here today," Sabrina says. "Did you have a good time?"

Everyone cheers, and Sabrina puffs with pride. "Well, now it's the moment you've all been waiting for. Scores have been tallied and combined with those from the previous challenges. Mr. Peterson, would you like to do the honors?"

She hands the microphone to Ken. "The winners of The Great Yeti Challenge are none other than..." He pauses, letting the suspense grow. "Coach Finley Blake and Beckett Kane!"

I stand, waving politely to the crowd as they chant Team-Blane.

"Smile," Sutton hisses quietly, and I pull my face into a grin, my gaze laser-focused on the opposite side of the arena from Beckett.

"Which means the Denver Yeti are very excited to be partnering with Wishes and Wings next year as our nonprofit partner!"

It takes almost a minute for the stands to settle down, but when they do, Ken adds, "We look forward to giving their team, plus a few special kiddos, a tour of our facilities in two weeks!"

With that, The Great Yeti Challenge is officially over. Beckett and I are simply player and coach once again.

So why do I still feel so guilty for the decisions I made?

Chapter 36
Finley

You can do this. Just how we practiced.

I stare at the white door in front of me, the hallway silent, except for the low hum of the overhead lighting.

Just knock.

Finally, I raise my hand and rap it twice against Beckett's apartment door.

There's no going back now. Not that I want to.

There's a pause before I hear, "Coming!"

Beckett opens the door. "Fin—Coach Blake?" He scans the hallway behind me like I might be hiding someone else. "Do you want to come in?"

"No," I say, shaking my head. "This should just take a minute."

"Okay. What can I do for you?"

"I crossed a line," I announce.

"You... crossed a line?" Beckett asks, like he's having a hard time keeping up.

"Yes. Getting romantically involved with a player was an unacceptable decision. What I did was wrong, and I'm sorry."

"You're... sorry?" He raises an eyebrow.

I nod, fighting my desire to ask him if he's a parrot. "I am. And I know it's too little too late, but moving forward, I promise to keep everything strictly professional between us."

He tilts his head. "Professional? Not even friendly?"

"No," I say, even as my heart is being ripped out of my chest. "I'm your coach. We're not friends."

His eyes scan my face, looking for an answer he's not going to find. One he *can't* find. "Are you worried someone is going to find out?"

I take a deep breath, reminding myself of what must be done. "It's not about that."

"Oh, really? So, if I could guarantee that no one would ever know about us, would you still do this? Still pretend like I mean nothing to you? That you mean nothing to me? Because I know that isn't true for me, and it damn sure felt like it wasn't true for you."

It's arrow after arrow straight to my gut. I know what I'm giving up. The future. The happiness. I know that once I answer, there's no coming back. No changing it.

"Yes."

Because *I* would know. Because *I* would never be able to trust myself again. Because I truly believe in the Yeti's culture of accountability.

Because the version of me I am supposed to be can't survive if I let Beckett mean something to me. Because I want him to mean *everything* to me. And that's certainly not something I'm allowed to have.

"Look," I say. "I want you to know this isn't about you or anything you did. You're great. I've enjoyed getting to know you. And it's not about people finding out. I know we could hide it if we wanted to. We were always professional at the rink, but we have to go back to being coach and player."

Beckett swallows hard, and it's all I can do to force my gaze away from the strong lines of his throat. "I understand. You've always held yourself to a higher standard than the rest of us. And we both knew what we were doing. It was certainly questionable, even if me being on IR made it a little bit more of a gray area than normal. But, just so you know, I don't think you ever treated me differently as a player. And I *never* felt like I had to be with you in order to play. So, while I completely understand why rules like this exist, we broke them in name only: not in spirit."

He raps once on the doorframe, as if he's preparing to leave, and the last threads of control start to splinter within me. But then he faces me again, a sad smile on his face. "And just so you know, I don't think you have to be the perfect Coach Blake who Sabrina and the team have tried to turn you into. You're more than just a coach."

The words should make me feel better, but they have the opposite effect. He doesn't understand. Coach Blake is Finley. Finley is Coach Blake. There is no difference between the two at this point. Maybe when I was alone with him, but never outside of that. Never with anyone else. The real Finley would've *never* made it to this level. This job would destroy her.

Not knowing how to explain that to him, I simply nod. "Thanks, Kane. See you at the airport tomorrow."

"See you," he says. He gives me a final, sad smile before shutting the door, leaving me alone in the hallway.

I suck in a deep breath, battling the sinking feeling of emptiness spreading in my gut, competing with the relief of finally being back in control.

Even if this version of myself willfully chooses survival over joy. Over happiness. At least I can do it with my head held high. Letting myself catch feelings was so far past my moral limits that I don't know if I can ever find the old version of myself again.

Now that I've closed that chapter of my life, I've cut myself off from wanting what would destroy me. Even if walking away seems to be breaking me apart piece by tiny piece. At least there's a chance I survive it.

I walk back into my apartment and drop on the couch. The silence causes my ears to buzz, the light over the table suddenly far too bright. Everything is too much and not enough.

I startle as my phone starts ringing on the arm of the couch next to me. I'm not sure how long I sat there, just staring out the window.

"Hi, Dad," I say. "Everything okay?" We already had our normal weekly call, and my dad only calls outside of those when I've done something that needs to be managed immediately.

Which has never happened on a day when I don't have a game. Usually, it's when I have back-to-back games, and he feels a decision I made was egregious enough that it needs to be stopped before the next game. Fortunately, those have been decreasing in frequency. But I suppose we are almost to the playoffs, and things are getting real.

"You should hard-match the second pair against their top line tomorrow."

Of course. Just wanted to make sure I'd thought of everything.

"Yes," I reply. "I discussed that with our team, but we decided it wasn't necessary for this game."

"You should reconsider."

"Our lines can handle Braun. We don't need to hard-match him. Plus, without home ice advantage, I'm not sure we'll be able to match him without changing on the fly."

"You have a better chance of winning if you keep your first pair on him. And you need this win, Finley."

"I know, Dad." We have to win all three of our final games to make the playoffs, and if we don't... well, I may be looking for a new job. Though if this guilt keeps eating away at my stomach, I'm going to need a new one anyway.

As if he can read my thoughts, Dad says, "If you don't win, they're going to cut you loose, Finley. They hired you out of desperation and kept you around this year out of some sense of loyalty. But if you don't win, I don't think they're going to keep you around. You've got to be prepared, Finley. You won't be at Denver forever, but if you don't see the writing on the wall, you won't have someplace to land."

"I think we can win these."

"Finley, you can't just *think*. You need to know. This impacts how people see you, and by default, me. This isn't just your reputation relying on this. It's mine as well."

"I know, Dad."

"Good. Then I'll let you get back to watching film. Watch the Titans again. You'll see that I'm right."

We hang up, and I pull up the Titans film, reconsidering every decision my team made about how we play. That said, I don't know if I should trust my decision-making right now.

As I sit alone in my apartment that night, watching hour after hour of game film, alone, I can't seem to ease the hollow feeling that has taken up residence in my chest.

Chapter 37

Beckett

"Jesus, Beckett," Rob says as he climbs onto the first bus the next day. "I was shocked when they said someone had already loaded up. You're headed to the arena this early?"

"Yeah. Want to make sure I'm good and warm before the game." I've been waiting here for ten minutes. I know two and a half hours before the game is early to warm up, but I need to ramp up slow and steady. Plus, then I have space. I have quiet. I have control.

Rob nods, settling into his seat as I click play on the game film I'm watching on my phone.

The pang of longing hits me as soon as the players on the ice start to move. Every day since Finley told me we have to go back to a fully professional relationship has been torture. To be in the same room as her. To hear her pre-game speeches. To listen to her game analysis. To catch glimpses of her dark hair around each corner at the arena. It's torture seeing her every day and pretending I don't care about her. Forcing myself to act like she isn't even my friend, when it feels like she's captured a part of my soul.

It's excruciating.

And the worst part is, I can't even be mad at her. Because I understand. What we did was reckless. Stupid.

And fucking amazing.

And now hockey, my one and only refuge from the storm of torment inside me, is a constant reminder of the woman I lost—the one I might never have truly had to begin with. So I'm forcing myself to focus more. No distractions. To burrow so deeply into my routines that no one and nothing can touch me.

It's kind of working.

Already in my workout clothes, I head straight to the training room, intent on spending ample time on my mobility work. It's all part of my new-and-improved plan. The room is blissfully quiet, the only sound my breathing timed with my movement.

When the next bus arrives an hour later, the room becomes too full, too loud, as men start doing some light warm-up jogging, sprints, and bounding work. I move on, rather than stay, as the other guys start to get warm.

"Sewer?" Li asks as I walk by, holding up the soccer ball the guys will use to help them get warm.

I shake my head. Sewer ball can get chaotic, and right now, I need to stay in control.

Hours later, I mentally check my pain levels as I go through my taping routine, making sure there isn't any crumpling or bunching to throw the feel of the puck off once I'm out on the ice. The *thwip thwip* of the tape pulling off its roll is the soundtrack to my meditation as I evenly cover my stick, leaving the tiniest hint of the toe showing.

I inspect my work, and when I realize there's a slight bunch in the center, I fight the rage that wants to bubble out of me. A completely inappropriate response to a minor inconvenience. With a jerk, I pull it all off, starting again.

Once I have it perfect, I do a few minutes of puck-handling drills before finally taking three minutes to do some mindfulness and breathing work to ensure I'm in the right headspace before we begin.

***

I slide back in the zone, tracking the Ironhounds' center as he looks to press their advantage.

"I've got middle!" I yell to Volkov in the net.

"Middle's yours."

"I've got puck!" Li calls.

When Li and I hustle over the boards for a shift change, I gulp down some water, making sure to track my pain levels. Low. We've been up since J.D. flew in a goal five minutes into the first period, so I've played it safe. Smart.

No unnecessary hits. No unnecessary movement. Just smart, sound hockey.

After the first score, the game became an offensive struggle. Both goalies were on tonight, and everyone struggled to find the holes. When the final buzzer sounds, we win with J.D.'s single goal. Beating Pittsburgh in Pennsylvania is a crucial win, and I climb onto the ice with my team to celebrate, but I opt to stay on the outskirts of the celebrations, rather than jumping into the fray.

As soon as we're in the locker room, I pull off my gloves and helmet before shoving on my headphones. I've never been a big music guy, always content to listen to whatever is playing in the locker room, but headphones give a certain go-fuck-yourself energy that I am desperate for right now. I can't focus when guys are chirping constantly about inane things like whether they should get two or three lines for their new tattoo, or if they're going to the club the bunnies like to hang out at, or trying to meet real women in normal bars. And if we're going to make it to the playoffs, I need to focus.

I've gotten most of my pads off and am working the tape off my socks when Coach Blake's double knock sounds at the locker room door. My pulse jumps slightly at the sight of her, but I don't let in any of the feelings that are trying to come along with it.

She made the right call, I remind myself for what seems like the millionth time.

"Well, gentlemen, that was a hard one, but we pulled it out. Our shots on goal numbers were right where they needed to be. Volkov, defense, excellent work out there. The plane will be wheels up in three hours, the bus in two. We've kept ourselves alive and in the hunt for this long—we're not letting the Bears stop us. Morning skate and then film tomorrow. Late schedule since it's going to be a long night. One more win and we're in the running."

I slide my headphones back on and move through my usual post-game routine. Now is not the time to cut corners or do anything but follow the plan—and to make sure I recover thoroughly, I've added even more post-game time to my plan. I've been on the bike for longer than any of the other guys when Larsen taps on my shoulder.

"What?" I say, making sure to only slide one of my headphones off.

"Okay, no need to bite my head off. A couple of guys are coming over for dinner tomorrow. I wanted to see if you were in before I told my chef final numbers."

"No."

He raises an eyebrow when I don't give him anything more than that, and when I pull my headphones back on, he rolls his eyes and walks away.

Getting to know the team is an important part of my strategy for next year, but they clearly like me. Larsen invited me to dinner. I don't need to eat with them every night.

If I let this injury slow me down, I might not even be on the ice next year. And then I'll lose my career and my new friends in one go. So, I have to stay healthy this season. Perform well. Position myself to take on a leadership role next year. And to do that, it requires one hundred percent focus on getting prepared, mentally and physically, for every game.

Deviation is dangerous.

So, connection is going to have to wait—even if no one knows exactly how long this season will last.

I grit my teeth through the ten minutes in the ice bath, thankful I'm the only one icing today. Young guys always think the ice bath is optional, but for me, it never is. Then, I find the stretching area, moving through my hip mobility exercises twice before working my hamstrings, glutes, lower back, and ankles. Once I get through the whole set, I do it again. When it's my time for PT, I head over to the tables, stripping to my boxers before I climb on.

"How you feeling today, Kane?" Glenn asks, working my hip.

I bite down hard on my back teeth to fight a grimace as his fingers hit a sore spot and work it.

"Fine."

"I'm going to need more than that."

"Range of motion was barely limited. I had a bit of a delay getting into my sprint, but I don't know if that's mental or physical."

"Any pain?"

"I'm an old hockey player. I always hurt."

The PT laughs, and I flash back to the last time I told that truth disguised as a joke: with the doctor when I first joined the Yeti.

Taking a deep breath, I try a different tactic this time. "It's at a three now. It hit five during the third period, but then I got that longer rest, and it was back to a four when I went back out."

By the time I finish with Glenn, almost everyone else is on the bus for the airport, so I quickly shower and dress before grabbing a plate of food to eat on the bus.

The ride is short, and as I climb onto the plane and settle in, the rest of the team following me on and taking their seats, all I can think about is the next part of my routine. It's late, and everyone is mostly subdued. My screen illuminates my face as the cabin lights dim overhead.

Larsen looks over at me from the other side of the aisle. "Are you watching film right now, Kane? Isn't it past your bedtime, old man?"

"I can sleep when I'm dead, Rookie," I say, pulling my headphones off my shoulders.

Plus, there's more I still need to do. Especially if there's a good chance I only have one more season.

So as the plane takes off, the engines humming outside my window, I log on to the Wi-Fi and keep watching the film reel Doctor Pearce put together for the Bears. I look up when the film ends, shocked to find over an hour has passed, and the rest of the team is asleep. My hip sends a small shock down my leg as I shift in my seat. Switching to the appropriate app on my phone, I schedule another PT session for tomorrow morning before skate starts. Then, with a sigh, I book sessions for every day this week.

Chapter 38

Finley

The clock above the ice trickles down to 00:00, and it's like every fan in the arena releases the breath they've been holding for the last sixty minutes.

It's still tied 0–0.

We're going to overtime against the Boston Bears.

Overtime always feels quieter to me. Though that's not what the average spectator would observe in the arena. God, no. The crowd is feral, on its feet, sound rattling the glass. We're lucky we're in Denver tonight.

But inside my head, everything narrows. Sharpens. The world is reduced to nothing more than ice.

Win, and we move on. Lose, and we're done. It's the scenario movies are made about.

I stand behind the bench, my arms crossed, the inside sliver of my cheek bleeding between my teeth.

This is not a moment for me to interfere.

I've done my part.

Every line, every matchup, every detail… perfect.

The guys hop over the boards, and my chest tightens with something like pride. They look calm. Focused. Ready. This is the team I've been building all season.

Not flashy. Not reckless.

Disciplined.

And they've played an almost perfect game tonight.

The puck drops.

And the Yeti players execute. No panic, no wasted stride. They take the zone, just the way they're supposed to. We cycle low. We're patient. We force them to chase. Force them to tire.

J.D. takes a shot from the point, and the rebound kicks wide, right where it should.

Lefevre gets another chance.

Then another.

I barely breathe.

This is what my system is supposed to look like. And it's working. The average professional hockey team scores once for every ten shots on goal. We've had thirty-four shots this game. Good fucking attempts.

Their goalie is on fire tonight.

The Bears rush the other way, but it's nothing. Angled wide. Our defense not letting anything into the middle. Volkov swallows the puck like he's done all game—like he's done a thousand times before.

We're doing everything right. And that's the cruel part.

Time stretches, those five minutes both flying by and standing still.

And suddenly there's fifteen seconds left. The puck slides into the slot, and my pulse spikes so hard I almost gasp.

This is the moment.

J.D.'s shot releases—hard, clean, right toward his upper glove side. The place where he and the rest of the goalies are most likely to let a puck go by.

But not this time.

Their goalie makes a save he had no business making. The sound the crowd makes is animalistic. Complete chaos and outrage, though the puck is still alive.

Players scramble. Sticks collide. Skates tangle.

We're going to sudden death.

But then—

"Puck!" the bench yells.

It's not a blown coverage.

It's not a lazy mistake.

It's not something *anyone* could've changed.

It's a bounce.

The puck hits the boards wrong and kicks out into open ice. Straight to a Bears winger who is behind the play.

And physics, the constant asshole that it is, betrays the Yeti.

They can't change their direction quite fast enough as the winger takes one stride and shoots his shot.

It's ugly.

Desperate.

Unremarkable.

And it slides right into Volkov's five hole.

The red light turns on.

And everything goes silent. Like no one quite believes it.

Then the horn sounds, and the Bears explode over the boards, gloves and sticks flying as they celebrate.

I don't move.

I watch Volkov drop to his knees, staring straight at the ice. My gaze shifts to J.D. as he bends forward, hands braced on his thighs, his gaze searching the crowd for... ah—his wife.

I wish I could look at Beckett. Get strength or comfort or that reassurance that someone still cares about me, like J.D. and his wife. But I can't. Instead, I focus on the sounds from the bench—the ones that echo the grief inside me.

They did *everything* right.

But the scoreboard didn't care.

We played better, we earned more chances, we played the cleanest game all year.

And we still lost.

I walk into the tunnel in a state of shock, the noise around me faded to a low hum.

I'm not even sure what I say to the team in the locker room. They don't need to hear from me right now. They did exactly what I told them to do.

And it wasn't enough.

I exit the locker room and have a quick debrief in the hall with the coaches, just long enough to tell them they did great work, and we'll start planning for the next season on Monday.

We all need a day off.

And then I see him. Standing at the door to my office.

My dad.

"You made it," I observe, pulling the door open and inviting him in.

"I wouldn't miss it for the world, Fin. Tough game out there."

I nod. Both grateful for his presence and already exhausted by the lecture that's sure to come. Because no matter how well I thought we did tonight, my dad will have critiques. Not to be mean, but because he's always wanted me to be the best. And that requires acknowledging and changing any action or thought that is less than perfect. Even if it's subjective.

But it is helpful: I can't change what I don't know.

"You coached not to lose," he says, eyes still sharp in a way that used to make grown men pay attention. "You trusted your system at a time when you needed your men to break it."

He paces, slow and deliberate. "Overtime isn't about control. It's about timing. You needed to unleash their killer instinct, not their discipline. You changed lines like it was regulation. You protected a structure that didn't serve the outcome you wanted. You should've unleashed your difference makers. You should've taken a risk. They didn't make any mistakes, but you didn't allow them to force one, either."

He stops in front of me. "Great coaches don't just eliminate errors. They decide which ones they're willing to live with."

I nod. Of course.

My dad sighs. "You're too young for this position, Finley. I wish they would've listened to me when I told them not to offer it to you, but they set you up for failure. This loss, whether it happened now or in a few weeks, would've happened. You're just not ready."

I know he's not trying to make me feel like this is my fault. I know he cares about making me better, but there's something about the way he says it that has the air whooshing out of me like I just took a hit to the solar plexus.

And while I know he was talking about playing it safe tonight, his words hit home in a different way. One that reminds me that I made a different error, one of potentially greater magnitude. One that I still have to deal with.

Chapter 39

Finley

"Coach Blake?" Paige says, popping her head into my office.

I look up from my computer. "Yes?"

"Ken Peterson is on the line and would like to talk to you."

"Did they say why?" I ask, my mind flying through every option that it could be. Very few of them are good.

I wish I could disappear. To drop off the face of the earth and then resurface again in five to ten years when I am no longer a story. Not because we lost. Though the pain of doing everything right and still losing still smarts at unsuspecting moments, even now, almost three days later.

We were disciplined. Professional. And we still failed.

But because I can't shake the hollow feeling that settled in behind my sternum weeks ago when I didn't hold myself to the same standard as the rest of the team. The one that I've codified in the culture of accountability.

Paige shakes her head. "No. But it didn't seem... important."

She says the last word like she knows what I'm thinking. Like everyone is thinking: Is this loss going to be the end for me?

"Okay," I reply, taking a calming breath before picking up my phone. "Hello, Mr. Peterson."

"Coach Blake, how are you today?"

"Doing fine, and yourself?"

"I can't complain. Look, I know you're a busy woman, so I'll cut to the chase. I know this is your first year as a head coach, and that wasn't the ending that we were hoping for. But I've talked to White, and I just want you to know that I'm pleased with how the season ended up. I mean, don't get me wrong, I want to get the Cup. But this was a rebuilding year for us, and we knew that going in. So still being in the running until after the last game of the regular season, it's as good as we could've hoped for. Plus, viewership is up: we didn't have a game after mid-February that wasn't completely sold out."

"I do think we're in a good place to move forward." My fear starts to disappear as I realize he might not be calling to fire me.

"We are. The press around you has died down some, and with the stability you and your culture of accountability have brought, I fully expect us to make the playoffs next year. So don't go sharing your résumé with anyone, ya hear?" he asks, giving the old-man chortle I've come to know means he's amused at his own joke.

"Yes, sir."

With that, we say our goodbyes. I hang up, his final words ringing through my head.

Yes. This is... I should be excited. Pleased. It's the call I wanted and could barely dream of getting after not making it to the playoffs. And there is a small part of me that is excited. The part that wants this more than anything. But the bigger part of me is crumbling. My chest aching at his praise of the culture I've intentionally been building here. The one that says to own up to your mistakes, to admit to them, and to learn from them.

"You have to be in the press room in five," Paige reminds me, sticking her head through my door. "Everything okay?"

"Good," I answer, giving her what I hope is a reassuring smile.

I walk into the hallway, surprised to see Larsen and Li, both in suits. "What are you doing here?" I ask, wiping my sweaty palms onto my pants.

"Press," Li replies.

I pull in a deep breath, trying to get air past the lump in my throat. "And you suited up for it?"

"Of course!" Larsen replies enthusiastically. "I knew you'd be in your game-day suit. Culture of accountability, Coach. You wouldn't ask us to do something you wouldn't do, so why should we ask you to do something we wouldn't do?"

My nose starts to tingle as the need to cry tries to overwhelm me. I bite the inside of my cheek hard. "Right."

"You okay, Coach?" Li asks, his dark eyes taking me in.

I nod, forcing out a cough. "Think I might be coming down with something."

We walk the rest of the way to the press room, Larsen's rambling filling the space between us, even if it refuses to fill the hole in my chest, the one that his comment made larger.

I go through the motions of the end-of-season interviews, and when I get back to my office, I pull out my cell phone only to discover I have a voicemail from my dad. Worried something happened with his flight home, I press play.

"Hey, Finley, just heard from a couple of contacts that the Yeti are planning on extending your contract. Congratulations. It never would've happened in my day, but I guess the Yeti likes what you're doing there. Both men I talked to mentioned your culture of accountability—whatever that is. Said they think it's going to pay off big in a couple of years. Anyway, good work."

Good work.

It might be the highest praise I've ever gotten from my dad. But of course, it has to be about the culture of accountability. I swallow hard, rubbing my face with my hands as I try not to get distracted.

Get it together, Finley.

I move through the rest of my day in a haze, trying to find the excitement I should be feeling from the calls from Ken and my dad, but it's lost beneath my shaking hands. The unease in my chest. The way my mind is constantly pulled from the present to the memory of what I did with Beckett. The guilt I feel for my decision, and my inability to regret the time I spent with him.

I keep hearing the players say, "culture of accountability" in the teasing way they do. Like it was a catchphrase they all found a little funny. Like it should maybe have a hashtag in front of it. But, fuck, they've bought in to it, and so have I.

I've sweated through my shirt and my suit jacket by the time I get back to my office that evening, and I realize I can't do this. I can't feel like this every day for the rest of my life.

The weight of it settles within me. With almost manic clarity, I realize what I need to do. I need to confess, and I need to resign, so the team isn't forced to fire me.

In a new email, I type a resignation letter to White and Mr. Peterson, one that explains what I've done and why I can no longer lead the team. But something about it doesn't feel right. It doesn't feel like I'm holding myself to the accountability I've preached since day one on the job.

Reading through it again, I make a few small edits, my mind continually caught on the words "my decision to step down is in the best interests of the team..."

The draw to send it sucks me in: I just want to have it done with. Then I can disappear, taking with me the burning guilt over the fact that, if any player confessed something like this to me, I would tell them they had to turn themselves in and let the system work out what the repercussions are. Culture of accountability, and all.

I hover the cursor over the large blue "send" button when I realize I am in no condition to be making this decision. My heart is pounding, my hands shaky. It's like I chugged fifteen cups of coffee and then walked through a haunted house. The relief I expect to feel isn't there. Instead, there is a slow trickle of ice falling down my sternum that feels wrong.

I don't examine it, though. With the push of a button, I save the email to my drafts.

Chapter 40

Finley

Today. I'm going to be unemployed starting today. Probably. I called an emergency dinner with Charlotte tonight, and after I confirm with my best friend that I'm not losing my mind, I'm going to press send. Or maybe she'll help me understand why resigning feels so wrong.

All I have to do is get through the next few hours of meetings. Then I can get away from the nagging pressure in my chest. The constant tremors in my hands. The slight smell of body odor that follows me around now that I'm losing half my body weight in anxious sweats.

"I'm headed to my meeting with Sutton," I tell Paige as I walk past her and out the door of my office.

"Have fun!" she sings, her tone almost sarcastic. She and Sutton have never gotten along.

I'm walking down the hallway, my tennis shoes squeaking on the clean floors when suddenly my face is planting into a large chest.

"Hey, Coach," Larsen says, reaching out to steady me.

"Larsen." I move to step around him.

He steps in front of me. "Do you have a minute?"

"Unfortunately, no. I have a meeting with Dr. Pearce."

"Well, she and Li just got into an argument about statistical diagonals, so maybe you can spare me a few minutes?"

I look into his unsmiling face. "You know that's not a real thing, right? Statistical diagonals?"

He shrugs. "It's as real to me as any other math term."

"Well, I'd better go anyway," I announce, starting to walk past him again.

"Don't leave," he says.

"What?"

"I had a coach leave after my sophomore year in college, and you're acting just like he did. You've not checked out, but you're not pushing forward, either. You're giving off a real about-to-bolt vibe."

"Larsen, that's..." I trail off. What?

Exactly correct?

Surprisingly insightful?

Not something I want to talk about?

He holds up a hand. "I just wanted to say, it was a hell of a game. Chaos is unfortunately the one thing you can't prepare for—trust me, it's the only reason I've made it this far." He tugs on the ends of his shaggy brown hair. "I know you hate losing, but we need you. And next year, we'll be there. Because we didn't fail this year... We just didn't win. There's always the possibility of a bad bounce, but there's nothing we can do about it."

This is not the conversation I need right now. I want to tie up loose ends with Sutton, reread my resignation email for the thousandth time, and go eat tacos with Charlotte.

I don't want to be lectured by the rookie.

"I... Okay. Well, thanks... I think."

I pull on the end of my ponytail to tighten it slightly. "Look, Larsen, I've got to go. But make sure you keep up your work with Rob over the next few weeks, okay?"

"Sure, Coach. I will." His smile is almost sad. Like maybe he knows this is goodbye, even if he doesn't understand why I need to leave.

Larsen may be insightful, but he's wrong about chaos. Sure, technically, sticking with the same matchups made the most sense. Structure and consistency win Cups. It was the safe decision. And maybe there are moments when choosing the safe option and the right one aren't the same thing. Or maybe Larsen's a meddling twenty-two-year-old who doesn't know how to stop chirping. He was still losing teeth—non-permanent ones—when I started coaching. He's never had to decide between the safe decision and the right one before.

After finding Sutton red-faced and breathing heavily after her argument with Li, the rest of my day is blissfully uneventful. When I make it back to my office just before three, I'm ready to ditch out early for a drink while I wait for Charlotte.

Unfortunately, the world seems to have other plans, as Sabrina knocks on my door no less than three seconds after I sit down.

"Coach Blake." Sabrina makes her way straight past Paige and through my open door. "I hope you don't mind, but I've got a little girl here who would like to see you."

My heart feels lighter as Lilly and her mom follow Sabrina into the room.

Lilly comes in, giving me a shy smile. "Hi."

"Hi, Lilly, I'm so glad you could come and see me." I stand to greet them.

"They were here as part of the Wishes and Wings tour this afternoon, and since we, unfortunately, didn't get to see many of the players, I promised Lilly I'd let her come chat with you," Sabrina says.

I smile. "I'm so glad you did!" And I really am. My short time with Lilly made a big impact on me. I was worried I might not have the opportunity to see her again.

"I thought your office would be bigger," Lilly announces, and I laugh as her mom's face turns a light shade of red.

"I did, too!" I agree, throwing up my hands in mock outrage. "I was promised enough room for my own hot tub."

I actually have no idea what I would do with more room—I barely know what to do with the space I have now, but I'm willing to play along.

Lilly giggles, the exact reaction I was hoping for.

"But I do have a pretty sweet view of the practice rink." I point out the tinted window behind my desk. "Want to see?"

She walks over and stares out at the ice. At the other end, the goalie coach is running a practice, despite me giving everyone the next couple of weeks off.

"That's Volkov," I say. "And he's out there with Nyquist, our goalie coach."

Lilly nods. "I know."

I love how confident kids are.

"I always wanted to be a goalie," Lilly murmurs as her mom and Sabrina start talking quietly behind us.

"There's still time," I offer, though my heart clenches at the thought that maybe there isn't. Not for me, at least.

"I don't know. With me being sick, there's so much that could go wrong. I think it might just be easier to stop wanting things, you know?"

I squat down to her level, thinking of the conversation I just had with Larsen. "There's always something that can go wrong. Just look at our game against the Bears. One bad bounce and it's all over. But that doesn't mean you shouldn't try… Though definitely talk to your mom and your doctor first."

I hope I didn't just saddle her mom with a big hockey expense and mentally make a note to send them some information about organizations in Denver that teach kids hockey for free.

"Mom gets bummed out when I'm too sick to do the things I want to do, though. I wouldn't want to make her sad just so I could do what I want."

This girl sure knows how to tug at the old heartstrings.

"It's not your job to protect your mom, though. I bet she'd be excited to see you out there, trying something new."

"Even if I fail?" she asks, and my heart clenches.

"*Especially* if you fail. That's how you get better."

"Have you failed before?" she asks softly.

I nod. "I have." It's an honest answer.

"Did you get better?"

No. I didn't. I'm getting out. I'm… quitting.

"Lilly, it's time to go, sweetheart," Lilly's mom announces as she steps around my desk to stand next to her daughter. "Say thank you to Coach Blake."

Lilly smiles up at me. "Thanks, Coach Blake. I hope you figure out what you're supposed to from your failure."

I force my face into a matching smile and say goodbye through the confusion burrowing its way into my gut, tugging at my mind to reconsider something that I've already decided on.

But I can't help the thought from crossing my mind: What if leaving isn't the right thing to do?

Chapter 41

Finley

"Okay, but here's a crazy idea," Charlotte says around a big bite of her chicken tacos. "What if you don't fuck yourself over and just promise not to sleep with any more of your players?"

I shake my head; glad I picked up tacos and came over to her place rather than meeting out at the restaurant like we'd originally planned. Charlotte is not quiet when she has an opinion on something.

"I'm not worried about sleeping with any more of my players!" I sputter.

Charlotte's eyes glitter with amusement. "So you're worried about sleeping with Kane again?"

While I am *very* worried about making sure my decisions don't negatively impact Beckett, I'm not interested in exploring that line of questioning... well, ever. Instead, I tell her, "It's not about the future. It's about taking accountability for my actions. It's about accepting I did something wrong and taking the actions to make it right."

"Or, you don't do it again, and no one will be any wiser," Charlotte retorts, frustration lacing her tone. "Just let it go and move on."

"You know that's not an option for me."

She shakes her head. "No. I know for a fact it *is* an option for you. You just have daddy issues, and so you're choosing to overlook it."

I almost choke on my bite of beef and cheese. "Excuse me? How does that have anything to do with anything? And, also, *I* have daddy issues?"

Charlotte lifts one slender shoulder. "Oh, I'm aware I have daddy issues. You don't grow up with Steve Langford and come out unscathed. The limit does not exist for the amount of therapy I need. But it makes me uniquely positioned to spot others like me."

The smell of steak and fresh tortilla lingers as I hold my taco suspended in the air. "What do you mean?"

Her eyes widen slightly as her mouth hangs open, showing me her half-chewed meal. "Oh shit. You think you don't have..." She chews thoughtfully for a moment. "I'm obviously not a therapist, so take this with a grain of salt, but have you ever considered that you hold yourself to unrealistic standards?"

"No one likes to do the wrong thing," I state the obvious.

Charlotte nods. "True. Well, in general. But, do you know what normal people do when they don't achieve their goals?"

I'm not sure I'm following. "They try again. I have failed before, Charlotte. Lots of times."

"Ah, yes. You and all the other female head coaches—oh wait."

I roll my eyes. "So I have daddy issues because I'm successful?"

Tilting her head slightly as if considering it, Charlotte says, "Nooo... But also, maybe? Do you think your dad would still love you if you weren't the head coach?"

"Are you serious right now? He didn't even think I should get the job. Hell, he told them *not* to hire me. He would probably love me more if I wasn't the head coach."

That settled, I dig back into my food.

After a moment, Charlotte asks, "You know how fucked up that sentence was, don't you?"

"What do you mean?"

"You just said your dad actively tried to keep you from getting the promotion you wanted. Shit. Definitely daddy issues, but maybe I was projecting my issues onto you. Yours are a *whole* different variety."

Don't love that evaluation of my life or my relationship with my one remaining family member.

"Love and support aren't conditional, Finley," Charlotte continues, and my chest tightens slightly. That's not my experience. "It's shitty that your dad would try to make it so you don't get a role you want. It's shitty that he calls you every week and spends hours telling you all the things you didn't do right in the last week—"

"That's not what he does!" I cut in, regretting the day she happened to walk into my office when my dad was on speakerphone. "We just review things. He knows what he's talking about, and he wants to make me better."

"Maybe," Charlotte concedes, "but that's a super fucking unhealthy way to go about it."

"Okay, well, we've veered way off course here," I say, trying to pull us back on topic. My relationship with my dad is fine. Normal. He shouldn't be proud of me when I make mistakes—I know I'm not. "Fortunately, I will have lots of time to seek professional help once I've been fired."

Charlotte rubs her temples with her left hand. "I'm going to need you to walk me through it like I'm five, because I still don't understand why you can't just do nothing and hope for the best.

Or, if you can't do that, just send the damn resignation email you've already written."

As if it's that simple.

But I do want her opinion, so I start with the easier answer. "I can't resign because it would be quitting. And people need to see that I didn't give up. People are counting on me, and I'm not going to walk away just to save face. I have to at least try to keep my job." It's the conclusion I came to after talking to both Larsen and Lilly today. Once I made it, it was like the weight I've been carrying around got lighter. It felt right. Resigning isn't holding myself accountable. Reporting myself is.

Charlotte leans back in her chair. "Okay. I understand that. But doesn't telling your GM that you slept with your player and getting fired for it have the same outcome as resigning?"

I chew on my lip. "Same outcome, maybe, but different optics. The team and the league will protect themselves. And it is possible—though not likely—that they *won't* fire me. We do have the whole IR-thing going for us. So, that slightly increases my chances of keeping my job, and it changes the narrative just slightly."

"But I still don't get why you can't do nothing. It's a viable option. No one knows. You're not at risk of being caught."

"Because it *did* happen. There are protocols in place, and I need to follow them. If I don't hold myself to the standard, how could I ever hold anyone else to one? And..." I chew on my bottom lip as I decide how to say the real reason I can't just resign and walk away from everyone who's counting on me.

"And you still want Kane," Charlotte adds unhelpfully.

"No. I don't think that's it," I answer. "I mean, my feelings for him haven't gone away in a few weeks. I still l—like him." I shift mid-word, catching myself before that feeling that's been lingering in my chest escapes. "But this is about me. *I* did something wrong, and I can't just let it go. If a slap shot is off, it doesn't just miss the net—it creates a rebound, a turnover, a goal against you. Acting like you didn't miss is how one mistake turns into five."

"You know I hate sports analogies," Charlotte reminds me, rubbing her temples again. "But I understand what you're saying. It's about owning your mistakes."

"I can't coach a culture of accountability if I'm not willing to live it myself when things get hard. Accountability only makes you better if you embrace it *when* things get hard."

Charlotte's gaze is locked on mine as she asks, "So you're going to do it? You're going to report yourself?"

I nod, cringing inwardly at the conversation I'm going to have with White tomorrow. "Yep. Tomorrow. Mondays are for hard conversations, after all. But I need to make sure it won't impact Beckett. I'm certainly the one in the wrong here since I'm in a position of power, so I should be able to limit his exposure, but there is a small possibility that they'll decide to keep me and trade him again."

"And we don't want that?" Charlotte asks.

"I will do anything to make sure my poor decision-making doesn't affect him."

"Then let's make sure you have your story straight tonight," Charlotte says.

I raise an eyebrow. "It's not a story."

"True, but there's a way to spin everything—even the truth. And we need to make sure you don't accidentally shoot yourself in the foot by giving them information they don't need." She pulls out her phone. "We're going to need some ice cream."

***

"Thanks for fitting me in this morning," I say, my stomach churning as I sit in the chair across from Greg White. I force my face into neutrality. Culture of accountability. I can do this.

"Of course," he replies with the warm smile I don't deserve. "You know I'll always make time for you. What brings you in today? Already researched who you think my department should trade for this off-season?" he asks, teasing.

I bite the inside of my cheek, telling myself to rip off the Band-Aid. Delaying this any longer isn't going to help anyone. "Unfortunately, no."

"Oh?" He lifts his eyebrows in surprise.

"No. I need to file an official report."

I almost miss the sharp inhale he takes as his hands dip into his right-hand drawer. "Okay. Let me get the templates. What kind of report are we filing today?"

It's clear he's done this before, at least a few times. Or paid a lot of attention during the training session. He's calm, making no assumptions.

"I need to file a formal report for inappropriate workplace relations."

His eyes betray him this time, narrowing with anger. "And who"—he takes a deep breath—"is the complaint against?"

The way he elongates the "s" in the word makes me realize that he's got it wrong. He thinks someone was harassing me.

I shake my head, a sad smile pulling my cheeks. "Me."

"I know, but who was the ma—*person* acting inappropriately?"

Damn my fucking heart and the way it's clenching right now.

"I was the one who acted inappropriately."

His gaze snaps to mine. "You?"

"Yes. I apologize for not being more clear."

He tilts his head, almost as if he doesn't believe what he's hearing. Finally, he suggests, "Why don't we start at the beginning?"

So I do.

I tell him about my crush on Kane in high school. Admit I should've been more open when I knew Kane may be considered for a trade. I talk about Lilly and how we fell in love with our selected charity. How we decided we had to win The Great Yeti Challenge. How we became reluctant friends. The doctor's decision to put him on IR. The snowstorm. Calling it off.

Just like Charlotte and I planned, I make sure I'm firm about the timeline. That we started spending time together because it was mandated by the team. That there was nothing romantic until the snowstorm, which, as I made sure to remind him, was after Kane was on the IR. That it in no way impacted my coaching decisions at any time.

White asks questions, making sure he understands everything.

I do not bring up what happened in the hotel room because, as Charlotte pointed out numerous times, we were not in the same room. We were not on the phone. We just happened to be engaging in solo-sexual activities at the same time, which is not a punishable offense. And it's for the best: I do not need to discuss masturbation with my coworker unless absolutely necessary.

"I think I have everything I need," he announces finally. "Can you sign on the bottom of this form?"

I flex my fingers, forcing them to stop trembling before wrapping them around the grip of the pen. "There you go."

"I have to talk with Eli in HR before anything is certain, but for now, I need you to go home. You can stop by your office if you need to grab anything, but don't send any emails or talk to anyone other than to say hello. Eli and I will follow up with you in a couple of hours."

It went exactly as I've been trained—from the other side—to expect it would. Which means I know better than to expect anything but the worst.

Chapter 42

Beckett

I'm lying on my back, windshield wipering my knees back and forth slowly as I wait for my ten-thirty appointment, to be evaluated by the medical team, when my phone buzzes.

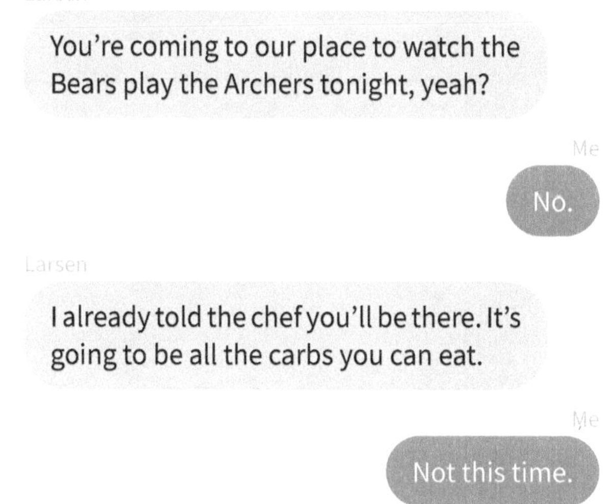

I set the phone back next to me and stand, dropping into a series of slow, easy side lunges and hip flexor stretches. The first few weeks after the season ends—especially if you don't make it deep into the playoffs—are all about rest and recovery.

So I'm resting. And recovering. And following the individualized programs the physical therapist, strength coaches, and doctors gave me. And it's been the longest three days of my life. Because it turns out, when you're prioritizing injury rehab, you spend *a lot* of time resting. And I hate resting.

My phone vibrates again, and I groan in anticipation of Larsen's comeback. This isn't what I need. Instead, though, it's someone much harder for me to ignore.

Li

> Come to the watch party tonight. I promise you can have the seat furthest from Larsen.

Me

> Can't tonight.

My fingers tap the screen, a guilty energy flowing through me at the white lie.

Li

> What could you possibly have going on? Lefevre said he saw you at the arena five minutes ago, so I know you're still in town.

> You know what? Don't answer that. I know it's nothing, and I don't want you to lie to me. Again.

> I'll see you at seven, or we're moving the party to your place.

I don't bother responding. Not that I need to. At least if I go to their place, I'll be able to leave when I want. If they show up at my place, they'll barge in and stay. And stay. And keep on staying, way past the time I want to go to bed.

Finally, Doctor Lowell calls me back for my end-of-season evaluation.

"Ready, Kane?"

No. Never ready for a physical evaluation.

"Of course!" I say instead, walking into the medical room, where Doctor Lowell and two trainers are waiting for me.

They have me run through a timeline of my hip symptoms, from onset to aggravating factors to when it improved. They map the various pain areas across my body, which extend beyond my injury to include my lower back and left shoulder. After talking for what feels like an hour, the doctor just typing away, documenting everything, we start the hands-on physical exam. I try not to cringe as they test my hip, though I can't help it when my groin strength is considerably worse than it should be.

It's another hour of tilting and turning, stretching, and engaging. They're trying to find out whether anything else hurts or if I've injured myself while trying to compensate for my hip, something that we'll need to take care of in the off-season.

Doctor Lowell doesn't say much, just tells me what to do before muttering, "Hmmm," and making a note. We move on to functional testing, a concussion and neurological screening, and bloodwork to inform my nutrition and supplement plan.

Just when I think we're done, Doctor Lowell announces, "We need to set up some imaging before you head out."

It's not what I want to hear, but I knew it was coming after my recent injury. So before I leave, I set up an appointment at their office in the city for X-rays, ultrasounds, and an MRI on my hip.

A few hours later, I'm freshly showered and riding the elevator to the party.

Larsen throws the door open after I knock, throwing his arms around me.

"Kane!" he practically yells in my face, and I catch the unmistakable odor of cheap beer.

I walk inside, a sinking feeling in my stomach as I take in the large group of people milling around the living space. There are at least five women squeezed into the kitchen, and the living and dining rooms are overflowing with people.

"Hey, Kane," Li hollers, waving aggressively as I attempt to navigate the crowded area to get to where he's seated on the couch.

"Li. What the fuck is this? I thought this was a casual hang."

"You've met Larsen; this is casual for him."

I groan, seriously considering covering my ears. This room is unbearably loud. "Why didn't he just do this at a bar?" I glance at the women in the kitchen before quickly looking away when I make eye contact with one of them. "Does he know how bad an idea it is to let random puck bunnies know where he lives?" I whisper.

Li laughs. "God, Maya would die if she knew you called her that."

"Maya?" I ask.

"My twin sister." He points his chin toward the petite woman with long, dark hair sitting on the countertop. "And Gloria might've been a puck bunny before she married J.D., but I've never worked up the nerve to ask either of them."

I know Gloria is J.D.'s wife, but as I've intentionally avoided spaces where I'd interact with family members, I can't be certain which of the other four women she is.

"The blonde is Gloria?" I guess as I take in the room through a whole new lens. It's not some random crowd. It's only players here. And apparently a few WAGs or family members.

"The brunette. Hair in the fishtail braid."

"The what?" I ask, unable to keep a hint of humor from my question.

"You know, the type of braid that looks like—Oh, fuck you," he says as I burst out laughing. "I have a *twin* sister. I didn't make it past middle school without learning all that stuff."

"This explains *a lot* about you," I tease, snagging the spot on the couch next to him when Herrera gets up.

Li runs a hand through his wavy black hair. "Probably more than I want it to." He pauses for a beat, his gaze locked on where his sister sits, all the women laughing at something Larsen says. "But I wouldn't give it up for the world. I learned how to be part of a team from the womb, and I'm not sure I'd be where I am today if I hadn't."

"Is she just in town visiting?" I ask, turning my attention to the television screen where the game is about to start.

Larsen interrupts Li, waving his hands in a shooing motion, "Make room for me, boys. This is my couch, after all."

I shove him as he starts to sit on my right thigh. "Don't some of the guys live in houses?" I ask. "Ones that could actually hold all of us comfortably?"

Larsen shakes his head. "No way. I begged J.D. to let me host this."

"Are you talking about me, Larsen?" J.D. calls from his spot near the food.

"Only to explain to Kane that, while your house could fit all of us, it wouldn't have had the special sauce that only a Matt Larsen party can."

"None of us want your special sauce, Larsen," Li's sister calls, and the room bursts into laughter as Larsen's cheeks turn a bright pink.

When the room quiets, we turn our attention to the Bears game, and I hear Larsen quietly ask Li, "It's a good party though, right?"

"Yeah, bud. It's a good party."

And it is. For as much as Larsen was talking up the carbs that would be available—and they definitely are in both solid and liquid form—there are a lot of other options too, which means I'll be able to eat and not feel like complete shit tomorrow.

After the first period, I make my way to the kitchen to grab the single beer I'll allow myself tonight. The women are all sitting on the counters now, every chair and stool in the place occupied by a Yeti.

"Beckett Kane, you're a hard man to pin down," Gloria says when I'm forced into the middle of their conversation to dig through the cooler.

I find the silver can I'm searching for before meeting her eyes. "I didn't realize you were looking for me."

She shrugs. "J.D. was excited when you joined the team. Just wanted to meet the man who had my husband's panties all in a twist."

"She's exaggerating!" J.D. yells, leaning away from the conversation he's having with Pike to focus on his wife. "No pantie-twisting was involved. Gloria just likes to know everything about everyone, so my vague answers about your life weren't up to her expectations."

"He told me you spent your free time sharpening your skates because you didn't trust the equipment managers enough to do it."

My eyebrows pull together in confusion. "What?"

J.D. throws up his hands. "I had to tell her *something*. She was trying to figure out, and I quote, 'the type of man you are,' so she can decide whether you need fed, fixed up, or friended."

"Gloria takes her role as team mom very seriously," Larsen adds, grabbing two beers out of the cooler without bothering to look at what kind they are.

Larsen sways slightly. "You ladies know I hid the desserts in the fridge, right?" I'm pretty sure it was supposed to be a whisper, but it did not land.

"Yes, Rookie," Maya replies. "You've told us five times now. You also got a ridiculous number of options. Who do you think is going to eat all those?"

"I didn't know what you'd want," Larsen explains as Maya completely ignores his puppy-dog eyes. "And you said you love dessert when we were all out at dinner the other night."

A lump forms in my throat when I realize I was invited to that dinner. And I chose not to go so I could watch game film at home instead. In April. When I don't have another game for six months.

"Of course I love dessert," Maya replies, as she and Larsen continue bickering about how ridiculous he is for filling his refrigerator with desserts instead of the drinks he has spread across the apartment in various coolers.

I make my way back to the living room, content to watch the game, occasionally commenting on plays, as the rest of the guys swirl around me, talking and laughing.

"You could do that once you're done, you know," Li suggests when I comment on the Bears switching their lines differently than they did against us.

"What? Coach?" I ask, my pulse picking up its pace at the mention of the word.

"I mean, sure," Li agrees. "But I meant the analysis. And the commentary. I bet one of the sports networks would pay you good money to look pretty and talk hockey all day."

I picture it. Spending my days watching film, talking to people who are just as obsessed with the sport as I am. It'd almost be like I was back—nope. Not going there. But it would be great.

"Maybe," I say, not willing to commit to anything other than hockey right now. But it is nice that, for the first time, I have something more than a black hole to look forward to once I'm done.

Chapter 43

Beckett

One of the things hockey analysts love to praise me for is my ability to wait. To hold the blue line.

But when I'm waiting to hear the results of the tests Doctor Lowell ran? Not patient at all. I'm so jumpy I'd certainly get beat wide if I were in a game right now. I've all but worn a path in front of his office when, finally, blessedly, the door swings open.

"You ready, Kane?" he asks.

No.

"Of course." I walk into his office, my stomach dropping as I notice we're the only two here. Almost like he told everyone else to clear out before he tells me my career is over.

Lowell doesn't sit right away. "Your hip flexor strain has healed," he reports. "Structurally, it looks fine now, after taking a few weeks off."

Relief sparks, warm and fast. Then it dies when he exhales, moving to the screen on the wall while tapping a few buttons on his tablet. Finally, an MRI image flares to life.

"But it was masking a more significant problem," Doctor Lowell explains, his voice too calm to be delivering that line.

He points to a shadowed area along the hip joint. The point where the ball and socket meet. "What we're seeing here is early degenerative change in the hip, as well as articular cartilage thinning here in the joint, along with an identifiable breakdown of the labrum."

My brain is trying to understand what I'm being told, what I'm seeing on the screen. Suddenly, the picture of my hip is replaced by three others. The only one I can truly identify anything in is the one of my pelvis, from the top of my hips to the middle of my thighs. He taps the left-most picture. "Do you see the thickness of this tendon?"

I squint at the black-and-white image. "Maybe?"

He taps his tablet again, pulling up another image below the one I'm currently looking at. "This is your left hip. Do you see the tendon there?"

"It's less bulky," I say, looking at the variance between the two, feeling like I've been assigned to spot the differences in a *Highlights* magazine. "And whiter?"

"Good catch. Yes. The bottom is a normal hockey player's. Yours? Well, that lighter signal is chronic tendinopathy."

I blink hard. "What?"

"Tendons should look dark and more uniform. The fact that yours has those white streaks suggests there is a degeneration of collagen fibers. So, it's wear. Not tear."

"What does it mean?" I ask, my heart braced for impact.

Doctor Lowell meets my gaze. "It means you can play next season."

Wait. I... Fuck. Yes.

"I can play?!" I want to celebrate. To jump up and dance. To find Finley and—tell her the good news that we can continue to be colleagues who never see each other.

The doctor nods. "There is no current medical reason to stop you. But the amount of pain you're in on a daily basis now? It's going to get worse. Likely a lot worse. And even once you're done playing, it's not going to get much better. This is chronic. It's not something that snaps. It's something that day by day stops tolerating load."

"But I *can* play?"

Lowell nods, turning to lean against the exam table so he's looking right at me. "At this point, I think the pain will be manageable with a concerted effort on the training and recovery side of things. And I don't believe it will have a big enough impact on your explosiveness or lateral movement to decrease your overall performance, particularly based on your position and how you play."

I can't believe what he's saying. After the buildup, the pictures and words like "chronic" being thrown around, there was a part of me that thought it was over. I might've even started coming to grips with it.

Wanting to make sure I'm understanding correctly, I ask again, "So I can play?"

"You can play, Kane. But as someone who sees a lot of retired athletes in my private practice, I have to warn you: you will feel the decision every moment for the rest of your life, moving forward." He says the last part slowly, like he wants to make sure I've heard it.

And I did.

I just can't seem to make myself care about future me with a bad hip trying to... I don't even know. What am I going to be doing five or ten years from now that's so important that I need to protect my hip? I'm financially stable. I've made a lot of money and have invested it well. Maybe I'll just buy a big, one-story house and sit around all day, watching hockey.

A small part of me wants to dig into how fucking depressing that sounds, but I push on through it. I'll find meaningful ways to live a fulfilling life after retirement another day.

"I understand," I say, knowing it's what he wants to hear.

We wrap up my visit, covering the basics of my new routine. He's already filled in the other members of the training staff on the findings. After I leave his office, I meet a rotating group of medical professionals to cover my new workout routine, the additional warm-up, stretching, and cooldown protocols to follow, and the pain management process.

Everyone has a plan. They also have a concerned look in their eyes.

Finally, I've met with everyone but Glenn to discuss my PT schedule. I have to wait for him to finish with another player before we can talk.

When Glenn's done with Volkov, we go through my updated plan, starting with the detailed breakdown of my recovery over the next four weeks and moving on to long-term care and a general overview of what the season will look like. When we reach the bottom of his checklist, Glenn sets down his tablet and meets my gaze. "You know we're all going to do our best to keep you healthy," he starts.

"I know," I reply quickly. "I appreciate you all for it."

And I do. The medical team is behind me. They've put in the work to make sure I can still play the game that means so much to me.

Glenn's sad smile doesn't match what I'd expect. "Look, I probably shouldn't say this, but I'm going to anyway. Because it's what I'd want someone to say to me. Even if I didn't want to hear it."

"Um, okay?" I'm not sure where he's going with this.

"Even though we'll do our best to make sure you're ready to play—because that's our job—it doesn't mean it's what we think you should do."

"What do you mean?" I feel like I've spent my whole day asking that same question.

He lets out a slow breath. "I can't speak for the rest of the medical staff, but if I were in your shoes, I would retire."

I lean back slightly, taken off guard by his blunt delivery. "Because you think I won't be able to play at the same level?" I ask.

He shakes his head. "Because every time you're on the ice, you're damaging your hip in a way that may never heal. Your labrum won't ever return to normal. Your tendons are already degenerating, and they're not going to recover under the strain of training. Even if you make it through the season, which isn't even close to a guarantee, you'll have fucked your hip up forever. And for what?"

I nod. "I see."

"No, it was a real question, Kane. For what? I truly don't understand. You're thirty-four. You've had an amazing career. You've won a championship." He rubs his eyes. "I get continuing to play until your body makes you stop. But your body is *screaming* at you to. I just don't get what you're getting out of one more season."

I understand where he's coming from, I really do. And even though I don't owe it to him, there's a feeling in the pit of my stomach that maybe I should tell him my truth.

Not that he needs a confession. We're not friends or teammates.

"I've never been team captain and won the Cup," I offer, hoping that will be enough to explain it.

He snorts, and then, with a glance at my face, widens his eyes. "Oh. Okay. I... Okay." There's a pause. "But to be clear, *that's* why you're about to endure years where you are in pain every time you move?"

The anger at his judgment hits me hard and fast, but I shove it deep. Who gives a fuck what Glenn thinks about my decision?

"Well, if that's all," I start, pushing back from the table.

Glenn stands, too, a look of horror on his face. "I apologize, Kane. That was out of line. Your reasons are your own; it's not my job to judge you for them. I promise, I'll make sure you're ready to go for next season. We'll get you exactly what you want."

I dip my chin in acknowledgement before leaving the room. I might not turn him in for the comment, but it doesn't mean I need to hang around and make him feel better for it, either.

He's right. It's not his place to judge my reasoning. And I will get exactly what I want: A championship as the team captain.

Except, as I think about it, I start to realize that maybe it isn't *exactly* what I want. Because I also want the woman I can't have. The one I still dream about most nights. And more than that, I want a life after hockey *with her*. I want to stay with her in a cabin and be able to go hiking with her without pain. I want to be able to throw our babies into the air and—

Oh, fuck. I shake my head.

I am not making a life-changing decision based on a future dark-haired baby with ice-blue eyes and a wide smile.

I'm *not*.

Chapter 44

Beckett

"Did you hear the news?" Larsen asks, barging into my apartment as soon as I open the door.

I follow as he strides past my kitchen and through the living room to stare out my windows. I'm too interested in what has him so worked up to acknowledge anything but a fleeting annoyance that he's in my apartment. "What news?"

Please don't let it be about my hip.

I haven't had enough time to process that information, let alone talk about it with a rookie who might have a decade left to play.

There's another knock, and Larsen flicks a hand at it like this is his apartment and I'm his personal door opener.

"Dude! You left me!" Li exclaims, glaring at his friend. "You literally ran to the elevator and hit the close door button."

Larsen shrugs his wide shoulders. "You can't expect me to wait after we just got news like that!"

"Do either of you children want to clue me in?" A nervous energy snaking up the back of my neck. I glance between the two men. Something doesn't feel right here.

"Coach is suspended!" The declaration bursts from Larsen like he just couldn't hold it in any longer, but then it sits, suspended in the middle of the room.

"Coach... Shaw?" I ask, naming the forwards coach, who I always felt was a little too sure of himself. I could see him getting up to some shady shit.

Li shakes his head, his eyes wide as he looks at me.

"Coach Blake," Larsen says, and it's like I'm hit square in the chest by a two-hundred-and-fifty-pound opponent moving at a full sprint.

They're both watching me, and I can't tell if it's because they expect me to already know, or if they suspect I had something to do with it.

"Why?" I ask, dropping onto the couch behind me as my legs all but give out.

Li starts doing something on his phone as Larsen turns back to the windows.

"They won't tell us!" Larsen complains. "I stopped by her office today, and Paige said she was out for the next few weeks. It was only after I asked about five hundred questions that she finally admitted that Coach was on temporary suspension while they investigated a self-reported possible conflict of interest."

Holy fucking shit.

That can't be...

Then one word hits me. Self-reported.

She did this.

But why?

"Here," Li says, sitting down next to me and holding his phone out. "The email from the team. You should've gotten it, too. And then here—" He swipes to a news app. "This is the official announcement they released about twenty minutes ago."

I skim through the public statement first, words like "tempo-rary administrative leave" and "self-reported potential conflict of interest," sticking out as I skim through the three sentences.

My insides are a mess of emotions. Is this about us? It can't be, right? Why the fuck would she tell them? We ended things so we could avoid this exact situation. If she gets fired, every-thing—the longing I've pushed aside, the evenings alone, the deep hunger for her that I tell myself isn't real—it's all been for nothing.

Or what if it's not about you? Maybe she's getting some spon-sorship deal that crossed a line. Maybe it's a super benign conflict, like the team wants to bring her dad on as an advisor or some-thing. Or maybe I'm not the first player she's slept with—I shake my head, dislodging the thought I know is a lie. I wasn't one of many. I—we—were something special. So, even though I'm not certain that I'm what she's confessing, I know there aren't loads of other men out there.

The comments section is already chaos, speculation ranging from basically nothing, to preferential treatment because of her father, to the league covering up the fact she's having a baby with one of her players.

I can't remember the last time I felt this nauseous.

Unable to stomach the toxic speculation, I pull up the email from White on my phone, handing Li's back to him. The mes-sage is essentially the same. Temporary leave. The organization is conducting a review. It's "procedural in nature."

I let out a choked laugh when I reach the line that says, "We ask that all players and staff refrain from speculation." Yeah. Like that will happen. Hockey players are bigger gossips than a women's coffee group.

"Don't laugh," Larsen demands, shaking his head. "This is a big deal. I mean, Coach is the squeakiest clean person I've ever met. She turned herself in, for fuck's sake. What if she leaves?

What if she gets fired? What if they get a new coach who trades me?" He drops his forehead to the window. "What if they bring up Shaw, and we have to listen to him showboat about how great he is every time he's on camera?"

"It's going to be okay," I say, not really believing it.

I hope this is just something minor. Because if she fucking told them about us... she'd *burn* for it.

An all-too-realistic image of Finley tied to a stake in the middle of the ice, while fans in Yeti jerseys throw fireballs at her, pops into my mind, and I almost sob.

She wouldn't put herself at risk like that, would she? *For you, she might* comes unbidden to my mind, but I know that can't be true. We could've stayed together and kept it secret until I retired, but she said no.

I clench my fists. She ended things with me to prevent this exact situation. So maybe this isn't about us. Maybe this isn't about what I pushed us toward. What she tried so hard to avoid, and I literally followed her into a snowstorm to convince her to do.

"This might be my fault." I clear my throat, the guilt sitting on my chest needing somewhere to go. I know I should be trying to pull those words back in, but—shit—I trust these two. Somewhere along the way, they became the first real friends I've had in a long time.

Larsen stops pacing. "What do you mean?"

"We... I..." I start, not quite sure how to say more without confessing Finley's secrets.

Li shakes his head at me. "You didn't."

Those two words were enough, it seems.

Larsen turns to me, getting right up in my face.

I relish the anger in his eyes. If this is about me, it's exactly what I deserve. "They told you not to! There was a clear, don't-fuck-Coach lecture given." His fist clenches, and I hope he hits me. Even if Finley's conflict of interest is something completely unrelated, it's still the least I deserve.

Instead, he stalks away.

"And she... agreed to sleep with you?" Li questions, his eyes narrowed, not out of anger, but in calculation. Like he's putting together the pieces Larsen is missing.

"Jesus Christ, are you asking if it was consensual, Li?" Larsen snarls, turning his ire on Li. "It's Kane, for fuck's sake. Of course he didn't fucking rape her."

I cringe. "Definitely did not—"

"Of course he didn't," Li jumps in, still calm, still rational. "I was just thinking. Coach doesn't sleep around. There's never anything in the media about her being spotted with different men." He looks at Larsen as he explains. "But she slept with Kane. Why?"

Jesus Christ. I regret opening my mouth.

"Because he's fucking stacked and has that silver-fox look about him."

I run my hands through my hair. "Am I going gray?" I know it's off topic, but I can't stop myself.

"No," Li replies, his attention still on Larsen.

Larsen, though, gives me a once-over, his lips pulled to the side in thought. "You just look like you're going to be a silver fox. I think it's the way your chin is, like, really defined."

"Can we please focus on the fact that our coach slept with her player and is now on leave?" Li asks. "Fuck. I thought there was no way this was a big deal. But, fuck. What if it is? If she told them about you, they're going to fire her. There's no way they won't."

I raise my palms in a placating gesture. "It might be okay."

Larsen starts pacing again. "Of course you would say that, asshole. That's probably what you told her, too, and look where we are now."

My pulse rises. "Jesus, Larsen." My gaze burns into his. "Do you think I somehow *conned* Finley Blake into sleeping with me? We both knew what we were doing."

Li cuts off Larsen's retort. "When was this?" He's clearly thinking much more logically than Larsen or me.

I lean back against the couch. "The night of the blizzard. She got locked out of her apartment and ended up staying here."

Li nods. "And it was only once?"

"It was only that one weekend," I hedge. Li subtly raises his eyebrows at the distinction but is fortunately classy enough not to act on it.

He runs his hand through his hair, his eyes darting back and forth. "But you were on IR that weekend, right?"

I nod. "Do you think it matters?"

"It definitely doesn't make it okay, but it helps." He walks toward the windows. "And you played less after it, not more. But that was the doctor's recommendation, not Coach's."

I'm not sure whether he's talking to himself or me at this point, but I let him keep going.

"But it's not going to matter. They'll never let her be your coach now that they know, and they can't trade you—that'd be so bad. You're the protected one here. They're going to have to fire her."

My throat closes. Hearing Li say it makes it real in a way it hasn't been so far. Finley and I were too wrapped up in each other to think logically. Larsen is a hothead. But, Li? Li is thinking it through. He evaluated it the same way the team will.

I drop my head into my hands, tugging at the ends of the strands.

"Unless..." He trails off, turning to look at me.

A faint glimmer of hope lights up my chest.

"Unless what?" I ask, my heartbeat increasing with anticipation.

"What's the plan?" Larsen asks.

Li taps a finger against his leg. "Unless you're not a Yeti any longer."

No. It's the only word in my frozen mind.

No, I can't. Or, maybe I should—for so many reasons—but I won't.

I can play through this injury for one more season. I can get that C on my jersey and fulfill the dream my dad had. The only thing I have left of the man.

I imagine skating onto the ice, hearing my name announced after the word captain. The crowd roaring with excitement.

A nameless, faceless man standing behind the bench, arms crossed.

And Finley, at home on her couch. No one next to her. Watching the game with her notebook open. Because she can't stop loving the game.

Even if it stopped loving her.

And my heart cracks open.

"But you can't retire for her," Larsen says.

"What do you mean?" I ask. "That's literally what Li just told me to do."

Larsen shakes his head. "One, we don't know whether you're what she turned herself in for, and two, Coach would never forgive you if you retired for her. If you're going to make that decision, you'd better be real damn sure you're doing it for yourself."

"I—" I pause. Would I make the same decision if Finley were completely out of the picture? If retiring didn't have the ability to save her career? The only way I'll ever know is if this blows over without HR ever contacting me to investigate.

"I'm starting to see a future for myself that isn't necessarily playing hockey," I admit, and it feels like a confession, one I need to be absolved from. "I know there is a chance that Finley isn't part of my future, but the future that I envision with her, I do want those things. Her, yes, obviously. But also, I want to be able to pick my kids up someday. To chase them around on the ice rink in our backyard. To go on hikes with my wife without needing to take a bottle of painkillers with me."

"Does that mean you want to retire?" Li asks.

"Would you?" I ask my friends.

Li purses his lips. "Yeah. I would. When my body tells me I'm done, I'm going to be done. I hope it's in a decade, but even if it's tomorrow, I've had a damn good run, doing something I love as a career."

"I have had quite the run," I agree.

"And you're getting old as fuck," Larsen chimes in, a smirk flashing across his face.

"There is that."

"Okay," Li says, heading toward the door. "You need to think about it. Like, really think about it. And we'll come back to-morrow and make a plan in case you are the reason she con-fessed. If you get a call from anyone on the HR team, just let it go to voicemail, and call them back tomorrow. And even if you don't decide to retire, well, maybe there's some other way we can make this okay... if it comes to that."

I watch them leave before dropping my head into my hands.

Do I want to retire? *No.* I love this game, and I love playing it.

But is it time? With every passing day, every painful step, it's looking more and more like the answer might be yes. Like I need to let go of the dream I've been chasing for my parents and focus on a new dream—one that's mine. One that doesn't require me to sacrifice my health for my own happiness.

Chapter 45

Finley

"Thanks for coming in today, Finley," White says from across the conference table.

Eli, the head of HR, is sitting at the top of the table, the only other person in the room.

"After a thorough investigation," White starts, and I force my expression into neutrality as I listen to him say the words from the HR script. This is it. This is the end of my career.

The hollow ache in my chest may never go away, but after spending two weeks at a cabin in the woods doing nothing but hiking and putting together puzzles, I've accepted my fate.

White continues, "And in light of new information, we found that you violated clause 4.2 in the Yeti handbook, by engaging in a romantic or sexual relationship with a player."

I swallow hard. I knew it was coming, but hearing it from the mouth of a person I have so much respect for burns.

White's gaze flashes to mine briefly before going back to the paper in front of him. This is the harsh reality of a termination—it has to be by the book. "There is no way around the fact that you engaged in a relationship with someone with whom you had power over. The investigation, however, showed that the relationship had no impact on playing time or roster decisions, specifically since the player was on IR and not participating in games during the time of the relationship. There is no evidence of favoritism or harm to the team."

"What are you saying?" I ask, looking between the two men, when he stops reading.

Eli takes a deep breath. "I want to be very clear: what you did was a violation of policy, and we are in no way condoning your actions. However, because the relationship did not compromise competitive integrity or workplace authority, we have decided not to enact the recommended punishment of termination. Instead, you will have a formal, written reprimand in your personnel file. You will have four weeks' unpaid suspension. As a condition of your return, you will have completed mandatory ethics retraining. You are on probation for the next twelve months."

I can't believe what I'm hearing.

"I'm... not fired?" I ask.

White shakes his head. "No. But you are in very big trouble, Coach Blake, and on very thin ice."

"Of course, sir," I say, biting the inside of my cheek.

"Oh, and you, Mr. Kane, and anyone else either of you has told about this will be expected to sign NDAs. You will make no public statements about your administrative leave or your suspension."

I rub the area just below my collarbone. The public speculation has to be out of control by now. A suspension will only make it worse.

As excited as I am to still have the job of my dreams, I don't know what to do with the fact I've lost the trust of everyone here.

We wrap up the meeting, signing documents and going through all the terms of my suspension. Finally, Eli says we're done with everything and leaves me alone with White.

"I am sorry," I apologize, hoping he understands just how much I mean it.

He nods, but I can tell from the look on his face how disappointed in me he is. "I know. Unfortunately, it takes a long time to earn back trust after something like this. We'll get there—we all will—but it's going to take some work. But no one can question whether you really believe in a culture of accountability now. Most people would've just hidden this under the rug."

"I know." My gaze locks on his. "I know."

As I start to leave, something White said at the beginning of the conversation flits back into my awareness. "What was the new information?" I ask, turning back to White.

"What?"

"At the beginning of the meeting, you said in light of new information. What was it?"

Uncertainty flickers behind his eyes. "Kane retired."

"What?" My heart drops to my toes. "No. You told him no, right?"

White shrugs. "I told him it might be for nothing. That it would in no way guarantee you wouldn't be fired. He knew," White says, standing from his chair. "I told him not to. He said it wasn't about this."

"What was it about, then?" I ask.

White stops next to me. "You'll have to ask him that. And now that it's not a fucking dumb mistake for you to be with him, I can tell you: I hope it works out for you two."

"I—Thank you. We're not still together, though."

White nods. "I know. We also confirmed that. Trust me. We looked into *everything*. Now, if you'll excuse me, I have a shitstorm to clean up, and I just lost my head coach for the next four weeks."

I walk out of the meeting in a daze. Beckett retired. Even though they told him it wouldn't save my job. It's enough to keep me from focusing on anything as I walk home: the sidewalk twisting by in a blur of sunshine and dogs on leashes. I know I should turn do-not-disturb off my phone and start interacting with the real world again, but I'm not ready yet.

I've talked to Charlotte, but she's been annoyingly optimistic about the whole thing, and positive thinking was not the point of my time in the cabin. The separation from my daily life was to come to terms with the fact that the life I thought I was going to live was gone. I didn't cry. I didn't mope. I walked. And I planned. And I did puzzles.

And maybe Charlotte was right. It didn't end up as bad as I thought.

My dad, well, I've avoided him like the plague. Though there were a few nights in the cabin when I would spiral and listen to the voicemail he left, in which he calmly walked me through all the reasons I'd ruined my entire life with one mistake. He doesn't know what the mistake was, but it doesn't matter.

Gray concrete shifts to the tiled floor of my apartment building, as I mentally shove my dad out of my mind.

I did make a mistake—and a really fucking big one—but no one is perfect all the time. Not even me. No matter how hard I try.

"Hey," a deep voice says from down the hall, pulling me from the recesses of my mind.

"Kane." My eyes meet his. I want to run and jump into his arms. To beg him to forgive me. I was never supposed to sacrifice him.

The sight of him standing in his doorway, a black T-shirt pulling across his chest, is like a balm on my burning soul. My gaze tracks his Adam's apple as he swallows hard.

"Did it... Are you still... What happened?" he asks. His hands twitch by his side, curling into fists.

And I wonder whether it's a reflection of the same tension running through me. The one that desperately wants me to run to him. The same one that's holding me back.

Not sure how to bypass the cracked earth that's spread wide between us.

"Fin?" he asks.

"I'm on unpaid suspension for four weeks," I say, the tears I've been holding at bay all day finding their way to my eyes.

He closes his eyes, letting out a sigh. "Oh, thank God. They said it wouldn't likely matter."

Suddenly, I'm standing right in front of him, between our two apartments. I glare up at him, the tightness in my scowl pulling me back into my body. "You shouldn't have done that! I was the one who crossed a line. I was the one who needed to pay for my mistake."

I bang his chest with my fist, and it lets out just enough of the swirling desolation in my chest that I do it again. And again. And again.

My fists crash into him as the tears pour from my eyes.

When I start to slow, he wraps his arms around my back, pulling me into him.

I lean my forehead against his chest. "Why would you do that?"

"Because I love you."

That's not...

I mean...

Could it be...

Do I...?

Yes.

As much as I don't want to, it's as inevitable as the puck dropping at the beginning of a game.

I jerk my gaze to his. "You... what? You can't."

He engulfs my hands with his, pulling me flush against him. His lips are millimeters from mine, his breath a warm caress as he says, "In fact, I can." He presses a light kiss to the corner of my mouth. "Which is for the best, since I do."

I shake my head. "That's not what I meant. You can't retire for me."

His thumb brushes over mine as he pulls away a little. "I didn't. I mean, it certainly was a factor, but—" He cuts off, sighing.

"What?" My air supply is running short, as if my nervous system is suddenly unable to keep up with the roller coaster that is my day.

He steps away slightly, a hint of something like guilt flitting across his face. "I found out right before the announcement that it was possible I wasn't going to be able to play next season, anyway. Or that I might seriously hurt my hip long-term if I did play." His thumb returns to stroking the side of mine.

"So you didn't retire in a romantic but ultimately ridiculous attempt to save my career?" I ask, feeling like I can breathe properly since the first time I heard Kane wasn't planning to play next season.

He shakes his head. "As much as I would love to tell you I sacrificed myself for you to have a chance at happiness, it didn't exactly go that way. And since I hadn't decided what I was going to do when I heard you'd turned yourself in—something I have a lot of thoughts about, by the way—I can't say for sure what I would've done."

The smile that breaks out across my face isn't one I can contain. "I love you, Beckett Kane."

His lips pull into a crooked, confused smile. "You what?"

"Love you," I repeat. Because it's true. Even if he's not sure whether he's the type of man to give up his dreams for a woman. Or maybe even more so because of that.

"How is that possibly your response to hearing I didn't retire for you?" he asks. "Do you have a weird kink for men with hips far worse than they should be at their age?"

Realizing we're talking about love and kinks in the middle of our apartment building's hallway, I grab his hand and pull him into my place.

Beckett laughs, following me. "You do, don't you?!"

"Hard to say." I push him against the closed door. "I can *definitely* confirm I have a thing for one guy with old-man hips."

He twists his hand in the bottom of my shirt. "Oh yeah?"

I kiss him deeply, his lips eagerly engaging mine in a dance that feels like fireworks and coming home.

He pulls me into him, his erection pressing into my stomach in a way that makes it impossible for me to keep in the low moan building in my throat.

"You want to know the best part?" I ask when we finally pull apart, my chest heaving.

"It's not that you get to keep your job?" he says on a disbelieving laugh.

I tilt my head back and forth. "Well, maybe, but I was thinking the fact that I happen to have a nice little vacation planned for the next four weeks."

He chuckles. "Is that what they're calling it these days?"

I bite my bottom lip and nod. "Want to spend it with me?"

"You couldn't stop me even if you tried."

Chapter 46

Beckett

"Elsie!" Larsen yells as he tries to pull Finley into a bear hug. She stiff-arms him to the side of the face, laughing as he dodges out of the way and tries again.

"Dude," Li groans.

"What?" Larsen asks. "I'm just excited she didn't get fired."

"Yeah, but I don't think you should hug her... like ever. It's how we got into this mess."

I meet Finley's eyes and want to laugh at the mirth there.

Larsen shakes his head. "We did not get into this mess from hugging. I'm pretty sure they were fu—"

His eyes go wide as my fist makes contact with his stomach. "I think that's enough of that. Don't touch Finley."

"Finley?!" Larsen says, his gaze darting between her face and mine.

Coach shakes her head. "Laps, Larsen."

"It's break!"

"You can't call me Finley. You can call me Coach Blake."

"Or..." Larsen leads.

"Coach Blake," she deadpans, her humor hidden where only I can see it.

"Come on! I don't think you understand how instrumental Li and I were in making sure you didn't get fired."

Li sighs, like he's exhausted by Larsen's existence. Which I understand. "I do not want to be included in this."

"But you were such an important part of the team," Larsen tells Li. "He was, Coach. Really."

Finley folds her arms, amusement tugging at the corner of her lips, even as she tries to smother it. It's the kind of expression that makes my brain short-circuit. Especially when I remember that I'm allowed to like it now.

"How did you even know I was back?" she asks.

Oh, fuck.

"Kane texted me," Larsen boasts, the look on his face suggesting Finley might be an idiot for not putting that together.

"Kane... texted you?"

"Yeah. He texted Li and me as soon as he found out you weren't getting fired. We're friends like that."

"Not right away," I tell Finley, giving her a wink. God forbid she thinks I was texting Larsen while kissing her senseless on the couch.

"Holy fuck! Did you just see that, Li? Did you? He winked at her! And he still has his balls. Holy shit. Honestly, I still wasn't completely sure any of this was real. I thought Kane might've been making it all up just to fuck with me. But it's real!"

I look at Finley. "Is it, though?"

"Seems pretty far-fetched. Me? Date a player? Terrible decision."

"Haha," Larsen huffed as Li laughs next to him. "I know it's real."

"Okay." I drag the word out like I'm unconvinced.

"Sure," Finley replies, her neutral expression matching mine.

"I'm regretting all the exclamation points I used when I told the team chat that you weren't fired. I want to take them back. You don't deserve all of them. One at most. Okay, maybe two."

Finley rubs her forehead. "Why are you texting the group chat about this, Larsen?"

"Because everyone was concerned that you were going to get fired. I let them know you weren't. You know, those guys would literally die for you. I mean, did you know they're the ones who told White to hire you? Like staged a coup or something."

"Larsen!" Li groans, trying to cut his friend off.

"They, what?" Finley asks.

"Don't really know," Larsen muses. "Wasn't here. But Li was."

Li tilts his head back, looking at the ceiling like it might offer him guidance. Finally, he says, "We just had a talk with White, put our names behind yours when they were deciding who to hire. They would've hired you even if we hadn't said anything, but we heard what people were saying about men not wanting to be coached by a female. And, well, we wanted to make sure we were clear that it wasn't true. You were the best. You made us better. That's all we said."

"That's..." Finley trails off, the indent in her right cheek appearing as she fights to keep her emotions from her face. But I can see them even if Li and Larsen can't. Every ounce of appreciation and love, and a little guilt, too. They're all there, pooling in her eyes.

"Don't mention it," Li warns. "Literally. The guys will make Larsen sleep on the ice or something if they hear he told you."

Larsen runs his hand through his hair, a sheepish look on his face. "It's just such a nice thing. I don't know why I can't tell her."

"Please pretend you understand the concept of a secret," Li urges.

"I do," Larsen argues. "I just think it's a dumb secret. I would want to know if the team said nice things about me."

"They didn't," I say, choosing to jump in.

"Never," Li agrees.

Finley lets out a sound that's half laugh, half exhale, like she's holding on to her composure by a thread.

"You guys are bullies; you know that, right?" Larsen accuses, pointing at each of us in turn.

Li sighs. "I regret everything."

"That's better."

"No, that's not..." Li trails off, apparently giving up on correcting Larsen. "You know what? I think it's time to go. Let's text Herrera and see if he wants to come play that new racing game."

"Yes!" Larsen agrees. "Oo. Let's just invite everyone over. You guys in?" he asks us.

"No," Finley answers, though she smiles at the end.

"Ah, come on!"

"Maybe next time, Larsen," I offer.

They disappear out the door, Larsen's voice echoing, loud as ever as he says, "I'm telling the group chat she almost cried. It's important. Character development."

"Larsen," Li groans, "I swear to God—"

Their voices fade, and suddenly it's just us again, in the quiet.

"I can't believe they did that," she admits.

"They knew you were the best option."

She swallows, and her gaze drops for a second, right to my chest, like she's wondering whether she can ask for a hug or not.

I pull her into me, tucking her head under my chin.

"I don't want them thinking I need—" she murmurs into my chest.

"Them to fight your battles," I cut in gently. "I know."

"I don't."

"They weren't doing it for you, Fin. They were doing it for themselves."

"I hope I didn't let them down."

"They'll get over it," I say. "Culture of accountability, and all that."

"What a terrible idea, in hindsight," she sighs.

"Nah." I lean down to kiss her forehead. "I think it's all going to turn out perfect."

Chapter 47

Beckett

"Are you ready?" I ask, pulling a suit jacket over my shoulders and taking one final look in the mirror.

"Ready," Finley replies as she walks into the room, still fastening her earring as she moves.

She looks amazing, in a black dress that hugs her curves and heels. Her dark hair is down, the curls she's been working on swaying slightly.

"Never mind," I say, caging her between me and the wall in our upmarket Parisian hotel room, "let's just stay here. You look far too good to go out."

It was the tenth day of Finley's suspension when I suggested we go literally anywhere people wouldn't recognize us.

For the first time in our lives, we both have unlimited free time. After spending eight days barely leaving my bedroom, we finally came down from the high of being together enough to realize that we needed to do something other than have sex.

Not that I was complaining.

And based on the way she woke me up with her mouth every morning, I don't think she was, either. But I wanted to take her on dates. To buy her dinner. To go to the movies. And Denver isn't exactly a safe place for that at the moment. Hell, the United States and Canada were both out, considering how recognizable she is.

But Paris? Well, it felt like it'd be a lot easier for us to go unnoticed here.

Plus, it was the most romantic place I could think of.

And since I tell Finley just how hard and fast I've fallen in love with her at least once a day, it felt fitting for our vacation. Even if Finley feels guilty about taking a vacation when she should be enduring her suspension.

Fortunately for her, I disagree.

So we booked our flights two days ago. And now, here we are with two weeks left before we need to return to Denver.

I lean down, brushing a kiss against her lips that deepens into something more.

When we finally pull apart, Finley wipes at the edges of my lips with her thumb. "My lipstick looks good on you."

"It'd look even better on my dick," I whisper in her ear, my voice teasing.

She quirks her lips to the side. "Only one way to find out, I suppose."

"We'll be late for dinner," I force myself to remind her, and it takes a Herculean effort to get the words out as she starts to drop to her knees in front of me.

She pauses, her hand on my zipper as she thinks about it. After a moment, she says, "We can be late."

"Fuck, yes, we can."

She looks up at me, her tongue millimeters from the head of my cock, and warns, "Just don't fuck up my hair."

"Yes, Queenie." I love this version of Finley. The one who is working on being okay with being late every once in a while, but still commands a room like a fucking drill sergeant.

She licks the tip of my dick before pulling me into the warm tunnel of her mouth. My hips jerk forward, and I have to fist my hands next to me to avoid gripping her head to take control.

Working me with her mouth and hand, I'm right on the edge quickly. It's fucking incredible how my body responds to this woman.

"Need to be inside you," I say, pulling her to her feet. I slide her dress over her hips and lift her up, spinning us so her back is against the wall. I shove her panties to the side, groaning when I feel how wet she is for me.

"Fucking love you," I murmur as I slowly push inside.

Finley's eyes flutter closed as I pick up my tempo, but she still manages to reply, "Love you, too."

As I make love to the most amazing woman against a wall in a Paris hotel room, I can't help but think about how lucky I am to have ended up here. How grateful I am that I realized the team doc was right: I would feel the decision to keep playing for the rest of my life.

But not because of my hip—because of Finley.

And that wasn't a hurt I was willing to try to play through.

Five minutes later, I slowly lower Finley onto her post-orgasm jelly legs. After grabbing a washcloth, I clean her quickly and tuck myself back in my pants before pulling her toward the door. "Dinner awaits."

We're almost to the restaurant when Finley's phone rings. Her dad's name flashes across the screen. When she goes to ignore it, I pull her to a stop. She's been avoiding his calls since the day the news of her suspension broke, and I can tell how much it's wearing on her.

"You can talk to him," I say.

She slips the phone into her purse. "He's just going to lecture me."

"You don't know that."

She laughs, a joyless imitation of her usual chuckle. "Right."

I squeeze her hand. "I don't care whether you talk to him or not. It just seems like *you* care."

Her right cheek pulls in slightly as she thinks it over. "Maybe."

We take a few more steps before she announces, "I'll call him after dinner."

"Sounds great."

As we walk in the warm June night, the lights of Paris glowing gold around us, I feel content in a way I never did before I stopped chasing my parents' dream for me and started chasing my dream woman.

"This is already the best decision I've ever made," I say.

"Coming to Paris with your favorite person?" she asks.

I bump my shoulder into hers. "You're assuming that's you?"

She leans into me, and I drop her hand to wrap my arm around her shoulders. "Yep."

"Was it the two-week trip to Paris?"

She laughs. "I was thinking the way you referred to me as your girlfriend when we checked in."

I raise my eyebrow as I pull her to another stop. "Wait, have you been functioning under the assumption that you're *not* my girlfriend? I know we're doing things a little out of order, but I assume the woman I love and sleep with every night falls into that category without us having that talk."

"I just like hearing it," she admits, pressing onto her toes to place a gentle kiss on my mouth.

"Then come on, girlfriend. Dinner awaits."

We make it to the restaurant later than predicted, but they still let us in. Candlelight flickers across white tablecloths, and music plays softly in the background as we're led to a secluded table. Though requesting the table in the back was likely un-necessary. No one points. No one stares. I'm not a professional athlete; she isn't Coach Blake. No microscopes, no adoring fans. Just Beckett and Finley.

I order a bottle of wine, and by the time we order, we've had just enough to attempt the French pronunciations, clearly butchering them by the look on the waiter's face.

When the man leaves, Finley starts laughing so hard she has to wipe her eyes.

"I needed this," she admits once she's recovered.

I reach across the table and lace my fingers through hers. "I needed you."

Her phone vibrates in her purse, the sound barely audible over the hum of the conversation. She stiffens a little, though she doesn't reach for her bag.

"You still planning to call him after?" I ask.

She nods. "Yeah. I am."

"Proud of you."

Her lips twitch. "I don't think I've ever had someone tell me they were proud of me so freely."

"You? *The* most badass woman I've ever met?"

She shakes her head. "I don't deserve that moniker. I'm scared of answering a call from my own dad."

"Doesn't change what I said."

"But you're right. I do need to speak to him."

That's Finley. Brave, even when it costs her something.

Dinner is slow and perfect. We talk about what we'll do when we get back. Who she hopes White trades for in the off-season. Where I'm going to live once I move out of the Yeti's apartment—I laughed when she mentioned the apartment across from Larsen is available to rent.

When she asks me what I'm planning to do when we get back, I consider deflecting. I know what I wanted to do for so long that I feel adrift right now. But I do have a few feelers out with old friends who have moved on but remained in the sports world. So I tell her about the most exciting one, an opportunity to be a hockey analyst, and in classic Finley form, she dives into the pros and cons without a second thought.

We walk back toward the hotel with the Eiffel Tower glowing in the distance. When her phone rings for the third time, Finley stops beneath a streetlamp to answer it.

"I'll be right back," she says.

"I'll be right here."

She steps a few paces away, straightening her spine, like she's about to be interviewed. I watch her chew the inside of her cheek, the only outward sign that she's nervous. The woman, who coaches a professional hockey team, is now standing on a sidewalk trying to work up the courage to talk to her own dad.

Whatever happens in that conversation, I already know one thing: even if they decide to cut ties—which I really hope they don't—she'll always have me.

And maybe a dark-haired, blue-eyed kid or two to keep us company.

Chapter 48

Finley

"You're here!" Callan yells as we walk into his backyard for his Labor Day party. The man is slightly tipsy already, and I can't help but laugh at his enthusiastic welcome.

Beckett is disappointed we can't go to the party Larsen and Li invited him to—apparently, the three of them became besties at some point while scheming how to save my job—but my suspension only ended a few months ago, and going to a players' party at a downtown bar felt like it might be flirting with my probation.

And, of course, Beckett would hear none of it when I suggested we split up for the night.

Luckily, Callan can provide the same golden-retriever energy Beckett secretly loves about Larsen.

"Of course we are," I say, returning Callan's hug somewhat stiffly.

"How was your trip to visit Finley's dad?" Callan asks. Before Beckett started his new job a few weeks ago, he was down for just about anything to keep himself entertained, and Callan's group of current and retired pro athletes became an integral part of that.

I think he was getting coffee with people more than once a day at one point.

"Great," Beckett replies, wrapping an arm around my shoulders. Callan assured us he was only inviting people he trusts completely, but even months later, it's still weird socializing with people we know professionally and being open about our relationship.

In fact, it's a bit surreal to think of the woman I was when I first met Callan. Beckett and I were still in full denial about what these feelings were between us. I was working so hard to control everything happening around me—fighting the impossible fight toward perfection.

"I wasn't asking you, Kane." Callan shoots him a mock glare. "It's not even vacation for you. It's just your life when you're retired."

My gaze meets Beckett's, and he winks. "Not retired anymore, unfortunately. I'm starting to miss being unemployed."

I miss him being around all the time, too, but I'm glad he found something he's excited about. Not all his options were in Denver, but I'm still secretly pleased he was hired by Colorado Sports Network to be part of the regional broadcast team for the Yeti. Even though it meant we had to sign a variety of relationship disclosure forms, and he's not allowed to comment on my coaching decisions. Fortunately, his co-analyst was happy to take on that role.

It was all a bit uncomfortable, especially knowing that the team at CSN was silently putting all the pieces around my suspension together.

He smiles down at me, pulling me closer as we chat with Callan and one of his teammates, who arrives after us.

My phone vibrates in my hand, and when I see my dad's name, I automatically start to answer it. Then, with a look at all the fun happening around me, I hit decline.

As much as I love my dad, my conversation with Charlotte made me reevaluate my relationship with him. After a very poorly handled call in Paris, where I almost cried on a public sidewalk, I started seeing an online therapist who is helping me understand that my worth as a human and daughter can't be solely centered on how well I perform at work. Which means, I've had to learn to enforce boundaries with him, including not dropping everything to answer his calls.

But we're both working on it. Our first call, when I refused to talk about anything related to hockey, was the most awkward thing I've ever been a part of: there isn't much we have in common without dissecting my games, so there were a lot of pauses. But they've gotten better since then.

I even found out he's been dating a woman for almost a year now and never thought to mention it.

Though I didn't ask.

It's another uncomfortable truth I've been forced to face—as much as I want to blame my dad for making me feel like I had to be perfect to be loved, *I* helped build that narrative. Fortunately, I'm starting to realize I don't have to sacrifice who I am to be accepted by those who care about me.

Beckett, however much he supports me in my decisions, talked hockey exclusively with my dad when we visited last weekend. He picked my dad's brain about off-season trades and what each team needs to do in order to be in the running for the Cup next year.

Not joining in may have been harder than not making it to the playoffs this year.

"How is the hockey analyst gig going?" Callan asks.

"So good," Beckett replies.

The man truly loves his job. Not that it's surprising. It's not that different than what we were doing when we first started spending time together: late nights watching hockey film.

I was worried Beckett wouldn't find something to replace hockey, or that he'd come to resent the role I played in his decision to retire, but I don't think that's the case. He doesn't seem to have lost anything. He actually seems like he gained something even better.

And I'm not just talking about us.

We talk with Callan and his teammate for a while before Beckett excuses himself, leaving me to argue with the Stallions' kicker about the reasons our arena needs to be upgraded before their stadium. I just about have him convinced when Beckett calls to me from next to a bag board.

"Fin! Come play!"

I say my goodbyes before heading his way. "I call being on Charlotte's team," I shout when I see who he's standing next to, surprised she came to Callan's party. "She's way too competitive for me."

"Oo, I'm out, then," Sage Sinclair says, giving Charlotte a quick hug. "You know I love you, but tonight is my only night off this week. I do not need competitive cornhole in my life."

"I'll play against Princess." Callan takes a long drink from his beer.

"Don't call me Princess, ball boy," Charlotte snaps.

Beckett meets my eyes, and we both try not to laugh. I want to defend her, but Charlotte looks exactly like an American princess tonight, in white slacks, blue-and-white-striped sweater, and red loafers. She's even wearing a strand of pearls.

As the two of them bicker, I stand next to Beckett, realizing just how relaxed I am. I'm not scanning to make sure everything is where it's supposed to be or preparing for every outcome.

"Girls versus boys?" I ask, confirming he's okay with me being on Charlotte's team.

"Sure," he agrees. "What are we playing for?"

"How about a kiss?"

He taps his lip as if thinking deeply. "How about a skate date before you come home tomorrow night?"

As happy as he is with the next chapter of his life, Beckett does miss skating and playing hockey. Even though he's trying to take it easy on his hip, he still likes to come to the practice facility and skate with me every once in a while.

"Will you help me with my slap shot?" I ask, smiling at the memory from so many years ago.

"Always," he replies, pulling me into him to kiss me. "But this time, no pads. I want to be able to feel you up when I show you how to hold a hockey stick."

I shove him away, laughing.

From a slap shot worth the coach's attention in high school to the streets of Paris, Beckett Kane has always made me feel seen.

And there's nothing more I could ask from the man I love.

Chapter 49

Epilogue

BECKETT – FOUR YEARS LATER

"Thanks for joining us in the studio today, Coach Blake," I say once the camera is rolling.

"Thanks for having me, *Mr.* Blake."

The glint in my wife's eyes is something I will never get tired of. I've never been happier than the day she agreed to marry me, except for maybe the day we finally got to say I do.

"We're still workshopping that name," I add to the camera.

Finley shakes her head, that teasing look still on her face. "I think it suits you."

I grin at my wife, hopefully reminding her that this is a big deal for me. My first full segment for a national sports network. Normally, I'm just breaking down the plays from the high-tech setup in our house and chiming in when they need a former player's perspective.

I clear my throat before asking, "You're about to start your fifth season as head coach with the Denver Yeti. I assume all our viewers watching know that I have a bit of a bias toward the Yeti, but for those of you who don't, I played with the Yeti during my last season. So, a lot of bias, some may say."

"If by bias you mean you are twice as hard during your analysis of us, I completely agree," Finley replies.

She's eased up a lot when it comes to her professional image in the past few years. Sure, she still wears her full-black pantsuits with the button-up white shirts at games, still has that little Denver Yeti pin on, and still pulls her hair up in her ponytail so tight that it gives her a headache. But off the ice, she's a little less worried about what the internet is saying about her. The Yeti's PR department is finally easing back from their rigid stance on never showing she's a woman, too.

I smile in the way I know makes her wish she could still make me skate sprints. "I just want to make sure that the audience doesn't think I'm giving you preferential treatment."

"You would never. Though, let's not forget the fact that, throughout the course of your career, you played with half the men that you're analyzing. And if we're going to start claiming favoritism, I don't think I've heard you say one bad thing about Larsen."

"This interview isn't supposed to be about me, Finley."

She shrugs. "I thought you preferred it when everything was about you."

I level my wife with a glare, looking over her shoulder to see the studio crew laughing behind us.

"Abel." I call out to my coworker. "Come out here and join us. I think we need a third party."

Abel walks out on screen, just like we had planned. He sits in the chair next to mine, so we're both looking across at Finley, who sits completely composed in yet another black pantsuit. Her hair is down, curled lightly, begging me to wrap it around my fist when we get back to our hotel.

"So," Abel starts, "you two got hitched this off-season, I hear?"

"We sure did," I agree.

"A small wedding up in the Colorado mountains," Finley adds.

"Small? You didn't invite the team?" Abel asks, as if he weren't there, too. As if he didn't do shots with Larsen and then proclaim it as the best night of his life.

I look at him in mock horror. "Of course they were there! They're her team. They're basically family."

Finley looks at Abel like they're co-conspirators. "They're coworkers... but Beckett talked me into it... eventually."

Abel nods solemnly. "Clearly a mistake. Can we expect such terrible decision-making from you this season with the Yeti?"

"While Beckett had a say in our wedding, he, fortunately, doesn't hold any weight when it comes to coaching the Yeti," Finley answers, and I smile. It's one of the many reasons we're putting together this segment right now. There's a not-so-small subset of hockey fans who like to think I'm calling the shots, and Finley is just a puppet. The people who matter know it's not true—there's a reason Denver had her sign a five-year contract. But we're putting that rumor to bed now, anyway. While also capitalizing on the Yeti's championship win to expand my career into more than just being a studio analyst.

"Okay, okay," I say. "I think our viewers want to hear what the Yeti have planned for this upcoming season. What changes are you hoping to make off-season to make sure you're holding the Cup above your heads come June?"

"You know there's nothing I like talking about more than Yeti hockey," Finley replies before leaning forward slightly and getting into it.

She talks about the off-season work the men are doing, the strategy the team has for the next year, and what she thinks their chances are of winning another championship. She's perfect and professional, and I've never loved her more.

And that night, when we both stumble into our hotel room in New York, I pull her into my arms, giving her a long kiss.

"You did amazing today," I whisper against her warm lips.

"No fair, taking advantage of my praise kink, Beckett," she groans, shoving lightly against my chest.

"I thought you said a little praise would get me anywhere."

She sighs, slipping out of her shoes while still holding on to me. "It will, but it's still not fair."

I lean down, capturing her lips with mine. When I finally come up for breath, I murmur, "You did so well today, Mrs. Kane."

She's not changing her last name, but she's still mine.

"I think it's the start of something big for you, Mr. Coach Blake."

"Even if it's not, I can't think of anything I'd rather do than sit around and talk hockey with you. Five years later, it's still my favorite thing to do."

"You're still my favorite thing to do," she flirts, a crooked tilt to her smile.

"Then what are we doing just standing here?" I ask, unbuttoning my pants and pulling off my shirt.

"Now that's the hustle I like to see." She follows suit, stripping to just her bra and underwear.

I pull her against me, my hands finding their home on her hips as I kiss her deeply. When she starts to rock against me, I slide one hand lower, running a finger over her center through her underwear.

"You're so ready for me. I'm going to make you feel so fucking good."

"It's always good with you." The last word comes out as a sigh as I bend down and take her hard nipple into my mouth.

I give it all the attention she deserves, licking and lapping as if my life depends on it. "You're so beautiful. So amazing. I could do this all day," I tell her, moving my attention from her breasts to her throat.

"I need you," she whispers, as close to whining as Finley ever gets. "Right now, Beckett."

I lift her up, and she pulls my cock free. I'll never get used to the feeling of her fingers wrapped around me.

"Fuck," I half grunt, half moan, as I reach between us, sliding her black underwear out of the way as I guide her onto my dick.

When I'm fully inside her, I stop, taking a moment to collect myself. To appreciate the fact that I can make love to my wife anytime I want.

That we got to the point where we could be together.

Her eyebrows pull together. "What?" she asks, and I realize I've been staring at her, unseeing, for an uncomfortable amount of time now.

"Just thinking about how lucky I am to have you," I say, slowly thrusting in and out of her.

She leans down, kissing the sensitive spot just below my ear. "I'm lucky to have you, too, Beckett."

I walk us both over to the bed and slowly lower her onto her back. She keeps her legs wrapped around me, my cock buried deep inside her.

I place my hands down on either side of her face. "You're so perfect."

She wiggles her hips against mine. "I'm so needy. Just make me come, love."

"Your wish is my command, Queenie."

With that, I rock into her, my eyes rolling back as her tight channel grips my cock. "You're amazing."

My mouth finds her nipple again, pulling it into my mouth as my right hand sneaks between us to find her clit.

She moans when I find it, thrusting her hips against me.

"So fucking perfect," I murmur in her ear.

I add a finger to her clit, continuing the slow circles, even as her breathing becomes ragged, her thrusts less controlled.

My pleasure builds deep inside me, my core clenching as my body demands its release.

"Come for me, love," I beg. "Let me feel your pretty pussy clenching around my cock."

She starts to unravel in my arms, and I talk her through it, barely able to get any words out. "You're such a good girl. You're—"

I cut off as I come, my head dropping to rest on her collarbone. "Fuck, you're perfect. I really am the luckiest man in the world."

"I love you," Finley murmurs sleepily.

"I love you, too, baby."

I cuddle her from behind, tucking her tight against me: the only place I ever want her to be. We lie like that, content to be tangled up in each other. Just when I'm about to fall asleep, Finley's phone dings once.

"Ugh," she groans, and I reach over and grab her phone for her from the nightstand. "Who could possibly need me right now?" She flops back down, one hand on her forehead like she's in need of smelling salts.

Seconds later, Finley sits up, her eyes wide as she stares at her screen. "Holy crap."

"What?" I ask.

"Look at this text from Charlotte." She holds her phone up to me.

I shake my head, reading my own text. "I don't need to. Callan just sent me a message. I'm sure it's about the same thing."

She's responding, her thumbs flying over the keys as she says, "Do you remember when we first found out they were working together? It was such a shit show."

"I mean, I fell in love with my coach," I reply, leaning over to give her a kiss on the smooth skin of her bare shoulder. "I don't know if it gets much worse than that. Though it turned out pretty well for us."

She lifts one dark eyebrow. "Pretty well?"

"So well," I say, pulling her on top of me. I run my fingertips down her waist, tracing the contours of her ribs. "Falling in love with my coach turned out so fucking well."

Not ready to say goodbye to Finley and Beckett? Neither was I. **I have TWO bonus scenes for you! One is SPICY, and the other is from before Her Slap Shot,** when Beckett is still in Florida. Get them free using the QR code below!

Get the bonus
scene

P.S. you'll be signed up for my super-fun newsletter that gets access to other VIP goodies.

***

Awkward author ask: If you loved Finley and Beckett's story (or even just liked it a lot), would you take 60 seconds and leave a review? It doesn't have to be long. "I stayed up until 2am.

Not sorry" totally counts. Hit up Amazon or Goodreads (or whatever platforms the cool kids are leaving reviews on these days) and tell the people what you thought!

***

Think you loved Finley and Beckett? Wait until you see Charlotte and Callan in book 2.

Charlotte has spent her entire life preparing to take over her father's entertainment dynasty. So when he tells her to prove herself by running his pro football team, she does what any strategic, determined woman would do: she finds a quarterback to fake date. Because apparently running a billion-dollar empire requires family values.

Callan Devine is the guy who always says yes. Too bad he didn't account for what saying yes to Charlotte would cost him.

Book 2 is a spicy football romance with fake dating, forced proximity, and the kind of tension that happens when faking it starts to feel dangerously real. Part of the In Her League *series, it can be read as a standalone.*

*Pre-order Book
2 today!*

Emma-verse Characters

There is nothing I love more than when random side characters have their own books. And if you're like me, you're in luck!

Charlotte Langford and Callan Devine – *Untitled Book 2*
Jameson Walker – *Forever Wild*
Lila Walker and JT Johnson – *Wildly Inappropriate*
Jaxon Steele – *Chasing Wild*

Also by Emma

Wild Bluffs
(Small Town Romance)
Forever Wild
Wildly Inappropriate
Wild and Free
Chasing Wild

***

In Her League
(Sports Romance)
Her Slap Shot
Untitled Book 2

Acknowledgements

A new series. A new map dot along my author journey. And somehow, it still feels just as exciting (and just as surreal) as the very first time I did this. Thank you for being here with me as I start something new. I am SO excited for you to meet the strong, badass women in the In Her League series.

While writing can be a solo sport, there are so many people I need to thank for their help and support along the way.

To Kelly, developmental editor extraordinaire, thank you for taking my chaotic first drafts and somehow turning them into stories with emotional depth, structure, and significantly fewer "why would she do that?" moments. This book is infinitely better because of you.

To Katie, thank you for reminding me that "says" has synonyms. "Groundbreaking," she declares. "Life-changing!" she yells.

To Judy, thank you for making sure every last detail was polished to perfection. I'm so grateful for your sharp eye and attention to detail.

To Sam, thank you for creating a cover that made me think, oh... these characters are really real. You bring this story to life before readers ever open the cover.

To both Megans in my life, thank you for the brainstorming sessions, the ideas, and for helping me talk through plot points until they actually made sense. Your brains are magic.

To Steph, thank you for being *in this* with me. For the conversations about publishing, algorithms, plot spirals, procrastination, and everything in between. Having someone who *gets it* makes all the difference.

To my mom, thank you for your constant support, and for being the best signed-book fulfillment service a girl could ask for. Truly unmatched. The 'Zon could never package a book bundle with such love.

And finally, to you, my readers—thank you for being here, for taking a chance on this story, and for continuing to support my books. It means more than I can ever fully put into words.

Until next time.

Happy reading,

EK

About the Author

Emma Kate is an author of rom-coms and contemporary romances. She lives in a small Colorado town with her rancher husband, three kids, a dog, and a whole lot of cows. When she's not writing or reading, she can be found chasing after her kids, eating ice cream and cookies, or binge-watching sitcoms.

www.ingramcontent.com/pod-product-compliance
Lightning Source LLC
Chambersburg PA
CBHW020905060726
47591CB00004B/1099